# ALEX WHEATLE

## *East of Acre Lane*

HARPER PERENNIAL
London, New York, Toronto and Sydney

Harper Perennial
An imprint of HarperCollins*Publishers*
77–85 Fulham Palace Road
Hammersmith
London W6 8JB

www.harperperennial.co.uk

This edition published by Harper Perennial 2006
1

Previously published in paperback by Fourth Estate 2002

First published in Great Britain by Fourth Estate 2001

PS™ is a trademark of HarperCollins*Publishers* Ltd

A catalogue record for this book is
available from the British Library

This novel is entirely a work of fiction. The names and characters
portrayed in it are the work of the author's imagination. Any
resemblance to actual persons, living or dead, is entirely coincidental.

ISBN-13 978-0-00-722562-0
ISBN-10 0-00-722562-8

Typeset by Avon Dataset Ltd, Bidford on Avon, Warks

Printed and bound in Great Britain by Clays Ltd, St Ives plc

This novel is dedicated to the life
and musical legacy of
Dennis Emmanuelle Brown

# 1

# Heady Heights

## 27 January 1981

It was 3am and Biscuit found himself being driven through the bad lands of South London. He was in the back seat, his heartbeat accelerating, flanked on the right by this big grizzly thing called Muttley, who looked like a young George Foreman with untamed facial hair. On Biscuit's left was the evil cackling dread nicknamed Ratmout', whose face would crease into a mask of sadism if anything humoured him. Nunchaks, the Brixtonian crime lord, was behind the wheel, displaying perfect calm. How de fuck am I gonna get out of this? Biscuit thought.

He wondered what he'd done to warm Nunchaks' wrath, and regretted leaving the party without Coffin Head and Floyd. It had been a dread rave. Plenty girls to dance with, strong lagers freeflowing, and Winston, the top notch selector of Crucial Rocker sound, spinning some dangerous tunes.

'Jus' ah liccle drive to tek in de sights,' Nunchaks said, smiling.

'Forget 'bout de herb, man,' Biscuit suggested, 'I'm too busy nex' week to do any selling, an' I was riding a serious crub wid a fit girl at de party.'

'De bitch can wait,' Nunchaks responded grimly.

'Don't fuck about, Chaks,' Biscuit fretted. 'Lemme outta de car, man, I ain't in de mood for one of your jokes.'

'Who de rarse says I'm joking. An', more time, I don't like yout' who joke wid *me*.'

The Cortina Mark Two pulled up at the foot of a cloud-seeking tower block, somewhere behind Stockwell Tube Station. The thick-necked Muttley yanked Biscuit out of the car as Nunchaks, in his cashmere coat and beaver-skinned hat, observed the skyline. He looked like a character from *Shaft*.

'What de fuck 'ave I done, man?' Biscuit panicked. 'I beg you. I ain't done nutten to you. Dis has gone too far.'

'You made ah wrong move, yout',' Chaks growled. 'If you can't listen good, den you mus' feel pain.'

'Wha' wrong move, Chaks, man? Wha' 'ave I done? I'm one of your best customers. My brethrens will be wondering where I am. Gi' me a chance to explain whatever I've done.'

'Stop grovelling, yout', you sound like weak-heart bwai inna beast cell.'

Ratmout' and Muttley dragged Biscuit towards the lift of the tower block. Before him Biscuit read the graffiti that decorated the bruised, hardwood swing doors of

2

the entrance. *Che Guevara, you're wanted in Brixton*, demanded one line. Biscuit looked up and saw hundreds of windows embedded in dark concrete reflecting the blackness of the night. He wanted to scream, but knew that if he did, his forehead would kiss Chak's steel-studded Nunchakoos. Ghetto youths, especially in Brixton, flocked to the late-night Ace cinema to watch the latest Martial Arts films, and they all considered the top ranking scene of all time was when Bruce Lee wielded his Nunchakoos in *Enter the Dragon*, mincing the brains of five assailants. The scene was not lost on Nunchaks.

How did I ever get hook up wid dis bad man? Biscuit thought. A cold sweat snaked down from his temples. He thought of his hard-working mother and his younger sister and brother, wondering if he would see them again. Only half an hour ago he was smoking a spliff and enjoying a serious smooch with a fit girl. Now he felt like he was approaching the end of his short life.

Muttley, wondering if the lift was in order, thumbed for the top floor and then ran his eyes over Biscuit, as if he was sizing up which part of the body he should eat first. As the mechanism of the lift echoed into a downward motion, Ratmout' emitted a throaty cackle, displaying his black gums and two missing front teeth. To add to Biscuit's torment, and to pass the time, he slowly ran his right index finger along his throat. Nunchaks was flicking his lighter on and off, cursing that it had run out of gas.

When the lift arrived and the steel doors had juddered open, Biscuit caught the scent of something a dog had left in the corner of the cramped compartment. They entered the confined cabin, Biscuit scouring Nunchaks' coat for any glint of custom-built brain scrambler. On the back wall of the lift was more graffiti in bold, red letters: *legalise it*.

A red-lit circle indicated that the lift had reached the 25th floor. The two flunkies shunted Biscuit through a wire-meshed door that led the way to the balcony. Biscuit ran the scene through his mind in trepidation. This was the end; he could see his eighteen-year-old body crumpled upon the concrete forecourt below, as lifeless as a black bag of rubbish. He felt an asthma attack gathering force in his chest and his fear rendered him speechless. Nunchaks was still fiddling with his lighter.

'Wha' yard number did you raid the uder day?' Nunchaks demanded.

'You can 'ave all de t'ings, man. Stereo, telly, everyt'ing. You can 'ave de lot, man. Jus' lemme go. Der's dis yard I'm working on nex' week an' you can 'ave all de t'ings we t'ief from der as well.'

'Wha' number!'

'Er, you told me twenty-seven, innit.'

Nunchaks turned to his cronies. 'My mudder always teach me dat if me can't hear, I mus' feel.'

'Don't frig about, Chaks, you'll get de t'ings back, no worries.'

Nunchaks managed to get his lighter working. He paused, took out a cigarette and lit it. 'Twenty-seven, you say?'

'Yeah, man. Dat's de number you gave me.'

'Can you remember me saying twenty-seven?' Nunchaks asked his goons.

'No, boss,' Muttley answered gleefully.

'I swear you told me twenty-seven. I swear, man.'

'You calling me a liar, yout'? You already raised your voice to me once. Do it again and you're flying t'rough de air.'

Biscuit glanced behind him and saw the communica-

4

tion towers of Crystal Palace blinking away on the horizon, overlooking the myriad of tiny illuminations that peppered South London. He could just make out the grey, flat tops of his home estate along Brixton Road. His eyes went eastwards and he took in the Oval cricket ground, backdropped by huge round gas tanks that looked like the crowns of poor giants. Surrounding all this were cousins upon cousins of council blocks. Biscuit wondered if there was anybody around to hear him scream. Maybe someone who lived below had witnessed his plight and would come to the rescue.

'I told you *seventy*-seven, yout',' Nunchaks said coldly.

'Does it matter?' Biscuit asked. 'De yard 'ad a top of de range JVC system, an' you can 'ave it, man. Free of charge wid nuff compliments an' t'ing.'

'Do you know who lives at twenty-seven?' Nunchaks asked eerily.

Biscuit hadn't a clue and wondered why it mattered so much to Chaks. He sensed his knees were buckling under the weight of his body, as if they knew he was going to die. My days are fucked, he thought. Knowing my luck I burgled a dealer's yard.

'My brudder's woman lives der,' Nunchaks revealed. 'When I sight her she was ah liccle upset. She couldn't believe dat while she was sleeping, some bastard bruk into her yard an' tek away her t'ings dem. You even t'ieved de friggin' ornaments!'

'Sorry, Chaks, man. If we did know we wouldn't 'ave gone near her yard. I'm sorry, man.'

'Shall we bruk him up, boss?' the smirking Ratmout' suggested, eager to earn his money for the night.

'Yeah, mon,' Muttley added, pulling up his sleeves and preparing his right fist. 'Mash up his knee cap to rarted.'

5

Nunchaks was more concerned with his lighter. He threw it over the balcony and into the night. Biscuit turned his head to watch it spiral towards the ground. He closed his eyes at the moment of impact.

'Fockin' wort'less piece of rubbish. I'm gonna drapes de bwai who sold me dat.'

He studied Biscuit and sensed the fear in the boy's lean body. Biscuit's petrified, narrow eyes were trained on Nunchaks' coat, yet Nunchaks knew that if he revealed what was concealed inside he would get an altogether different reaction from the youth. He looked at Biscuit's rangy legs and had to admit that he would never catch him in a long chase. He searched the teenager's features again. Biscuit's brown eyes were set in a diamond-shaped, chocolate-mousse-coloured face that showed the hint of a moustache. His top lip bore the scar of a recent spliff and infant sideburns lined his jawbone. Nunchaks had Biscuit cornered now; he could really *frighten* him.

Biscuit awaited his fate, breathing heavily and wondering if it wouldn't look too pitiful if he used his inhaler.

'Me 'ave ah liccle business in Handswort' to attend to,' Nunchaks announced. 'I should be back by de end ah nex' week. An' when I reach, if me don't see de t'ings dat you t'iefed, I'm gonna personally peel your fingers like raw carrot wid my machete to rarted. Y'hear me, yout'?'

'De t'ings will be back before your 'pon de motorway, man. Considered done.'

Nunchaks glared at Biscuit for five seconds, before reaching into the inside pocket of his coat. He pulled out a polythene bag of top-range cannabis, rubbing the fingers of his free hand together. 'You 'ave de corn, yout'?'

'Yeah, course.'

Biscuit took out the wad of notes, totalling £250, from

the back pocket of his Farahs and made the exchange. Nunchaks about turned and made his way to the lift, tailed by his minders.

'By de end ah nex' week, yout'.'

Biscuit watched them enter the lift and sighed heavily as the door closed. He shuddered at what might have been and tried to get the image of Nunchaks' lighter dropping to the ground out of his mind. 'Fuck my days,' he whispered. 'Dat was close.' He felt a ridiculous urge to peer down to the concrete below, but stopped himself. 'Fuck my days.' He attempted to compose himself, and after a few minutes of trying to get his breathing together, he decided he would have to step back to the party and alert Coffin Head. 'Shit! A one mile trod in my crocs.'

He made tentative steps to the lift, afraid that Nunchaks and his crew were lurking about in the shadows. Impatiently, he pressed the button, then wondered if it would be a better idea to run down the concrete steps. Before he made his mind up the lift arrived. He stepped inside, comparing the metal box to a square coffin. On reaching the ground floor, he made a quick check to see who was about before sprinting to Stockwell Tube Station. He remembered the many times he had partied and smoked good herb with his crew in the buildings adjacent to the tower block. Now the place had an altogether different atmosphere. He wondered if this was Nunchaks' regular site for scaring the shit out of youths. Perhaps he had killed someone here. He looked behind at the great monolith and raised his sight to its highest point. 'Fuck my days.' He christened the building mentally, calling it Nunchaks' killing block.

He turned right into Clapham Road, only too aware of the dangers that might come from any lane, shadow or building, but this was a hazard he had come to accept as a natural aspect of living in the ghetto. He passed a supermarket on his right and noticed ten or so trolleys keeled over on their side. Vandalism touches everything around here, he thought. He pondered on taking a short cut through a council estate but decided against it; he had seen enough council blocks on this night. On his way, he mentally cursed the boarded-up housing, the rubbish on the streets, the graffiti that covered the railway bridges that made up his habitat. Nevertheless, it was home, and he was a part of his environment just as much as the run-down church he now passed by.

Cars were parked and double parked around him as Biscuit heard the music thumping out to greet the morning. Gregory Isaacs' 'Soon Forward' filtered through the snappy Brixton air, the smooth and delicate vocals riding over a slow, murderous bass-line with a one-drop drum.

He knocked on the door of the house, its windows covered by blockboard.

'Pound fe come in, an' if you nah have the entrance fee, I will cuss your behind for wasting my time.'

'Paid my pound already, man. You don't recognise me?'

'Don't boder try fool me. One pound fifty fe come in, especially for you. I don't like ginall.'

'Crook your ear, man. I entered de dance wid Nunchaks.'

The doorman thought for a moment.

'Alright, enter, yout'.'

The stench of Mary Jane made Biscuit's nostrils flare as he made his way to the jam-packed room he had left with Nunchaks, his sight aided only by a blue light-bulb. Girls were dressed in thin, ankle-length, pleated dresses. Most of them sported hot-combed hairstyles; black sculptured art finished off with lacquer. By this time of night, a generous share of the girls found themselves enveloped by their men, smooching away to the dub version of 'Soon Forward'. Sweet-bwais were dressed in loose-fitting shirts that were often unbuttoned to reveal gold rope chains. The latest hairstyle was semi-afro which was shampooed and 'blown out', giving an appearance of carved black candyfloss. No one calling themselves a sweet-bwai would go to a party without their Farah slacks and reptile skin shoes.

As Biscuit threaded his way to the room in which he'd last seen Coffin Head, the ghetto messenger Yardman Irie grabbed hold of the Crucial Rocker sound system microphone, ready to deliver his sermon. Dressed in green army garb and topped by a black cloth beret, Yardman Irie waited for the selector, Winston, to spin the rabble-rousing instrumental 'Johnny Dollar'.

'Crowd ah people, de Private Yardman Irie is 'ere 'pon de scene. Dis one special request to all ghetto foot soldier.'

*Me seh life inna Brixton nah easy*
*Me seh life inna Brixton nah easy*
*Me daddy cannot afford de money fe me tea*
*Me mudder cannot pay de electricity*
*De council nah fix de roof above we*
*De bird dem a fly in an' shit 'pon me*
*Me daddy sick an' tired of redundancy*
*We 'ad to sell our new black and white TV*
*De rat dem ah come in an' 'ave ah party*
*Me look out me window an' see ah plane nex' to me*
*Me feel de flat ah sway when we get de strong breeze*
*We are so high we cyan't see de trees*
*De flat is so damp dat me brudder start wheeze*

*De shitstem is bringing us down to our knees*
*But de politician dem nah listen to our pleas*
*Me seh life inna Brixton nah easy*
*Me seh life inna Brixton nah easy*
*Me don't know why we left from de Caribbean sea.*

The crowd hollered their approval of Yardman Irie's lyrics while flicking their lighters in the air; those without clenched their fists in raised salutes. Everyone wanted an encore. 'FORWARD YARDMAN IRIE, FORWARD!' Yardman Irie refreshed himself with a swig of Lucozade and a toke from Winston's spliff.

Amidst the excited throng, butted against the wall, Biscuit made out Coffin Head, riding a disgusting crub that sorely examined the wallpaper.

'Coff! Coff!'

Coffin Head looked up and saw his spar threading his way towards him. What does he want now, he thought. Probably needs a pen so he can write down a girl's digits.

'Coff, need to chat to you. Urgent, man. Step outside.'

Coffin Head's dance partner, who was wearing a flowing pleated dress that was thin enough to expose her bra, looked upon Biscuit. 'Can't you wait till de record done?'

'Who's chatting to you? Jus' quiet your beak an' lemme chat to my spar.' Coffin Head had read the worry upon Biscuit's face. 'Dis better be important, man. I was gonna ask de girl back to my gates an' deal wid it proper. She's fit, man!'

'Trus' me brethren, dis is important. Where's Floyd?'

'He jus' chip. He lef' wid some light skin girl. Said to me he's gonna service her if possible.'

The two friends walked out of the party and Coffin

Head led the way to his Triumph Dolomite. 'You get de herb?' he asked.

'Yeah, yeah, but don't worry 'bout dat. We're in serious shit.'

'Whatya mean?'

'De yard we burgled the uder day . . .'

'Wha' about it?'

'It was de friggin' wrong yard!'

'Who cares a fuckin' damn? Got some nice t'ings, innit.'

'It's Nunchaks. His brudder's woman yard!'

Coffin Head looked disbelievingly out through the windscreen. 'You're not ramping, are you?'

'Course I ain't friggin' ramping. He told me dis as he was jus' 'bout to fling me over de balcony of some dirty tower block. I t'ought my forehead was gonna kiss de friggin' concrete. We've got to get de t'ings back.'

Coffin Head shook his head in dismay 'I always said don't deal wid dat man, I always said. But oh no, you jus' wouldn't listen. It'll be cool, you said. Well, fuck my days. I'm fucked, we're fucked. You jus' don't wanna listen to reason, man. Didn't I say Chaks is into all sorts of shit. Pimping, money-lending, protection racket, drugs, cheque book. He even owns a Rottweiler dat fights uder dogs in Brockwell Park, to rarted. De man's well versatile.'

'Look, Coff, we can chat to Smiley an' he might give us de t'ings back. We jus' got to give 'im back his corn.'

'Did you tell Chaks we sold de t'ings to Smiley?'

'Are you cuckoo? Course I never! If I did you t'ink I'd be here now?'

Coffin Head turned the ignition key and pulled away. Barrington Levy's 'Bounty Hunter' came on the car stereo, the lyrics backed by a hot-stepping rhythm that was full of menace. The song filled the two teenagers with dread.

'Wha' we gonna do, man?' Coffin Head asked, turning into Brixton Road.

'Check Smiley tomorrow.'

# 2
# Homestead

The council estate that housed Biscuit's family and countless others, stretched between two bus stops along Brixton Road, and was three blocks deep. Biscuit made his way to his home slab and climbed four flights of concrete stairs, eyeing the graffiti that seemed to have been written when the block was built. The sight of the dark brown brickwork brought a powerful relief that not even the filthy syringes that were breeding in dark corners could repel. He winced as he observed the panoramic view of the tower block where Nunchaks had threatened his life. The sky was a malevolent grey, and to the east, beyond Kennington, he saw the hint of a threatening sunrise creeping over the tower blocks of Elephant and Castle. 'A new day,' Biscuit thought to himself and smiled. It was a phrase his mother had taught him when he was young. 'A new day is full of hope.'

As a child, Biscuit had witnessed at first hand the eroding of his mother's dignity, set in motion by the death of his father from pneumonia in 1963 after one of the worse winters the country had ever suffered. Biscuit could not remember his father at all, but his mother had described the details of his death. Working outdoors to service telephone lines, Mr Huggins had battled with the ferocious winter that chilled the country for nearly six months. In April of that year, flu claimed him first.

Pneumonia paid him a visit soon after, sending him to his grave in Streatham cemetery in early May. Biscuit's mother had hated the sight of snow ever since, and she still swept it away, cursing under her breath, whenever it made an appearance by her front door. Immediately following her husband's death she also vowed never to enter a church again, citing that God had made her suffer too much. During his childhood, Biscuit was sometimes awakened by his mother's rantings against the Most High. He would creep along the hallway and spy her holding her head between her hands in the front room, crying.

Biscuit turned the key and entered the flat.

'Lincoln! Is dat you? Wha' kinda party gwarn till de lark dem sing inna tree top? Ah seven ah clock ah marnin y'know. You know me caan't sleep when you out der 'pon street ah night-time.'

'I keep telling you don't wait up for me, Mummy. Didn't I say I wouldn't be back till morning?'

He took off his leather jacket and hung it on a peg in the hallway, which was lit by a naked bulb. Last summer, he had bought and put up the cheap white wallpaper and glossed the skirting in an attempt to brighten up the

14

corridor. Unfortunately, he had forgotten to pull up the wild-patterned, multi-coloured carpet while he was decorating, and it still bore the white paint and paste stains.

The bedroom that he shared with his brother, Royston, was nearest to the front door with the entrance to the right of the hallway. On the left-hand side, two paces further up, was Denise's room, which was next door to his mother's chamber. Moving on, the bathroom was situated on the right. Beyond this and to the right was the lounge.

The centrepiece of this room, sitting on a mantelpiece above the gas heater, was a large framed, black and white photo of Mr and Mr Huggins on their wedding day. Other photos, propped on the black and white television set or peering out of an old wooden china cabinet and sitting on a window ledge, were mostly of a young Biscuit. The wallpaper in this room was a more stylish pink and white pattern, disturbed only by a Jamaican tourist poster, boasting a golden beach and turquoise sea. To the rear of the room was the kitchen door, where a calendar, published by a Jamaican rum company, was hanging from a nail.

'You waan some breakfast?' Biscuit's mother called from the lounge. 'I'm gonna cook up some cornmeal porridge after me done de washing up.'

'Nah, t'anks. I jus' wanna get some sleep, Mummy.'

'Den tek off your clothes dem. Me gone ah bagwash when it open. Me nah like to reach too late, cah de place cork up come de afternoon.'

Biscuit sat on the bed and smiled as he witnessed his brother Royston trying to pretend he was asleep. He looked upon his round-headed, dimple-cheeked sibling as he peeled off his crocodile skin shoes, then ambled into the kitchen where his mother was busy rinsing pots and dishes.

Biscuit kissed his mother on her left cheek and offered her a home-coming smile. Her hair was braided into short plaits, all pointing in different directions. The hue of her black skin was dark and rich, but her eyes sparkled whenever she looked upon Lincoln, her first born and only child from her beloved husband.

'Here, Mummy, control dis,' he offered, presenting his mother with a five-pound note. 'For de bagwash.'

'But you jus' gi' me ah ten pound yesterday fe do ah liccle shopping.'

'Jus' tek it, Mummy.'

She took the note and placed it on top of the fridge, her face curving into the kind of smile that mothers only reserved for their children. Biscuit acknowledged her silent thanks. 'I'm gonna ketch some sleep.' He turned and made for his bedroom.

The room was dominated by the double bed he shared with his nine-year-old brother. A single wardrobe housed Biscuit's garments and Royston's school uniform. A simple blue mat was the racing ground for Royston's matchbox cars, and a small chest of drawers had both siblings' underwear fighting for breath. On one side of the room, above Biscuit's side of the bed, spawning from the join of ceiling and wall was a damp stain in the shape of South America.

'Royston, I know you're awake,' Biscuit said.

'No I'm not.'

'Den how comes you answer me?'

'You waked me up.'

'You was awake from time.'

16

'No I wasn't, you waked me up.'

'Go on! Admit it. You were waiting up for me.'

'So . . . It's horrible when I wake up in the middle of the night and you ain't der.'

'Come 'ere you little brat.' Royston leaped up and viced his brother's neck with his chubby arms. 'Well, you ain't got no excuse now. Go back to sleep.'

Biscuit undressed down to his Y-fronts and slipped under the covers. Royston was still sitting up, and watched as his brother's head hit the pillow. He tried to think of something with which to restart the conversation.

'Did you get any rub-a-dub at the party?' he asked, wondering how his brother would react to the latest addition to his vocabulary.

'Stop using word if you don't know wha' dey mean. Quiet yout' an' go back to sleep.'

'I do know what it means.'

'Good fe you. But you don't ask dem kinda question to big man. Know your size.'

'You ain't a big man.'

'I'm a lot bigger dan you.'

'But you ain't a man yet. A man goes out to work. You don't work.'

'Royston, quiet your beak. Why is it every weekend I come back from somewhere, you wanna keep me up?'

'Not my fault your bedtime's when everyone else is getting up.'

'Look, Royston, I'm tired, an' der's a lot of t'ings 'pon my mind. I'll talk to you later on. Oh, one last t'ing, I want you to help Mummy at de bagwash.'

'I ain't going. Last time I went my friend saw me and made fun out of me at school.'

'You're going.'

'No I ain't.'

'*Yes*, you are.'

'No I ain't. Mummy's always cussing me cos I drop the clothes on the floor.'

'Den be more careful.'

'Why can't Denise go?'

'Cos she 'as to help wid de cooking.'

'Don't wanna go.'

'Look, if you go, I'll buy you some sweets.'

'I wanna Mars Bar and a Kit-Kat.'

'You liccle blackmailer,' Biscuit sighed. 'Alright den, but make sure you go.'

Several hours later, Biscuit's mother was ironing Royston's school uniform in the lounge, watching *The Waltons* on the black and white telly. She draped the pressed clothes over a worn armchair and kissed her teeth as Royston played around her feet, jumping on her nerves.

Denise was sprawled on the sofa, thinking of what her friends, Hilary and Jackie, would wear to a forthcoming party. Perhaps those new split skirts with a small, gold-coloured chain at the front which were catching on fast. Or maybe them fashionable waffle slacks.

The owner of an Olympic swimmer's physique, Denise had a complexion that looked like dark honey. Her Siamese cat-like eyes, framed by perfectly arched eyebrows, were seductively attractive, making her a just challenge for a top-notch sweet-bwai. Her cheeks were not blessed with flesh but her lips were generous and sexy. Her pitch-black hair was beautifully styled in corn-row plaits, lending her an appearance of innocence. Dressed in seamed jeans and an oversized pullover,

Denise wondered if Hilary and her boyfriend had patched things up after their argument.

'Mummy, can I have some money to buy a dress dis week,' she asked. 'I've been invited to a party Saturday.'

'You 'ave plenty dress inna your wardrobe – wha' is wrong wid dem?'

'Nutten. But I've 'ad dem from time an' I wanna wear somet'ing diffcrent for once.'

'Waan dis, waan dat. You always waan somet'ing. Electric bill affe pay nex' week but you nuh worry 'bout dat.'

'I haven't asked you money for clothes for long time. Anybody t'ink me ask you every week.'

'Why don't you find ah nice gentleman fe buy dem t'ings der.'

'Cah men don't give somet'ing fe nutten.'

'You say dat cos you mixed inna de wrong crowd. Pure rude bwai you ah deal wid.'

'What d'you expect! Dis is SW9 not SW1. No gentlemen 'round dese sides.'

'You would meet some nice gentlemen if you gwarn ah church wid Auntie Jenny.'

'Dem man who go Auntie Jenny's church – most of dem go raving on a Saturday night. Besides, why should I go to Auntie Jenny's church when you never go?'

Hortense rested her ironing arm for a while, sat on the limb of a chair and tried to look meaningfully at her daughter. 'Me nuh see why you 'ave problem getting ah nice man fe court wid,' she said, ignoring her daughter's last remark. 'You pretty in your own way an' not fatty or maaga. Y'know me caan't feed two big people inna de yard.'

Denise shook her head. 'But you'll always feed Lincoln, innit.'

'Me nuh say dat.'

'You might as well.'

'Stop putting word inna me mout'.'

Biscuit entered the lounge, rubbing his eyes, not at all embarrassed at wearing only his Y-fronts. 'Bwai, every Sunday you two ketch up inna argument. What's de beef now?' he asked.

'Mummy wants to marry me off quick time,' Denise blurted out, getting in first.

'Me tell you before, stop putting words inna me mout'.'

'It might not be de *exact* words, but I get de drift.'

'You're so damn facety!' Hortense barked, getting back to her ironing. 'You're jus' looking argument.'

'It tek two to 'ave one.'

'Quiet your mout', girl! Me 'ave nutten more fe say to you.'

Denise cut her eyes at her mother and then turned her fierce gaze to the TV.

Royston, who was rolling about underneath the ironing board, playing with a matchbox car, sprung up on sight of his brother. 'Where's my Mars Bar and Kit-Kat?'

'What's wrong wid you? I jus' get up, an' stop ramping under de ironing board.'

'You waan ah cup ah tea, Lincoln? Mebbe some toast?'

'Please, Mummy. But I have to dally soon and link up wid Coffin Head.'

'Never mek me a cup of tea when I get up,' Denise snapped.

'An' you never mek me one!' Hortense retaliated.

Biscuit ate his breakfast of cornmeal porridge standing up in the kitchen, his worries interrupted by the stop-start bickering of his mother and sister. He knew it all came down to money; that was the bottom line. He

20

wouldn't have to wake up to family debates so often if there was more of it around. Maybe he could give Denise the money for the dress if he sold a decent amount of herb in the next few days. That would get her off her mother's back. Perhaps he could even buy Royston his much-needed new shoes for school if things went alright. Biscuit's mother had mentioned to him a few days before how she had had to box the young bwai for kicking stones. He knew it was a hint he couldn't ignore. How much is dat? he asked himself. A pair of new shoes might cost a tenner – and a new dress? Maybe twenty notes for a decent one. Might be cheaper if Denise could be persuaded to shop at the market.

He weighed up his financial position as he took Royston to the sweet shop. If Coffin Head and himself sold their herb on the Front Line in Brixton, they could clear £400, especially if he bagged the weed sparingly. I've got a few loyal customers around this area, he thought, but no serious herb man would rely for his corn in and about Cowley estate.

When they got to Vassal Road, Biscuit grabbed his brother's hand so they could cross together. At that moment he saw Wilson Walker, an old school brethren who now lived in Stockwell Park, depart the off-licence.

'Walker! Walker! Yo!'

Wilson crossed the road, brew in his hand, looking like he had two years of sleep to catch up on. Biscuit and Wilson had been firm friends at school but their paths split when Wilson won an apprenticeship at British Aerospace. Now Biscuit only checked Wilson when he had herb to sell.

'Wha'appen Walker. Where you rave last night?'

'Diamonds blues near Fiveways. Cork me ah tell you.

Checked a leg-back fe de morning. Said to her I'm going shop but I'm dallying home. I got my delights so I t'ought, why 'ang around? She lives in your estate . . . wassername? Katrina Conley – used to go Stockwell Manor.'

'Yeah, I know her. Ain't seen her for a while t'ough. She got her own yard?' Biscuit queried.

'Yeah, well, she 'ave pickney now. Eight months old.'

'Who pumped the seed?' Biscuit asked, keeping an eye on his impatient brother.

'Some Filthy Rocker sound bwai, don't know which one but I feel so it could be Liccle Axe.'

'Bwai! She's playing wid fire.'

'Yeah, well. She got a flat out of it.'

'Man! De t'ings girl do to get flat.'

'I could do wid my own yard. Maybe I would do the same t'ing if I was a girl!'

Biscuit laughed as Royston tugged his arm. Wilson offered his brethren a cigarette as his face turned serious.

'Katrina knows one of de people who dead in de fire last week.'

'Dat t'ing at Deptford?'

'Yeah, friend of friend business. Everyone was chatting 'bout it at de dance last night. Maybe dey were t'inking dat some National Front bwai would fling petrol bomb inna de dance. It's like all an' all so vex y'know. Me sight a white yout' get bus' up down Acre Lane de uder day. De poor sap only went to buy a pattie, but when he came out, some man who were in de bookie jump on 'im an' mash up his claat. People are vex me ah tell you.'

'So how many are dead now?' Biscuit asked solemnly.

'Ten. T'irty are injured or inna hospital. De beast ain't made no arres' yet an dat's why people are so vex. Der's talk of some kinda march if de beast don't do nutten. An' de nex' National Front march der's going to be nuff trouble.'

'So nobody sight who did it?'

'Nah. It was dark an' t'ing an' one minute everybody's wining an' dining, de nex' minute de yard ketch a fire. Some jus' escape. A serious business.'

'So if it was de beef'eads, you t'ink dey will try de same t'ing?'

'Nobody knows. I can't see dem trying it in Brixton. If dey do it will be pure almshouse business. Some beef'ead mus' ah dead, believe.'

'Yeah, it's dat. But somet'ing gonna snap, man. So many yout' get bus' up inna cell dese days. Y'hear wha' 'appen to Sceptic? Beastman arres' 'im outside Kentucky inna Brixton, tek 'im to cell an' bruk up 'im nose an' boot up his rib-cage. An' now, fockin' beef'ead might 'ave fling petrol bomb inna one of our dance. Man an' man waan life fe life. Dat's wha' dem Brixton panther man say, innit.'

'Seen. Somet'ings gonna blow up . . . Listen, man. You dealing?'

'Yeah, man. Jus' get me batch last night.'

'I wanna check you for an eighth later on, yeah.'

'Seen. You know where to check me, innit.'

'Yeah, man. But don't gi' me a draw wid too much seed in it. Laters.'

Biscuit and Royston watched Wilson cross the road before they entered the sweet shop. Royston had listened attentively to the conversation, as he did when his brother's friends turned up at home. He was scared for his brother but didn't know what to say. He had heard how Biscuit's friends were beat up by the beast, locked up in jail, or stabbed by some bad man. He knew the tale of Brenton Brown and Terry Flynn, which went down in the annals of Brixtonian folklore as one of the most violent confrontations anyone had ever heard of. Whenever Brenton visited the Huggins' home, Royston's eyes could not be deflected from the scar upon the man's neck as he listened attentively to every word the 'Stepping Volcano' uttered. A real life Brixtonian bad man in *my* house, he told himself. He repeated the description of Brenton to his classmates, and would go into detail on how his hero walked.

As the brothers ambled towards home, Royston munched his Kit-Kat and asked, 'Do white people always throw fire in black homes?'

'No. But dey might do it more often if we let dem.'

'The beast won't catch the white people who done it, will they?'

# Roadblock

Coffin Head palmed his car horn and waited for Biscuit. Dressed in thick, green corduroy trousers and a cream-coloured puffy anorak, he had time to smoke a cigarette before Biscuit came down. He looked out of the passenger window and thought to himself that Cowley was the ugliest council estate in the area. Why did they use the colour of old shit for bricks, he wondered. An elderly black woman passed his view, wearing a Sunday-best white dress underneath her unbuttoned blue trench coat. His eyes tailed her as Biscuit, dressed in blue seamed jeans and a thick black sweater, filled the passenger seat.

'You're an hour late,' Biscuit rebuked.

'Char, I 'ad t'ings to do, innit. Drop my mum to church.'

'Church! I can't see why so many of our mudders

forward to dem boring service,' Biscuit remarked.

'Your mudder don't.'

'Cos she's always busy 'pon Sundays wid bagwash, cooking an' dem t'ing der.'

Coffin Head restarted the car and drove south along Brixton Road, turning left into Mostyn Road.

'I've been to Smiley's flat before one time wid Floyd,' Biscuit said. 'But you know what Myatts Field is like – one big friggin' maze. I'll never find it again.'

'Yeah, but I know where Dyer's flat is,' replied Coffin Head. 'We'll head der first. He lives wid his mudder.'

Biscuit scanned the interior of the car. 'When you gonna fix up dis car, man? Look how my seat is eaten out! No girl will sit 'pon dis. Dat yellow fluffy stuff is all coming out. An' when you gonna get a new handle for de window? An' bwai, you better get some more carpet to cover up de rust an' t'ing 'pon de floor.'

'I'll fix it up nex' week wid de corn I'll make off de herb. An' stop your complaining; dis car has saved you nuff trods on a cold night. We coulda walked to Myatts Field anyway, it's only a five-minute trek.'

'I don't like walking across dat green wid all de amount of untold dog shit . . . An' who de rarse is Dyer?'

'Luther Dyer, jus' come out of Borstal. He went to Kennington Boys an' used to walk wid de Sledgehammer posse.'

'Wha' did he go Borstal for?'

'Drapes a handbag an' t'ing off a girl at Cats Whiskers. Beastman were waiting for him outside de club and he tried to chip but dey caught him jus' outside Brixton Bus Garage. He shoulda known dat de beast always patrol outside de club. I t'ought it was a bit extra for de beast to 'ave van, nuff dog and truncheons blazing.'

'How much bird did he get?'

' 'Bout a year. Beast went to his yard an' found whole 'eap of uder t'ings. His mudder went cuckoo, cos she didn't know nutten.'

Coffin Head turned into the Myatts Field Estate, driving down a narrow road with alleyways and paths leading off in all directions. Tiny sections of grass, dissected by cheap wooden partitions, fronted two- and three-storey blocks that seemed to have been built by an agoraphobic architect.

Coffin Head found a parking space and eyed a trio of black teenagers smoking cigarettes and shooting the breeze. 'I ain't leaving my car here for long,' he commented.

They climbed out of the car and surveyed the low-level concrete jungle around them. Coffin Head led the way up two flights of stairs to a path that offered no view outside the estate and was hardly touched by the sun. It was hard to tell where one home started and another finished. They kept a close watch over their shoulders, only too aware that even bad men got mugged around here. After many turns, they finally arrived at Dyer's fortressed door. Coffin Head knocked impatiently.

'Who dat?'

'Coffin Head an' Biscuit.'

'I ain't got no corn to buy telly, hi-fi or anyt'ing like dat.'

'But we're selling some nice collie, what you saying?'

The callers heard two mortice locks click back. The door swung open to reveal Dyer wearing a thick pullover and woolly hat.

'Gas man cut off de gas to rarted,' he began. 'My mudder tried to reason wid dem but dey weren't 'aving it. Friggin' stinkin' gas man dem. I have it in mind to break

27

in to one of der yards an' turn de gas on, fling a match an' chip. Dey couldn't wait ah nex' week for us to pay de bill. An' my mudder gets bronchitis . . . What herb you 'ave? Sinsemilla?'

'Nah, jus' collie,' Coffin Head answered. 'What d'you want? Ten pound draw?'

'Yeah, but I wanna sample it first. Nuff imitation herb 'pon street.'

Dyer led his acquaintances along the narrow hallway to his bedroom. Once inside, Biscuit took out his rizlas and built a smooth spliff.

'So what brings you two 'round 'ere? Don't usually get 'ome delivery – more time I affe get my herb 'pon de Line. An' you know dat's a dangerous t'ing.'

While rolling the joint, Biscuit gazed at the Che Guevara poster that overlooked the bed. 'Well, apart from dealing,' he replied, 'we're trying to find Smiley.'

'Smiley! Dat ginall. He's trying to check my sister. Told my sister dat he's got six pickney already but she ain't listening.'

'So where's his yard?' Coffin Head butted in.

'Five doors away, an' if you see him tell him to stay away from Chantelle. She's only sixteen.'

After tasting the herb, Dyer nodded with a half-grinned satisfaction and paid for the merchandise.

'It's alright,' he remarked. 'Ain't got too much seed in it an' burns OK.'

'Yeah,' Coffin Head agreed. 'It's de best herb we've 'ad for a while. You should buy up some more before we sell out.'

'Nah, my budget's kinda sad right now.'

'So you've come out of de import–export business,' laughed Coffin Head.

'Yeah, I got to see a friggin' probation officer every Friday. An' my mudder says dat if she finds out I'm t'iefing again, she'll fling me out wid de chicken bones.'

'Well, wish I could stay an' chat but we've got some runnings to do,' announced Biscuit, and the two wasted no time in leaving.

Following Dyer's instruction, they found Smiley's flat. The door was made of a varnished hardwood and had two spy-holes. Looking at the three locks, Coffin Head thought it funny that Smiley worried about burglars. Biscuit knocked ferociously.

'Ah, who de backside beat down me door!' stormed a voice on the inside.

'It's Biscuit. Open de door nuh, man.'

Smiley opened the door, wearing only his football shorts and a not-this-time-of-morning expression on his face.

'Look, right, I ain't buying nutten. Dis is Sunday, man. You wanna observe de rarted Sabbath.'

'Char! Shut your mout' an' let us in de yard. Serious business we come to discuss,' announced Coffin Head.

Smiley, taken aback by Coffin Head's temper and wondering if his two associates had had a recent visit from the police, stood aside and let Biscuit and an impatient Coffin Head pass inside. Reaching the lounge, the visitors recognised the expensive furniture and top-of-the-range Sony hi-fi system from a burglary they'd done two months back. The hardware was totally out of sync with the crudely painted blue walls, the home-made coffee table and ageing burgundy carpet.

'If you ain't selling den why are you beating down my gates,' inquired Smiley.

'Dose t'ings we sold you de uder day – we got to 'ave dem back,' answered Biscuit.

'What d'you mean 'ave dem back?'

'We raided the wrong friggin' yard! It turned out to be Nunchaks' brudder's woman yard.'

Smiley fell on the sofa in hysterics. 'You two raided the wrong yard! What a palaver. Nunchaks mus' ah been well happy.'

Biscuit and Coffin Head looked at one another, both thinking that a punch on Smiley's jaw was not totally out of the question.

'Dis might be a joke to you but I nearly get fling over a friggin' balcony cos of dis,' said a solemn Biscuit. 'Where's de t'ings, man? You ain't sold dem on yet 'ave you?'

Smiley needed a few seconds to compose himself. In his mind, Biscuit was suddenly transported back to the top of the tower block and his confrontation with Nunchaks. Coffin Head shifted his feet uneasily, fearing Smiley's reply.

'No, not yet,' he finally answered. 'Lucky you, innit. Der still in my van. I ain't had time to put dem in my lock-up yet.'

'Thank fuck fe dat,' sighed Biscuit. 'Where's de van?'

'Behind the block. But before we go down, we affe chat 'bout de money side.'

'Char,' Coffin Head scoffed. 'You paid us two hundred notes for de t'ings an' we jus' gi' you de money back, innit.'

'No, dat can't work, man,' Smiley argued. 'You affe gi' me a nex' twenty notes for my inconvenience.' He rubbed his fingers together, gesturing a little payback.

'Inconvenience? Char! Wha' inconvenience? Your backside weren't on the job so fuck your inconvenience. I should inconvenience your fockin' backside wid a drill to rarted,' Coffin Head threatened.

'I had to cancel some runnings I had to do dat T'ursday night. Like my sound was s'posed to be playing up Settlement in Peckham, but I had to reschedule.'

'Reschedule which part!' contested Coffin Head. 'Since when your sound plays in Settlement? You've got barely got enough boxes to play in a t'ree room blues, let alone a hall like Settlement.'

'Look, I ain't arguing wid you. Gimme a nex' twenty notes.'

'Char! After all de favours we done you.'

'Give 'im his twenty notes, Coff. You know how he's grabilicious from time.'

'Char!'

Coffin Head pulled up his trouser leg, rolled down his sock and took out a wad of notes bound with elastic bands. He carefully counted out £220 and begrudgingly handed it to Smiley, who checked the amount again.

'It's nice doing business wid you,' grinned Smiley. 'I'm gonna rinse off my BO, pull on one of my Cecil Gees, den I'll drive de van 'round to your lock-up. You can follow me in your mash-up car.'

'Fuck you! It gets me from A to B,' Coffin Head argued. 'Jus' 'urry up, man.'

Twenty minutes later, Smiley was opening up the back of his van. 'No damage,' he proclaimed. 'You can check everyt'ing. I even got one of my girl to polish an' clean de goods de uder night. Bwai, you wanna see de legs she's got; Dawn's her name.'

Coffin Head, not entirely convinced by Smiley's assurances, leaped into the back of the vehicle and cast a critical eye over the stolen goods. He noticed a small tear on the back of one of the armchairs, but remembered that was done while loading the van. He hoped Nunchaks wouldn't see it. 'Yeah, he's right, man, everyt'ing looks alright.'

Keeping a keen eye out for any nosey-parkers, Biscuit caught sight of a moving net curtain. 'Coff, 'urry up an' close de shutters, man. Don't trus' de people in dis estate. Some of dem are squealers.'

'Wha' did you see?' asked Smiley.

'Someone's watching us,' replied Biscuit.

Coffin Head jumped down and hurriedly closed the shutters behind him. 'Let's remove from dis place, man. I'm parked up jus' 'round de corner. Follow us, yeah. We're going to Biscuit's lock-up behind Cowley.'

'Yeah, I 'ear you. Don't boder drive off too fast cos dis van is a crawler – second gear don't work.'

'Seen.'

On their way to the car, Coffin Head and Biscuit walked past the teenagers they had seen earlier, who glared at the two as if they wanted trouble. They returned the challenge with cut eyes of their own before jumping into the Dolomite.

'Better be careful, Coff,' advised Biscuit. 'Dey could be members of de Field crew.'

'Char! If dey wanted to start somet'ing, dey would 'ave!'

Coffin Head U-turned and drove slowly out of the estate, waiting for Smiley to catch up with him. Biscuit, more concerned about the twitching net curtain than the ever watchful gang, silently urged him to speed up; he didn't trust anybody from this place.

Turning right into Brixton Road, Coffin Head pulled out in front of a police car. Shit! Why didn't I see de beast wagon? he cursed himself. 'Char, beast. Let's hope dey jus' drive past.'

32

Biscuit slapped his palm on the dashboard in irritation and glanced over his shoulder to see if Smiley was immediately behind. He was. '*Shit!*'

'I'll slow down,' Coffin Head said. 'Hopefully, de beast will jus' drive past.'

The patrol car accelerated ahead then veered across the road, forcing Coffin Head to brake sharply. Smiley, in the van behind, bottomed his brake pedal to stop himself from driving into the back of the Dolomite. The stolen cargo shifted forward and Smiley heard a faint crushing sound. He looked out through the windscreen and saw he had missed the back end of Coffin Head's car by six inches. He then met Biscuit's frantic gaze before looking ahead to the white and blue Allegro with two officers inside.

'Ah wha de blouse an' skirt!' screamed Smiley. 'You waan kill me?'

'Oh my fucking days,' cried Biscuit, shaking his head. 'We're fucking jinxed, man.'

Coffin Head looked down to the floor of the car and closed his eyes. 'We're fucked, totally fucked. An' Smiley's gonna go into one.'

A tall, twenty-something officer, sporting a crew cut with long ginger sideburns, stepped out of the patrol car and surveyed the scene in front of him. He quickly strode past Coffin Head's car to Smiley's vehicle. Smiley looked to the heavens and prayed that the hot goods had not yet been reported to the beast. The policeman stood in front of the window and gestured for Smiley to wind it down. Coffin Head and Biscuit looked on, their heartbeats resonating through to their throats.

'Good morning, sir,' the officer said. 'I take it you do have the relevant documents for this vehicle?'

Smiley regretted ever opening his door to Biscuit and Coffin Head, wishing he had taken up the offer to stay at Dawn's yard for the night. He would be nice and cosy in bed still, probably having a breakfast of fried plantain, eggs and ardough bread. 'Yeah, I'm legal,' he finally replied, staring ahead through the windscreen, refusing to meet the eyes of the policeman.

'Do you have your licence on you, sir?'

'I don't carry it 'round wid me, it's at my yard.'

'Let's hope it is. But all the same, I will give you a producer. If you have your documents, then you will have nothing to worry about.'

'Can't you take my word? I don't lie y'know, I'm a Christian.'

'Now, sir, if I did that all the time, eighty per cent of people around here would drive safely in the knowledge that they were *not* legal.'

'Look,' Smiley said, shaking his head in exasperation. 'Your people 'ave stopped me before, man. I'm safe. Ain't you got nutten better to do? Shouldn't you be finding out who fling a petrol bomb in dat party at Deptford de uder day.'

Coffin Head had wound down his window in an attempt to eavesdrop on the exchange. He couldn't hear much, but saw Smiley apparently being asked to step out of the van.

'And what do you have in the back,' the officer demanded in a superior tone.

'I'm jus' helping my brethrens move, innit. Jus' doing a favour.'

'Open it up!'

Biscuit and Coffin Head heard the demand. They looked at each other and decided to emerge from the car, their minds furiously whirring as to what to do. On seeing Biscuit and Coffin Head approach his colleague, the second policeman, who had remained in the patrol car, busied himself with his radio before stepping out, imagining the worst of scenarios.

'Do you understand English!? Open it up!' the ginger-crowned officer repeated.

Smiley's delay gave Biscuit time to think. 'He's jus' helping me move, innit. Nutten going on funny, officer.'

'I'll be the judge of that. Open it.'

Smiley lifted the shutters, thinking he was going back to his home of four months ago: Wormwood Scrubs. The two officers peered inside. 'I hope you've got receipts for this lot?'

'You know how it is, officer,' Biscuit answered. 'When you're moving house, t'ings get lost an' t'ing.'

'Do you have the receipts or not?'

'It'll take a while to look for dem. Let it pass an' I'll come up to de station tomorrow an' show you nuff receipts.'

'Let it *pass*! Do you take me for a fucking idiot? This van stays with us until we complete our checks.'

'What d'you mean de van stays wid you?' Smiley bemoaned. 'I was jus' helping a brethren move. My van's got nutten to do wid it.'

'We don't even know if the van belongs to you, do we?' the officer snapped.

'You lot 'ave stopped me untold times already an' gi' me producers,' Smiley argued again. 'I've 'ad more producers dan Hollywood.'

'Wanna entertain my colleagues with your remarks down the station, do you?'

The policeman doing all the talking turned to his

colleague and together they ambled out of Smiley's earshot. 'Have you got the form, Denis? Make out one for that Dolomite over there as well. Look at the state of it. I bet that thing never passed an MOT – it looks like it's been in a stock car rally.'

Coffin Head wasn't amused. The policeman scribbled down the registration numbers of the van and the Dolomite, then handed it to his colleague who returned to the Allegro and picked up the car's radio.

'Right, you lot, names and addresses, and don't give me no bullshit because it ain't worth it.'

Smiley responded first. 'My first an' middle name is Smiley Stopped-By-Beast. My surname is Suspect.'

The policeman paced towards Smiley with menace. Biscuit shook his head while Coffin Head whispered, 'We're fucked, totally fucked.'

'Now, you might think you're funny,' the policeman said soberly. 'Perhaps you want to be charged with obstructing police inquiries?'

'Stop friggin' about, Smiley,' rebuked Biscuit. 'Tell him what he wants, we ain't done nutten.'

'Jus' winding you up, officer,' Smiley laughed.

'*Name and address!*'

'Charlton Forbes,' Smiley answered. He gave the officer his address and Coffin Head and Biscuit did likewise.

After a five-minute wait, during which the officer wrote in his notebook, the other policeman emerged from his car and spoke quietly to his colleague. The three black youths crooked their ears in an attempt to listen. Coffin Head knew he was legal, but he wasn't sure about Smiley.

'Seems like you lot are who you say you are,' one of the officers stated. 'But both vehicle owners will be required to produce their documents to a police station of their choice. The form tells you exactly what to do.'

'I'm an expert,' Smiley grinned.

'Within seven days,' the policeman added.

Biscuit thought of Nunchaks' ultimatum: seven days to get the stolen goods back to him. He produced a wry smile as he realised he was halfway out of the hole he had got himself into.

After a check on Coffin Head's car lights, indicators and tyres, the policemen returned to their car and were on their way. The black youths watched them drive northbound, towards Kennington.

Biscuit sighed. 'Dat was fucking close. It's a good t'ing de goods weren't reported, otherwise we'd be yamming oats for breakfast.'

'Speak for yourself,' said Smiley.

The trio continued their journey into Cowley estate, turning into a side road where blue-painted garages with flat-topped roofs stretched out for a hundred yards or so. None of the pull-up garage doors had escaped the signature of a graffiti artist called Howling Lion. Biscuit was especially careful as he off-loaded their cache from the back of the lorry into the garage, telling Smiley and Coffin Head to cover the stereo with black bin liners and look out for any passers-by who might have an interest. Soon Smiley was on his way, telling his spars that some girl was expecting him. Coffin Head and Biscuit remained in the lock-up, surrounded by car parts, odd bits of furniture, all sorts of hi-fi equipment, a top of the range camera, a brand-new food mixer and other miscellaneous items, all overlooked by a huge poster of Bob Marley, the Gong.

'So what's your plans for de rest of de day?' Coffin Head asked.

'I'm going up de Line, try an' sell some herb, den after dat I will check Carol. Ain't seen her all week.'

'You going up de Line?' Coffin Head said in alarm. 'Why don't we jus' sell the herb to people we know?'

'Cos I wanna mek up de corn we lost on dat burglary.'

'Bit drastic, innit? You don't know who you're going to meet up der so.'

'I'll be safe, man.'

'Char. Sometimes you're so headstrong. I'll catch you tomorrow.'

# 4

# The Front Line

Biscuit made his way to the Front Line – Railton Road – which led from the heart of Brixton to Herne Hill. It was just after 6pm. The wind was growing wilder by the hour, blowing empty lager cans and failed betting shop receipts along the kerb. Biscuit pulled his brown leather beret further down and pushed his hands deeper into the pockets of his black leather jacket. He turned left from Coldharbour Lane, heard a John Holt song as he walked past Desmond's Hip City record store, and nodded to a rasta cyclist he recognised.

As he reached his destination he clicked into cautionary mode, looking out for the police, bad men, madmen, or any other occurrence that might need a swift reaction. Almost all the housing on this terraced street was in need of repair. Every other house seemed to be boarded up, and the pavements were full of rubble and bits of wood. As he walked on, he knew he was being watched from countless windows and slightly open doors. 'Man, de t'ings a man 'ave to do to sell ah liccle herb,' he whispered to himself.

Biscuit knew this environment well, and his eyes were keen and his hearing acute as he found himself a clear spot from which to sell his wares, near to a row of four shops that sold West Indian produce such as tinned ackee, fish fritters, fried dumplings and rum cakes. One of the outlets was an off-licence. He sat on a wall outside a crumbling house, ignoring the comings and goings of suspicious men. He took out an already rolled spliff and lit it, observing the street for any potential customers. A green 3.5 Rover pulled up and out stepped the beaver-skin hatted Sammy Samurai, wrapped in an ankle-length black leather coat. The gangster walked past Biscuit, his metal-tipped soles echoing on the concrete, and offered him a faint smile of recognition as he disappeared into the residence. From somewhere above, Biscuit heard the shouts and yelps of a domino game in progress: 'Your double five *dead* to bloodclaat,' growled a voice. 'Gi me de rarse money *now!*'

Biscuit watched the Filthy Rocker sound bwai DJ Pancho Dread, whose dreadlocks were tucked into a moth-eaten sombrero, practising his latest rhymes about ten feet away, sitting on an unstable milk crate. '*Beast affe dead, me seh de beast affe dead, cos dem raid de party where me sister get wed, dem mash up de front room an' push over me bed, me gwarn tek me ratchet knife an' cut dem in dem head . . .*'

Biscuit's eyes lingered on a trio of whores walking up the street in perverse dignity. Their faces were caked in white powder and burgundy lipstick. The imitation fur jackets they wore were not long enough to cover their ridiculously short skirts, and the holes in their fishnet stockings were big enough for a hand to slip through. Black Uhuru's 'Shine Eye Gal' blared from a ghetto-blaster that Biscuit couldn't quite locate.

Zigzagging across the road in a drunken stupor was a bare-footed man dressed in only a string vest and stained trousers that were cut off at the calves. 'Everyone's gonna die,' he cried, his face giving way to an enormous smile as he waved his arms about. 'Do you know wha'appened in Sodom an' Gomorra? Sleeping wid Satan will be de sinners reward. *I* am de reincarnation of John de Baptist, so mark my words, Judgement Day will be soon upon us.' The population of the street jeered and laughed as the wild-haired man followed his haphazard course.

Biscuit didn't have to wait long for custom. A white girl in an African-type head-wrap approached him. 'You selling?' she whispered.

'Might be,' he replied.

'I've got ten pound and I want some grass.'

'Happy to oblige, madam.'

'It better be good stuff.'

'Char, man. You want de t'ings or not?'

The girl, no older than fifteen, showed Biscuit her ten-pound note. He nodded and delved into his inside pocket. He'd already portioned his weed into matchbox size polythene bags. His inside right pocket contained his five-pound draws, his inside left the tens.

Not bothering to check her merchandise, the girl turned and disappeared into the passenger seat of a Cortina Mark Two with tinted windows. 'Poor bitch,'

Biscuit whispered to himself. 'What's she doing out 'pon dis street at her age?'

Within two hours, he had made over £160. He still had over seventy-five per cent of the herb left, and guessed that if he continued at this rate, he and Coffin Head would make over double their outlay. He knew he'd been fortunate because Soferno B sound system had wired up their set in a run-down terrace about 100 yards away, testing out some new speakers. They had attracted a sizeable crowd which proved to be a good customer base for ganga, and Biscuit got his share.

He was preparing to depart the Front Line when he saw a familiar face approach him. His greying locks falling over a large forehead, Jah Nelson fixed Biscuit with the glare of one eye. His other eye was misshapen and half closed. A familiar figure to Brixtonians, Biscuit always saw Jah Nelson at Town Hall dances, especially when Shaka sound system was playing. But he wasn't sure whether to believe a story that his friend, Floyd, had told him.

Apparently, Nelson had been arrested at the front door of Westminster Abbey with a 'disciple' of his, both of them carrying pick-axes. Defending himself and his disciple in court, Nelson told the magistrate that since European man had continually desecrated the tombs of ancient Egyptian royalty and got away with it, he didn't see no reason why he couldn't destroy the tomb of an English monarch. The magistrate sentenced him to six months in prison.

'Biscuit's de name, innit?' Nelson asked.

Biscuit nodded at the dread. The rasta was dressed in what could only be described as Jesus Christ's line of fashion, but on this particular street he didn't look out of place. 'Wha'appened to de army trousers, dread? You gone all African 'pon me.'

'I haven't gone all African 'pon you. I's been an African from time.'

'So, Jah Nelson, you come up here for your supply of collie?'

'What's it to you?'

'Might be able to help you out, dread,' Biscuit said with a wink.

Nelson glared at him accusingly. 'Ain't you ah bit young to walk an' go' long dis street an' sell 'erb?'

'What's it to you?'

'Cah dis is ah dangerous place. You mus' know dat all kinda man get jook up on dis road fe liccle more dan nutten.'

'Look, right, a man's got to survive an' I'm old enough to do wha' I want fe do.'

'Ah man you call yourself. Ah man would try fe do somet'ing better, and nah get 'imself moulded by de environment where 'im live.' Nelson watched Sammy Samurai return to his car, then set his one eye upon a whore who was idling on the pavement. Realising that her employer was waiting in the car, the prostitute ran to the 3.5 Rover and climbed inside. Biscuit tailed the car as it pulled away, heading to Herne Hill.

'I don't get involved in dat kinda shit,' he finally replied. 'I'm jus' 'ere to sell my liccle herb.'

'But you will. Given time.'

'Wha' you on 'bout, Nelson? You've lost me. Do you want to buy or not? If not, den stop wasting my time.'

'I want ah quarter ounce, but on one condition.'

'A quarter! Dat will be 50 notes. What's de condition?'

'Dat we mek de exchange in *my* yard.'

'Where you live? I ain't trodding nuff miles, I've 'ad a busy day.'

'Jus' up near Fiveways.'

Biscuit knew the place, it was not two minutes' walk from where he lived. 'Alright den, lead off.'

He followed the dread, thinking of his mother's smile when he would give her the money to buy Royston's new shoes, and his sister's grin when he handed her the cash for her new dress. He felt it wasn't an ideal situation and suffered a tinge of guilt, but it was the best he could do for now. Survival was the game.

Jah Nelson walked slowly, looking like a modern-day Nazarene, satisfied with a flock of one. The dread didn't talk much on the way along Coldharbour Lane, choosing to survey the people he passed, which only added to Biscuit's suspicion. Ah well, he thought, if the dread was gonna give him fifty notes, he didn't care how weird he looked. But he hoped the police wouldn't see him. They were more likely to stop or arrest somebody who walked with Jah Nelson.

Following his release from prison in the summer of 1979, Nelson had taken to delivering lectures on racial pride in Brockwell Park. His audience would sometimes consist of a few dreads and curious kids, but the police deemed him a stirrer of racial hatred, asking him to leave the park at every opportunity. Recently, Nelson had decided to protest about his persecution on the steps of Brixton Police Station. This led to a charge of disturbance of the peace. He served another month's sentence.

On reaching Fiveways, Nelson led Biscuit down a narrow road to the entrance of Loughborough estate. The dread lived on the third floor of a faded yellow-bricked council block. About forty paces along a rubber walkway from the flight of concrete stairs, he unfastened the mortice locks to his front door and led Biscuit inside.

Biscuit was immediately drawn to the pictures and paintings that hung in the hallway. He ambled slowly along, taking in images of Haile Selassie, Malcolm X, Bob Marley, Mahatma Gandhi and the great pyramids of Giza. Nelson looked at Biscuit's wonderment and smiled, then led the way to his front room. On entering, Biscuit thought to himself that the dread should rename it a library. There were books everywhere: upon shelves, covering the home-made coffee table, beside the hi-fi and on a table where Biscuit thought a telly should have been.

Nelson told him to sit down in an armchair while he went to ignite an incense stick jutting out of a vase that was resting on another home-made table in the corner of the room. Biscuit made himself comfortable and began to study the walls. In front of him, hanging over a gas heater, was a large painting of an African woman breastfeeding her child. Scanning clockwise, he saw a smaller sketched drawing of a slave ship crossing the Atlantic. In the corner of the room was a painting that depicted the selling of slaves in a Western market, while staring from the adjacent wall was a photo of Jack Johnson, the first black heavy-weight champion, and beside that was a portrait of Malcolm X. Biscuit looked behind him and a huge map of ancient Africa filled his sight. He felt as if he had stepped into a different world. Nelson smiled as he studied Biscuit's face.

'You're pretty serious 'bout your stuff, innit?' Biscuit said, still looking around.

Nelson took out his rizlas. 'Yeah, mon. Being a rasta-man is not my religion, it's my life.'

Biscuit felt uncomfortable and wanted to finish the deal. 'You said you wanna quarter?'

'Dat can wait. Hol' on ah liccle.' Nelson went to his bedroom and returned with a red, gold and green scarf in his hand. 'Get up,' he ordered.

Biscuit did as he was told.

'Right, walk to the door,' Nelson instructed.

'Wha' for?'

'Jus' do wha' I say, man. I want to show you somet'ing.'

Biscuit walked to the door. 'Hey, Nelson, man. You've been smoking too much herb, dread. Wha' kinda tom-foolery is dis?'

'It's tomfoolery dat so many yout's don't know dem history.' Nelson stood impassive. 'Now, walk to de middle of de room.'

'What? Wha' you up to, dread? You mus' tek me for fool.'

'Jus' do what I say, an' be patient.'

Nonplussed, Biscuit walked to the centre of the room. 'Right, now we got the palaver out of the way, show me your corn, dread, and I will give you de herb.'

'Patience, man, you mus' 'ave patience. Attum-Ra, why de yout's dem nuh 'ave no patience?'

'Wha' now?' Biscuit asked. 'If I knew you'd 'ave me prancing about like an idiot I wouldn't of come here.' What is de dread up to? he asked himself. I'm friggin' glad dat Sceptic ain't 'ere, he'd be rolling on de floor by now, laughing his head off.

'Jus' hol' on,' the dread persuaded. 'I jus' wan' to teach you somet'ing.'

Nelson approached Biscuit with the scarf in his hand. 'I'm gonna put dis scarf to cover your eye dem. Den, you try an' do wha' you jus' done before. Start from

46

de door an' walk to de middle of de room.'

'Nelson, man! I t'ink you've gone too many days without socks, dread. It's turning you fool to rarted.'

'Jus' do what I say.'

Biscuit took the scarf and covered his eyes, securing it at the back of his head. He then tried to make his way to the centre of the room, feeling his way around the furniture and stepping uneasily around the coffee table. Nelson laughed heartily, but Biscuit tolerated the humiliation, thinking it was worth his while if he was going to make fifty notes.

After stumbling twice, he found the door. 'Right, now try an' walk over to de under side of de room,' Nelson ordered.

Biscuit felt his feet brush against the sofa, and as he went further he suffered a sharp pain as his hand met the corner of a hardback book resting on the arm of the sofa. The book fell and Biscuit almost felt himself follow it to the floor.

Nelson had seen enough. 'Alright, tek de scarf off an' si' down.'

Satisfied that the dread had had his entertainment, Biscuit sat on the sofa. Nelson disappeared off to his bedroom and returned with fifty pounds in his hand. He gave the money to Biscuit and sat beside him, grinning like a smug teacher. 'Now, you might t'ink I'm jus' teking de piss, as de Cockney man say. But de image of you stumbling around an' not knowing quite where you were is somet'ing you should remember.'

Biscuit was still none the wiser, gently shaking his head. Nelson eyed the boy's confusion.

'Now, 'ear dis,' the dread continued, pointing a scholarly finger at Biscuit. 'A long time ago, two different nations were virtually wiped off de earth by a terrible flood, hardly anybody survive. One of de nations used to keep records an' books written on tablets an' so forth. But de uder nation never kept nutten like dis. De survivors from de nation dat keep records an' books rebuilt der country by using old documents dat dey found, an' dey became prosperous again. De uder nation, although once ah great civilised country, der survivors were forever blinded by de flood an' dey did nuh know how to build nutten. To dis day dey are living like cave man.'

Nelson pointed to the map of Africa. Biscuit took no notice and decided to fish out his client's herb. The dread needs serious help, he thought. He's probably been licking de chalice too much.

Nelson seemed disappointed at the lack of interest Biscuit took in his lesson. He examined the herb and nodded when he felt satisfied. 'When ah man wanders far an' decides to settle down near ah village of huts,' he resumed, 'should he do wha' de locals do an' buil' 'imself ah hut? Or should he do somet'ing new an' buil' ah 'ouse wid brick?'

'Wha'?' Biscuit replied, preparing to leave. 'Nelson, man. I ain't got time for your funny stories dem. I affe dally.'

Nelson stroked his stringy beard. 'You t'ink you could come to my yard every two weeks an' sell me some collie?'

'Yeah, dat could be arranged. But don't expect me to walk 'round wid some scarf over my face.'

The dread laughed, but shook his head as he watched Biscuit depart.

# Oh Carol

'Shouldn't you be sleeping?' Biscuit rebuked his younger brother. It was past nine when he finally made it home from Jah Nelson's estate. The flat was quiet for once and he had found Royston alone, sitting on their bed.

'Shouldn't you have been home for dinner?' asked Royston mischievously.

'Put de damn cars away an' go to your bed. I wish I never bought you de damn t'ings. De uder day I went to my bed an' one of your blasted cars 'cratched me in my back.'

Royston hid himself under the covers, but his brother could still hear the stifled laughter coming from under the blankets. Biscuit ignored him and placed his herb and money on top of his wardrobe. He then took off his zip-up bomber jacket and pulled off his beret, revealing knotty, tangled hair. He headed for the lounge.

His mother was sewing buttons on one of Royston's grey school shirts, occasionally looking up at the news bulletin on the telly. Denise was sitting on the sofa, chatting away to one of her friends on the phone. She was talking about some party or other and asking if she could borrow a pair of shoes.

'You waan me to warm up your dinner, Lincoln?' Hortense offered.

'No, it's alright, Mummy, I can do it.'

Biscuit went to the kitchen and lit two gas rings. He put a dab of margarine in the rice and peas saucepan and replaced the lid, then poured half a cup of water into the boiled chicken pot, stirring it with a fork. He checked his watch, wondering if it wasn't too late to travel up to Brixton Hill and call on Carol. She was expecting him and he hated letting her down. His thoughts were interrupted by a manic banging on the front door.

'Who ah bang 'pon me door so?' Hortense queried. 'Lincoln, 'ow many times 'ave me tell you fe tell your friends dem not to bang down me door!'

Biscuit went to the door. 'Easy nuh, man. You sound like beast to rarted.'

A frantic thirty-something white woman, whose elfin-like face didn't quite match her heavy frame, stood on the balcony. The woman seemed to have been crying for days. Her long auburn hair wouldn't have recognised a comb, and underneath the tear stains her face was a pink mass of sadness. She was wearing a tatty dressing gown and slippers.

'Where's your mum, Lincoln?' she asked desperately.

Before Biscuit could reply, the lady was past him and inside the lounge. Hortense stopped sewing and looked up in concern. Biscuit returned to the kitchen and peered through the doorway as his mother got to her feet and switched off the telly. Denise paused in her conversation and ran her eyes over the white woman's blotched face.

'Hortense, I just don't know what I'm gonna do,' the white woman whimpered, holding her temples within her palms and then shaking her head. 'I haven't seen Frank for two days, they cut off the electric yesterday, the kids are hungry, I ain't got no money.' She covered her face with her hands, shifting her feet in an unsteady semi-circle. 'I just can't carry on, Hortense. I've had it up to 'ere. Fucking social are no use, the gas people are on my case and Frank's gone. He's *fucking* gone, without a fucking word. He's just fucking gone!'

'Stella, slow down, you're talking too fast,' Hortense replied, ushering her friend to sit beside her. Stella wrapped her arms around her stomach as if she was suffering some cramp, then dropped herself on the sofa.

'I might as well fucking kill myself. Frank's gone, how could he just go like that? I'm at my wits' end. I dunno where I'm turning. How could he fucking leave me like this!'

Hortense put her arms around the shoulders of her friend. Biscuit watched from the kitchen, embarrassed by Stella's sobbing and cursing Frank under his breath. Denise said a quick goodbye to her friend and looked on, wondering what she could do to help.

'Denise! Don't jus' sit der! Run downstairs an' get Tommy an' Sarah. Den gi' dem somet'ing to eat,' Hortense ordered her daughter aggressively. 'An' mek Stella ah cup ah tea.'

Royston poked his face around the door frame to see what the commotion was all about. 'Royston!' Hortense yelled. 'Go back to your bed before me bus' your backside.'

'I just can't take it no more,' Stella wept. 'Frank went for a job interview for a labouring job the other day, but he didn't get it. Since then he's been acting all funny. I thought he might snap out of it after a while. But he's gone. I've phoned his mum but he ain't been 'round there. I even phoned his brother in Birmingham. I dunno where he is.'

Denise returned with two bewildered children in tow. The youngest child, a girl, gripped her teddy tightly as her brother held on grimly to an old *Beano* magazine. They edged into the room as if embarrassed to see their mother in such a state. The girl covered her face with the bear.

'Hiya, Tommy,' Royston greeted, braving the hallway once again. 'Hiya, Sarah.'

'Royston!' Hortense screamed. 'If me 'ave fe tell you again your backside will be sizzling like fried chicken-back! *Go to your bed*!'

On sight of her children, Stella palmed away her tears, trying to regain her composure. Hortense tenderly stroked her friend's hair. Denise stood at the kitchen doorway waiting for instructions, while Biscuit guiltily prepared his dinner. 'Gi de pickney dem some bun an' cheese,' Hortense ordered. 'De last time we baby-sit fe dem, dey did favour it.'

Biscuit didn't want to get stuck with all this woman's business. He took his dinner to his bedroom on a tray, catching Royston standing by the door, feeling pushed out of the drama.

'Wha' did Mummy say?' Biscuit scolded. 'Get to your blasted bed.'

Royston did as he was told while he watched his brother

52

eat his dinner. 'Why was Stella crying?' he asked.

'Cos Frank's gone missing an' she ain't got no money.'

'Did Frank go missing cos he can't find a job?'

'Somet'ing like dat.'

'So, when people been looking for a job for a long time, and they can't find one, do they do what Frank done? Just go somewhere and go missing?'

Biscuit didn't answer. In a strange way, he thought his brother was right. People did go missing when they couldn't find work. They went missing in the head. Some, like Biscuit himself, sought to provide by illegal means. Every Saturday morning he witnessed the exodus of single mothers to various prisons throughout the country to visit their providers, rationing the week's social security cheque to afford the fares. He knew that some of these desperate women, especially the ones with children, had already shacked up with other men who came by their incomes via illegal means, starting the cycle all over again. He wondered when the day would come when his mother would have to visit him only on Saturdays.

Frank was a decent guy, always offering Biscuit a can of beer if he could afford it. And he loved his kids, forever taking them out to the park. But he hadn't worked in a steady job for nearly three years. From the smart-dressed guy Biscuit knew as a child, Frank had transformed into an unshaven figure who raged at the staff in the job centre for a chance of work, any work. With Frank's brooding and getting under his wife's feet at home, the rows with Stella had increased, and so did the money they owed.

Biscuit dropped a naked chicken bone on his plate then reached up to take two tenners from the top of his wardrobe, calling out to his mother, 'Mummy, come 'ere for a sec, I waan chat to you.'

Hortense ambled into her sons' room, shaking her head as she searched her eldest son's eyes. 'She's inna right state,' she said softly, bringing her gaze down to the carpet. 'Me nuh know wha fe say to her, I really don't. She jus' bawlin' an bawlin'. Frank dis an' Frank dat. If me see 'im me gwarn gi' 'im two bitch lick. Me cyan't tek Stella noise inna me 'ead. An' de two pickney dem jus' ah si' down quiet like mice, looking at dem mudder.'

Biscuit glanced quickly at the top of the wardrobe to check if his bags of herb were out of his mother's sight. A powerful surge of guilt took hold of him as he slowly raised his right hand that clutched two ten-pound notes. 'Control dis for her,' he offered.

Hortense looked at the cash for five seconds before opening her left palm. 'Y'know Lincoln, yu 'ave ah 'eart. Like I said before, me nuh waan to know weh yu get your money from. But yu 'ave ah 'eart. God bless.' She departed with a stolen glance at the top of the wardrobe.

Half an hour later, Biscuit caught a 109 bus, climbing up Brixton Hill to visit Carol. He had time to think about what he had done, and although moral questions echoed inside his head, he satisfied himself that survival was the game. He got off in front of a high steepled church opposite the narrow road that led to Brixton prison; he could just make out the high walls and spotlights in the distance. Walking into Carol's road, he heard the familiar screaming of police cars. Carol lived in the shadow of Strand secondary school, a building that could have been used for Gothic horror films with its pointed arches and sharp angles. She was one of the only friends Biscuit had who lived in a decent-sized house with a garden, which her father tended faithfully. Biscuit thought that if his own father was still alive, then perhaps his family would be living on a street like this.

Mentally polishing his manners, he rang the buzzer once. The door opened to reveal Carol with a comb in her hair, one half of it plaited, the other half afro. The hue of her skin was like perfect milk chocolate and her height was suitable for the catwalk. Her figure was slender, giving way to curves just where men liked them. Her onyx-coloured eyes were generous and kind, giving her an all round appearance of sensitivity. Wearing seamed blue jeans and a white polo-neck sweater, she smiled at her visitor. 'Alright, Biscuit,' she greeted. 'I was expecting you a liccle earlier. I'm jus' plaiting up my hair.'

'Yeah, well,' Biscuit said, his face yielding to a full grin. 'Got a liccle delayed.'

'Come in.' She gestured him through the door. She touched his arm as he passed and leant her face next to his, whispering, 'Remember to say hello to my parents.'

Biscuit followed her through the hallway, looking up to the high, white-glossed ceiling then dropping his sight to the richly embossed, beige wallpaper. Intimidation crept within him. Carol led him to the kitchen at the end of the hallway where her parents were sitting around a circular glass table, sipping coffee. Her father was a tall man with a neat, trimmed moustache. The hair he had was combed back behind his ears, leaving the top of his head naked. Carol's mother was wearing a black head scarf that crowned an unlined, angular face. She had the same dark eyes as her daughter.

Biscuit took in his surroundings and thought that his own mother would love to possess a washing machine and wash up her dishes in the two sinks he saw in front of him. He doubted that all the cupboards in Carol's kitchen would fit in the cramped cubicle where his mother cooked.

'Evening Mr Windett, evening Mrs Windett,' he greeted them.

'Evening, Lincoln,' Mrs Windett returned. 'An' a late one it is, too.'

Biscuit looked up at the clock that stood high over the double sink: nearly half past ten.

'Don't worry, Mrs Windett, I won't keep Carol long. I know she's got work in the morning.'

'You 'ave no work to go to inna de morning, Lincoln?' Mr Windett asked, peering over his reading glasses.

'No, but I have to get up early an' look about some interviews.'

'Good, dat is good,' Mr Windett replied, before returning to his gardening magazine.

Carol led Biscuit upstairs to her bedroom. It was decorated in peach-coloured wallpaper that gave it a warm feel. The burgundy carpet was deep enough to lose your toes in, and alongside the double bed was a white rug. The twin wardrobes each had a full-length mirror, and Biscuit lost count of the perfumes and toiletries upon the dressing table. On one side of the bed was a small, white-painted cabinet with a lamp resting on it, and in the corner of the room was a JVC stereo. Denise would love all this, he thought.

She invited him to sit at the foot of her double bed and then went over to her stereo system where she inserted a cassette tape. The Cool Notes' 'My Tune' sang softly from the speakers.

'Biscuit, you look troubled, man. Wha's de hard time pressure?' Carol asked, joining him on the bed and snuggling up close to his side while adjusting his brown beret.

'Nutten dat I can't sort out,' he replied, twirling his

56

right index finger around one of Carol's plaits. 'T'ings are running smoothly, man.'

'You know I don't like de business you're in.'

'Den wha' is a yout' like me s'posed to do?' Biscuit asked, dropping his hands to his thighs. 'You know my liccle hustling helps out my mudder. If it weren't for me we'd never pay de bills an' t'ing.'

'So wha' you gonna do in twenty years' time?' Carol asked, now fingering Biscuit's hair. 'Still sell herb down de Line?'

'No,' he answered, his eyes now shut. 'Hopefully I'll 'ave some kinda job by den.'

'You'll have to. Cos I told you before, I ain't going out wid no man who's hustling. One day we'll be raving out somewhere, de nex' you might be locked up. I ain't dealing wid dat, Biscuit. An' I don't business how much money you mek.'

'Wha's your problem, Carol? We rave together anyway, we spend a lot of time together, innit. An' besides, nuff innocent man get jail up by de beast.'

'Yeah, well. But wha' you're doing you 'ave more chance being jailed up. An' we rave as friends, only as friends. An' besides, Floyd an' Sharon would always come wid us, an' Coffin Head an' Brenton.'

'Wha's wrong wid dat? Dat's always been the case. Our posse always go everywhere together, innit.'

'Biscuit, listen to me proper, man,' Carol asserted, removing her fingers from his hair. 'You said you wanted to marry me one day. Now tell me, how can I marry a somebody who meks his money selling herb or doing whatever. Me an' you won't even get to first base if you're still carrying on wid dem t'ings der.'

Biscuit searched her eyes and realised she wouldn't

back down. He'd been after her a long time, since the third year of secondary school. After the school day finished, Biscuit would make a detour across Brockwell Park in the hope of seeing her after school hours. She and a few of her friends would walk from Dick Shepherd school into the park and shoot the breeze, sometimes fending off apprentice sweet-bwais. On the few occasions Biscuit did see her, fearful of rejection in front of his crew, he wouldn't say much, just a hi and a hello, but it made his day. One afternoon, he plucked up the courage to wait outside Carol's school gates, with the intention of asking her out for a date. She said no, telling him he was not her type. It felt like a mortal blow, but one his pride accepted after time healed his ego. When they both finished their education, they lost touch for a while; Biscuit knew where she lived but was too shy to knock on her door. It was only when Floyd started to go out with Carol's friend Sharon that Biscuit decided he'd better make a move, especially when Coffin Head expressed an interest in her. Now he wanted her as much, if not more, than ever before.

Louisa Mark's 'Caught You In A Lie' played quietly from the stereo, the anguished vocals giving the lyrics extra power. Carol studied her long-time friend and thought of the many if onlys between them. Biscuit's commitment to her she never doubted. Her wish was for him to rid himself of all crime and search for a career or a worthwhile job. Then they could make plans for the future, and perhaps even marry.

Deep down, she loved Biscuit. He had kind of grown on her through the years, like getting on terms with a glass of Guinness – the first you could hardly swallow, but by the seventh it's a cool taste. She dared not tell him of her true feelings, however. Things might get complicated.

58

'Some youts are going on dat YOP scheme run by the Government,' Carol suddenly announced. 'De money ain't brilliant but at least dey've got a chance of getting a permanent job when dey finish de six months course.'

'Yeah, I know,' Biscuit replied. 'Sceptic tried it. He quit after two weeks. He told me de money is only seven pounds a week better dan dole money. De government are only doing it to cut down on de unemployment figures, innit. An' besides, dem employers who use de scheme are jus' using de youts dem – a kinda slave labour. After de six months done dey don't offer any yout' a permanent job, dey jus' get anoder yout' to do a nex' six months, innit.'

'Yeah, I s'pose,' Carol agreed. 'It's depressing all 'round, innit?'

'How 'bout you?' Biscuit asked. 'How's your job? You get promotion yet? Got your own office an' t'ing wid your name 'pon de door?'

Carol laughed, thinking that there was absolutely no chance of promotion with all the white girls at her place of work. For the time being she could see no way of climbing up from her VDU operator title, although checking orders and typing invoices was getting a little boring. Her bosses at the mail order catalogue company made it clear to her that she was lucky to even have a job. 'Nah, I'll 'ave to be der a long time for dat. Probably when I'm a greyback.'

'How's Sharon getting on at college?' Biscuit asked, wanting to deflect any attention from his career prospects.

'She's doing alright y'know. You know dat last year she got all her O levels, well, she's jus' done her mocks for her A levels an' she reckon she done alright. She told me she wants to be a social worker.'

'Social worker? Rarted. At least one of us is going places.'

'Yeah, well, you know Sharon, always reading book an' t'ing. She don't even rave too much dese days. Wha' about Floyd? When is he gonna change his ways?'

'Floyd's the same, man. Den again he ain't the same. He's getting more vex by de day. He really hates white people y'know. All he does dese days is listen to Peter Tosh an' Burning Spear, an' last week he went down to the library down Brixton an takes out dese books 'bout communism an' dat Marxist t'ing. He's got talking to some of dem man who sell dat newspaper outside de tube station. He better mind 'imself cos man an' man say dat dem newspaper man get followed by spy an' shit.'

'Wha' about Brenton? I haven't seen 'im for a few weeks.'

'He's jus' got a flat in Palace Road. Don't see him too much meself dese days, he kinda keeps 'imself to 'imself. You noticed he's calmed down a bit since de Terry Flynn t'ing. He's doing alright y'know.'

'You see,' Carol said. 'If Brenton can get his runnings alright, den why can't you?'

'Cos I'm not good at nutten. I dunno wha' I can do. An' even if I did know, der's many youts all in de same queue for de one job.'

'Keep trying, man. You can't carry on what you're doing, an' dat goes to Coffin Head too.'

'Yeah, I know. But I got to survive, man. Wid all dis talk of de future I've got to pay for today. I don't like to see my mudder go widout.'

Carol had heard these words about Biscuit's mother often. It was a bond she found overbearing. With all the cash Biscuit accumulated, he didn't drive a car or overindulge in clothes. He had no expensive rings or heavy gold chains. And he didn't have an expansive music catalogue. She knew his money went to the maintenance and well-being of his family and she respected him for it.

'I better chip now, your parents will start cussing soon.'

'Yeah, alright den. You going to Maxine's wedding in two weeks' time? Floyd an' Sharon are going and I t'ought your mum would get an invitation. She knows Maxine's mum, innit?'

'Oh yeah, I forgot 'bout dat. Yeah, I should reach, all my family should reach.'

Carol escorted Biscuit downstairs where he bade goodbye to her parents. He met the cold Brixton air with a heaviness in his heart, wondering why Carol kicked up such a fuss about where his money came from. If we both like each uder, den wha's de problem, he asked himself. I s'pose I'll jus' 'ave to 'ave patience, he sighed. He recalled the thoughts of his brother: when a man hasn't got any work, they go missing. He felt that Royston should also have added that a man without work can't have the girl he loves. He looked into his future and dreaded that Carol might not be in it.

'Wha' de fuck am I gonna do?'

# Delivery

## 2 February 1981

'Why can't we jus' tell Nunchaks where to pick up the goods?' asked Coffin Head, bracing his shoulders to protect himself from the biting wind.

'Cos I don't trus' him,' replied Biscuit. 'I want man an' man to sight us leave together.'

'You're too para, man.'

'It wasn't you who was standing 'pon de top of de tallest tower block inna SW9.'

The pair were walking into Brixton High Street, leaving behind them the police station on their left-hand side just as twenty policemen emerged.

'Hey, Coff, we'd better step it up,' whispered Biscuit.

Coffin Head looked over his shoulder. 'Char! You're right.'

The heavens tried their best to offload a Christmas card amount of snow, but the storm clouds were shoved by a strong-armed wind. Beggars outside the tube station rubbed their mittened hands in resignation, for they knew that a cold day meant less offerings; people couldn't be bothered to take off their gloves to search for their loose change. The doom-mongers and bible addicts that usually frequented the lobby of Brixton Tube Station had obviously decided that the world would not end on this day.

'You sure Nunchaks will be in Soferno Bs record shack?' queried Coffin Head.

'Yeah, he always checks de place out on a Saturday afternoon. He don't buy much tune but he poses off his jewellery at the counter, innit, an' passes 'im comment to any girl who steps by.'

'He might not be der-ya today cos it's so friggin' cold,' replied Coffin Head, inwardly pining for his car.

'Stop bitchin', man,' Biscuit scolded. 'Anybody t'ink you were born in Jamaica, de way you go on. You been bitchin' since you left my gates, screwing up your face 'bout de cold.'

Passing underneath the railway bridge, the friends turned left into Atlantic Road where they saw a familiar face peering into a menswear shop window.

'Mikey, long time me nuh see you, brethren,' hailed Biscuit.

Mikey, Sharon's cousin, was wearing a sheepskin coat and a woollen hat. 'Biscuit, Coffin Head,' he greeted. 'Wha's appening? Still in de garden game?'

'Yeah, man,' Biscuit replied. 'So if you want your plants don't go to no one else.'

'If me get a discount . . .'

'Could work out somet'ing. Listen, yeah, we 'ave to step so we'll sight you later.'

'Seen.'

Coffin Head and Biscuit, now strutting like bad men, passed the section of Brixton market that was behind the main-line train station. Shoppers were studying a variety of wares that ranged from cheap digital watches to multi-coloured rugs. The street was carpeted with bits of soiled fruit, broken palettes and food wrappings. But even this could not wipe out the smell of fresh fish wafting through the air from the doorway that led to the arcade area of the market.

Soferno Bs record shack, on the corner of Atlantic Road and Coldharbour Lane, was populated by sound men and idlers who were all nodding their heads like stepping chickens. The shop boomed out Johnny Osbourne's 'To Kiss Somebody', a hot-steppers favourite with a relentless drum and bass rhythm. Sound boys leant over the counter giving affirmative nods to the busy assistant whenever they liked a tune. On the counter were stacks of seven-inch import records that were marked down to play at numerous blues and raves all over London over the weekend. Jamaican patois filled the air as sound men tried to make themselves heard over the murderous bass-line. Reggae album sleeves covered the walls, along with flyers promoting the gigs of untold sound systems.

Nunchaks stood in the corner of the shop, wearing his cashmere coat and his black felt Stetson hat. The sound boys kept a respectable distance from him as he bopped his head and drummed his gold-clad fingers on the counter.

Coffin Head, taller than Biscuit, peered over the crowd

64

and saw Nunchaks first. 'See 'im der. In his corner.'

Biscuit was surprised to see Nunchaks without his minders. He suddenly felt more confident and threaded his way through the horde, Coffin Head in tow.

'Chaks, Chaks,' Biscuit greeted. 'Wha'appen?'

Nunchaks turned around and grinned a dangerous grin. 'So yout', you find me. Me 'ope you can deliver.'

'Yeah, I can,' answered Biscuit confidently, his eyes darting east and west, conscious of all eyes on him.

'Let's step outside, yout'.'

The trio walked out of the shop and made their way inside the arcade. Standing outside a West Indian bread shop, Nunchaks had trouble torching his cigarette with his lighter. 'If de t'ings are damage in any way, yout', den you haf fe get damage.'

Biscuit smiled nervously. 'No, man. Everyt'ing in working order an' t'ing. Don't worry yourself 'bout dat.'

'Yeah, man,' Coffin Head concurred. 'Not even a stain.'

'Well, I 'ope so. Cos if you're wrong, you know wha' it like to try an' walk wid no kneecap?'

Biscuit didn't answer. He stood silently as the smell of recently baked ardough bread laced the air. Coffin Head shifted his feet uneasily.

'De t'ings are in my lock-up,' revealed Biscuit. 'Pick dem up when you're ready. Try an' mek it early morning cos de beast send cars up and down my estate during de night. An' in afternoon time der der-ya 'pon foot, sometimes t'ree ah dem together.'

'Why should I boder 'bout radication? Me nuh t'ief nutten – ah my family's property me ah come for.'

'Yeah, but we don't want no beast to sight us off-loading t'ings from the lock-up,' said Coffin Head. 'If dey do, der gonna mark us down, man. Char.'

'Alright,' Nunchaks agreed. 'I'll send ah van first t'ing tomorrow. An' you'd better be der-ya. Cos I don't like wasting my people dem time. Y'hear me, yout'?'

'Understood, man,' Biscuit said.

'Alright, dat is settled,' Nunchaks concluded. 'But de warning is der: me find anyt'ing wrong wid de goods, you know wha' will 'appen.'

Biscuit, his gaze dropping to the concrete, remembered what Bruce Lee had done with his Nunchakoos in *Enter the Dragon*, while Coffin Head took a deep breath.

'I might wan' you two fe a liccle job down by Dorset Road sides,' Nunchaks suddenly announced. 'Y'hear me, yout'?'

'I don't know, Chaks, man,' Coffin Head fretted. Dorset Road, within throwing distance of the Oval cricket ground, was home to Nunchaks' rival, Cutlass Blake. Cutlass called his gang the 'Trodding Blades' and any visitors to their turf were not greeted warmly.

'Wha' you mean you don't know? Remember it's me who put money inna your pocket! An' me de reason no one trouble you. When people know you working fe me, dey lef' you alone. You don't fockin' know, you ah say. When *I* tell you fe do somet'ing, you don't rarse tell me you don't fockin' know!'

Coffin Head shook his head in submission. Biscuit looked at his friend in surprise.

'I 'ope we understand each uder,' Nunchaks said ominously.

Biscuit nodded.

'Alright, dat is out of de way,' Nunchaks said. 'Come, follow me to me car.'

Biscuit and Coffin Head were led up Railton Road, listening to the Lone Ranger's 'M-16' resounding from

66

Desmond's Hip City record shack. The Front Line was relatively quiet at this time of day, apart from one doom-monger dressed only in cut-down jeans and a smart waistcoat. Marching down the middle of the road, he shouted, 'Brimstone an' fire will soon come. *Believe it!*'

Ignoring the doom merchant, Nunchaks turned to the teenagers. 'Come, yout's. Me car is jus' parked up by T'umper's takeaway.'

The trio walked on, Biscuit wondering where all the whores and bad men went to during the day-time. Nunchaks opened the door to his car and ushered his two employees into the back seat. He pulled away and drove along the Front Line before turning left into a quiet road. Although the Line was quiet, Nunchaks knew there was always a chance that an informant or rival dealer could be watching, so he stopped the car a half mile away. He got out and opened the boot then returned to the driver's seat with a small plastic bag. 'You sell de last bag alright?' he asked.

'Yeah,' replied Biscuit. 'No problem. Sold de last draw T'ursday night.'

'You 'ave de corn?'

Coffin Head stooped to remove the elastic band that gripped the wad of two hundred pounds inside his sock. He passed the cash to Nunchaks who didn't bother counting it; there was no way his juniors would cut him short.

'Right, *remove ya*,' Nunchaks ordered.

Biscuit and Coffin Head vacated the car and watched as Nunchaks performed a three-point turn and headed off to central Brixton.

'Char,' Coffin Head grouched. 'He's always doing dat, telling us to get out of his car an' trod.'

'Would you expect anyt'ing different?' said Biscuit.

'Can't we get our herb off someone else?'

'Oh yeah, like who? To rarted.'

'Slim Lamb Harry, innit. He lives up Palace Road, in de estate up der. Brenton knows him.'

'Nah, he's too hot, man. An' he deals wid dem white man down Rotherhithe sides. He's into cocaine, speed an' all kinds of shit. An' he charges 'bout two t'irty for an ounce of herb. An' he carries a fockin' Remington. I ain't dealing wid no man who's got a rarse gun under his trench.'

The friends walked along Shakespeare Road, both looking at the huge council block on their left. With its lack of windows, locals called this expanse of concrete 'The Prison'. They could hear some rootshead testing out his bass speakers in a third-floor flat. On another floor, they heard a child being severely disciplined by his mother. The various noises intermingled into a soundtrack of foreboding. Coffin Head wondered what Nunchaks would do to him if he knew what Coffin Head was thinking.

'Coff, your turn to sell at de Line dis week,' said Biscuit, knowing his spar hated to trade his stock there.

'Char, in dis fockin' weder?'

'I done it last time. Stop your moaning, man. I t'ought you wanted to buy some garms for de wedding?'

'Yeah, I do. I jus' don't like de Front Line. Too much man who 'ave gone cuckoo. Too much man wid a blade who would wet you for nutten.'

'You'll get used to it, man.'

'How can you get used to madman who tell you dat your heart's gonna be melted by de rarse fires of hell?'

The pair turned left into Loughborough Road. Coffin

Head dwelt on the perilous act of selling herb on the Front Line. Just two months ago, while idling with Brenton and Floyd, he had seen a youth get his stomach carved with a machete. Coffin Head had seen men get cut before, but this incident had disturbed him. In the middle of an argument about the quantity of herb the youth had bought, the dealer walked calmly up to the naïve teenager and, without warning, took a mighty swing.

Biscuit's mind was on Nunchaks and the next assignment. 'I ain't doing it,' he announced. 'I ain't bruking into no more yards. I've had enough of dat shit. It's too dangerous, man. We don't know whose yards we bruking into. Say we run into a man who's got a friggin' gun or somet'ing? Especially if we do a job up Dorset Road. Gonna 'appen one day, y'know. Jus' a matter of time. An' it ain't like we're meking too much out of it, eider. Nunchaks jus' gives us half what we sell. Nah, man. I ain't doing it again. Fock dat runnings.'

'I didn't wan' to do it in de first place,' revealed Coffin Head. 'How we gonna get out of it?'

'I affe think 'bout it, man. I'll come up wid some excuse.'

The friends reached Mostyn Road where they went their separate ways. Biscuit headed off home and Coffin Head to his place off Denmark Road. Back at the flat, Biscuit found his mother placing food in the cupboards after a shopping trip. Royston was helping her, glad to be inside the warmth of his home. He loathed the queues in Brixton market.

'Lincoln, you're 'ome,' Hortense greeted. 'Wha' you waan' fe your dinner today? Mutton or some beef.'

'Don't mind, Mummy. Whatever.'

'My God it col' outside. Why you nuh wear de scarf me

69

knit fe you. Col' will ketch your backside if you nuh wrap up.'

'I'm alright, Mummy. I'm wearing two T-shirt, innit.'

He retired to the lounge, where he turned on the television and watched the wrestling. His mother prepared the dinner as Royston played with his favourite toy cars.

Denise arrived home two hours later, and immediately made for the gas heater in the lounge. 'T'anks for the twenty notes you gi' me. Controlled a nice dress for de party.' Still standing in her black wool coat and beige corduroy trousers, Denise switched the heater to its full capacity.

'Dat's alright,' replied Biscuit. 'Jus' when you need somet'ing, don't run to Mummy. She's got enough worries already.'

'So, wha' you saying? When I need somet'ing I affe run to you?'

'Widin reason.'

'Wha' gives you de right to tell me when I should ask my mudder fe somet'ing?' Denise asked hotly. She placed her hands on her hips and primed her tongue. 'I'm sick an' tired of you playing daddy for me. Don't you remember? I ain't got no daddy, never 'ad one. Not like *you*.'

'I'm not trying to act like a daddy, I jus' don't like it when you an' Mummy ketch up inna argument 'bout money. Besides, you know Mummy don't earn much at de cleaning job.'

'At least I know it's legal corn she's bringing 'ome!'

'Survival's de game.'

'Don't t'ink I don't know where you get your money from. You t'ink I like buying clothes wid your money?'

Biscuit paused, refusing to look his sister in the eye. 'Instead of worrying 'bout dat, why don't *you* look a job.

70

Even a part-time job would help a liccle . . . An' keep your voice down.'

'Why don't you look a job,' returned Denise, leaning towards her brother aggressively. 'Cos wha' you doing ain't no blasted job.'

'But it buys you a friggin' dress t'ough, innit,' Biscuit retorted, pointing his right index finger near to his sister's face.

'If I did wha' you do, you would soon complain.'

'Dat's cos you're more brainy dan me. Why don't you put dose CSEs to use instead of loafing around.'

'You t'ink cos me 'ave some CSEs dat will get me a job? You don't see de news lately. Even people who jus' come out of university wid initials after dem name can't find work. I went job centre yesterday an' de only jobs dey had was for chambermaid in some hotel. Ain't no way I'm cleaning up after people who can afford to stay inna top-ranking hotel.'

'Our mudder cleans up after people.'

'Don't mean I affe do it. It's humiliating.'

'An' our mudder's humiliation put food on de table.'

'Me nuh partial. Don't mean I affe do de same t'ing.'

'You can't satisfy, man.'

'I don't call satisfaction wid a rarse broom in me 'and,' dismissed Denise, swishing her left hand in front of her face contemptuously.

Knowing her brother loved to watch Saturday afternoon wrestling, Denise switched channels on purpose, trying to gain his full attention. Biscuit stopped himself from giving her a severe cussing; he hated to argue with his sister within earshot of his mother.

'It's alright for you t'ough, innit,' she whispered through pursed lips. 'Doing wha' you like cos Mummy t'inks dat liccle halos an' expensive perfumes comes out of your batty. You can't do nutten wrong in her eyes. It mek me sick when she says Lincoln dis an' Lincoln dat, describing you as some liccle Jesus. Maybe she would treat me de same if we 'ad de same daddy.'

Biscuit fidgeted uneasily. His tongue wanted to answer the charges with venom, but his common sense decided otherwise. 'I'm going to my room, can't tek your shit, man. Sometimes you're so red eye you're coming like devil pickney, to rarted.' He kissed his teeth, got to his feet and cut his eye at his sister.

Denise laughed. 'Like mudder like son, innit. She tells me nuff times I come from de devil.'

'She mus' be right wid de mout' you got.'

'Yeah? Why don't you all jus' call me Jezebel.'

Biscuit departed the lounge.

# 7
# Sons of SW9

Biscuit had just eaten his dinner of stewed mutton, yams and green banana. His mother had cooked the meat and vegetables in one pot, making a delicious broth, and served it with boiled brown rice. After telling Royston to tidy up his bedroom, Biscuit bear-hugged his brother goodnight. As he was leaving the flat he found his mother leaning over the balcony, looking out over the concrete landscape. The lights were coming on in the streets below.

'You alright, Mummy?' he asked, noticing a sadness in his mother's eyes.

'Course I am,' she smiled. 'You t'ink de troubles of life cyan overcome me?'

'No, Mummy. Nutten can get de better of you.'

Hortense stood up straight as she saw her son hiding his worry with a smile. She grabbed the zip of his bomber jacket and pulled it up to his throat. 'Now, you be safe, don't mek your mudder worry over you, especially in dis cold.'

He set off into the blackness of the estate, on his way to Coffin Head's place. On route, he saw two boys trying to gain entry into a car that was parked in Calais Street. Bwai, dey start early dese days, he thought. They're barely old enough to be in secondary school.

A car horn interrupted his thoughts and he saw Coffin Head's battered Dolomite brake sharply. Biscuit wasted no time in filling the passenger seat. 'Put de heater on, Coff, its friggin' cold.'

'Char, you know so it don't work. Somet'ing wrong wid my electrics.'

'Der's always somet'ing wrong wid your car, innit,' Biscuit remarked. 'Can't you fix it up? I t'ought you was a scientist when it comes to mechanics.'

'Shut up, man. You should be glad you ain't trodding to Floyd's yard.'

Coffin Head turned left into the shadow of Kennington Boys School, an institution that bred many bad men. Biscuit looked at the school and wondered if the pupils would turn out just like him. Coffin Head's eyes stayed on the road, driving past the tall, white council blocks on Loughborough Road before turning towards central Brixton. In the distance he saw the dark outline of a still windmill as he turned into the estate where his friend lived. Floyd's block was only two storeys high, but it was a three-minute walk to get from one end to the other.

'You bag up de herb in ten-pound draws?' asked Biscuit.

'Yeah, four draws I bagged up. One for Floyd, Sceptic an' Brenton, an' one extra in case any brethren turns up.'

Floyd lived on the second floor, and two minutes later

they reached his front door. Biscuit knocked as Coffin Head checked to see if he had parked in a well-lit spot. 'If joy rider trouble my car I'm gonna gi' dem two lick an' sen' dem hospital,' he threatened under his breath.

'Backside!' greeted Floyd. 'De herbmen cometh.'

'Char, let us in, man. You don't know it's col' outside?' complained Coffin Head.

The flat was in a state of redecoration. Pots of white paint were huddled in a corner of the half-painted hall-way, next to a soiled black bucket. The visitors admired the posters of Jacob Miller and Dennis Brown; the rest of the wall in the passage was filled with flyers of raves and blues gone by. Floyd led the way to his uncarpeted lounge. Three bean bags sat in the middle of the room. A hazy-looking black and white television set, placed in the corner, had just finished a news broadcast and a Brixton suitcase thumped out Horace Andy's 'Natty Dread Ah Weh She Want', the fragile vocals riding over a sensuous rhythm.

On one of the bean bags sprawled a slim black guy with a goatee beard and high cheekbones. Sporting a wide green beret and a gold-toothed grin, his black polo-neck sweater was falling off his meagre torso. 'Wha'appen Coff, Biscuit,' he said. 'You got de herb?'

'Sceptic,' Biscuit replied, 'you t'ink me's a dud salesman to rarted?'

Coffin Head and Biscuit crashed on a bean bag each. Floyd disappeared into his bedroom and returned with a wooden chair in one hand and two ashtrays in the other. He joined his friends in front of the television set. The latest episode of *Dallas* was showing silently, with JR blackmailing a rival by placing drugs at the victim's home and calling the police.

'Gwarn, JR, you're bad,' hailed Sceptic. 'Anyone

who troubles 'im always end up inna cell.'

'You shouldn't praise 'im too much, Sceptic,' remarked Biscuit. 'It's man like dose dat are working for JR who fucked you up inna cell.'

'Tek out your corn, man,' Coffin Head dictated, ignoring the TV show. 'No squeeze or freeness fe anybody. I get frigged off wid friend an' friend looking for credit.'

'An' a rarse good evening to you,' laughed Floyd. 'You should be blasted lucky we're buying from you. Don't forget before I bought off you, my herbman was Chemist, an' he ain't too contented wid you teking his business. He was all complaining an' shit when I sight 'im up inna Crucial Rocker blues.'

'Fock Chemist,' said Biscuit. 'He always sold me short anyway.'

'Yeah,' Sceptic concurred. 'I never did trus' him. One time I went to his yard an' he searched me up like he's a beastman, to blowoh. Somet'ing funny 'bout him.'

Coffin Head took out three bags of Jamaican bush. 'Where's Brenton?'

'Gone to Shaka dance wid Finnley an' Lizard,' answered Floyd. 'He told me to control his bag for him.'

'Where's Shaka playing tonight?' asked Biscuit.

'Acton Town Hall,' replied Sceptic. 'I would of gone but I don't trust dem West London bwai. Dey kinda go on funny an' always look 'pon you like der looking fight.'

'You don't even trus' Brixton man,' said Coffin Head.

'I don't trus' anybody I don't know too good,' affirmed Sceptic. 'Too much informer der 'bout an' trickster an' ginall. 'Pon de Front Line der is pure undercover beastman, to blowoh. An' you can't tell de coconuts from de pure chocolate, man.'

Floyd took out a tenner as Coffin Head gave him his

weed. 'Shut de fock up, Sceptic, man. You're too suspicious of anybody to rarted. You're so fucked up wid dat police beating you get, you probably t'ink your mudder is an informer.'

Sceptic paid Coffin Head for his herb and snatched the rizlas off Floyd. '*Don't* chat 'bout me mudder. You know I don't like dem t'ings der.'

'Char!' Coffin Head rebuked. 'De man's only ramping wid you.'

'Don't like anyone ramping wid my mudder's name,' snapped Sceptic.

'Stop your sulking,' Biscuit said. 'Jus' wrap your lips round a spliff an' cool.'

'Alright fe you to say,' moaned Sceptic. 'If it was your mudder he was meking joke 'bout, you'd be de first one to ketch a rage.'

'For fuck sake!' cried Floyd. 'I'm sorry, yeah. Double sorry, plead guilty an' t'ing. Whip me if you t'ink dat is nuff punishment.'

'Anybody got any liquor?' asked Coffin Head, building a spliff for himself.

'We drank it,' replied Floyd. 'Bought some Tennants dis afternoon. But it's so friggin' cold we never went outside my gates again. So we kinda drunk it off while we were slapping down domino.'

'Char,' Coffin Head complained. 'Could of done wid a liccle liquor.'

'We can toss a coin to send someone off-licence,' suggested Sceptic.

'Fock dat shit,' scolded Biscuit. 'Every time we 'ave toss up, I lose.'

'Talking of being a loser,' said Floyd, 'you get to first base wid Carol?'

'Don't ask me no question I won't tell you no lie,' replied Biscuit.

'Don't get all evasive on me!' snapped Floyd. 'Wha's de score, man? I know so you've been going round to her gates, an' you mus' be determined cos I know her paps don't like you a damn.'

'Carol's paps goes on weird, man,' butted in Sceptic. 'He don't wan' 'im daughter to go out wid any yout'. He's funny, man.'

'An' how you know Carol's paps don't like me?' queried Biscuit.

'Sharon told me,' retorted Floyd. 'He t'inks you're some kinda hustler. He don't trus' you a damn, an' he would rather buy Enoch Powell a drink than let Carol marry you.'

'Who said anyt'ing 'bout marrying?' asked Biscuit.

'Everybody knows you love Carol off, to blowoh,' said Sceptic. 'You t'ink we forget wha' you bought for her birt'day dis year?'

Biscuit had bought Carol a gold rope chain last September. He had asked her to keep the gift quiet, but she couldn't help herself and told her friend, Sharon. Floyd got the secret off Sharon, and since then it was common knowledge.

Biscuit pastried his spliff and lit it, not caring too much that his friends knew of his love for Carol. In a strange way, he felt relief. Carol knew of his feelings for her, and anything his friends said about the matter meant nothing to him. 'Wha' me an' Carol do or don't do is none of your friggin' business,' he affirmed. 'I don't 'ave to tell you nutten.'

Sceptic pulled on his spliff. 'You know so dat Carol used to love off Brenton . . . She might still do.'

Biscuit became serious. 'Sceptic, if you keep on wid dis

subject, den I will quiet your beak like how de beast did quiet your beak.'

'Touchy touchy,' retorted Sceptic, trying to laugh off Biscuit's anger.

'Char, leave de man alone,' appealed Coffin Head, noticing the vexed breathing of his friend. 'Besides, everyone knows dat Brenton weren't interested in Carol. If Biscuit wants to go to her yard, dat's his business. An' if he can't get to bone it, well, dat's his business as well. Anyway, I t'ought we don't get involved inna brethren's love life.'

Floyd nodded as Coffin Head glared at Sceptic, indicating he'd better leave the subject alone or there'd be trouble.

Biscuit looked at the telly, telling himself that he must master his feelings whenever Carol's name cropped up in conversation.

'Talking of Brenton,' remarked Floyd, wanting to change the subject, 'where's his draw? You know so he gets mad-up if he's left out of de herb runnings.'

'Here, man,' answered Coffin Head. 'Brenton will like dis draw. Makes your mout' dry but gives you a nice slow creeping buzz. Still, could do wid a liccle liquor t'ough.'

Each of the quartet had a spliff in hand, and the smoke billowed lazily above their heads. As more cannabis was smoked, they became more horizontal. They watched each other, wondering what the next topic of conversation would be. The herb ate away at their inhibitions and taboo subjects were discussed. Michael Prophet's 'Warn Them' blared out from the ghetto-blaster as JR closed a shady deal in *Dallas*.

'Hey, Sceptic,' Floyd called out. 'You gonna deal wid dat Bajee girl?'

'Are you sick?' Sceptic spat with scorn. 'I ain't going out wid no Bajee girl. Dey yam monkey an' gibbon an' t'ing. No brethren, don't trus' dem Barbadian people dem. I might go round to de girl's yard an' who de fock knows wha' I'm eating. An' if I stay de night I might be yamming lizard 'pon toast. Wha' a blowoh.'

'She fit t'ough,' offered Coffin Head. 'I wouldn't say no. I would jook dat proper an' lock her in my bedroom for furder use, man. You're too damn picky, Sceptic.'

'I don't like dem small island girl,' insisted Sceptic. 'Wherever dey blasted come from, whether it's St Kitts, St Lucia or any uder small island dat ain't big enough to hol' cricket match. An' I bet dat girl's parents hate Jamaicans.'

'Char, man,' Coffin Head rebuked. 'Der's too much man like you inna Brixton, wid your ism an' schism 'bout girl from different island. An' you t'ink cos you 'ave Jamaican parents you're superior. Well, fuck dat. If dat was me I wouldn't partial 'bout where she come from. I would deal wid it proper an' give it a good examination.'

'Wha' you know 'bout examining a girl,' joked Biscuit. 'De only t'ing you know 'bout examination is de ones you failed in school.'

'Fock you, man.'

'I mus' admit, man,' Floyd said, 'when I see you rub down de girl in dat blues, me get red eye to rarted. She's fit badly. Her leg-back is jus' demanding a stroke . . . You never tek down her digits?'

'Look, right,' Sceptic responded. 'When I hear say de girl is a Bajee, I tell her, *later*, goodbye an' 'ave a nice life. No, man. Gi' me a brown-skin Jamaican girl every time. I don't deal wid no monkey yamming girl dem.'

'Dat's low, man,' said Biscuit. 'So you don't want no

small island girl an' you don't want no dark skin girl. Looking 'pon your face, if I was you I'd accept anyt'ing coming, dread.'

Everyone laughed.

Sceptic tugged on his spliff as he prepared his response. 'I don't business, man. I know de kinda girl I wanna move wid, an' she's brown-skin an' got Jamaican parents, man. An' she 'ave nice hair an' a fit batty an' a serious pair of toned leg-backs. An' she would smoke herb an' be able to cook a wicked curry goat. An' she be quiet an' shy an' respect my mudder. She would affe like D. Brown an' Linval Thompson. An' in de bedroom, she would affe gwarn like dat Emmanuelle in dem sex film. An' when I gi' it to her strong she 'ave to bawl out like her crotches ketch ah fire. An' liccle after me sex her, she affe shower me. Wha' a blowoh!'

Hoots of laughter filled the room once more. As they subsided, Coffin Head started to build his second spliff. He turned to Sceptic. 'You're a hypocrite, man. Char. You say you don't like dark skin girl an' dat you love your browning. But ain't your mudder dark?'

'Dis ain't got nutten to do wid my mudder. An' I t'ought I told you not to bring my mudder into any conversation? Bring her name up again an' see if me an' you don't rumble!'

Biscuit and Floyd chuckled, thinking Sceptic's skinny body was no match for Coffin Head's tall, muscular build.

'I don't partial wha' you say, anyway,' Sceptic asserted. 'I jus' prefer dem lighter skin girl dem, widout any apology.'

'You're fucked up, man,' scolded Floyd.

'Well, at least I don't run around town boning anyt'ing dat wears a blouse an' skirt, an' den telling everyone dat if

Sharon lef' you, you'd go cuckoo. An' people call *me* a hypocrite.'

Floyd concerned himself with his rizla papers. Coffin Head chuckled as Biscuit shook his head. His friends had had many similar run-ins in the past, he thought, but this one was up there with the best of them.

'As Brenton always says,' added Sceptic. 'Sharon's wasted on you, man.'

'Fock you.'

'An' fock you, too.'

'You don't say fock you to Brenton, do you?'

'Dat's cos he ain't a fockin' idiot.'

'Who you calling idiot you big lip fool. See your lips are big like Hovercraft bumper,' responded Sceptic.

'Fock you, your lips are two times the size of mine. I'm surprised de tyre people don't give you a contract, nuff tread in your lips, dread. Dey could use de tread an' bounce in your lips for car to go on rally round Russia to rarted. You don't need no umbrella when rain is falling, you can jus' pull your lips dem over your 'ead.'

Coffin Head and Biscuit were rolling about on the floor. Sceptic didn't have the wit to reply. Instead, he drew on his spliff and exhaled the smoke in the direction of the TV.

Satisfied, Floyd got up and went to the kitchen to pour himself a glass of water; the herb had made his throat dry. He returned with a triumphant grin on his face. 'You t'ink you can test me? Don't even try, Sceptic, cos you ain't my match.'

'Fock you, man. You carry on, an' see I don't tell Sharon dat you're palaving wid uder girls.'

'An' if you do, I'll cut out your lips an' mek imitation sausages to rarted. Whatever 'appened in not getting involved inna brethren's love life?'

'Char!' Coffin Head rebuked. 'Shut de fuck up, man. It seem like you two been seeing too much of each uder.'

'Yeah,' Biscuit agreed. 'You see more of each uder dan man seeing his girl.'

'Least I got girl to see,' snapped Floyd. 'When's de last time you examined a girl?'

'Oh, so you wan' start 'pon me again now?' confronted Biscuit. 'Don't mek I tell everybody how you drop inna dance when you had too much herb an' dat girl slapped you in de face cos you was crubbing wid a serious erection. An' don't you mek me tell everyone 'bout dat girl Rosene who tell her friend dat she sack cos you come quicker dan Concorde. An' how anoder girl say your armpit reek like cabbage water an' your toe nails are clog up like ghetto sewage drain. An' how you went Bali Hai an' you pull some girl to dance an' she say she don't dance wid no man who hasn't yet discovered deodorant. Den der was dat girl in Cubies who gave you her supposed telephone number an' de nex' day you dialled de number for Streatham Cemetery to rarted. Don't even start 'pon me, Floyd. Cos I know so many t'ings about you, if I was to reveal dem, you'd affe walk street wid Tesco bag over your head an' some serious ear muffs, cos de laughter you might hear would drown out Shaka speaker boxes.'

Sceptic and Coffin Head laughed until their bodies nearly gave away, both of them recognising that when it came to after-herb cussing, Biscuit was still the undisputed champion. 'Wha', what a blowoh,' Sceptic gasped. 'Ki', kiss me neck, Floyd get cuss like him never get cuss before. Cabbage water . . . wha' a blowoh.'

Floyd sucked on his dying spliff. 'You finished?' he asked. 'You 'ave any more secret you wan' tell de world?'

'You started dis shit, man,' replied Biscuit. 'Asking me when's de last time I examined a girl. Like I said, it's nutten do wid you, an' you wanna stop t'inking you're some kinda hero jus' because you go round boning anyt'ing dat wears a frock. I know who I want an' I will wait for who I want. So don't gi' me any grief on de subject.'

'Char, jus' cool, man,' said Coffin Head. 'Come round here for a nice smoke an' you lot jus' start cussing each uder like you wanna fight. Do we always affe do dis? Who's gonna go off licence?'

Sceptic was still chuckling. He tried to restrain himself, but the thought of Floyd being told by a girl that he hadn't yet discovered deodorant proved too much. He burst out laughing in full force.

'*Shut* de fuck up, man! You're coming like hyena watching a *Carry On* film.'

Sceptic looked upon Coffin Head and sensed he was serious. He tried hard to control himself.

'Sharon was reading de *South London Press* de uder day,' Floyd changed the subject. 'Dey done some survey an' dey reckon der is over fifty per cent of young blacks unemployed.'

'Der telling lie,' commented Biscuit. 'More like ninety-five per cent. Who do we know who's got a job? Apart from dat foolish YOP scheme where dey pay you jus' enough corn to buy a gobstopper an' tek bus to work.'

'Lizard an' Brenton, innit,' answered Sceptic. 'Lizard's working in some electrical shop an' you know dat Brenton works as an apprentice carpenter for de council, innit.'

'Jus' de two of us den,' remarked Floyd. 'It's like de Government jus' kinda forget 'bout us—'

'No dey don't,' Sceptic butted in. 'Dey don't forget to

84

tell de beast to arrest you for nutten, an' to beat you up inna cell.'

'Friggin' wort'less, renkin beast,' cussed Floyd. 'Dey still ain't made no arrest for de Deptford fire. I still can't believe it, man. Ten dead. Most of dem even younger dan us. Mus' 'ave been hell, man.'

'Beef'ead bwai do it,' insisted Sceptic. 'It 'as to be dem.'

'Some man 'pon de Line are saying it's de beast dat fling petrol bomb in der,' Biscuit replied.

'Wouldn't surprise me,' said Floyd. 'Since de beast kill Blair Peach in broad daylight, an' nuff people see it, an' no one get charge for it, nutten de beast do or might do to us in de future will surprise me.'

Everyone nodded their heads, thinking that if the police could get away with killing a white teacher from New Zealand, then what chance did they have?

Coffin Head turned to Sceptic. 'It could of been worse.'

'Yeah, I know,' Sceptic replied quietly, peering at the floor. 'It gives me de shits ah night-time when I realise I could of died in that beast cell.'

'We're in de middle of a friggin' war,' stated Floyd. 'De outside world don't know nutten.'

'Mebbe one of us could jus' fin' a gun an' blast one of dem away,' said Sceptic. 'Dat will get everyone's attention. Yeah, hol' one of dem beastman down an' put de gun barrel right up his nostril an' pull de trigger. Mek his blood decorate the *rarse* claat road. An' den send de bits of his brain to Westminster to de 'Ome Secretary. Wassis-name? William Whitelaw, innit?'

'Dat's kinda spooky, man,' commented Biscuit. 'White law.'

'Dat could be our own message to de fockin' Govern-ment,' added Sceptic. 'Mess wid one of us, an' we'll kill one of dem. De 'Ome Secretary would quake in his cabinet chair to blowoh, an' t'ink twice 'bout sending order to murder we.'

Even Floyd was stunned by the depth of Sceptic's hatred. He peered into his friend's eyes, and though reddened by the Jamaican bush, he knew Sceptic was speaking with an intensity that even scared him.

'I'm going off licence,' announced Coffin Head. 'You lot love talk 'bout doing somet'ing, but dat's all you really do – jus' *talk* . . . Brews all round, yeah?'

He was answered in lazy nods. As he departed, Floyd dropped himself on to the vacant bean bag. The Wailing Souls 'War' thunderclapped out of the ghetto-blaster as Sceptic commenced the building of another spliff.

# Sisters

## 3 February 1981

Biscuit wanted to go back to bed. He had just seen
Nunchaks off, driving away in his van from the lock-up.
As he reached his balcony, he saw his mother standing
outside their flat.

'Lincoln, me an' Royston are on our way to Aunt
Jenny's,' she announced. She was wearing a head-tie
that covered her eyebrows, and didn't look all that enthu-
siastic about visiting her sister. 'Tell your sister fe meet
us der if she wan' her dinner. She's still sleeping. An' I
expect you fe reach, cos you nuh see Aunt Jenny fe ah
long time.'

Biscuit entered the flat. 'It's Sunday, Mummy. Ain't
Aunty Jenny going to church?'

'Wha' time you get 'ome las' night?' Hortense asked. She controlled her voice to hide the fact that she had stayed up until 2am when sleep finally claimed her; she was awakened by the front door slamming just after 4am. 'It's gone past ten, an' Aunt Jenny gone ah church an' come back.'

'I was at Floyd's,' Biscuit revealed. 'Can't remember what time I got back.'

'Wha' you doing round de back dis time of morning?'

'Jus' doing some tidying in de lock-up,' Biscuit lied.

'Well, I'll see you later.'

'Bye, Mummy.'

Holding the reluctant hand of Royston in his Sunday best, Hortense made her way to the bus stop. Biscuit watched them catch a 109 bus before collapsing on to his bed.

'Hortense!' Jenny hailed as she opened the front door. She took off her glasses and hugged her sister. Hortense patted Jenny's shoulder with one hand and smiled without using her eyes. Jenny, slimmer and taller than her sister, was dressed in a smart yellow jacket and matching skirt. As Hortense dropped her eyes to her sister's calves, she thought that white tights didn't suit black women. Jenny's frilly white blouse was the same colour as the flower pinned into her hair. Coming up behind Jenny was her daughter, Ruth, sporting a neat black trouser suit, displaying a look of perfect politeness. 'Ruth, put 'pon de kettle an' mek your aunt ah cup ah tea.'

In the hallway was a rubber plant that was taller than Royston. The lush carpet was protected by a see-through rubber mat and a telephone was sitting on a small glass table near the staircase. Blue-flocked wallpaper covered the walls, disturbed only by a waist-high radiator, situated past the staircase. The lounge was the first room on the right, and the dining room was further on. The hallway led all the way to the spacious kitchen, where the smell of boiling chicken licked the air.

Royston scampered to greet his cousin and hopefully win a chocolate treat if he charmed her with enough smiles.

'Royston,' Hortense yelled. ' 'Ow many times me affe tell you fe stop run around inside people 'ouse.'

'Let him be,' Jenny soothed. 'Him an' Ruth were always close, an' he don't see her fe quite ah while now. I'm sure she 'ave some sweetie fe him . . . Royston! Come 'ere darling.'

Royston ran to his aunt's side. 'You forget your manners? You can't say hello?'

'Good morning Aunty Jenny . . . Where's Uncle Jacob?'

'Oh, 'im doing God's work at de church. He's very busy setting up t'ings for de Reverend from America who's going to talk to us again tonight. Jacob an' de rest will 'ave to set up more chairs, cos if tonight's service is anyt'ing like dis morning, it will be packed out.' Jenny clasped her hands together and closed her eyes. 'Everyone sing so nice an' de sound of de musicians jus' mek everyt'ing so joyous.' She opened her eyes and smiled broadly. 'An' den, dis minister from Chicago jus' raise up everybody's spirits wid his speech.'

'If God's got so much work to be done,' Royston said suddenly, 'why can't He get Lincoln and Denise a job, and Frank?'

'Cos de Lord wants us to help ourselves,' smiled Jenny.

'We can't jus' pray an' expect everyt'ing . . . Why don't you find Ruth, I'm sure she 'as ah nice surprise fe you.'

'OK.'

Royston skipped off to the kitchen as Hortense controlled her tongue, not liking anyone to spoil her son.

Jenny gently pulled her sister into the lounge. Hanging on the chimney breast, above the mantelpiece, was a framed portrait of Martin Luther King, whose eyes seemed to follow Hortense around the room, putting her on edge. The beige and red curtains were neatly tied by velvet-looking ropes, and the immaculately clean white net curtain showed off an intricate design. Upon the wall opposite the window were various framed family photographs, mostly of Jenny's wedding day and her parents. Overlooking a red, buttoned sofa was a canvas painting of Jesus Christ upon the cross. Red weals lined his naked white chest, and it was apparent he was close to death, his head wilting limply on to his right shoulder. Hortense always avoided this painful image and purposefully sat with her back to it. Two smoked-glass coffee tables were in the centre of the room, each with a white doily upon it, and Hortense eyed the new wood-panelled drinks cabinet in the corner. Jenny love fe keep up wid de Joneses, she thought.

Jenny sat on the thick-limbed sofa and snuggled up close to her sister. 'Say, how's de children, dem,' she asked.

'Nutten change,' Hortense answered sedately. 'Lincoln an' Denise are still looking work. An' Royston still asking all kinda question dat me don't know how fe answer.'

'De boy's inquisitive,' replied Jenny. 'It means he's hungry fe learning. Ah good sign dat.'

90

'Wha? A good sign when de bwai wan' to know wha'appen to 'im daddy?'

'You should tell him, Hortense. You can't jus' leave it to his imagination. An' you should of told Denise 'bout her daddy from time.'

Hortense primed her tongue to reply, but before she could, Ruth entered with two mugs of nutmegged tea. 'It's brown sugar you take innit, Aunty?'

'Yes, me love. You always cyan remember.'

Ruth returned to the kitchen. Hortense glared at her elder sister. 'Should do dis, should do dat. You always tell me I should whatever. It is fe me to decide fe tell me pickney 'bout dem daddy. An' besides, Denise daddy ain't much fe tell, an' as for Royston daddy, Royal George! Me nuh like to even refer to 'im as ah daddy. 'Im jus' ah rudie who came an' den went. Bot' ah dem cyan't match up to Cilbert.' She paused as she remembered her first husband. 'Don't you t'ink dat Lincoln favour Cilbert?' she asked.

'Well, he does, I'll give you dat,' replied Jenny. 'Lincoln 'as his daddy's eyes. But you 'ave fe stop comparing Cilbert wid Royston's an' Denise's daddies.'

'Dat's alright fe you to say. You 'ave never los' your 'usband. Der was ah time when people did respeck me. People use to walk by an' say 'ow do you do Mrs Huggins an' exchange nice pleasantries. But now, everyone jus' see me as ah penny ketcha.'

'You can't blame dat on Denise's dad,' replied Jenny.

Hortense sipped her tea. 'Well, like ah damn fool I went in search for ah so called fader figure fe Lincoln. You an' everybody else say dat it would be 'ard bringing up my son 'pon me own. But me ah tell you – Denise's daddy? Wort'less me ah tell you! 'Im lucky me never t'row his backside over de balcony after de first week he did ah live wid me. He only stayed cos I was pregnant wid Denise, an' cos he was yamming ah cooked meal ah night-time. All 'im good for was to check 'im loose woman an' to tek me money an' put it 'pon 'orse an' maaga dog!'

'But you can't blame Denise for her daddy's ways. Wasn't we told long ago dat de sins of de fader should not be brought against his children?'

'Yes, me remember Daddy saying dat. But I'm sorry fe say dis, but Denise jus' remind me of de mistake I mek when me tek up wid dat batty-scratching fool. She 'as his cantankerous ways . . . Me could nuh believe it when me find out Denise's daddy related to Pastor Thomas.'

Jenny placed her hand on her sister's forearm. 'Why you don't come to church again? Pastor Thomas is always asking fe you.'

'Church! *Your* God 'as taken away de man I truly loved,' charged Hortense, edging away from her sister. 'If 'Im so kind an' merciful, He wouldn't 'ave lef' me wid a young chile fe bring up 'pon me own. I will never step inna church no more. Me made dat vow after Cilbert's funeral, an' me will *never* bruk it.'

Hortense's voice was splintering with emotion, and the recollection of her husband's funeral had made her bitter. The Almighty had control of all things, she had learned as a child in Sunday school. This was affirmed by her parents in Jamaica. So why did God let her husband die? Was this the compassionate God that everybody kept preaching about? She recalled childhood Sundays where she walked three miles to a church that was no more than a large hut. Spellbound, she would listen to the preacher, an elderly man who she never heard speak quietly. God *knows* our needs, the preacher would shout, banging his fist on the pulpit. *He* will provide us with all our needs, he would repeat, his arms outstretched, inviting shouts of 'Praise The Lord' from the congregation. Hortense would always join in, standing on her feet and clapping her hands.

'*Your* God never listened to me prayers when Gilbert was in such pain,' she charged. 'Never listen at all.'

Jenny fell silent. She was glad that her parents were thousands of miles away in Jamaica, relaxing in their wicker chairs upon their veranda and well out of earshot. They would have died from shock to hear Hortense's bitter words. Their belief was something that they had all shared, but Jenny knew that the loss of her sister's husband had gnawed away the joyous faith that they had all been part of.

Jenny missed the unity of family and community from her hometown of Claremont. Her family and neighbours lived mostly in two-room wooden shacks but there was a dignity within the people that Jenny hadn't seen matched. People were respectful to each other and the advice of the elders was eagerly sought. Men worked the fields singing spirituals while women scrubbed everything that was worth scrubbing, fed the chickens and milked the goats. The whole village acted as baby-sitter for bare-footed children and there was no reason to lock any doors. Everyone woke up with the rising sun and retired to their shacks when it set; even the local sages were afraid of the dark.

Jenny remembered the beacons of fire that lit the steep hills surrounding her hometown and beyond at harvest-time. Big dinners were cooked in outside kitchens, using every available vegetable and prize goat. Men would go into town and buy the best overproof rum. African Anancy stories were told to mesmerised children around the bonfire. Courting couples, sitting on felled branches, embraced and fed each other as local griots interpreted biblical tales. The bouncy rhythms of mento bands drifted on the Caribbean night breeze, to a backdrop of gossiping unseen crickets, filling the valleys and hollows in this mountainous part of Jamaica with sounds Jenny would never forget.

'What about Royston?' she enquired. 'I could pick him up on Sunday mornings an' tek him to church, an' he could spend de rest of de day wid us. It will give you ah liccle respite 'pon Sundays.'

'You better mek sure me's well underground before you even t'ink 'bout dat,' barked Hortense. 'Me pickney nuh get poison by promises of mercy an' going to heaven, an' of ah God dat listen to people's worries an' give people dem der daily bread. I'd rather walk 'pon burning bush nettle an' stan' up before 109 bus dan let me young pickney go ah church an' listen pastor-man posing in der t'ree-piece suit.'

Jenny glared in disgust, restraining herself from spilling the tea upon her sister. 'Your contention is wid God, an' it's you alone who defy him in dis family. Don't bring your own flesh an' blood to fight your battle wid you. Leave Royston outta it – he's jus' ah small boy an' you 'ave no right to turn him 'gainst de Almighty.'

'Don't boder try an' scare me wid your hell talk,' Hortense snapped. 'Royston alright how he is, an' dat's 'ow it's gwarn stay. So don't you boder come wid your ketch a fire scare-mongering tales. Cos dem t'ings don't boder me no more. I 'ave more concern dat dey start

94

charge more fe breadfruit ah Brixton market.'

'If dat's de way you want it, then let it be,' Jenny said, knowing the argument was far from over. It would fire up the next time, and the next, as surely as the sun rises in the east, she thought.

In the silence of the armistice, Hortense finished her cup of tea as Jenny informed her sister of the goings on at the church. Pastor Thomas had initiated a recruitment drive, telling all and sundry that it was up to the church to save the souls of the youth. He had castigated the 'ignorant rastamen' who were trying to lead the youth down a dangerous and unGodlike path. And he had called on God's wrath to bear down on the people responsible for the unemployed masses.

Hortense imitated a favourable ear but her mind was elsewhere.

Two hours later, dressed in faded blue jeans and a thick green pullover, a surly-faced Denise arrived. She said a brief hello to her aunt and mother before disappearing into the kitchen to help Ruth with the dinner. Her cousin was basting the roast potatoes and Denise decided to prepare the salad.

'So, how's the job hunting?' Ruth asked.

'Dat's a laugh, innit,' Denise replied. 'De only jobs I sight down de job centre de uder day were for chambermaids. Two pounds an' a liccle an hour dem offering.'

'Don't give up,' encouraged Ruth. 'You'll find something if you keep looking.'

'Find somet'ing? I'll find a millionaire to love me before I find a job. Dat's what mummy would like anyway.'

'So you don't find your sweetheart yet?' Ruth laughed, pouring water into a steaming pot filled with red kidney beans.

'Sweetheart? Don't give me joke. All de bwai dem who ask me out ain't got nutten to offer. Wha's de point of going out wid a bwai if he's on giro money. Wha' we're gonna do? Stay at my yard 'pon Saturday night an' listen to Rodigan 'pon Capital Radio while my mudder der inna armchair sewing socks wid her screw up face? Dem bwai can't tek me anywhere. Dem don't even 'ave money for a blasted Kentucky, an' dey can't afford to go barber saloon an' get dem head trim. I ain't moving wid no cruff.'

'You wanna be more open-minded,' Ruth suggested, turning her attention to the onions. 'Start going to different places and meet all kinds of people.'

'Whadya mean different places?' replied Denise. 'Don't expect me to go to dem soul clubs where dem white bwai try to act black an' dem black bwai skin up dem teet' checking dem white girl an' try to act white. An' when de stupid black bwai gets his piece of pork dey say dat black girl are too facety an' unapproachable.'

'Denise! That is racist!'

'Well, it's true. Dem idiot soul 'ead black bwai jus' wanna dilute, man.'

'That is no excuse for referring to white people as pork.'

'Alright, sorry fe dat. But it mek me sick when I see dem banner-check black fool wid a smiling white bitch 'pon der arm. Dey don't know dat dey could of got lynched for dat in Marcus Garvey time.'

Ruth fell silent, wondering if her mother's charge that reggae music was corrupting the ghetto youths was true. Why else would Denise mention a rabble-rousing black power-monger like Marcus Garvey? Ruth wondered whether her cousin smoked herb as well.

'Can you do the gravy?' Ruth asked.

'Course, dat's why I'm here for, innit,' grinned Denise.

Half an hour later, Biscuit arrived. He said a quick hi to his aunt, not wanting her to question him on what he was doing with his life. He went to the kitchen next, greeting Ruth by slapping her backside. On seeing Denise he kissed his teeth. 'You let *her* in de kitchen?' He turned back to Ruth. 'Bwai, family's gonna dead tonight.'

Denise picked up an onion and threw it at her brother's head.

'Behave!' scolded Ruth. 'Mum will go mad.'

Biscuit found Royston sitting halfway up the stairs, and on closer inspection saw that his brother's hands were caked in chocolate. 'Go wash your hands, man. You can't eat at Aunty Jenny's table like dat.'

Biscuit tested out his cousin's new stereo for an hour or so until Ruth and Denise brought out the dinner of boiled chicken legs, rice and peas, stuffing, roast potatoes, hot corn cobs, Yorkshire pudding, spicy gravy and a wide variety of salad. The family ate around an oval-shaped table in the dining room. Biscuit ignored the salad but filled his plate with rice and peas while Royston looked upon his generous dinner with trepidation. Denise shied away from the roast potatoes, saying they made her put on weight, as Hortense glared at her youngest, trying to mentally force-feed him. Royston started on his chicken, but a little later received more cussing from his mother for not eating his vegetables. Then he complained of a funny stomach but was promptly banned from eating chocolate for a week although not before Jenny gave him some ice-cream. Biscuit drank his after-dinner wine like it was lemonade, and when he finished that, went to the off licence to buy a *proper* drink. Denise, drinking from a lager can her brother bought her, moaned to Ruth about her stagnant wardrobe, and Hortense whinged about the price of mutton and chicken legs while downing a glass of Aunt Jenny's Guinness punch, made with her own special ingredient. Jenny sat at the dinner table, observing and listening, wondering when her husband would return home. She enjoyed the monthly ritual of sharing dinner with her extended family, although Hortense used her as a sponge to absorb her bitterness. She realised that luck had long deserted her younger sister and, looking at Lincoln and Denise, she felt that God had many trials for her yet. Prompted by Denise's Brixtonian dialect and her unladylike manner, she feared that the girl was already sexually active. As for Lincoln, she wondered how he always had money on him when he didn't have a job. But she adored Royston. Jenny thought he would have a better chance in life if she looked after him and sent him to a decent school in Norbury or somewhere similar. His intelligence would be doomed if he went to a school in the ghetto. But how would she persuade her sister to think likewise? she pondered, watching Hortense fill her glass again.

The Huggins clan returned to their block just before nine o'clock. Royston, who sprinted up the stairs ahead of everyone else, saw Frank first, smoking a cigarette and peering over the balcony. He was a tall, well-built man topped by long, ginger hair. His square chin was covered with shaving spots and his squashed nose betrayed his amateur boxing days. The freckles on his face were too numerous to count and his sea-green eyes seemed to display many hardships. Royston ran towards him, leaped up and gave him a high five.

'Hi ya, Smokin' Joe,' hailed Frank. 'Been out for the day?'

Before Royston could answer, his mother appeared on the balcony. 'So you fin' your way 'ome,' spat Hortense. 'You realise de amount ah distress you cause Stella by your disappearing act. Do you know your pickney ah walk around like duppy, all confused an' bawling cos dem t'ink you might ah get run over by truck. Do you—'

Frank interrupted, speaking in a quiet, defeated tone. 'I 'ad to sort out my head, Hortense. Honest. Things just got on top of me and I sorta just flipped.'

Biscuit ambled lazily along the balcony, and saw his mother eyeballing the tall man. Denise looked at Frank, offered him a polite smile, then walked by and opened the front door, not prepared to stand out in the cold for anyone.

'Easy on him, Mummy,' said Biscuit.

'Easy 'pon 'im? Stella should beat him till his ginger hair drop out.' Hortense kissed her teeth as she went inside, leaving Frank and Biscuit leaning over the balcony, observing the traffic on Brixton Road.

'Your old girl's not happy, is she?' said Frank, swatting away strands of hair from in front of his face.

'Why you walk out, man?' interrogated Biscuit. 'Mummy's right, y'know. I thought Stella was gonna go completely cuckoo.'

'Like I said, I just 'ad enough. It just kinda got to me. The other day I was even turned down for a labouring job. Geezer said he wants people to 'ave a little know-how of bricklaying. I told him I've done a bit but I ain't got no level or tools or anything.'

'Der's more dan one building site in South London,

y'know,' Biscuit encouraged, touching his fist on Frank's shoulder.

'Sometimes I think I might take my chances doing a hustle,' commented Frank.

'Nah,' replied Biscuit. 'You've got kids, innit. You don't want to end up like Snowman – you know 'im, used to live in de block behind.'

'Yeah.'

'He's doing seven years' bird after de beast catch 'im in dat container wid all dat charlie at Dover. Karen was four months pregnant when he went inside. An' as for his t'ree uder kids, it can't be no joy to visit der paps in Wandswort' jailhouse.'

Frank smiled wistfully. 'We went to school together, me and Snowman. Back then he was plain old Simon. Who would 'ave thought it, eh? Simon, who used to skive off games lessons, and now he's doing time for bringing in charlie. Mind you, Snowman was the guy who thought of the decoy raid.'

'Wha's dat again?' Biscuit asked.

'You know, that shoplifting thing where three black guys walk in a store. All the attention is on them wherever they go. But they don't see the white accomplice who's tea-leafing all sorts of stuff. Snowman and his crew used to work Oxford Street every Saturday.'

'Dat Snowman was kinda smart,' Biscuit laughed. 'But he should a kept to de decoy runnings instead of running wid coke.'

'Yeah. But I bet when he comes out he will do the same again.'

Two floors up, someone had turned their stereo on. An unseen woman sang along to UB40's 'One In Ten'. One floor down, a drunk joined in the chorus but failed to keep up with the rhythm. Frank and Biscuit laughed.

'They got it about right, innit,' commented Frank. 'One in ten *are* unemployed. How much is that in the whole country?'

' 'Bout five million,' answered Biscuit. 'An' you can add on all de sad saps on Yops schemes. An' you can also add on all de hustlers who mek so much dey don't 'ave to worry 'bout signing on.'

'I saw that weird dread in Ruskin park yesterday,' said Frank. 'You know, the one with one eye?'

'Yeah, Jah Nelson.'

'Well, I was just sitting there, feeling really pissed off, and he came up to me. He told me he sometimes sees me in the park with my kids.'

'Yeah, wha' did he say to you? Start chatting rubbish, did he?'

'Nah, he made sense in a funny way.'

'About wha'?'

'I was telling him of my situation, totally fucked off with everything. And he told me about the fucking potato famine in Ireland years back. Then he told me about how loads of Irishmen slaved away building all the tracks for the trains in England. After that he really went into one, telling me about St Patrick, Pope Celestine and some bishop called Palladius . . . How the fuck did he know all that?'

'He's a walking library.'

'He then said that while those Irish workers were toiling away for little money, they hoped their children would do something better, 'ave a better life, and I owe it to them to make something of my life and not give up.'

'Well, frig my days,' commented Biscuit. 'So wha' he said made you go 'ome?'

'Yeah. But fucking hell, what is the world coming to when it takes a one-eyed dread to make me see reason.'

Frank and Biscuit laughed before they disappeared into their respective flats.

# Six Babylon

## 6 February 1981

Coffin Head, working his pitch on the Front Line, had sold £120 worth of herb in two and a half hours. Apart from a safari-jacketed black guy with a Scottish accent, who asked for 'some good dope', and a wildly optimistic ghetto youth, who promised to pay for his 'weed' when his giro turned up, there had been no cause for alarm. What had troubled him most was the horizontal rain, which forced him to squint under his beret and take extra care when handling his merchandise; customers didn't like smoking damp cannabis. During his sales shift, however, the heavens turned to a promising white hue, with the rain relenting to an irritating patter. But none of this deterred the illegal entrepreneurs who fast-talked the herb buyers while they ate Jamaican meat patties.

The scar-faced Chemist was there, leaning against a lamp-post, crowned by a Sherlock Holmes-style hat and wearing a puffy black anorak. He offered Coffin Head a respectful nod. The huge Cutlass Blake, wearing a parka jacket with the hood up, was sitting on the kerb counting notes. Coffin Head decided not to dwell on Blake's massive figure for too long.

An hour later, with the time approaching 3pm, Coffin Head decided that his stint on the Front Line was over. Relieved, he made for home via Shakespeare Road, his wad of money safely tucked inside his right sock. As he walked, he pondered on what outfit he should buy for the wedding this coming Saturday. Maybe blue slacks and a silk cream shirt, he thought. Or perhaps a new Slazenger polo-neck and beige waffle trousers. He liked the look of those new green crocs in the shoe shop on Atlantic Road. Coming from the 'prison' estate, Sugar Minott's 'Mr DC' blared out from a second-floor flat, causing Coffin Head to glance upwards. A mischievous gust of wind caught his beret, dislodging it from his head. The purple cloth fluttered and landed neatly next to a pile of sodden dog shit. 'Fockin' breeze, man.' He stooped down to pick it up, grimaced at the wet stain and dusted it down. Then he heard synchronised shouts all around him.

Still bending down cleaning his hat, he raised his sights and saw six dark uniforms converging on him and heard the dull echo of the polished black boots walking across the concrete. 'Wha' de fuck ah gwarn?'

'Put your fucking hands up and don't go near your pockets. *Now*!'

Coffin Head rose slowly, adopted a rebel pose and cut his eyes, feeling confident as he had no more herb on his person. The beast will let me go in a few minutes, he thought. Just a sus stop.

One policeman handcuffed his wrists behind his back. Another went through his pockets, revealing a bunch of keys, some loose change, a box of matches, a stick of Lipsyl and a steel-toothed afro comb.

'So,' smiled the senior policeman, studying the comb. 'That's two charges already – selling drugs and carrying an offensive weapon.'

Coffin Head stilled his tongue, but his eyes betrayed his fear.

One of the policemen picked up the beret, which had fallen to the kerb during the handcuffing, then dropped it theatrically on the dog shit. 'Oh, clumsy me.'

'You're nicked,' said the sergeant.

Coffin Head was roughly escorted to a waiting police van on Mayall Road. Sensing many hands around his torso, he found himself being hurled into the back of the vehicle and cried out as his stomach thudded on to the metallic floor. Five seconds later, he felt two boots pressing upon his spine. He sensed his right cheek flattening against the cold floor and smelt the stench of a thousand arrests. He tried to look up but all he saw were legs, there were no windows at the side of the van, and he could not see out the front.

He had no idea where he was being taken; they can't be going to Brixton police station, he thought, they were taking too long. The cuffs were tight around his wrists and he cursed inwardly. He hoped the beast wouldn't locate the wad of notes inside his right sock. He moved his head to give his neck relief, and realised that grit had

105

smothered his right cheek and his brown suede jacket; he wondered at the cost of the dry cleaning if any blood was spilled. How long were they gonna keep him? Would he be able to go to the wedding? Was it a case of mistaken identity? What would his parents think of it all? And Denise – what would she think? Linvall Thompson's 'Six Babylon' sang inside his head: *Jus' ah lock dem up cos der smoking a spliff, Babylon, cool down your temper, sa.* He tried to rid himself of the image of Sceptic's story of woe inside a police cell, and concentrate his ears on what was being said by the chuckling uniforms around him.

'Can't believe the judge let Bailey out on bail,' one officer moaned.

'He'll go down, just a matter of time,' another assured.

'But he ain't got no stable address,' someone answered. 'He's bound to do a runner.'

'If I know Bailey, he'll be on the line soon enough,' the sergeant said. 'That's the only way he makes his dosh – he can't resist it.'

'He's got himself a good brief, though.'

'That won't save him this time. For fuck's sake, we found five thousand pounds worth of cannabis under his bedroom floorboards. If he don't get about five years I'll eat my fucking helmet.'

'Yeah,' the driver concurred. 'There ain't no judge who disputes a policeman's word.'

The van came to a halt. Coffin Head felt two arms around his neck, lifting him up. He suffered a kick on his backside. As the doors at the back of the van opened he tried to look around for any clues as to where he was, perhaps a road sign or the name of the police station. All he saw were the wheels of police vehicles. He felt himself being bundled out on to a police station's parking lot.

106

This ain't de friggin' entrance, he told himself.

Coffin Head felt more pressure around his neck, forcing his head to bow and his back to bend. The handcuffs were cutting into his wrists and he wondered if he was bleeding. His shoulders were taut from the pressure of the cuffs pulling in an unnatural direction. He wondered what idiot had designed the handcuffs. A skinny man mus' 'ave tried on de prototype, he thought. He smelt the cocktail of exhaust fumes and spitting rain.

'Keep his head down,' the sergeant instructed.

Coffin Head was led through a back door and into the station. Two right turns later, he found himself face down inside a cell. The cuffs were unclipped and he was left alone. He rubbed his wrists, wondering why he hadn't been presented to the charging officer. His watch read 3.45pm. He still felt that he might get out soon, once the police realised their mistake. He would still be able to check out his new clothes.

All the men's fashion shops had closed before Coffin Head saw his cell door opening again. A bearded, plain-clothes detective with eyebrows that joined led five uniformed officers into the cell. The door shut with a fort-like clang behind them. From his seat, on a jutting slab of cold concrete, Coffin Head pushed his knees against his chest and wrapped his arms around his legs, expecting a beating. He felt the cell shrink as the officers appeared, and turned his head away, closing his eyes.

'No need to be alarmed, my friend,' the detective said quietly. 'If you co-operate you'll be out of here before you know it. Do you want a fag? Something to eat?'

Coffin Head shook his head, wondering what his

mother would be cooking for the family evening meal.

'Maybe something to drink?' the detective offered. 'Cuppa tea?'

Coffin Head didn't reply.

'You sure you don't want nothing?' the detective asked, showing his palms to Coffin Head, faking hospitality. 'I'm sorry you had to wait for me for so long, but as you might realise, we are very busy people.' He turned around and smiled at his fellow officers.

Coffin Head wasn't sure what to make of the apology, but allowed himself a forlorn hope that he wouldn't be harmed.

'Now, my young friend,' the detective said in a neighbourly tone. 'Let's not be vague. Your situation is not good. You have been seen by my colleagues, and many other witnesses, selling a banned substance on the Railton Road.'

Coffin Head thought of the strange black guy with the Scottish accent. Char! Fockin' traitor.

'The evidence is so overwhelming that it would be laughable for you to deny these allegations,' his interrogator continued. 'Before you are charged formally, you can tell me your name and address.'

Coffin Head stared at the wall for a few seconds before co-operating in a quiet but wrathful voice.

'OK, Mr Beckford, or can I call you Everton?' the detective asked, playing up to his colleagues and speaking like Regan in *The Sweeney*. 'To be honest, my superiors are not really interested in picking up the likes of you and charging you for peddling a few scores of dope. I mean . . . how can I put this? You're not worth more than two for a penny. Me and my colleagues won't get no pats on the back from the superintendent. Do you get my drift?'

Coffin Head nodded slowly, realising his worst case scenario was about to happen. His sweat became a downpour, and the single light-bulb reflected brightly from his dampened face.

'But if you can help us out, we'll try and help you,' the detective offered. 'Won't we guys,' he chuckled, turning around.

'Yeah guv,' a burly policeman answered, his colleagues nodding and gesturing in the affirmative.

Coffin Head felt a spike-booted caterpillar crawling down his back. He kept quiet and watched the men pace the cell, closing in around him.

'All you have to do is answer one question. That's all, just one.'

'What?' Coffin Head asked, more a nervous reaction than a question.

'Who's selling heroin and cocaine on the Front Line,' his inquisitor demanded, his voice suddenly brutal. 'Name?'

'I . . . I dunno.'

'This is not good, Everton,' the detective murmured. 'You're a popular kinda guy, I reckon. You know a lot of the inhabitants on Railton Road. I reckon you're a streetwise kinda kid. NOW GIVE ME THE FUCKING NAME WHO'S SELLING?'

'I dunno, I ain't got a clue.' Coffin Head replied in a whimper.

The detective gestured to one of his colleagues, then made for the cell door. 'Everton, this is not good. I've got some business to attend to. By the time I get back let's all hope you are more helpful.'

The clang of the closing cell door shook Coffin Head's bones. He looked up, and what he saw was not good. A brawny policeman advanced towards him with serious intent, backed up by three colleagues, leaving a young policeman by the door.

'Give us a fucking name.'

Coffin Head remained silent, and for a millisecond, considered giving his oppressors a name that didn't belong to anyone he knew. He blinked, but the name didn't come to him, as if his brain was on pause.

'A fucking name, Midnight!'

'Don't know one.'

Coffin Head felt the knuckles of a fist detonate against his stomach, knocking him off his slab and propelling him to the floor. He thought he was going to bring up his cornmeal porridge breakfast. He felt himself exhale vigorously and he doubled up in pain. There was a slight pause as the other officers looked at each other before deciding to get in on the action. Coffin Head covered his privates with his right hand and used his left to cover his face. This is it, he thought. Don't give dem de pleasure of screaming. *Don't*. He gnashed his teeth, closed his eyes tight and tensed every muscle that he knew of. Then he felt the severe pain of boots hacking at his torso. He didn't know which way to roll to escape as he was kicked in from both sides, his back, chest, shoulders and backside. The stench of dead urine rose from the floor and filled his nose, causing him to sneeze violently.

The young policeman by the door winced and turned his face away. 'I'm going, I don't want no part of this,' he muttered, before opening the cell door.

'Wassa matter with you, Milton?' one of the assailants mocked. 'You fucking wuss. Welcome to the real world, pal. This ain't nut and choc cookies at fucking Hendon.'

Coffin Head thought of Sceptic before momentarily

taking his hand away from his face and offering a glance to Milton. The young officer looked into Coffin Head's eyes and the reality of his new post in the inner cities struck home. He disappeared out into the corridor, closing the cell door behind him, shaking his head in disbelief.

Coffin Head stopped rolling about, realising that it was pointless. He sobbed quietly, closing his eyes again, and felt the shape and form of the boots indenting his upper body and rattling every bone in his frame.

Suddenly, he heard the boots march out of the cell door, some echoing off the concrete more than others. He opened his eyes slowly and found he was alone in the cell. He looked up at the shaft of sunlight coming in from a small misted window. High in the corners, he could just make out spider webs that were flecked by dirt. He dropped his gaze to the concrete floor and noticed the many tread prints formed in the fine dust. It was only now in the quiet of the cell that the nerves in his torso shrieked and a monumental pain cascaded over him. He didn't know where to rub first.

Three and a half hours later, the detective returned and found Coffin Head laying on his back on the floor, peering aimlessly at the ceiling. The shaft of sunlight had disappeared and the cell was lit by a flickering, naked bulb. His body didn't stir, he just lay silent, as if he was offering himself as sacrifice. You t'ink you 'ave conquered me, he thought. I'm still 'ere! I can go t'rough dat shit again! Come, I'm ready for you, give me all you've got!

'Get up, Everton,' the detective commanded.

Coffin Head rose slowly, trying to control his face, refusing to show the man his pain. His eyes met the

111

detective's fierce glare, and he held the gaze as he returned to his seated position on the concrete slab.

'Everton,' the detective addressed, fighting the urge to smile. 'I'm sorry if my friends were a little impatient in their methods. It's unfortunate that you can't be more helpful.'

'Dat's cos I don't know nutten,' retorted Coffin Head, returning the detective's stare with interest.

'Now, Everton, that is no tone of voice with which to talk to an officer. I will get the information sooner or later. You've been a good boy, Everton, your name and address checks out. You know what that means, don't you?'

'No.'

'Let me enlighten you. My colleagues can arrest you at any time; we can still charge you for your infringement today. But I'm a fair sort. I'll let you off with a warning. I might as well be honest – my colleagues can't be bothered with the paperwork. But I expect you to make a friendly call within two weeks. Do you get my drift?'

'Dat's friggin' blackmail.'

'I'd say helping with inquiries,' answered the detective. 'Giving your friendly bobby some information. I *want* that name, Everton. And you're going to find it for me.' The detective scribbled a phone number on his note-pad along with his name and gave the page to Coffin Head. 'Two weeks, Everton. Otherwise . . . it won't be good. If I'm out when you call, then just leave a message. Who knows? You might even get a reward,' he laughed.

The detective about-turned and departed the cell. Coffin Head was grabbed by rough hands, handcuffed once more, and forced to walk in a stoop. The corridor outside the cell was dark and he could hear the shouts of a drunk in another cell. He noticed names written with

112

chalk on boards beside cell doors and wondered how many sufferers passed through this place daily. Seconds later, he felt the night air cooling his head and heard the clomping of boots on asphalt.

Before he could look around to try and guess where he was, he felt himself being dragged inside the back of another police van. His left shoulder met the floor of the vehicle with a dull thud, his cheek kissing the floor once again. He felt the rubber sole of a boot upon his upper back.

Fifteen minutes later, Coffin Head was launched out of the van and into the air. He grazed his shoulder and cut his left knee as he landed. He groped for the bankroll inside his right sock and exhaled a heavy sigh when he realised his beating wasn't for nothing. He looked across the road and saw the castle-coloured brickwork of the vast Lansdowne council estate, fronted by a long, narrow green. Looking up the street, he could make out the buildings of the South Bank college and knew he was on Wandsworth Road. In a shop doorway, a tramp, more red-faced than white, and wearing a balaclava, peered at him with watering eyes. 'Look like you need a drink, young man?' The vagrant gestured at the flask of Pernod in his mittened hand. 'Dropping you home, were they?'

Coffin Head struggled to his feet, sniffed the air and got a strange aroma of aniseed and urine. Someone might as well piss 'pon me, he said to himself. 'Tek yourself off de friggin' street, man, an' look soap!' He kissed his teeth and tried to gather his bearings, then limped off, searching for a cab office, as the drunk took a generous swig and cried goodbye.

'Wandsworth Road,' Coffin Head muttered to himself.

'Char, where's de fockin' cab station round dese sides?'

He checked his watch. 11.45pm. He remembered there was a cab station near the college, he guessed about fifty yards away, so he set off, cursing the police under his breath. De beast mus' be after Slim Lamb Harry, he told himself. But he don't sell cocaine an' shit 'pon de Line, he reasoned. Friggin' bloodclaat beast, I'd rader tek beating from dem dan 'ave it known dat I'm a squealer. Harry would put out me living light jus' like dat, an' de beast wouldn't protect me. I wonder if Sceptic went t'rough de same shit. Friggin' pussy'ole beast dem, he cursed inwardly. I'd love to get one of dem one on one. Not five 'pon one.

He finally found a cab station ten minutes later. He walked inside and saw a cigarette-puffing white woman behind a shoulder-high wooden counter. Sellotaped to the wall behind her, and written in black felt tip, were various fare prices to parts of London and beyond. Coffin Head looked through a doorway that led to a hallway. At the end of the corridor was a smoky room where five men played cards around a battered table.

'I wanna cab,' he demanded.

The lady stubbed out her fag in a overspilling ashtray, then walked to the doorway. 'Number two! That's you, Clive.'

Clive put down his hand of cards and stepped through the hallway. 'Denmark Road, off Coldharbour Lane,' Coffin Head told him.

'Denmark Road? Then I want paying now, sunshine.'

Coffin Head kissed his teeth as he paid the driver. 'I'm in no friggin' state to do a runner. Char, jus' drive me home, James.'

# Crisis

## 7 February 1981

The next morning Coffin Head waited until his father had departed for work before rolling out of bed. His ribs throbbed like a Shaka speaker cone working to the max. Maybe he should have taken his mother's advice last night and gone to the hospital for an X-ray. But the prospect of sitting on a hard plastic chair in the casualty foyer in the early hours didn't interest him, especially after suffering batty ache from the concrete slab in the police cell.

Coffin Head's small bedroom was ordered and clean. Numbered cassette tapes formed a neat pile on the dresser, and behind them was a top-of-the-range Brixton suitcase. Toiletries, a gold-coloured wristwatch, combs and some dry-cleaning tickets scattered the rest of the surface. A mirror about the size of a record album jacket was set above the dresser. Boxing and cricket magazines were piled beside the bedside cabinet, which had a small radio and one polished glass ashtray upon it. A Dennis Brown poster kept watch over his single bed. Four pairs of shoes and three pairs of trainers formed a line against the wall at the foot of the bed.

The events at the police station replayed in his mind, sound-tracked by Black Uhuru's 'General Penitentiary', chomping away at his self-worth. The fockin' beast thought of him as so insignificant, he fumed, that they couldn't even be bothered to charge him with anything. All they wanted was to test out their boots on a black youth. Fockin' devil people dem.

Once dressed and washed, he moved into the kitchen where he found his mother, wearing a head scarf and apron. She had tolerant, chestnut eyes and her unlined forehead made her look younger than her 41 years. The colour of her skin was rusty-brown and her taut cheeks showed a hint of laughter. She was scalping the skin from a tray of chicken legs. She scrutinised her son as only mothers can. 'Everton, why you nuh tek yourself to Kings College? Dey will gi' you an X-ray an' mek sure everyt'ing alright. Char, man, sometime you're so stubborn.'

'I'm alright, Mummy. If my ribs are broken, den I would be feeling more pain, innit.'

'I 'ave ah good mind fe go to dat damn police station an' gi' dem one piece of fire from me tongue, me ah tell you. 'Ow can dey jus' beat up ah somebody an' nobody say nutten?'

'I don't even know wha' blasted police station dey tek me to.'

'Wha!'

116

'I told you last night. Weren't you listening? Dey held me down, innit. I didn't know where me der.'

'I will mek ah complaint. Yeah, me t'ink I will affe mek appointment wid our MP. He will affe do somet'ing.'

Mrs Beckford hoped that one day, she and her family could escape from Brixton. In her part-time job as a consultant to Lambeth social services she had seen too many family lives ruined by the area. Too many youths walked the streets with nothing to do and no aspirations. Teachers in schools were having to deal with kids who had massive social problems rather than educating a class. She thought the Government should address the root of the problem, rather than just offering sound-bites to middle England, telling them they were going to get ruthless with crime and increase the police presence in the inner cities. Mrs Beckford knew her son had joined the ranks of the underclass. You can only influence your children to a certain extent, she thought, but the environment where that child grows up will have its undeniable effect.

Coffin Head eyed the cereal boxes and the ardough bread on the kitchen table, but hadn't the stomach for breakfast. 'No one will listen to you, Mummy. How do you expect politician to believe us when my own paps don't? Look at dat time last year when I was arrested on sus. He t'ought I really was 'bout to raid a jeweller's.' He met his mother's eyes for half a moment, before retreating to the hallway to pick up his leather jacket which was hanging on a peg.

'Where you going? You should be resting yourself an' not walking street.'

'I'm going Biscuit's.'

'Biscuit? Me never hear seh Biscuit turn doctor. 'Im can't do nutten fe your ribs dem.'

'Got to chat to him 'bout somet'ing. Soon come.'

Coffin Head disappeared out the front door, leaving his mother worried and regretting that she had not taken him to the hospital. We 'ave to get away from dis area, she promised herself again.

Before setting off for Biscuit's flat, Coffin Head checked on his car. He kicked the tyres, testing the air pressure, then gave the windscreen a wipe with a chamois cloth. He also made a quick check to see if there were any police about. On his trek over the grassy knolls that stood between Cowley and Myatts Field estates, his anger mushroomed inside him. Why should the beast get away with beating up a black youth? he asked himself. He felt his damaged ribs, and wondered if there was any way to get his own back; maybe he could cut the tyres of a police vehicle, he grinned.

Hortense answered Coffin Head's impatient knocking. 'Everton,' she greeted, reading his face. 'You going ah funeral today? Why you so glum? You favor dem idiot man who step outta bookie shop who curse dem maaga dog, an' dem tut an tut till dem mout' get tired.'

'Nah, I'm jus' tired, Mrs Huggins. Had a late night. Lincoln up an' about?'

'Come in, man. Come in. You cyan wake him up yourself. Lincoln inna 'im bed drawing some ugly piece ah snore.'

Hortense returned to her chores as Coffin Head made for Biscuit's bedroom. Once inside he had to dodge and walk over items of clothing, cassette tapes and Royston's matchbox cars. A wasp and a dragonfly seemed to be having a fight in Biscuit's nose, and Coffin Head felt sorry for any future wife of his brethren.

118

'Char! Get up, man. Wha' do you?'

Biscuit stirred into life. 'Carol?' he mumbled.

'Wake up you damn fool. You t'ink me 'ave voice like a girl?'

Biscuit rubbed his eyes, shook his head, sat up and set his sight on his long-time friend. 'At dis time ah morning, I only expect girl in my room. Wha's de emergency, man?'

Coffin Head parked on the foot of the bed. 'Char. Don't mek me laugh. De day I sight Carol in *your* bed will be de same day I'm drawing serious pension.' Fully awake now, Biscuit noticed Coffin Head's grim expression. 'Wha's de score, man? Since when 'ave you been round to my gates dis time of morning? We're in serious shit, innit.'

Coffin Head kicked the bedroom door closed, kissed his teeth and covered his face with the palms of his hands. 'Beast arrested me, innit. I dunno where de rarse dey tek me. All I know so is dey did boot me up inna cell an' dey didn't even charge me, to rarted. After dat, dey fling me in de beast wagon, tek me to Wandswort' Road, an' fling me 'pon de kerb like how dem council sweeper fling rubbish bag.'

Biscuit cradled his chin with his thumb and forefinger. 'Fuck my living days, man. You're alright t'ough?'

'Not too bad. My mudder wanted to tek me Kings College last night. But you know wha' it's like in der, an' I was well tired. So I didn't boder in the end, I jus' went to my bed.'

'Can't believe it, man.' Biscuit shook his head. 'First Sceptic, an' now you. I'm telling you dem beast man are looking war y'know. Der lucky man an' man ain't flingin' no bomb an' shit in dem station. Nah, man. Dis can't gwarn. Somet'ing 'ave to be done.'

'Oh yeah, like wha', to rarted?'

'Sen' a letter to de Commissioner man, innit. Wha's his blasted name? David Knee or somet'ing.'

'McNee!' Coffin Head corrected. 'Dat's like asking de fader of a murderer to be de judge of de trial.'

Biscuit got out of bed, grabbed his denims and slipped them on. 'You must ah get ketch by SPG to rarted. You know so dey 'ave der own rules an' play dat game – to truncheon butt a sufferer. You know how it is, dey pick up a black yout', brutalise dem inna cell, an' dey expect crime to drop.'

'Biscuit, man. Don't mek joke 'bout it, y'hear me. I was in dat rarted cell for some long hours before dey come in an' cramp an' paralyse me. Dey wanted to know who's selling charlie 'pon de Line. I weren't saying nutten, so dey decide to gi' me some bitch lick wid der government boot. Char! I thought I was gonna dead, to rarted.'

Biscuit switched on his blaster. 'Maybe you shoulda listen to your mudder an' gone ah Kings College. You might 'ave some bruk up ribs an' t'ing. How you gonna crub girl at de wedding if your ribs dem are mash up?'

'Fuck crubbing girl at wedding! Char! Dat don't even pass my mind. I don't even know if I'm going to de damn wedding.'

'Wha' you saying, man? Everybody's reaching. Jus' come, dread. It will tek our minds off business an' mek us relax for once widout worries of juggling de herb.'

Coffin Head thought of Nunchaks and the rest of the jugglers on the Line, and wondered if they'd received similar beatings from the police. He knew the dangers of selling herb, and although it provided him with money to buy clothes, a beating was a high price to pay. In his mind, he suddenly made a decision. 'Speak for yourself, brethren, cos from dis day I ain't juggling no more, I'm finished wid dem t'ings. It's giving me too much grief.' He hid his face with his hands. 'Almshouse business is wha' I'm dealing wid now. I will never forget dem faces, man. Never. An' when I sight dem faces again, there'll be yamming lead an' clocking de inside of a burns unit, to rarted. Babylon *affe* burn!'

Biscuit watched his friend with dismay. He had never seen him so troubled, and he tried to find words of comfort. He reached up to the top of his wardrobe, grabbed his bag of herb and rizlas and threw them to his spar. 'I'm jus' gonna dash 'way my BO. An' I affe say I don't like to 'ear wha's coming out of your mout', dread. Buil' up an' we'll chat 'bout dis inna minute. De herb will calm you down.'

He plucked his towel from the wardrobe door and disappeared. Burning Spear's 'Jah A Go Raid' played from the blaster, and Coffin Head couldn't help but concentrate his ears on the haunting lyrics. He rewound the cassette to the start of the tune.

Biscuit returned five minutes later. 'Listen to me, Coff. Don't boder do nutten stupid, y'know. I don't wanna hear dat you beat up some beastman an' doing time, y'hear? Touch de herb an' dat will mek you cool down.' Coffin Head began to construct a seven-paper spliff. Biscuit found his Vaseline jar and buttered his torso. 'So de beast dem tek your corn an' herb?'

'Nah. I sold all the herb, an' you know I always put the corn in my sock.'

'I can kinda understand why you don't wanna juggle no more, but you know so we affe clear it wid Nunchaks first. You know how he stay, he don't like man an' man working fe him an' den stopping cos der feeling a liccle heat. An' den after dat dey start work for a nex' dealer.'

Coffin Head set fire to his roach, inhaling deeply. 'Right about now, I don't give a fuck wha' Nunchaks might do or say. It's you who 'ad de idea of working for dat lighter-clicking madman, *not* me.'

Biscuit shook his head, then snatched the rizlas off his brethren. 'You forget wha' appened to Rough Neck Rasputin?'

'Who de rarse is he? An' what kind of rarse name is dat?'

'He used to be in dat sound, wassit called . . . Marxist Hi-Fi. Dey used to play in dat shubeen on Landor Road on a Friday night. Nuff leggo beast an' blue foot were always der, you know, dem whores who operate from Bedford Hill, in der mini-skirt, tight blouse, suspender an' t'ing. Greybacks would reach an' crub dem 'gainst de wall . . . Anyway, 'ear de blow by blow. De sound did bruk up cos one of de sound man t'ief de takings one night from de shubeen. Nuff palaver an' contention did ah gwarn an' two sound man get ratchet sketch. Sir Lenin, de owner fe de sound, kick out Rasputin.'

'Gi' me de score, man,' Coffin Head rebuked. 'You love make a novel of everyt'ing.'

'Anyway,' Biscuit continued, disliking his flow inter-rupted, 'Rasputin checked out Nunchaks to do a liccle juggling. Two weeks later, Rasputin was offered more corn to juggle an' look out for Herbman Blue. Nunchaks 'eard 'bout it an' set him up neatly. Rasputin went to check Nunchaks at his brothel to collect his collie. Muttley and Ratmout' t'ump up Rasputin inna serious manner. Fat up his lip, bruk him nose, blast his cheekbone, an' mash up his eye-corner. Dey dragged him to Nunchaks and Nunchaks went all Bruce Lee on him wid his *Enter the*

*Dragon* weapon. Den Nunchaks tol' him, 'Your days as a salesman are over, yout' '. Bwai, Rasputin still concuss till dis day to rarted.'

Coffin Head chuckled and admired the way Biscuit told a story. 'He had it coming, man. Idiot bwai.'

Biscuit opened his wardrobe door, pulled out one of his many Gabbicci tops and covered his trunk with it. The zip-up cardigan was light blue with wide lapels and dark blue suede trimming on the cuffs and around the collar. 'Wha' did your parents say, man?'

'I told my mudder 'bout it. T'ough I didn't tell her why I was arrested. I didn't tell de old man, you know how he stays. When she did hear 'bout de beating she did wanna complain. But y'know, who's gonna listen to her? Beastman only understand force, not complaints.'

Biscuit torched his roach, and realised that Coffin Head was talking more and more like Sceptic. Just the other day, Sceptic told him he would like to kidnap a policeman and give him some serious Japanese torture, just like he'd seen in a war film. Biscuit hoped Coffin Head would not develop this train of thought. 'Listen up, Coff, yeah,' Biscuit said softly. 'We'll jus' chill out till de wedding an' review de situation after dat, seen. Jus' don't boder do anyt'ing stupid an' don't do nutten widout telling me, seen.'

'Char! You sound like my mudder to rarted. If you affe know, I'm going to check Sceptic dis morning.'

'Wha' for?'

'Cos I wanna know the full SP of his tribulation inna beast cell. He's never told me de full story.'

Biscuit went to the bottom of his wardrobe where his selection of hats was resting. He picked out his weatherman hat, a black cloth cap with a peak and a red, gold and green star of David sewn on the top. He put the hat on, and although tilting it to almost cover his right eye, it still looked three sizes too big. 'I'll sight you later den. Don't let Sceptic talk you into anyt'ing stupid. You know how he's bragga bragga from time, whole 'eap of talk but no action.'

'Char,' Coffin Head scolded, 'I told you stop chatting like my mudder.' He kissed his teeth as he headed out the door.

Denise was in the passage, wearing a two-tone skirt and a light brown cardigan. 'Alright, Coff,' she greeted. 'Wha' brings you round at dese times?'

'Ask no question, I'll tell you no lie,' came back the reply.

'Bwai, you can't answer simple question?'

After an admiring glance at Denise's backside, Coffin Head departed the flat. She looks nice today, he thought.

Back in Biscuit's room, Denise sat down on the bed. 'Wha's troubling 'im?' she asked.

'Dis an' dat. In uder words, none of your business.'

'Only asked!'

'Wha' do you want, anyway?'

Denise twiddled her hair, appearing a touch embarrassed. 'Jus' wanna say t'anks for de corn for de dress. I do appreciate it, y'know.'

'T'ings irie. No problem 'bout dat. Jus' keep off Mummy's back, yeah.' Biscuit peered into his broken mirror to style his hat. 'Will you stop de red eye business? Sometimes Mummy don't let on what she really feels. Believe it, Denise, she feels for you jus' as much as she feels for Royston or me.'

Denise sprawled along the bed, immersing her face in the covers. 'Sometimes I feel so unwanted, y'know. Like Mummy don't want me around.'

Biscuit turned from the cracked mirror, regarding his sister with suspicion, as if she had broken an unspoken family rule. 'Nah, Sis. Don't grudge Mummy for dat. You ain't seen dose photos of Mummy when she was young. She was pretty like any beauty queen. But now you can say de years 'ave taken its toll. An' she look 'pon you jus' growing to be a young lady. So don't tell her I said so, but she getting a liccle red eye. Auntie Jenny always say dat you an' Mummy are spitting image.'

Denise stood up and approached her brother. She offered him a motherly look before adjusting his hat for him. 'Der, dat look better. You 'ad it like any uder man 'as it. Got to be different, innit.'

Biscuit smiled. 'You're gonna look criss in dat dress at de wedding, Sis. You're gonna look even crisser dan Maxine . . . But not Carol.'

Denise punched her brother on the shoulder. 'You feisty wretch. An' speaking of Carol, you an' her an item yet?'

'None of your damn business.'

'I s'pose I'll find out at de wedding, innit,' Denise grinned.

# 11

## The Wedding

### 9 February 1981

Hortense stood on her balcony, picking strands of hair from her shoulders. She was wearing her favourite yellow sleeveless dress that reached down below her knees. Her legs were covered in dark tights. A silver oval-shaped brooch sparkled above her left breast and her head was crowned by a white bonnet that was pinned into her hair. She was trying to decide whether she should wear her old mac to protect her from the cold, which she knew would surely invite dismissive stares from her peers, or to just go as she was. Around her right wrist was a gold-coloured watch her husband had bought her for their first wedding anniversary. She read the time. 5.45pm. She went back inside her flat, deciding against the coat. 'Lincoln, wha'appen to your square head friend? 'Im s'pose to be 'ere fifteen minutes ago. You t'ink 'im bruk down car bruk down fe de last time?'

'He's on his way. Stop fret, he jus' dinged me.'

She found Royston in the front room. Wearing a navy-blue blazer, white shirt and black slacks, he was buffing his black shoes, hoping his mother wouldn't thrash him for his giggling behaviour during the church service.

'If you as so much breathe at de reception,' Hortense warned, 'I will gi' your backside so much grief dat to si' down will be an agony. Y'hear me?'

'Yes, Mummy. Is der going to be chocolate cake at de reception?'

'If der is, nuh boder mek yourself sick. You know wha' will 'appen if you dutty up your pretty clothes dem.'

Hortense then went to Denise's bedroom and kissed her teeth as she watched her daughter reapply her make-up. 'Come, Denise. Everton soon come wid his bruk down car. Lord me God, wha' an uncomfortable ride. Me backside ah still pain me after 'im drop us off from de church.'

Coffin Head's car whinged and wailed to a halt on Brixton Road. He slapped his horn and Biscuit, boasting a fresh hair trim and wearing a double-breasted white jacket and sharply pressed black slacks, was the first to appear on the balcony. Five minutes later, they were in the car and ready to depart.

'Wha' tek you so long, Everton?' Hortense enquired.

'I changed my shirt, innit. After checking it, de colour didn't quite match my blue slacks.'

'Bwai, you go on like a woman,' Denise mocked.

'Do you wanna trod?'

The wedding reception was at a church hall somewhere

near Streatham Vale. At six-thirty, Hortense's party entered the hall. They found it bedecked with balloons and glitter. Middle-aged black men wearing dark suits and skinny ties stood in huddles talking about cricket and their retirement plans. Their wives and girlfriends, wearing bright-coloured dresses, different styled hats and plenty of pearls, sat on wooden chairs, looking as ladylike as possible with their legs crossed. Young children ran across the hall playing tag, while others asked their parents for soft drinks. Tables skirted three sides of wall, dressed in white tablecloths and fancy doilies, and held the polished cutlery, bunches of flowers, champagne glasses and commemorative napkins. The bride and bridegroom's table had the added luxury of extra flowers, a bowl of fruit, a huge loaf of duckbread and two champagne bottles, submerged up to their necks in a silver bucket of chilled water. On its own stand beside the bridal table was a three-tiered, square wedding cake, decorated with a light blue ribbon. At the opposite side of the room was a table laden with gift-wrapped wedding presents, cards and envelopes containing money.

The sound system, Tupper King, had their control tower wired up in a corner, well away from the bridal table. The sound boys, sifting through their music collection and checking wiring, were playing Nat King Cole's 'Unforgettable'. They were clad in jeans, weatherman hats, donkey jackets and trodder boots.

Young men, who all seemed to have paid a visit to their favourite hair trimmer, displayed their violently ironed Farah slacks, flower shirts, double-breasted jackets and snake and crocodile skin shoes. A few of them were wearing gold bracelets and gold sovereign rings. Others wore tailor-cut suits with gold rope chains draped over their fat ties. Those not so affluent looked uneasy in their bright safari suits and Hawaiian shirts.

The young ladies all seemed to be wearing pleated skirts, frilly blouses and blazer-type jackets in cream and burgundy. Some wore light-coloured suits and wide-lapelled blouses, showing off their gold belcher chains. Most of them walked in suede, high-heeled, gold-buckled shoes. Tights were the order of the day due to the snarling weather, and it seemed a battalion of curling tongs had styled endless black waves of hair. Light brown and cherry-coloured lipstick added a touch of glamour, and smiles would sometimes expose a gold tooth.

The aroma of heavily spiced jerk chicken and curried goat blended with the tasty smell of Jamaican patties being gently warmed in the oven. The bar, situated on tables outside the kitchen door, offered strong beers and soft drinks. Pink Lady, Thunderbird and Canei bottles were also in evidence, along with the smaller bottles of Snowballs and Cherry Bs. Surrounding all this were columns of paper cups. The hosts were clever enough to have hidden the Jamaican overproof rum and other spirits. The Guinness punch bowl was guarded by the father of the bride, looking natty in a black three-piece suit, sipping from a tumbler, posing as he'd never posed before and greeting guests with more enthusiasm than was necessary.

Biscuit, who thought that Denise looked seriously stunning, saw his posse members lounging near the sound system. He made his way over, followed by Coffin Head, an eager Royston and a self-conscious Denise. Hortense found a friend of hers and proceeded to complain about the organisation and the seasonal timing of the wedding.

Biscuit and Coffin Head greeted their crew. Biscuit was immediately struck by Carol's natural beauty. She was wearing a sky blue suit with a white frilly blouse that complemented her dark complexion perfectly. Her wavy, permed hair graced her shoulders and he noticed a gold cross, hanging from a gold link chain, resting teasingly on her cleavage.

'Wha'appen Floyd, Shaz, Scep, Finn, Carol,' he hailed. Then he turned to Brenton. 'An' not forgetting the stepping volcano.'

Everyone nodded their greetings, including Royston, who gave all his elders a high five. Denise prised Sharon away from Floyd, and along with Carol proceeded to gossip swap. The guys, especially Coffin Head, all looked at Denise, thinking she had finally grown into a very attractive lady. Meanwhile, Hortense, who had to admit her daughter looked beautiful on this night, stole a glance at Carol, trying to guess how close she was to her son. You'll 'ave to meet my approval before you ketch my son, she thought.

After the meal and all the speeches, the best man sat down and the music rose to a rumbling pitch. Biscuit and his crew scouted for dark corners where they could build their after-dinner spliffs. He feared that wherever they went his mother would find him and give him more than a red look, so with Floyd, Coffin Head, Brenton and Sceptic in tow, he ventured outside, leaving Finnley at the bar.

As the February chill greeted the posse, they saw a figure coming from the car park. The man, fiddling about with a lighter, was dressed in a cashmere coat and sharp slacks, sucking a thumb-thick Havana, and bearing the countenance of a black Clint Eastwood. They all recognised him and looked at each other in alarm.

'Nunchaks,' Biscuit greeted, his voice cloaked in surprise.

130

'Didn't t'ink you go to dese sort of t'ings?'

'Maurice ah my cousin y'know,' Nunchaks replied, eyeing Biscuit's spars with contempt. 'Me jus' come to wish 'im luck an' t'ing.'

'Sout' London a small place, innit,' laughed Biscuit. 'Laters.'

'Hol' on yout'. Before you chip, now I 'ave touched down, we can talk ah liccle business. So tell your spar dem to run an' go'long.'

Biscuit turned to his crew and told them he would meet them outside to smoke his zoot. 'Wrap de spliff good, man. Don't wanna smoke paper.' The posse kissed their teeth and headed for Coffin Head's car.

Nunchaks played with his lighter. 'When are you checking me for your nex' batch ah collic?'

'Monday.'

'Don't check me in Soferno B's shop. I hear so beast-man got some undercover squealers der 'bout. Check me in Desmond's Hip City. Y'hear me yout'?'

'Yeah, wha' time?'

'Mek it 'bout two. An' if I don't reach on time, wait for me, yout'. Y'hear?'

'Yeah, man. I'll reach.'

Nunchaks relit his cigar, eyed his lighter with contempt, and entered the hall like a bounty hunter stepping inside a saloon bar. He surveyed the scene, went to the bar where he grabbed a can of Special Brew, and then his eyes rested on a pretty young lady who strutted across the room like only Brixtonian girls could. Wearing a red velvet, figure-hugging dress and white high-heeled shoes, she carried her head high with the knowledge that she looked good. John Holt's 'Queen Of The Ghetto' pounded from the crusty speaker boxes, and Nunchaks felt the

131

song was made for her. He caught her eye, his smile revealing the golden dentistry in his mouth and a money-making opportunity in his eyes. The girl smiled back, thinking now here's a chilled out sticksman . . . I wonder how he makes his corn? He might 'ave a Jag.

Half an hour later, Hortense was helping dish out the Jamaican patties. Looking for her eldest son, she found him in the hallway, returning from his after-dinner spliff. 'Lincoln, go tell dat damn Royston fe stop jumping 'pon de balloons dem or I will jump 'pon 'im.'

As he entered the hall, Biscuit saw couples crubbing against the walls to a slow groove, and mothers sitting down on chairs sipping wine, complaining to each other about their teenagers. Men besieged the bar, asking where was the overproof rum, while children ran here and there, evading their parent's clutches. Biscuit found Royston gleefully stepping on a balloon with a newly acquired friend. 'Move your backside to de kitchen an' when you reach don't leave Mummy's side.'

Royston did as he was told. Right, thought Biscuit, where's Carol? I haven't had a chance to chat to her tonight. Scanning the crubbing couples, hoping she wasn't with someone else, he saw Nunchaks, wearing a grin that exposed his gums and crubbing some girl. Biscuit stood transfixed, all sorts of scenarios running through his mind. 'Oh shit,' he said to himself. 'Double shit, serious palaver.'

Before he could drop any further into the pits of despair, Carol tugged his arm. 'Been avoiding me 'ave you?'

'Nah, nah.' Using his head, he pointed to his sister. 'Check dat out. Der getting kinda entwined, innit. Der doing de figure eight, man.'

132

'Cool yourself, Biscuit, man. It's jus' a dance. She has a right to enjoy herself. Leave Denise alone.'

'I'm kinda fretting wha' might 'appen once de crub is over. Check how she is smiling.'

'So you wan' her to dance wid a long face? Leave dem, man. It's 'bout time you give *me* some attention.'

'But I affe warn Denise . . .'

'Wha' do you expect? She's bound to ketch a man's eye. She's looking criss tonight.'

'Yeah, but it's '*im*. Look how he's chatting to her in her ear!'

Carol kissed her teeth and led Biscuit by the hand to where the crew were dancing. Finnley, who was now on first-name terms with the barman, was almost pissed. Brenton was hoovering a cigarette, eye-drilling anyone he didn't know. Sceptic was trying to locate his courage so he could ask a girl for a crub. Floyd and Sharon were performing an elaborate smooch, and Coffin Head was emptying a Special Brew can down his gullet, pinching looks at Denise while feeling a river of emotion flow through his body.

Biscuit, you got to do somet'ing, man, Coffin Head thought, hating the way Nunchaks placed his left hand just above Denise's backside.

Yet Biscuit could do nothing, for Carol linked her hands around his neck, smiled sweetly, headbutted him gently and settled for a one-step groove, rocking away to 15, 16, 17s, 'Emotion'. He could only regret giving his sister the cash to buy the red, off-the-shoulder dress that she now sparkled in. He looked across and found her throwing her head back, laughing.

Three hours later, Coffin Head's car asthma-attacked to a standstill outside Cowley estate. Biscuit picked up a sleeping Royston and slung him over his shoulder, then bade laters to his friend as Hortense and Denise got out the other side.

On reaching home, Biscuit unclothed his brother, wrapped him in his pyjamas and put him to bed. Meanwhile, Hortense had sparked out on the sofa, feeling the effects of the Guinness punch and rum cake. Shit, he thought, I'm gonna 'ave to move her later on to her room. Shit, an' she's so grumpy when you wake her from sleep.

Finally, he headed for his sister's bedroom. He didn't knock. Denise's room was the smallest in the house, but she had made the best of it. A single wardrobe, painted creatively in red, gold and green, dominated the room. The petite chest of drawers matched the wardrobe, giving the room a rasta vibe. Overlooking the single bed was a large picture frame, made for Denise by Brenton in appreciation of her helping him with his English studies. He knew that Denise loved photographs. Within the frame was a multitude of photos, flyers and articles about reggae music. The Cool Ruler – Gregory Isaacs – dominated the frame, caked in sweat, wearing a red, gold and green headband and smoking a spliff.

'Can't you friggin' knock? I'm sick an' tired of you jus' stepping into my room as if you's any beastman wid warrant.'

'Quiet your beak an' listen to me keenly. I don't t'ink you know wha' kind of palaver you might get into.'

'Wha' you chatting 'bout. Wha' palaver?'

'You an' Nunchaks at de wedding.'

'Wha' 'bout it?'

'Wha's de score, man? I hope you haven't given 'im our phone digits?'

'An' wha' if I 'ave?'

'Den der's gonna be pure tribulation.'

'Biscuit, man, wha's your problem? Yeah, I know so Nunchaks got a bit of a bad rep, but den so 'ave you. He was kinda polite to me, showed me some manners, an' he's taking me to a club nex' week.'

Biscuit closed the door behind him, not wanting to wake his mother. 'Oh no you ain't. You ain't raving wid 'im full stop. It's not even negotiable, it ain't gonna 'appen, an' I will personally stand outside your room to mek sure you ain't moving wid dat man.'

'Since when 'ave you been my jailer? I see who I like, when I like. An' I'm not sure if your maths is fucked up or you 'ave forgotten, but I'm seventeen now, an' I can do wha' I please. Who do you t'ink you are putting some kinda curfew 'pon me?'

'Denise, listen to me, man. Nunchaks is bad news. Believe. He's a Line man, into all sorts of shit, an' he juggles nuff crime an' terrorises nuff innocent people.'

'Yeah, well, you listen to me good. Friends of mine say de same t'ing 'bout you.'

'Alright, I admit I juggle, you know dat already. But Nunchaks is a different story. He could be your downfall.'

'Look, Biscuit. I don't need for you to look out fe me now. I can look out for myself, I know wha' I'm doing. An' as far as I'm concerned, he offered to take me out, to pay for it an' t'ing, an' he was polite 'bout it. Ain't dat wha' Mummy an' you want?'

'Not wid 'im!'

'Move yourself from my room, man. You jus' wanna control my life an' tell me wha' fe do. An' by de way, who are you to accuse of badness? I know from a good source dat Carol won't deal wid you cos you juggle. You wanna deal wid dat before you come 'ere telling me wha' fe do.'

Biscuit caught a rage and clenched his fists. His eyes narrowed in frustration. She could do with a rarse lick, he thought. He firmed his lips and bared his top row of teeth. Denise backed away, thinking her mouth had gone too far. Biscuit fish-eyed her fiercely before turning around to open the door. He departed, breathing heavily, and the impact of the door against its frame drowned out Denise's sigh of relief.

She dropped on to her bed, regretting her words. At least her brother showed some concern, she thought. Mummy had sighted her figure of eight crub with Nunchaks but she didn't say nutten. She don't give a damn, Denise concluded.

# 12

# Gunman Connection

## 11 February 1981

Monday morning after the wedding, Sceptic was inside the unemployment exchange, leaning against a white-painted wall and sucking a cigarette. East-westing his eyes while keeping his head still, he looked around him. A bad man once told him he would make a great lookout as he was so alert, and today he was in lookout mode. Dressed in a faded blue denim jacket and black corduroy trousers, and topped by a white leather beret, Sceptic flicked his ash on the thin-carpeted floor.

To kill time, he decided to take a stroll around the job boards in the middle of the room. He noticed the 'latest vacancy' board had only eight jobs on it, while the Youth Opportunities board was full. He saw a man take off one

137

of the job cards, place it in his pocket, then walk out. Sceptic kissed his teeth at the jobs that were on offer, before returning to his previous position at the wall. He looked beyond the job boards and watched the unsmiling civil servants sitting behind a long wooden counter, rib-cage high. In front of them were aluminium cartons, about the size of shoe boxes, which housed the files of the unemployed. A cross section of the Brixtonian public queued up in thirteen rows, clutching their cards, ready to sign on for benefit. On the far side of the room were a few booths separated by shoulder-high partitions. Sceptic knew this was where the job advisors had their desks and interviewed the public. He looked around at the walls again, which were covered in posters about how to claim all sorts of benefits, before resting his gaze on the entrance. He pulled out another cigarette, lit it and checked his watch.

Five minutes later, looking neat in a black leather jacket and blue Farahs, and crowned by a burgundy beret, Coffin Head strolled through the entrance of the exchange.

Sceptic stepped up to his friend. 'Wha'appen, Coff. Bit late aren't you? It's gone past ten, man. An' I signed on nearly half an hour ago.'

'Well, sorry fe dat. I kinda got up late an' like it's cold outside, I ain't leaving my yard widout hot Weetabix, dread.'

'It's dat, innit. My hat ain't leaving my head-top, rasta . . . Let's step, man.'

The spars left the warmth of the job exchange and ambled into Coldharbour Lane, near the junction of Atlantic Road.

'So, Scep, man. You set t'ings up.'

'Yeah, neatly. You know me, nuff contacts. He's expecting us. 'Ave you got de wad?'

138

'Of blasted course, man. Blue ain't gonna tek me seriously if I turn up widout nutten.'

'Yeah, seen. Dat would of been a blowoh.'

'Wha' d'you know about 'im, anyway? I mean, man an' man know he's a bad man, but wha's his score?'

'He's a dangerous man, believe. Man an' man say he come from yard, an' some Line man say he come from de States, New York side. Personally, I t'ink he comes from a rarse madhouse, believe! No one ain't too sure, dread. He's like Wilkinson Sword, man. Cross him an' you get wet up like razor 'pon baby flesh. You know so he wet up dat Chinee Jamaican juggler, Clinton Wong.'

'Yeah, wha'appened?'

'One of Wong's crew t'ump up one of Blue's whores cos she wouldn't gi' 'im a free grind. Blue 'eard 'bout it an' set up Wong neatly. He got some fit girl of his to chat up Wong inna Filthy Rocker blues. Wong, who t'ought he got lucky, was looking forward to gi' de girl a serious service back at her yard. When Wong reached de yard, de girl ran up de stairs an' Blue appeared wid Barrabas. Dey t'ump up Wong to de ground an' Blue tek out his ratchet an' etched Wong's face from chin to eyebrow. Den Blue tek out his 'ammer an' demolished Wong's elbows. Serious t'ing. Wong's still inna hospital wid all tube an' shit running t'rough his face an' his arms inna plaster. Word 'pon street is dat Wong's face is looking like underground train map to rarted.'

Coffin Head knew he was taking a risk. He hadn't slept soundly since the beating, suffering nightmares of being thrown into a gladiatorial arena armed with just his fists, and having to fight a hundred truncheon-wielding policemen. A crowd of politicians would yell their approval as the Home Secretary, sitting on a regal throne, signalled a thumbs down. Coffin Head had awoken every morning since the beating with a burning desire for revenge. The other day, Floyd had given him a book about the Black Panthers in America, and he had read it at night, the story of Eldridge Cleaver and his fellow Panthers adding to his anger. One of those friggin' beastman gonna suffer, he repeatedly told himself. Cos a violent oppressor only takes notice of violence, not words.

The two friends crossed the road, strolled for another thirty yards or so, passing two drunks on the way, and a crusty dread yanking along a barking Rottweiler. Sceptic turned left into Rushcroft Road. Small terraced houses filled the street, most of them with boards covering the windows and doors. Sceptic feared the mad and bad men who always walked along here. Coffin Head, knowing that even the police were cautious on this road, felt his heart thumping inside his chest.

Sceptic rattled the letterbox of a house with broken windows. Ten seconds later the door was opened by an unshaven black man with baby dreads spouting from his head, like a junior Medusa. 'Wha'appen, Barrabas,' hailed Sceptic, using a smile to protect his anxiety. 'Blowoh, we're catching a deat' 'pon street y'know. England friggin' cold.'

Barrabas said nothing. Instead, he scrutinised Coffin Head from his eyebrows to his trodder boots. He let Sceptic into the hallway. 'Hol' on, skipper,' Barrabas halted Coffin Head. 'A regulation t'ing, y'understand?'

He frisked Coffin Head's sleeves and then gave his belly a slap. 'Nuff detail der ya, boss.' Coffin Head felt an aching pain, a small reminder of why he was there in the first place. He hid his discomfort as Barrabas went on to check his trouser legs, before spinning him around

140

and palming his back. 'Alright, skip, you're safe. Follow me.'

Coffin Head was led through an unlit passage. At the end of the hallway they entered a room which looked like it had once been a kitchen, but which had been converted into a kind of office. Lit by a naked blue bulb and darkened by black curtains, the orange-painted room looked like a good place to take LSD. A framed black and white picture of Robert Johnson, strumming his guitar, hung from the wall to Coffin Head's right. John Lee Hooker's 'One Bourbon, One Scotch, One Beer' played from a suitcase in the corner of the room. Lounging behind an impressive teak desk, on which were scattered boxes of black women's hair products, was a man big enough to be a bouncer at a wrestling party. He was wearing a sky blue three-piece suit and a navy blue fedora. A black felt-tip thin moustache crossed his face like an old scar. Herbman Blue, Coffin Head thought to himself. Sceptic stood silently near the entrance, not wanting to get too close to Blue's penetrating gaze.

'So,' Blue began, in bank manager mode. 'What can I do for you? Mr . . . What is it?'

'Brethrens call me Coffin Head. Coff for short.'

'Yes, I can see why.'

Coffin Head's nerves jangled as he felt Barrabas behind him. The sight of Sceptic's twitching head also did his courage no favours. Barrabas would wet me before I blink, he thought. Maybe there's another way I can get what I'm looking for.

'I'll ask you again – what can I do for you?'

'I wanna buy a gun.' As he said it, Coffin Head looked at the two henchmen standing behind their boss who slipped their hands inside their jackets at the same time.

Coffin Head allowed himself a long blink while Sceptic inched towards the door.

'And what do you know about guns, Mr Coffin Head?'

'Er, not much. Nutten really.' He felt the confidence seep out of his trodder boots.

Blue laughed. His employees chuckled in unison. Coffin Head felt like he was being inspected for any sign of weakness. He closed his eyes again and saw himself being brutalised by the police for the eighty-seventh time. He felt the courage surge through his body. 'I was kinda hoping dat you would point me in the right direction cos I wanna blow away a beastman to rarted. Dey done me somet'ing I can't forget, man. Radication affe get eradicated. Char.'

'Don't you work for Nunchaks?' Blue asked, rising to his feet.

'Yeah, wha's dat got to do wid it?'

'Mr Coffin Head, I ask the questions.' Blue rounded the table and met Coffin Head square on, glaring at him with scornful intensity. 'You sure it ain't Nunchaks who you want to eradicate?'

Coffin Head started to sweat, and he felt Barrabas's Special Brew breath upon his neck. The word on the street was that no one was quicker with a ratchet blade than Barrabas; some Brixtonians called him Lee Hand Grief. Glancing into the man's eyes, Coffin Head could well believe it. He took a small sideways step, palming his forehead.

Coffin Head held Blue's gaze, knowing that to look down would be as good as asking Blue to crush his elbows with a ball hammer – Blue's trademark. He tried not to blink and to keep his stance upright. 'Nah, man, I don't wanna do Nunchaks nutten,' he finally replied. 'I've

142

stopped juggling for 'im. It's getting too dangerous to sell 'pon de Line. An' I didn't want to do any more burglaries.'

He continued to binocular the man in blue. Satisfied, Blue returned to his chair. 'What kind of handgun you looking for?'

'Er, I dunno. Somet'ing easy to use, innit.'

'Well, Mr Coffin Head, let me enlighten you. There is the single-action revolver which might interest you. This is a gun where you have to pull back that lever thing before firing. My contact can do an American Colt for four hundred pounds.' He used his hands to demonstrate the action. His fingers pointed towards Coffin Head and he cocked the thumb with his other hand. 'Click . . . Then you have the double-action revolver. Now, this gun is like the single-action revolver, except that you don't have to pull nothing back. The sort of gun Clint Eastwood uses in those spaghetti westerns that ghetto youths love. I could do a Smith and Wesson for six hundred pounds.'

Coffin Head offered a vague nod.

'Then, lastly in my contacts catalogue is the single-action semi-automatic pistol,' Blue continued. 'Man, it gives me a buzz just to say that.' He laughed, but stopped abruptly as he realised his employees were not laughing with him. 'Single action semi-automatic pistol,' he repeated. 'With this gun you have to pull back some kind of slide, and then, as they say, you can fire at will. We can do a German Luger for six hundred pounds.'

Barrabas giggled, which prompted the men behind Blue to follow suit. Blue spotlit Coffin Head with the whites of his eyes. 'What's it gonna be, Mr Coffin Head?'

'I'll tek de American Colt.'

Again, laughter filled the room. 'Mr Coffin Head,' Blue snorted, 'we don't stock the guns here. The local constabulary might take offence. As you can see, the only thing we stock here is black ladies' hair products. I am not a stupid man, Mr Coffin Head.'

'Den where do I get the gun?'

'From my contact in Rotherhithe. But before I give you the address for the pub, I hope you will give me my introduction fee of sixty pounds. After all, I am a business man.'

Coffin Head had money all over his person: inside his briefs, around his ankles and hidden in his shoe. He decided to unwrap the money within his right sock. He counted the cash carefully before leaning over the desk and handing £60 to Blue.

The crime duke banked the cash inside a drawer. He then made a phone call to his contact in Rotherhithe, altering his accent to a New York drawl. 'Good morning, Blue here. Business doing well I hope . . . I have a gentle-man with me who requires a forty-five. Do you have it in stock? . . . Splendid. Four hundred? . . . Yes, I'll make sure of that. Yes, he is black . . . He'll be coming with another gentleman called Sceptic . . . One's wearing a black leather jacket with a burgundy beret, the other's got a denim jacket on and a white beret . . . You heard about that? . . . Hah, hah . . . You're right there, Wong won't be sniffing Charlie like he used to . . . OK, I'll send them on their way. See you at the same place next Monday.'

As Coffin Head looked at the boxes containing hair grease, wigs and shampoo, he wondered who the hell Blue was talking to.

After putting the phone down, Blue began writing something down on a piece of paper. B.B. King's 'Payin' The Cost To Be The Boss' twanged from the speakers. Blue quarter-mooned his eyes and began to rock his head, feeling every single lyric and each pluck of the guitar.

'Mr Coffin Head.' He suddenly opened his eyes again. 'Here's your address and name of contact.' He presented Coffin Head with the slip of paper. 'Don't tag anybody along; he knows what you and Sceptic look like and he ain't expecting any surplus. Do you comprehend?'

'Yeah, t'anks an' t'ing, yeah. Appreciate it.' He turned to leave. A relieved Sceptic prepared to follow his spar.

'Blow one away for me, Mr Coffin Head,' Blue laughed. 'And for all of us.' He flicked them out of the room, nodding to Barrabas to show them the door.

Out on the street, Sceptic snatched the slip of paper from Coffin Head's grasp. 'Some pub in Rotherhithe, The Cheeky Bell Toller, what a blowoh. National Front country, believe. I ain't stepping into no pub down dem sides, nah, man. De place is full up wid Hitler's brudders. Dem white man down dem sides tek a piss wid der gun hangin' out, dread. An' dey 'ave dat Nazi sign tattooed on der willys to rarted. Hey, Coff, you're on your own on dis one.'

'Char! You liccle mouse! It's you who set up de Blue t'ing, an' if you don't step wid me to Rotherhithe den I'm gonna beat you up like you're inna beast cell to rarted.'

'Don't say dat. I still 'ave to smoke a spliff before I go to my bed cos of dat tribulation. An' besides, didn't you get your ribs blasted inna beast cell?'

'Whatever, whatever. But you're coming wid me, an' if you don't, I'll drag your backside to de nearest beast station so you get blast up again, y'hear.'

'Alright, alright. Frig me, I was jus' ramping wid you, an' you wanna get militant. What a blowoh, Rotherhithe to rarted. Black man wid sense don't walk der. An' I'm gonna step in a pub der. I don't believe it.'

145

'Wha's de name of de contact?' Coffin Head asked.

Sceptic read the slip of paper. 'Gonzo. Dat's clicking somet'ing inna my brain, man. Where 'ave I heard dat name before?'

'De Muppets, innit. One of Kermit's brethrens. Gonzo looks like some kinda half rat, half bird t'ing wid a bitch of a nose.'

'So dis Gonzo, you reckon he looks like a troll or somet'ing?'

'I dunno. Maybe he's got a big nose or somet'ing, we'll jus' 'ave to wait an' see, innit.'

'How do you get to friggin Rotherhithe?' Sceptic wondered.

'I'm not too sure, but I know so you 'ave to get to Elephant first, den hol' a bus from der. An' you know so dat anyt'ing east from Elephant is Beef'ead country. So beware.'

'You ain't gonna get your car?'

Coffin Head pondered the idea. 'Nah. Say on de way back I get pull by de bull. Nuff tribulation, rasta. When dey find de gun, der gonna lock me up, boot me up inna beast cell, fling de key inna River Thames off Tower Bridge, an' den forget 'bout my sad backside. My mudder won't see me again till her head top turn white, to rarted.'

'She won't see you a damn if you blow away a beastman an' get ketch. De beast would reintroduce de sparky chair, dread. Your backside will fry like egg.'

'Why you affe get so negative, man. Char. We're teking bus an' I don't wanna 'ear no more worries.'

Forty-five minutes later they were walking the streets of Rotherhithe. The council blocks were smaller than the Brixton ones, they noted. And although they thought the small terraced housing was similar, they hadn't yet seen a boarded residence. There was more graffiti sprayed on walls than they were used to; mostly football slogans supporting Millwall. Coffin Head was trying to read the map that Blue had drawn. 'Hey, Scep. Wha' street is dis?'

'Albion Street. Dey should call it black-people-don't-belong street. 'Ave you seen de way de pagans are clocking us?'

'You're para, man. Char, stop being so sof'. Come, de road we're looking for is de second right.'

Cautiously they ambled on, with Sceptic looking behind more than in front of him, Beefheads were on his mind. Fifty yards on, Coffin Head found his road. 'See it der, no problem, I'm a dread navigator.'

The Cheeky Bell Toller public house was situated at a T-junction at the end of a row of terraced houses. Its brickwork was painted blue and the pub's large windows were veiled by long net curtains. A cartoon image of a grinning man pulling the rope to operate a massive bell hung over the brown-panelled, wooden doors. Opposite the watering hole was a brown-bricked junior school. Coffin Head and Sceptic could hear the screams and sounds of pupils enjoying their dinner break.

They stood for a moment outside the pub before entering, both thinking of the bad scenarios that might confront them once they stepped inside, but neither wanted to lose face in front of the other. 'Char, let's mek a move, man. No time fe weak 'eart business.'

Sceptic followed his pal as he went to open the brown double door. It was locked. 'Oh well, we'll 'ave to dust, innit. De place is closed.'

'Hol' your corner,' demanded Coffin Head. 'Blue wouldn't sen' us down 'ere for nutten.' He used his keys to rat-a-tat the door, then stepped back, looking up at the windows to see any movement. Sceptic was five yards behind him.

Eventually they heard the crunch of someone turning a key in the lock of the front door. The two friends made out a figure through the misted glass, then the door opened to reveal a tall man with a bald head. Sceptic immediately thought of the National Front. The skinhead was wearing a black Crombie overcoat and a collarless white shirt. A three-lioned tattoo was on his neck and a silver ring hung from his right ear. His Doc Marten boots almost laced up to his knees, where blue jeans were rolled up, exposing his white football socks.

'So, you find us then,' the white man said.

'No worries,' replied Coffin Head.

The pub was dimly lit and the wooden tiled flooring had specks of sawdust here and there. Small round tables, each with a plastic, lager-labelled ashtray, were surrounded by sets of wooden stools. A battered dartboard was in the corner, hanging beside a narrow blackboard. Stuck up behind the bar was a large Union Jack, next to a framed photograph of Winston Churchill. In another corner was a jukebox, Harry J's All Stars 'Liquidator' playing from it. Next to this, bolted to the wall, was a cigarette machine.

The spars were led to a round table surrounded by three chairs. Filling one of the seats, smartly dressed in dark slacks, polo sweater and leather jacket, was a neatly shaved white man, in his mid-thirties, pulling on a roll-up. He owned a nose that a parrot could have perched on, and his eyebrows met in the middle of his forehead. He killed the burning tobacco stick in a clean ashtray, then watched Coffin Head and Sceptic take their seats. 'You got the four ton?' he asked in a heavy East End accent.

148

'Yeah, no problem,' Coffin Head replied.

'Let's see your credentials,' he demanded.

Coffin Head stood up and proceeded to unwrap the money from all parts of his body. Carefully, holding his gaze, he presented the wad of notes to the man. Gonzo nodded to the Beefhead, who disappeared behind the bar. There was a pause in the proceedings.

Coffin Head lit a cigarette, thinking that the people he was dealing with were big-time villains. He eyed Gonzo with a false confidence. The heavy-booted man returned with a plastic bag containing a Corn Flakes box. Gonzo prepared another roll-up. 'Now, I don't give a blind fuck who you blow away on your own turf or what you do with the merchandise. But I'll tell you one thing. I don't wanna see your face, or your friend's face here again. Ever. And if the merchandise is traced back to this place, I might as well give you a spade now to dig your fucking graves. Is that clear?'

'Yeah, no problem.'

The bald-headed man passed the carrier bag and its contents to Coffin Head. Gonzo continued, 'At the top of the road you'll find a waste paper bin. In there you'll find instructions on how to use the merchandise, and your bits of lead.' He looked at Coffin Head and Sceptic as if they were kids preparing to steal sweets from a shop. 'Now, fuck off.'

Sceptic was the first to rise to his feet, accompanied by Desmond Dekker and the Aces 'Israelites'. He was followed by a cool Coffin Head, clocking the prize-fighters on the wall. Sceptic caught sight of another Beefhead coming out of the gents. The two spars quickened their pace as they reached the door, meeting the cold air with visible sighs.

'Fuck me grand paps,' exclaimed Sceptic. 'De place is crawling wid Beef'eads. Let's remove from dis area.'

'Hol' on,' Coffin Head ordered. 'Where's de bin Gonzo was chatting 'bout?'

'See it der.' Sceptic pointed, indicating a council bin across the road, adjacent to the school.

Coffin Head wasted no time in retrieving the plastic carrier bag. Inside was a Weetabix box. And within this was a sheet of instructions enclosed in a polythene bag, along with ammunition. The shells felt like small fish in his hand, running through his fingers. There was a feeling of unreality about the whole thing.

An hour later, back in Brixton, Coffin Head and Sceptic parted company. Sceptic went in search of Floyd, while Coffin Head made for home. Turning the corner at the junction of Carew Street and Denmark Street, Coffin Head paused, stunned by the sight of a light blue Panda car parked outside his block, with a policeman standing beside it. The policeman saw Coffin Head and smiled. Coffin Head felt his pulse beat inside his neck and through to his throat. His ribs ached more than ever, and sweat dripped from his temples.

He picked up his pace as he approached the block, his head down, ignoring the policeman who was watching him.

'Afternoon, Everton,' the policeman greeted. 'Been shopping?'

Coffin Head didn't reply. Instead, he simply nodded.

'Saw your dear mum earlier. Lovely blue coat she's got.'

Coffin Head walked past the officer, recognising him as one of the bastards who had assaulted him.

'Just dropping by to let you know that me and my

friends expect to see you within the week.'

The officer grinned, then stepped into the panda. Coffin Head looked behind him until the car pulled away, then diverted his gaze to the bag he was carrying.

# 13
# The Teachings
of Jah Nelson

## 16 February 1981

David Rodigan, the reggae DJ who had the 10pm slot on Capital Radio, opened his show with the Wailing Soul's 'Old Broom'. Denise was listening inside her room, rocking her head in time with the bass, wondering where Nunchaks would take her for their date. Maybe All Nations up Hackney side, she thought. Or the Bouncing Ball in Peckham. Perhaps Cubies up Dalston. Oh well, as long as we don't go to a club in South London, she decided. I wanna go for a bit of a drive, and to check out Nunchaks' Cortina Mark Two.

Denise imagined the red eye stares from other girls as they clocked her getting out of Nunchaks' car outside a club. The arrival of Biscuit in her room blew the image away.

'Careful wid dat man y'know,' he stressed. 'Jus' go to de club an' come back an' don't forward nowhere else. Believe, Sis, he only wants to sniff somet'ing.'

'Biscuit, stop daddying me. How many times do I affe tell you dis week – I can look after myself.'

'You don't know him like I do. He's a terrorist, trickster, a conman. Bwai, everyt'ing dat's bad under de sun.'

'You work for him.'

'Yeah, but dat's different. Jus' promise me you won't go to de man's yard.'

'Promise!' Denise raised her voice. 'I'm seventeen, a liccle more dan a year younger dan you. An' you want me fe promise? Go away wid dat, I ain't into brudders trying to heavy manners me.'

'You're too damn tacety,' Biscuit yelled. 'You want two slap in your head.'

'An' you're gonna give it?' dared Denise, pushing her face towards his while grinning snidely.

Biscuit raised his hand. 'Char! One of dese days. You're too friggin 'ard of 'earing.'

'Denise, stop your noise!' Hortense reprimanded from the kitchen. 'De mad deaf man who walk 'pon Vassal Road ah night-time mus' ah 'ear you. Stop your noise!'

Denise turned up her blaster. Madoo's 'Joe Grine' filled the room. Hortense cussed again, but wasn't heard. 'She never say anyt'ing 'bout your shouting, innit,' Denise remarked. 'It's always me. You can never do wrong.'

Biscuit kissed his teeth and left the room. He collected his suede jacket and his scarf from his bedroom, where Royston was building something with a Meccano set, and bade his mother goodbye. 'Mek sure you nah walk-pon street inna de early hours,' she said in place of a farewell.

'I'll be OK, Mummy,' Biscuit answered. 'Jus' checking

a spar.' He disappeared into the starlit night.

He headed for Fiveways, where he turned into Lough-borough estate. Walking along the rubber walkways, he looked down from his first-floor vantage point and saw two dealers he knew, plying their trade in a Mark Three Cortina. A white man had just walked away from the vehicle, putting something in his pocket, and although the car was stationary, the driver had the engine running and the radio tuned to Capital radio. 'Crooks, Louis!' Biscuit hailed. 'Wha' appen.'

'Wha'appen, me bredren', Crooks answered. 'You're forwarding ah I Spy blues tonight?'

'I dunno, but you might see me der . . . Later perhaps.'

He ambled on, hearing Rodigan's selections from many homes, mixed with the sounds of babies crying and dogs barking. In a forecourt, he watched members of the Dread Diamond sound system loading up their van with huge speaker boxes. 'Lawson,' Biscuit called, recognising one of the boxboys who was wearing a parka jacket. 'Where you playing tonight?'

'Tulse Hill estate, the block near de adventure play-ground,' came the reply, as another boxboy yelped in pain, suffering from a splinter.

Biscuit arrived at Jah Nelson's front door and knocked aggressively, not wanting to wait in the chill for any length of time. Jah Nelson's one eye shone brightly through the crack of the doorway. 'I was expecting you yesterday.'

'Yeah, well, I had t'ings to do.'

The dread led Biscuit to the lounge and invited him to sit down. The smoke from the incense stick projecting from a plant pot in the corner of the room spiralled lazily upwards. Burning Spear's 'Jordan River' preached from the blaster. An open book sat on the armchair opposite

154

Biscuit. The ancient map of Africa looked down from the wall. Nelson turned down the volume a notch and moved to the centre of the room. 'So, my young friend. How is you keeping?'

'Can't complain. Still yamming t'ree meals a day, rent paid an' t'ing.'

'Good. So, my yout', you 'ave some nice 'erb fe me?'

'You don't affe ask, dread. You know so I only deal wid top of de range merchandise.'

'Well, before me purchase my t'ings, I wan' you fe do somet'ing fe me.'

'Nelson, man. I ain't got time. I wanna see my woman tonight.'

'It won't tck long. Patience, man. You mus' 'ave patience.'

Biscuit sighed, then decided to wrap a zoot so Nelson could taste his herb.

'You cyan't wash one 'and widout de other,' Nelson suddenly exclaimed.

Biscuit looked up curiously as he halved a cigarette, watching Nelson wrapping one hand into the other and then shaking them. 'Nelson, man, I ain't staying a damn if you gonna start chatting foolishness in my ears.'

He allowed himself a long look at the dread, and tried to guess the man's age. It was masked behind his heavily bushed face, but his eyes were kind and calm, curious, and forever analysing, trying to read other people's thoughts. Biscuit delved into the inside pocket of his jacket and his hand emerged with his personal stash of top quality, green Jamaican export.

'Nelson, tell me dread. Where you come from? I'm kinda curious cos you gave my neighbour, Frank, some good advice de uder day.'

'Yes, he was feeling very down. Rasta don't discriminate . . . You 'ave time, yout'.'

'I've always wondered, man. Wha's your story?'

Biscuit presented the spliff to the dread. Nelson studied it, went over to the burning incense stick, and lit his cannabis stick. His lips pulled on it mightily, exhaling the smoke to the ceiling and creating a small fog. He observed the young man.

'I was born inna Old Harbour,' he began. 'Ah liccle town, 'bout fifteen miles or so from Spanish Town . . . People still say dat Old Harbour Bay supplies de bes' fish in de island.' He smiled. 'My mudder an' fader bot' worked on a government farm called Bodles. I spent my childhood walking wid cows an' goats. From me reach sixteen me turn rasta.'

'Why?' Biscuit asked, leaning forward.

'I used to 'ave ah uncle who lived in de hills. He was de first rasta me ever did see. He would come down from his place now an' again to visit my family. An' every time before 'im set off he would tell me fantastic stories.'

'About wha'?'

'Oh, first of all Anancy fairytales, an' den when me get a liccle older he would tell me stories 'bout African Kings.'

'Wha's Anancy?'

'You don't know? Anancy is like a clever spider who can change into any shape he wants. He gets into all kinda adventures, but really Anancy stories are for children.'

Biscuit nodded his head as he sucked his own ready-made spliff.

'Anyway,' Nelson resumed, 'it was not de done t'ing back in dose days to wear locks. Me fader did not want anyt'ing to do wid me, so me ran away to ah place near Spanish Town, where de rasta dem find ah coch an'

156

coulda live somet'ing resembling life. At dis place not even de beggar man would go near it. An' I 'ad to get used to people who t'ought we were de lowest of de low.'

Michael Prophet's 'Hear I Prayer' sounded from the suitcase. A herb seed cracked and emitted a sweet smell.

'We moved to Kingston in de early sixties cos we were not wanted near Spanish Town,' Nelson went on.

'Where?' Biscuit asked. 'Trenchtown?' He primed himself to sing the opening line of the Gong's 'Trenchtown Rock': *'One good thing about music, when it hits, you feel no pain.'*

Nelson laughed loud, throwing back his head. 'We did live in ah place called de Dungle in Kingston,' he continued, regaining his composure. 'It was more or less a rubbish dump but we made of it wha' we could, living in small huts an' t'ing. In 1966, ah liccle after de Emperor visit Jamaica, de government decreed dat de Dungle should be mosh up. Dey destroyed de area completely.'

'Why?' Biscuit asked again, thinking that it was not just the English police that were bad.

'Basically, cos no one at dat time liked rasta. Anyway, after dat, me an' some of me rasta bredrens moved to downtown Kingston, or more precisely ah place call Rema. Sufferation me ah tell you. But me hook up wid ah cabinet-making job an' learn de trade from dis old rasta man, who taught me nuff 'bout life, religion, an' all dem t'ing der.'

Biscuit leaned further forward, snared by the dread's tale. 'Did you live near Trenchtown?' he asked again, hoping for an eye-witness account of that legendary part of Kingston immortalised in song by the Gong.

'Yeah, mon. Used to sight nuff artist round dem ways. It was ah desperate time, but talent seemed to be everywhere. Me smoke 'erb wid de Gong one time, an de Stepping Razor.'

'Yeah, seriously? Ain't lie your telling jus' to impress? You smoke herb wid de Gong?'

'Lie me nuh tell. It nuh jus' me, y'understand. Nuff people der 'bout, an I was jus' passing tru'.'

'Raaar! Can't believe I'm chatting to a man who's smoked wid de Gong.'

'An' nuh nutten. De Gong jus' ordinary dem time, jus' like everybody else . . . Anyway, me was ah man who always wanted to travel. So me save an' scrape up an' t'ing, cos me wanted to reach Africa.'

'Wha' appened to your eye?' Biscuit enquired.

'Ah police gun butt where me use to live inna Rema. One morning everybody woke up to de sounds of gunfire. From me tenement yard me see de police dem moshing up people dem yard an' arresting some bredrens of mine. Me start complain, an' before me know it, rifle butt sent me spinning to de ground.'

'Shit. So Jamaican police don't joke.'

'No, yout'. Dey used to brutalise you first, den ask question.'

'Did you go hospital?'

'Yes, some bredrens tek me der. But de doctor dem could nah do nutten wid de liccle facility day 'ad. I coulda gone ah Miami fe de operation me eye did need, but me wanted to use me money to go Africa.'

Biscuit started to build another spliff. 'So when did you reach Africa?'

'In 1969. Me tek ship an' land ah Sierra Leone on de west coast. Me found ah liccle work as a carpenter, an' I did work all along de coast of West Africa, until me sight de place where de slavemaster tek de slave dem to

158

de ships . . . It was ah moving experience.'

Biscuit remembered seeing something similar on *Roots*. The scene of Kunte Kinte being manacled in the bottom of a ship was a vision he would never forget. And now he was sitting in front of a man who had been at *that* place. Biscuit felt that the reality of slavery had finally touched him in human form. The young Brixtonian looked serious and was eager for Nelson to continue. The dread obliged.

'Den me decide to go east, working me way 'cross de continent. An' I find dat de Muslim influence was everywhere. Until me reach ah country call Mali.'

'Wha' did you find der? Mud hut an' t'ing?'

'Me come 'cross a tribe who call demself de Dogon. Der was ah tribesman who could speak French, an' as me mudder come from Haiti, an' could speak French, me could speak wid de tribesman jus' 'bout. Some of de words change up, but we understand each uder . . . Him tell me somet'ing dat changed me life.'

'Wha'?'

'Dat his people worshipped de stars an' de ancient sun God, Attum-Ra. Dem tell me dat de pyramids were not burial place, an' dat dey were built to represent de stars 'pon de very eart'. Dem tell me so de Sphinx is over twelve t'ousand years old. Dey exposed de lie dat de so called professor an' powers dat be 'ave uttered, who say de Sphinx was built 'bout four t'ousand years ago. Ah lie dat only told cos dem cyan't admit dat black people 'ad a civilisation when dem living inna raas cave. De mighty people who buil' de pyramids t'ought de Sphinx was ancient.'

Nelson paused and checked Biscuit's eyes, to see if he was showing interest.

'De Dogon tell me dat de Sphinx at one time 'ad ah

159

lion 'ead which looks out to de east to catch de sight of de constellation of Leo as it rise, over ten t'ousand years ago.'

'Hol' on, dread. You've totally lost me.' Biscuit shook his head. Nelson smiled, encouraged by Biscuit's apparent enthusiasm.

'Wha' birt' sign are you?' the dread asked.

'Capricorn, innit. I was born jus' before Christmas.'

'Well, Leo is round 'bout July an' August. An' de signs of de zodiac get dem name from groups of stars inna de sky. Y'understand?'

Biscuit nodded.

'Now,' Nelson continued, 'you mus' ah 'ear 'bout dat de world will soon be inna de age of Aquarius?'

'Yeah, der was some song 'bout it.'

'Right, so now we are living inna de last years of de age of Pisces, cos in astrology we work backwards, seen . . . De sign of Pisces is de fish. An' as you should know, de early Christians use de sign of de fish fe identity. De sign of de cross was *not* de first sign of de Christian dem. Dis was de start of de age of Pisces. Dat was 'bout two t'ousand years ago inna de time of Christ. So every sign 'ave ah period when it rise in de east fe 'bout two t'ousand years, y'understand?'

'Not really.'

'You will, my yout', you will. Liccle bit more teaching.'

'So wha' does all dis mean?' Biscuit asked, torching his joint.

'Dat as a people, we are much more intelligent dan de so-called establishment gi' us credit for. An' from t'ousands of years before Christ we 'ad our own religion, civilisation, government, schools, an' all dem t'ing der. You descend from de greatest civilisation in de world.

160

Don't you t'ink dat it kinda funny dat de establishment use de t'ree lion inna dem flag. You ever see lion inna England?'

'Only inna zoo,' replied Biscuit.

'It's a crucial symbol, which means dominance an' power. An Haile Selassie's title is the Conquering Lion Of The Tribe Of Judah. It nuh jus' ah t'rowaway title. It 'as some serious meaning. Der are Sphinx's all over de upper Nile an' Nubia, which now dey call Et'iopia, wid lion 'ead.'

'You're losing me again, Nelson, man.'

'Come to me yard regular an' you will understand. You affe unlearn wha' you 'ave learned, an' den you will see dat our people 'ave been lied to by de so-called establishment an' t'ing. Jah know! An' den de education me can teach you will be your key.'

Biscuit slowly nodded, but wondered what Nelson could teach him. Nelson smiled again, his eyes shining with a deep wisdom. 'So you call yourself an African, den?' the teenager enquired.

'Yes, from birt'. As de bird fly over de ocean an' get sick an' drop inna de sea. It don't turn into no fish. It still ah bird. An' if you listen to the lyrics of Culture's "Natty Never Get Weary", it tells us how our people crossed the Atlantic in sufferation. Now, if you imagine dat de Nazis captured de British army at Dunkirk an' took dem fe prisoner an' dey was still der to dis day, even der children, do you t'ink de English prisoners would call demself German?'

Biscuit shook his head and checked his watch. Jah Nelson is interesting, he thought, but he really wanted to see Carol. Don't stay for too long, he told himself. 'Er, no. Not dat I really give a damn . . . Nelson, man, you gonna deal wid me or what, dread?' he laughed. 'Can't stay here an' jus' smoke off my herb. Pay me some dollars, dread. I've got someone to see.'

Nelson chuckled, rising to his feet and shaking his locks, making them dance in the air and exposing his greying temples.

' 'Erb,' Nelson stated. 'Dat's a story in itself . . . It was decreed by de very God dat India will be blessed wid nuff 'erbs an' spices. An' de land of India will be called The Healing of De Nations. De ancients say dat 'erb grow 'pon Solomon's grave. Inna de last century, de Indian man bring it come to Jamaica.'

'Indian man provide de collie?'

'Yes, me yout'.'

'So you believe in all dis Selassie t'ing?'

'I'm still searching fe de trut' to de matter, an' I still 'ave learning fe do. But you affe believe dat you come from ah mighty people. Even de Greek writers admit dat during the siege of Troy, Memnon, who came from Nubia, an' everybody say was de bes' looking man ever born 'pon dis eart', arrive wid his mighty army to lend ah 'and to de Trojans in dem war 'gainst de Greeks. Nuff scholar travelled from all over de known world to learn at de Alexandria library inna Nort' Africa. Dis library 'ad all de books, maps an' manuscript dat man needed – ah lot of dem supplied by de priests of Heliopolis. Until de so-called Christians come wid der badness an' burn it. Uder races an' peoples 'ave always tried to obliterate our history. Jah know!'

'Yeah, but dat's de past, dread. Won't 'elp me now, will it.'

'But as I show you de first time you come round, you affe know ah beginning to know where you going to end

162

up. So many of you yout' are ignorant an' don't know your roots. But if you did, your esteem would grow sturdy like Sycamore tree, an' you will believe ant'ing is possible.'

'So, when you reach England?' Biscuit asked.

'Early 1975. I was on me way to Shashamane Lan', birt'place of Haile Selassie, when ah whole 'eap ah violence bruk out all over Et'iopia. It was a shame, cah my final intention was to sight de holy church in Axum where de Ark of the Covenant rests. I had to flee sout' to Kenya; me was surprised cos nuff Indian inna Kenya. Me work me way 'cross de continent, going tru' Tanzania, Zaire an' de Congo. Den me work up de west coast which took up de bes' part ah two year. Me finally reach Casablanca an' tek ship to Englan'.'

'Backside, you done some serious travelling, innit.' Biscuit pulled himself to his feet, not wanting to arrive at Carol's place too late after his promised 10.30 visit. He felt a hot rush inside his head; the herb smoked good.

'To see uder peoples an' different lands is an education,' Nelson said. 'Me eye dem are fully open now, albeit jus' de one, but it still can open liccle more.'

Biscuit presented Nelson with a quarter ounce of Jamaican collie. The dread smiled his thanks, passing £50 to the young dealer. Biscuit studied Nelson's bad eye, and saw that the reddened eyelid was clinging on for dear life. Between the gaps in the locks that partly concealed Nelson's head, he noticed a lined forehead that had wrestled with many thoughts.

'Before you go,' Nelson continued, 't'ink 'bout dis. It says clearly in de scriptures dat when Christ approached John de Baptist, people were telling Him not to go near 'im as John de Baptist looked so rough wid wild, untamed hair an' t'ing. Christ ignored his advisors an'

163

bowed before de prophet, letting him baptise Him.'

'I don't know 'bout de Bible, dread,' Biscuit replied. 'But I know wha' you trying to say.'

'When King James edited the Bible, he didn't do it for black people benefit. But he wasn't thorough in dis an' didn't omit certain clues. He also left out fifteen books which are called de *Apocrypha*. Dese books included de trio of de Maccabees. But de powers in de church at de time didn't t'ink dese books followed de church's traditional teachings. So dey were not included. But it's clear dat dey weren't included cos dey detailed certain t'ings 'bout de black race dat were very uncomfortable fe de powers dat be. De Jews say de books is 'bout dem but I disagree.'

'Whatever, whatever. As I said, never read de Bible anyway, my mudder don't keep it in de yard.'

Jah Nelson look surprised. He changed the subject. 'So you 'ave ah girl?'

'Yeah, sort of,' Biscuit replied, realising the time was nudging past 10.30.

'Mek sure you tell her she ah Nubian Queen.'

Biscuit folded his bounty into his back pocket, and took another look at the impressive African map. 'Yeah, she's definitely dat.'

Nelson watched Biscuit take his leave, admiring his Brixtonian strut.

# 14

## Queen Majesty

On the top deck of the 109 bus Biscuit thought of Jah
Nelson's life story and his words of wisdom. He wondered
about the peoples Nelson had met on his travels, and the
sights he had seen. He made a mental note that he had to
travel to a foreign country one day. Nelson should chat
to Floyd, he thought, remembering Floyd's interest in
African history, I ain't got no time for it, I'm too busy
hustling, but Floyd spends nuff time inna library dese
days, he reasoned.

Biscuit couldn't remember the last book he had read,
and he thought that if Nelson expected to take him on as
some kind of student, then he might be disappointed. It's
alright for Nelson, he told himself. He can spend all the
time he wants on his books because he don't have to
worry about no one but himself.

Carol opened the door, smiling, dressed in dark slacks and a cream-coloured, frilly blouse. Her burgundy lipstick glistened under the light of the nearby lamp-post, and her hair, free of its rollers, topped the look off neatly. Biscuit's eyes were drawn to her gold ear-rings and neck chain that seemed to sparkle on her dark-chocolate skin. He could only think of one tune, 'Queen Majesty' by the Techniques. The song told the tale of a poor man visiting his beautiful queen's magnificent palace and asking for an audience with her.

'How comes you ain't dressed,' rebuked Carol, hands on her hips.

'Dressed? We going on a rave?'

'Don't tell me you forgot. I left a message wid your mudder last night.'

'I didn't get it.'

Carol threw Biscuit an accusing glare, but let him into the hallway. 'You'd better come in. I s'pose we'll 'ave to stop at your yard so you can put some garments on.'

'We? Who else is coming 'pon dis rave?'

'Sharon an' Floyd, innit. Der's a Crucial Rocker blues up by New Park Road, near where Sharon lives. Yardman Irie's gonna be der.'

She led him through to the front room. Biscuit loathed the sight of the neat doilies resting on the limbs of the furniture; it made the room appear so formal, as if Carol's parents always expected someone important to visit. Then there was the huge radiogram situated in the far corner of the room which doubled as a bar. Bottles of whisky, red wine and overproof Jamaican rum teased Biscuit's dry throat. A wall cabinet filled with assorted glasses and commemorative plates reminded him that Carol's parents worked hard for their respect.

'Your parents in bed?' he asked hopefully, parking himself in a doily-clad armchair.

'Yeah. From 'bout ten o'clock dey go upstairs an' watch TV, regular like anyt'ing.'

'Your paps don't like me, does he?'

'He don't like any guys who I chat to. Dat's how he stay.'

'But wid me it's more intense, innit. If one day you tol' 'im you was gonna swap ring wid me, he would leggo some serious tears. I feel so he would come looking for me wid an M16 to rarted.'

Carol laughed. 'He ain't dat bad. But den again, he won't 'ave to feel dat bad cos if it 'appens, by dat time you will 'ave a safe job, innit?'

Biscuit took his time to respond. He wondered if he would live to see a day when he might go legal, get married and remove himself from the madness. He peered into Carol's eyes, like black opals, and fearful that he might be caught staring, diverted his gaze. You're dreaming, man, he told himself. How am I gonna control a decent job? 'I left school wid nutten, you know de score.'

'Den learn somet'ing,' Carol snapped, shocked by her own frustration. She paused and composed herself. 'Don't boder gi' me no blasted excuse. If Sharon can go college an' look after her family, den why can't you?'

Education is the key; Biscuit thought of Jah Nelson's words. He wondered if he did attend college, could he resist the temptation of selling herb to other students? What would his family live on? Maybe he could get a grant. 'Yeah, maybe you're right,' he finally answered. 'Brenton goes day release at Vauxhall, innit. An' remember how he got us a squeeze at de Christmas dance dey 'ad.'

'Yeah, de place was cork. We weren't de only ones getting squeeze dat night.'

'I affe chat to de Steppin' Volcano 'bout it. See wha' uder courses dem 'ave. Cos you know so I ain't no Michael Angelo wid my 'ands dem. In woodwork man an' man use to bus' nuff laugh at my efforts.'

Carol chuckled. 'Yeah, you do dat. Chat to Brenton 'bout it.'

'Talking of Brenton, where's he forwarding tonight?'

'Him an' Lizard gone up north east sides to dat club dat Shaka play at. Noreik club I think it's called. Boof, bang bing business. Dem two love up der steppers music.'

'It's true. An' I 'ear so dem two always 'tand up by Shaka bass-pin box to get de full impact. I'm surprised dey got any ear-piece lef'.'

'You wanna drink?'

'Yeah, gi' me ah liccle portion of your fader's whisky an' drop ah liccle orange wid it.'

Carol chuckled once more, a hint of laughter lines showing at the corners of her eyes. 'You know so I can't gi' you any of dat . . . Oh, wha' de hell, we ain't got no orange but I'll mix it wid some sarsaparilla in de fridge.'

'Alright, I'll control dat. Your fader mean like rough-neck doorman outside de Bali-Hai club.'

Carol covered her mouth with her hand as she departed, not wanting her father to hear her laugh. She returned with a half-full tumbler and a plate supporting a cheese sandwich. Carefully, she poured a measure of whisky into the glass and presented the refreshments to a grateful Biscuit. 'Remember dat time in de park?' she recalled. 'When we was all about thirteen, after school one day.'

Biscuit indulged in a generous bite before answering. 'Der were nuff times we met up after school. You didn't wanna know me dem time. Yeah, you used to ignore me an' chat to Finnley an' Coffin Head.'

'But der was a time when we did chat 'bout wha' we wanna be when we grow up. Sharon was der, also Coffin Head an' Sceptic, an' dat guy, wassisname, Mooker, Mooker Vohn. He was always going to watch *Star Wars* an' telling everybody dat he's got de force. Looks like de force got him; he's doing time now for armed robbery.'

'Oh yeah, de damn fool, how can man go to rob bank an' queue up to rarted in de middle of de summer wearing his trench coat. 'Im get ketch before de blasted fool could mek his demand. He used to go clear 'bout *Star Wars* innit. One time at de park we were chatting 'bout films an' he's going all Yoda 'pon me, telling me not to join de dark side.'

Carol sat beside him. 'He did wanna be an astronaut, innit. Where he is now, he can't even see de blasted sky.'

Biscuit washed down his snack. 'It's dat, innit. Yeah, I remember dat day. Sceptic wanted to be a hat designer, innit. Wha' kinda blasted job is dat? Ain't no corn in it, cos he can't buy a yard wid a garden or his t'ree point five litre car an' a piece of gold bracelet chops. I can't t'ink of anyt'ing as boring as making blasted hats.'

'An' Floyd wanted to be a footballer. He was always telling us 'bout Clyde Best who played for West Ham, innit.' Carol grinned deliciously as a pleasant memory hit the spot. 'An' you wanted to be a doctor, Biscuit. Wha' was dat programme you used to tell us 'bout . . . *Marcus Welby MD* or somet'ing, 'bout dat greyback doctor.'

Biscuit's mind rewound to those days at school. He had been good at Biology and Physics, and always told the

169

teachers he wanted to be a doctor. But in the last year of school a career advisor told him that becoming a doctor was unrealistic, and that he didn't think Biscuit could make it through his O and A levels, let alone university. He was told that he should get himself a trade. But at the time he had been more worried about making sure he collected the calor gas twice a week to heat the family home, and how to get a one on one conversation with the girl who was now sitting next to him. 'Wha' did you wanna be?' he asked.

'A newsreader, innit. Or present *Blue Peter*. Sharon wanted to be a politician, reckoning she could run de country better dan any man.'

'She could run it better dan de Ironheart lady. Can't do no blasted worse.'

The couple paused, looking at each other and sensing they both shared the same thoughts. Biscuit recalled Jah Nelson's words earlier on in the evening, when he had said that black people have a proud history that should be recognised by all, and that anything is possible. 'You know Jah Nelson, innit?' he asked.

'Yeah, de rastaman, innit. He kinda gives me de creaks, man. My mudder one time sight him when we were doing shopping, an' she told me Nelson's a duppy.'

'Nelson ain't no ghost!' Biscuit rejected. 'If you gi' 'im a chance, he's kinda wise. He tol' me some t'ings I never knew before.'

'He's jus' like dem bible t'umping man who chant outside Terry's Waterloo inna all weders.'

Biscuit shook his head. 'Nah, if you get to know 'im, he chats sense. You can't compare 'im to dem labba labba doom-mongers outside Brixton Tube Station.'

Carol couldn't hide her disagreement. 'Anyway, 'bout

tonight. You're gonna 'ave to dally 'ome, sweet-lick your armpits, slap on some clothes an' meet me at de blues.'

'But I dunno where de blues is. I tell you what, you wait here an' I'll come look for you inna cab an' we forward to de blues from here. You can ding Sharon an' tell her so we'll sight her at the blues.'

'Alright, but don't tek too long. You know so I don't like to reach to blues when it's cork.'

Seventy minutes later, Biscuit, dressed in blue corduroys and a blue suede jacket, escorted Carol to a housing estate just off New Park Road. He didn't need the address as a heavy bass-line pierced the Brixton air, reaching and hovering over the South Circular Road. The street lamps were tall, and behind a row of shops that consisted of two off-licences, a newsagent and a grocery store, they could see the top balconies, lit by naked bulbs, of a brown concrete jungle.

As they reached the forecourt of the estate, Carol recoiled at the sight of an overturned council bin. Forgotten cars with smashed windscreens and tyreless wheels stood on one side of the parking area. On the other side, vehicles were double and treble parked, some of them with young black men inside, preparing spliffs. In others, black girls used rear-view mirrors to apply late touches of make-up. *Blair Peach Was Murdered By Babylon* protested red-painted graffiti on an outside wall. Weary-looking brown bricks were stacked eight storeys high, and some residents looked over their balconies in their dressing gowns, smoking cigarettes and sipping hot drinks. Pablo Gad's 'Hard Times' sang out a unified despair as a Parka-wearing ragamuffin sat on a concrete stairwell rolling cigarette butts that he found on the floor.

Biscuit paid his and Carol's door tax of two pounds,

peering into the blue-lit hallway for any signs of Floyd and Sharon. In the passage, Biscuit recognised a rasta, dressed in ankle-swinging slacks and a track-suit top. Biscuit offered him a nod, hoping the dread wouldn't bother him for herb on this night; he didn't like to sell while with Carol.

Squinting his eyes so he could see through the cannabis and cigarette smoke, Biscuit looked at the cables that were taped to the ceiling. Passing the kitchen, where a girl was selling cans of lager, wearing a flimsy black dress that barely covered her knickers, Biscuit and Carol forced their way through the crowd, heading for the room in which the sound boys had set up their control tower. Carol latched on to Biscuit's jacket as he led her into the road-blocked room, passing a man in the doorway who was selling herb. He was dressed in an open mac and a knitted red, gold and green hat. Using the lights that lit the control tower and record deck, he saw Floyd and Sharon beside a neck-high speaker box, chatting to the toaster, Yardman Irie.

Hatted by a green beaver, not quite housing his wild, infant dreads, the ghetto-rapper was covered in green army garb and booted in trodders. He had a goatee beard and a permanent smile that made him approachable. Ravers were patting him on the back and offering him fist-clenched salutes as he scanned the crowd, waiting for his moment.

Satisfied that the vibes were right and downing the last drop from his Coke can, Yardman advised the selector of what tune to play as he grabbed the microphone. The anticipation of the crowd grew. The selector spun the legendary 'M16' instrumental by the Revolutionaries.

'Crowd ah people,' Yardman began. 'Listen to me

keenly. Respect to de Tulse Hill Crew an' de Stockwell posse, an' special dedication to me bredren Remington Moses . . . Dem say life is not ah easy road, but ghetto yout' affe persevere. Jah know! Yardman Irie nah bow, an' everybody know, me nah yam no sow. So 'ear dis ghetto yout'.'

*Dem beat I inna cell an' me look straight into hell*
*But dem cyan't conquer de Yardman*
*Dem give me bitch licks and der corrupt politricks*
*But dem cyan't conquer de Yardman*
*I cyan't pay me rent so me pitch up me tent*
*But dem cyan't conquer de Yardman.*
*Dem always harass me call me public enemy*
*But dem cyan't conquer de Yardman*
*Dem gi' me ah false mentality an' tell me wrong history*
*But dem cyan't conquer de Yardman*
*I still feel de chains an poverty jus' rains*
*But dem cyan't conquer de Yardman*
*Since me was born me live 'pon Government corn*
*But dem cyan't conquer de Yardman*
*My mudder cyan't tek de col' an' me fader 'pon de dole*
*But dem cyan't conquer de Yardman*
*Oh no, me say dey cyan't conquer de Yardman*
*You never cyan conquer Yardman Irie.*
*An' if you love wha' me say bawl forward.*

'*FORWARD!*'

Fists and cigarette lighters were raised in salute of Yardman's lyrics. Brixtonian girls dressed in denim skirts and crew-neck sweaters hollered for more. Young men, topped by all kinds of head-wear and wrapped in puffy anoraks and jeans, yelled their approval. 'GWARN,

173

YARDIE, GWARN!' Battered speaker boxes were slapped in appreciation as wise dreads nodded, inhaling fiercely on four-inch spliffs. The selector's torch-light exposed the collie smoke, like a veil suspended from the ceiling.

'Before me carry on wid de Brixtonian news,' Yardman announced, 'I wan' fe introduce to you de ghetto dub-poet call Prester John. Forward to de microphone, Prester John, an' chant out your prayer to de Brixtonian people.'

Emerging from behind the control tower, a tall bearded man wearing a white turban, a red, gold and green scarf and a red tunic with the Star of David stitched upon the chest surveyed the crowd and stepped up to the ghetto-rapper. Prester John then embraced Yardman Irie, congratulating him on his lyrics.

'Forward, Prester John,' someone shouted. The crowd surged forward and Biscuit and his crew felt themselves being squeezed on all sides. Expectant arms went up in the air. Someone gained a vantage point by climbing up and sitting on a speaker box. There was a jam at the doorway. All eyes were on the poet. Drinkers stilled their cans of lager. Yardman Irie gave Prester John the microphone and the dub-poet grabbed it, holding his head high as if no one in the world could belittle him.

'Greetings to each an' everyone,' Prester John began. He signalled to the selector and seconds later the Revolutionaries instrumental 'Drum Song' cranked out of the speakers. The intro was full of Nyabinghi hand drumming, then a pulsating bass took hold, along with the riff of what seemed a distant organ. 'Dis one call *Fear Not*. Dedicated to all freedom fighter all over de world, an' especially to de children of de dispossessed.'

174

*Fear not, my brethren, for we shall gather the sweet*
*fruits of our fathers' toils*
*And the wails of our mothers shall transform into*
*joyous smiles of emancipation*
*Brood not, for the pain of the heavy heart shall beat in*
*the oppressor's chest*
*Weep not, for our sore wounds shall heal, and only the*
*scars shall remain of our mighty struggles.*

Whistles were blown. Speaker boxes were thumped.
Small, oval flames filled the room, giving it a yellow glow.
'FORWARD!' the crowd yelled as one, wanting to hear
the next verse. The selector turned up the bass and the
whole room shook.

*Concentrate your ears, for the hymn of our mother*
*land is now heard among us*
*Be of sure foot, for we shall be led to the blessed*
*greenland by the righteous*
*songwriters who play the golden harps of deliverance*
*Their footprints shall be employed by the gifted*
*musicians and the spirit dancers*
*Unchain your doubts, for our sufferation shall be no*
*more*
*Sing out loud, for glorious things have been written of*
*our triumphant redemption*
*Yield not, for the oppressor shall not find haven from*
*the tablets of judgement*
*Stride proudly, for our path has been sign-posted by*
*the martyrs of equal rights*
*The end of our perilous journey is near, and I can see*
*the ark of our homeland, glitter in the distance*
*Fear not, my breathren, for we shall soon be free.*

Prester John gave the microphone back to Yardman amid roars of acclaim all around him. He looked at the crowd and offered them an open-palmed salute. The selector offered Prester a spliff as a rasta in the corner shouted, 'JAH!'

In unison, the ravers responded, 'RASTAFARI!'

Moments later the crowd settled while the selector played the Heptones' 'Crystal Blue Persuasion'. Yardman Irie returned the microphone to the selector and turned to Floyd. 'Ah reality we ah deal wid, y'know.'

'Yeah,' replied Floyd. 'But you're lucky I ain't in de mood, cos oderwise de crowd will be chanting my name.'

'Seal your beak,' censured Biscuit, arriving at the control tower with Carol in tow. 'Andy Pandy 'as better lyrics dan you.'

Sharon and Carol paired off to swap gossip as Biscuit and Floyd enmeshed themselves into an argument on who was the better toaster. Yardman Irie looked on impatiently. 'Biscuit, man. Stop your noise an' deal wid me.'

'Not so loud, man. You want my woman to 'ear?'

Biscuit found a dark corner and sold ten pounds worth of herb to Yardman. 'Floyd said you was gonna reach, an' Chemist was bugging me 'bout his draw. But I'd rader buy off man I know, y'understand?'

'Yeah, safe, man. Nice draw dis, get ah creepin' buzz.'

'So, Biscuit. T'ings cool?'

'Well, to be honest, not really. I've got nuff boderation 'pon my mind.'

'You wanna chat 'bout it?' Yardman asked softly, putting one hand on Biscuit's shoulder.

'Not now. Not 'ere in dis place,' Biscuit replied, looking around him.

176

'Den we affe link up,' Yardman insisted. 'Long time since me an' you chat. I haven't seen you too much since we lef' school.'

'Yeah, it's dat . . . Yardie, why don't you write a lyric 'bout de Deptford fire?'

'I am. I'm gonna bus' de lyrics maybe nex' week inna Crucial Rocker blues.'

'Seen. Anyway, I'll hook up wid you later, yeah. Carol don't like me leaving her too long inna blues dance; too many crub-hungry yout's around.'

'Seen,' Yardman laughed.

Biscuit returned to his crew. He and Floyd shared three spliffs before settling down to a crub with their girls. Janet Kay's 'Rock The Rhythm' boomed from the speakers as Biscuit wrapped an arm around Carol's waist. He pulled her towards him, placed his other hand around her neck and gently touched her cheek with his.

'I dunno why you try hide it, Biscuit. I sight you selling to Yardman.'

'He's a brethren, innit. Know 'im from school days, he was in my class.'

'I don't like you dealin' when you're wid me. Can't we ever 'ave a night together when you're not juggling?'

'I'm gonna stop soon anyway. I'm coming out of de juggling business. Believe.'

'I've 'eard dat before somewhere.'

'Jus' gi' me ah liccle time, man,' he replied curtly, not knowing how much time he would need.

He escorted Carol home as the first hint of daybreak threatened. It was at these times that both of them thought that Brixton was not a bad place. There were hardly any motorists on the road and the birdsong in the trees that lined Brixton Hill was audible. The council blocks to the east, caught by the orange glow of the sunrise, appeared less harsh, and the clouds above were parting to reveal a purple sky. Biscuit, walking with his right arm around Carol's shoulders, was free of worry and lost in Carol's beauty. He stopped walking and kissed her on the forehead, caressing her hair. Their eyes met and Carol wondered how long she could resist making love to him.

On reaching Carol's front door, Biscuit stood on the doorstep shuffling his feet, hopeful of something.

'Soon, man,' Carol soothed. 'Soon. I'm jus' not ready yet. Besides, my mudder get up well early.'

# 15
# Babylon Pressure

Biscuit, dressed only in his briefs, was lying on Carol's bed, watching her unbutton her blouse . . . Then the Lone Ranger's 'Rosemarie' blared out from nowhere, and he found himself waking up from his dream. He checked his watch and saw the time was nudging past 1.00pm. 'Char! Why does Denise 'ave to tune into Tony Williams show at dis time of day?'

He got out of bed to tell his sister to turn down the music. Now almost fully awake, he wondered where Nunchaks had taken Denise last night. With only a pair of football shorts on, he carefully prised his sister's door open, hoping the hinges wouldn't squeak as they usually did.

'Come out of de room, man,' Denise objected, lying on her bed in her dressing gown with her feet against the wall. 'So, wha'appen? You can't remember where your blasted bedroom is?'

'Mask your mout', girl. I'm jus' checking dat you reach 'ome safe.'

'Well I'm sleeping! So remove.'

'Facety wretch.'

He closed the door, feeling nervous for his sister, then headed for the kitchen where he saw Royston climbing on the table, trying to reach the biscuit tin on top of a cupboard.

'Get your backside down from der before I conk you wid de Dutch pot.'

Looking guilty, Royston jumped down, landing awkwardly on the thin tiled floor. 'Mummy put my cars up there.'

'Yeah, an' Fred Flintstone's smoking inna de front room. Where's Mummy?'

'She went bagwash.'

'Ain't you s'posed to go wid her, you lazy wretch. How can she cope wid all dose clothes?'

'She put them in the shopping basket.' Royston scampered away, thinking he may yet be forced to go to the dreaded launderette.

Biscuit enjoyed a late breakfast of toasted ardough bread and a glass of fruit juice as he listened to the radio. 15, 16, 17s 'Only Sixteen' made him think of Carol and the conversation they had had. He wondered how his interrupted dream would have finished; maybe it was a sign that he was gonna get physical with her soon. A clattering from the front door interrupted his musings. Royston was quick to answer the knocking, and he opened the door to reveal Frank smoking a roll-up. 'Afternoon Smoking Joe. Give me a high five.' Royston jumped up and slapped Frank's mighty hand. 'Where's your brother? Is he home?'

'Yeah, he's yamming his breakfast.' The youngster led Frank to his bedroom where Biscuit was sucking toast crumbs off his fingers.

'Wha'appen, Frank. How's t'ings? Stella an' de pickney alright an' t'ing.'

'Not too bad. I had a couple of days of work last week; a bit of labouring up Catford way.'

'Dat's sweet. Any chance of somet'ing permanent?'

'Dunno, manager says he'll give me a bell. You never know.'

'Does this mean that you and Stella won't argue no more,' Royston remarked.

Frank didn't answer. Biscuit shook his head, half-grinning.

'You're good, Frank, man. I can't tek forwarding to de blasted job centre for mont' after mont' an' all dey gi' you after all dat time is ah two day labouring t'ing.'

'Well, you know I've got a criminal record,' Frank reminded him. 'If I as so much nick a packet of biscuits I'll be going down below.'

'Yeah, ah true dat,' Biscuit concurred. 'De beast don't appreciate your Irish backside cider.'

'Yeah, you can say that. Since the Birmingham pub bombing they haven't left my family alone, even though they sent down six. Especially as my brother was living in Wolverhampton at the time. Questioned him seven times they did. Bastards. Smashed down his door and ripped up all his floorboards; his wife was in a right state. Then they came down to London to question me.'

'Believe me, Frank, I've been der. But not as much as Coffin Head and Sceptic. Dey get brutalise inna cell, innit. Coffin Head get it so bad he's given up de juggling.'

'Nothing surprises me any more. They done the same thing to my brother, but Sean's a tough bastard. He wouldn't tell them what they wanted to hear. They just think that cos he's Irish, he must be a member of the IRA.'

'I remember you telling me 'bout it. I mus' ah been 'bout twelve, innit. Wha' was de year? 1974 wasn't it?'

'Yeah. Sean came down for a while to escape all that was going on up there. They wouldn't even serve him in his local.'

Biscuit laughed. 'Ain't Stella English?'

'Yeah, but she's so eccentric. Just this morning she decides to get up early and scrub the landing outside the front door. Half past six it was. She's still in a cleaning mood now. That's why I hopped it.'

Biscuit found a pair of jeans in his wardrobe and put them on. 'Don't you ever t'ink 'bout being a bouncer, Frank? You 'ave untold detail an' t'ick vein in de arm section, an' a neck t'ick like Nelson's column, to rarted. If I didn't know you I wouldn't flex my temper inna your direction, man. You an' Brenton would mek ah good boxing match.'

Frank smiled, exposing his crooked teeth. 'I'd get too bored,' he replied. 'Can't see me standing outside a club all night tending to drunks. And as for Brenton, I don't think he would hear the bell; he ain't the type to play by rules.'

'Stella used to tell my mudder 'bout you fighting all comers in de pubs,' Biscuit said in a low voice, looking into Frank's eyes.

Frank paused for a moment and glanced at his right hand. He dropped his sight to the carpet. 'It wasn't that often, but people who've heard of me would like to offer me out, usually after a few pints when their courage was up. Most of them were just wankers.'

Biscuit chuckled, not totally convinced by Frank's response. He reached to the top of his wardrobe where he found his herb bag and rizlas. 'Do you wanna spliff before you go?'

'Nah, the last spliff you gave me made me all sleepy. Don't wanna drop off in the park, do I?'

Biscuit laughed, most of the sound coming from his nose. 'One day you'll get used to it.'

Two hours later, Biscuit took a bus up to Floyd's estate, which was within throwing distance of Brixton Prison.

Floyd, topped by a furry black beret and wearing a suede trimmed cardigan and brown waffle slacks, led his friend into his flat. 'Wha' ah gwarn, me bredren? T'ings irie?'

'Dis an' dat, you know how it go.' He followed Floyd into the kitchen where he was offered a can of lager. 'Nah, man,' he declined. 'Can't drink liquor so early in de day.'

'You shoulda stayed at de blues till de end, dread,' said Floyd, opening a Special Brew for himself before leading Biscuit to the front room. 'People were reaching up to seven o'clock. Yardman Irie was moshing it up 'pon de mic, an' dat Prester John is a serious poet.'

'Carol wanted to forward home, innit. She was all tired up.'

'More time, maybe it was kinda wise to dally early. Cos der was nuff radication der 'bout. I see dem harass de Dorset Road posse. Der car get searched an' t'ing. Bwai, good t'ing me an' Sharon only 'ad a short trod to my yard. You jus' miss Sharon, she 'ad to forward 'ome to cook dinner fe her mudder.'

'Radication an' badness everywhere,' Biscuit said, throwing up his arms and shaking his head. 'I heard some yout' get bore up by Fiveways last night. When 'im lick de ground he weren't moving, to rarted.'

'Yardman Irie was telling me 'bout de Flaxman Road posse,' informed Floyd, switching on his suitcase in the corner of the room. 'Some Lineman, I t'ink it was Round-head, wet up Elfego Barker from de Flaxman road crew.' Floyd drew a finger across his chest. 'Word 'pon de street is Barker's fighting fe 'im life.'

Biscuit agreed, nodding his head. 'Elfego went Ken-nington boys, innit? He 'ad ah t'ing wid Mary Bad Mout'. But I dunno if de pickney she 'ave is for Barker.'

Johnny Osbourne's 'Too Sexy' bassed out of the blaster; it was one of Biscuit's favourite recent tunes. Enjoying the moment, he decided to build a joint as Floyd fingered his infant beard. 'Bwai, ah man mus' be desperate to clinch up wid Mary Bad Mout'. She 'as some cuckoo brudders, believe.'

The letterbox rattled and Floyd went to see who was rapping so hard. Coffin Head stood in the doorway.

'Wha'appen Coff,' greeted Floyd. 'Bwai, don't tell me. You get boot up by radication again?'

'Char! Let me in, man.'

Coffin Head was ushered into the front room where he saw Biscuit hoovering a spliff. 'Wha'appen, Biscuit. Called round your yard jus' a while ago. Your mudder told me you was round Floyd's. She also asked if you'll be 'ome fe dinner.'

Biscuit passed on the joint to Floyd, who was eyeing Coffin Head's bag. 'Wha's wid de bag?' he asked, gestur-ing with his free hand. 'Dallying from 'ome?'

'Could say dat,' replied Coffin Head, his mood not

improving. 'I'm staying 'ere so fe a few days.'

Floyd sucked mightily on the weed and viewed Coffin Head from the corner of his eyes. 'An' do I 'ave ah say in dis?'

'Stop your complaining!' Coffin Head raised his voice, dismissing Floyd with a swish of his right hand. 'Char! After all de favours I done you. Drive you 'ere an' der like I'm your blasted chauffeur, to rarted. You owe me nuff.'

'Ease up, dread,' cooled Floyd, surprised by Coffin Head's over-reaction. 'Wha's de rush business?'

'Beast keep blocking outside my yard, innit,' he replied, dropping his angry tone. 'I'm sick an' tired of der good morning's an' shit. Char. An' my mudder's getting para an' my fader's clocking me like I jus' rob de crown jewels, to rarted. So I t'ought it wise to leave dem no scent.'

'Dat's wha' dey done to Sceptic,' remarked Floyd. 'Like dey wanted 'im to be ah grass.'

Coffin Head seated himself on a bean bag, not letting go of his holdall which was gripped tightly inside his fist. 'Char! Ain't no blasted way I'm gonna be a reporter.' He eyed the spliff Biscuit was sucking. 'Fling me de rizlas an' herb. I could do wid a liccle mellowing.'

Biscuit passed on the green wonder with the cigarette papers. Coffin Head finally let go of his bag, but viced it between his feet. Biscuit eyed the holdall and offered Floyd a curious glance. General Echo's 'Bathroom Sex' soft-porned out of the suitcase.

'I'm kinda glad you two reach my yard today,' announced Floyd.

'Why? You run outta herb?' asked Biscuit.

'Well, yeah, an' dat. But fe anoder reason as well.'

'Char, I ain't got no money fe lend you.'

'Nah, nah. I've got a corn mission, innit.'

'Forget it dread,' rejected Coffin Head. 'Your corn missions are too dodgy, man. I gotta keep outta jailhouse mission.'

'At least 'ear me out.'

'Alright den,' allowed Biscuit. 'But if it's for Spinner, tell 'im to find another sap to do his t'iefing.'

'Nah, nah. Dis is bona-fide. For us dread, nutten in-between an' when you 'ear de plan you're gonna kiss me foot-bottom an' gi' me some free herb cos it's so easy.'

'Char! Tell us de friggin' plan,' Coffin Head urged impatiently, gesturing with his right hand.

'Loudspeaker warehouse, dread. By T'ornton Heat' sides. Doors are padlocked an' t'ing but de building ain't so high. We can go t'rough de sky-light, innit.'

'You mean you are going t'rough de sky-light,' grinned Biscuit, finally getting a smile from Coffin Head.

'Whatever. I'm de fittest an' most agile from our crew anyway.'

'Only cos you've been chased by de beast de most times,' returned Biscuit, pumping his arms as if he was running. Coffin Head stopped himself laughing out loud.

'An' how you gonna carry dese loudspeakers to your yard?' interrogated Coffin Head, fearful of the answer.

'Your sweet Dolomite, innit,' smiled Floyd. 'I'll gi' you petrol money dis time . . . Do you t'ink your wheels can mek it to T'ornton Heat'?'

'Char! An' you say I should keep a low profile?'

'Stop fret, man. T'ink 'bout de money we'll get from dem sound bwai. Winston from Crucial Rocker is well interested.'

'Fuck you, man,' rejected Coffin Head, forming his face into a picture of mock anger. 'I'm t'inking 'bout de serious stretch I might get.'

186

'Bwai, you two going sof' 'pon me,' mocked Floyd.

'How much corn you gonna sell dese speakers for?' asked Coffin Head.

'T'ree browns each. So even if we only get six speakers, dat's sixty notes each.'

Biscuit thought about it. He knew Coffin Head was short of money now he'd stopped juggling. So maybe Coffin Head's vexness towards Floyd was just a cover. I'll do the job, he decided. Put some corn in Coffin Head's pocket.

Two minutes later, Coffin Head picked up his bag and went to Floyd's bedroom. 'I'm hanging up my garments in your wardrobe,' he called too loudly from the hallway. 'You know I 'ate my garments to get creased up.'

Making sure he wasn't followed, Coffin Head unzipped a small compartment in his carrier and felt for his gun, wrapped up in kitchen foil. It felt cold, but every time he touched it he sensed a surge of confidence. 'Beastman gonna dead soon,' he whispered. He resealed the holdall with the gun inside.

# 16

## Bounty Hunting

### 2am, 22 February 1981

Coffin Head parked his wheezing Dolomite on a quiet road in Thornton Heath. Floyd pulled on his gloves as Biscuit wound down a window and threw out a chocolate wrapper, then put on his balaclava. Coffin Head lit a cigarette.

At the end of the street, the terraced houses gave way to a small industrial estate of a few warehouses and office buildings. A placard on a wire meshed perimeter fence of about ten feet high projected a warning to any intruders: GUARD DOG PATROL.

Floyd was sitting in the passenger seat, clad in a night blue woollen hat, donkey jacket and black leather gloves. He looked up to the star-lit canopy, noting the frost on the roof tops. Biscuit flexed his fingers. Floyd looked up and down the street. Coffin Head, fretting about his overcooking engine, turned off the ignition before addressing his brethren. 'Well, my car made it, but I don't like de sight of dat dog patrol sign. Dis could be a waste of time. If we do mek de corn from dis mission, I'm gonna spend it 'pon a service for my damn car.'

'Don't worry, man,' Floyd said, eyeing the fence. 'Der ain't no rarse dog. Dey jus' put up de sign to scare man an' man away, innit. Nuff of dem warehouse try de same skank.'

'Well, if I get seriously nibbled by a rarse mad up dog,' Biscuit remarked, 'I'm suing your backside.'

'Der ain't no friggin' dog, man,' Floyd insisted. 'If der is, den I'll yam Pedigree Chum tomorrow. You lot are shapers, to rarted. Come, let's get dis over wid. Coff, lif' up your boot, dread.'

The trio climbed out of the car and Coffin Head opened the boot. Floyd grabbed the two lengths of rope and placed them over his head like a fireman. Biscuit collected a glass-cutter, a selection of screwdrivers and a mini-size crow-bar and placed the tools inside his pockets. Coffin Head looked on, shaking his beret-topped head. Floyd scanned the street once more, then made for the fence. 'Eighteen-inch speakers are coching in my yard in de morning,' he said to himself.

'Coff, don't fall asleep,' instructed Biscuit. 'If beast come an' you don't gi' de shout, I'm saying you're de brains 'pon dis planned mission.'

'Char. Jus' 'urry up, man.'

Floyd was the first to clutch the triangular mesh of the fence. 'Gi' me a leg up, man.'

Biscuit interlocked his fingers into a cradle. He sank

189

low, cupping Floyd's right foot, and hoisted his body up straight. Floyd was up and clambered over the other side of the fence. Biscuit took more care, climbing slowly and deliberately. Coffin Head retreated to the car, looking up at the drawn curtains in the terrace. Expecting to hear the bark of a guard dog at any moment, he glanced behind him.

Biscuit and Floyd crouched by the fence and held their breath, trying to catch any sound of nearby movement. All they could detect was the distant whoosh of night-time cars cutting through the frost-infected air.

'Told you der's no blasted dog,' whispered Floyd. 'Dese people mus' t'ink we're stupid.'

He led the approach to the warehouse wall and looked up at a black, scaly drainpipe. Biscuit tried to peer through the misted windows. Floyd shook the drainpipe, trying to guess if it would take his weight. He began to climb, gripping the corrugated roofing with one hand and pulling himself up. Crouching on top of the wall, he pressed his left foot on the corrugated roofing. Satisfied, he composed himself. Then he unhooked the thick rope from his shoulder and secured one end to a stone chimney which was jutting out about three foot away from the guttering. Kneeling down, trying to spread his weight evenly, he waved at Biscuit to join him. Biscuit made it up in two minutes, then crouched unsteadily upon the roof. He rubbed his hands free of grit and gave Floyd a thumbs up.

'Don't stand on your feet, dread,' Floyd advised. 'Use your knees to get mobile. Bwai, don't wanna see you dropping t'rough, bredren.' He bound the other length of rope to the chimney before turning back to his accomplice. 'One is fe me to get down, an' de uder is fe de speakers dem. Comprehendo?'

'My 'ead ain't dense, dread. I know de plan.'

A sky-light was on a sloped incline about two metres above them. Biscuit told himself this was the last time he'd be doing any raid. Too friggin' dangerous. Can't keep on putting myself at risk just for friends. He crawled to the sky-light as Floyd carried the ropes behind him. As Biscuit waited, he took in the panoramic view. He could see the oblong, dark shapes of tall buildings in central Croydon and the nearby railway station of Selhurst. The yellow glow of the street lights reflected off bedroom windows in the terraced housing. He looked below and saw Coffin Head nodding his head to a reggae beat inside his car.

He felt the cold in his nostrils and upon his fingertips as he scrimmaged for the assorted tools in his pockets.

'So, wha' ah gwarn?' asked Floyd, inspecting the sky-light. 'Can you get de t'ing open?'

'Yeah, should be no major worries.'

He inserted three screwdrivers under the window frame and, using his crow-bar, prised open the window to a one-inch gap. Something broke inside the frame and dropped to the blackness of the warehouse floor. He felt a rush of adrenaline flow through his body. 'I should start t'iefing jewels to rarted,' he boasted.

Floyd pulled the window frame open and unleashed the rope down inside the warehouse. 'Fuck me, it's dark in der. When I climb down, mek sure the window don't close up. If it does I'm fucked.' He tested the strength of the rope and, once satisfied, coiled it around his right arm and gradually eased himself into the blackness, his own weight forcing him to swing gently.

As he descended, Floyd could make out the outlines of cardboard boxes and a fork-lift truck. He saw a tiny red light in an office. His body was warming with adrenaline as his feet searched for stable ground. He landed in the middle of a gangway, looked up and raised his thumb to Biscuit. He then searched for his matchbox in his trouser pocket and stroked a light, revealing sealed cardboard boxes stacked in shelves of ten feet high. He turned around and saw a long table on which a range of speakers were ready to be packaged.

All of a sudden, he saw something indistinct moving; a shadow near the offices about waist high. It moved rapidly. A fierce barking cut through the night as the rhythm of four paws drummed on the wooden floor. 'Friggin' dog!' Floyd cried.

'Jump up! Jump up!' echoed Biscuit.

Floyd leapt up, grasping the rope for dear life. His left calf felt the smooth coat of the Alsatian sentry as Biscuit peered downwards. Floyd climbed frantically, raising his feet to the height of his waist as the dog bounded hungrily below him.

He reached out a hand and grabbed the edge of the window frame. Biscuit gripped his other hand and pulled him up. 'Fockin' rarse 'ole dog,' Floyd spat, the palms of his hands stinging due to the quick ascent. 'I'm gonna come a next time an' club your rarse wid a Viv Richards cricket bat, to rarted.'

Biscuit surveyed the street and saw Coffin Head get out of his car. Floyd sat down, palming his forehead as Biscuit hastily unlatched the ropes.

'Bloodfire!' heavy-breathed Floyd. 'Fuck my living days! De dog's ah fockin' man-eater. I t'ought my days were over an' out, dread. Bwai, de somet'ing tried to yam my leg to rarted! Fockin' dog, man. We should ah come wid nuff bonio an' rare steak an' t'ing to keep de blasted dog 'appy.'

Biscuit couldn't hide the smile on his face, although he realised they could still be in danger. 'Backside, if dat rarse dog did ketch you, I dunno wha' you would 'ave expected me fe do.'

'Come down an' help, innit,' Floyd replied, his tone serious. 'Lace de friggin' dog on his 'ead top wid your big screwdriver, innit . . . Dat dog 'as los' me nuff corn.' He stamped his right foot on the roof in frustration.

'Mek no sense de two of we get yam,' said Biscuit, shaking his head.

'Bwai, let's remove from dis place, man,' said a sweaty-faced Floyd, looking down the street.

On reaching ground level, they saw a tense-looking Coffin Head on the other side of the fence. 'Blouse an' skirt! Get in de car, man,' he gestured around him with his hand. 'Someone mus' 'ave 'eard.'

Biscuit and Floyd scrambled over the fence as Coffin Head ran to his car and started the engine. A bedroom curtain moved in the house at the end of the terrace and a shadowy face looked down on them. Biscuit and Floyd slammed the car doors and Coffin Head hit first gear. He U-turned over the pavement and floored the accelerator.

Fifteen minutes later, the motor was huffing and puffing through the streets of Streatham. In the passenger seat, Floyd slouched, deflated. In the back, Biscuit contented himself with a Twix chocolate bar. The pavements were mostly deserted. Coffin Head drove slowly and attentively, looking out for SPG vans and police cars. 'I shoulda gone by Knights Hill way,' he said. 'Not so many beast are on dat route.'

He drove past the Cats Whiskers club and Brixton bus garage on Streatham Hill, checking his rear-view mirror continually.

'Drop me off at Brenton's,' asked Floyd. He chucks his keys over to Coffin Head. 'Let me in when I get back.'

Coffin Head nodded as Biscuit closed his tired eyes.

Three minutes later, the Dolomite spluttered to a halt outside Brenton's ground-floor flat. Situated in a new two-storey block, Brenton had put in the hard-wood front door himself. Plain net curtains covered the windows, and Brenton had recently varnished his front gate. Untamed grass grew in his tiny garden.

Floyd emerged from the car. 'Wha's a matter wid you two? Brenton don't bite, y'know.'

Two minutes later, rubbing away the sleep from his eyes, a yawning Brenton, dressed in track-suit bottoms and a thick, stringed vest, opened the door. 'Don't you friggin' sleep? You're like a friggin' vampire, man. Not seen during the blasted day but stressing people during the night.'

'Just cool, man,' Floyd replied, not waiting to be invited in. 'Coffin Head jus' drop me off. Jus tried to t'ief some speakers from T'ornton Heat' sides. We 'ad to chip cos of a friggin' mad dog. An' you can't complain anyway. I ain't been to your gates fe over a week.'

Brenton sighed. 'Bwai, you're still doing dat t'iefing madness.'

'You got anyt'ing to yam in de fridge?' asked Floyd, stepping towards the small kitchen.

'Nah. An' you still owe me for that Ploughman's Lunch I bought you a while back.'

Floyd made his way to the front room, admiring the new wallpaper in the hallway. He plonked himself on a bean bag on the uncovered floor and greeted the Bruce Lee poster which overlooked Brenton's black and white television. A small teak table in the middle of the room held a framed picture of a baby, and next to it a glass ashtray. In one corner of the room was a large DIY book that was sitting next to a paint-specked ghetto-blaster.

Brenton went over to the mantelpiece, which framed a gas heater. He picked up his herb bag and rizlas and threw them over to his spar. 'You buil' up, man. You always wrapped a better zoot than me.'

'You know dat.'

Floyd began to construct the spliff scientifically. Brenton looked on in envy. 'So wha' is Biscuit and Coff up to these days?' he asked, walking to the suitcase. 'Do they still juggle for Nunchaks?'

'Nah. Coff decide not to juggle again. I t'ink de rarse beating 'im get inna cell discourage 'im a liccle. An' as for Biscuit, he ain't buying his t'ings off Nunchaks again. Cos Nunchaks is moving in on Denise. Scrious t'ing. Biscuit can't chat her out of de situation.'

'Backside!' Brenton raised his voice while pushing the play button. 'She's living dangerous, innit.'

'Yeah, it's dat. But you know Denise, she's too head-strong an' 'ard of listening to advise an' t'ing. I was t'inking of putting Sharon 'pon her case. She might listen to her. As for Biscuit, worry an' stress is jus' licking 'im.'

Dennis Brown's 'Cassandra' played softly in the background. Brenton scratched behind his ear, wondering if he could do anything about the problem. 'Maybe I can chat to Nunchaks, tell him not to do anyt'ing to her.'

'Bwai, you're bold, dread. But believe, Denise won't t'ank you for it. Mind you, she listens to you more dan anyone else. You might get t'rough to her . . . I 'ave a feeling you tickle her fancy.'

'Nah. We jus' get on good. Anyway, if I sight her I'll drop a word in her lug.'

Brenton watched his brethren spark the joint. Floyd toked hard as a thick smoke rose like the spirit of a dead man.

# Sister Love

## 1 March 1981

'Mummy said you've got my pocket money,' exclaimed Royston, holding out a keen hand.

'Did you go bagwash wid Mummy?' asked Biscuit, sitting up in bed and opening his eyes.

'Yeah, an' I hoovered the bedroom.'

Biscuit inspected the brown carpet. Mus' ah been tired, he thought, to sleep t'rough a hoovering. 'You should do it every day, not when you're jus' looking money.'

'So I can 'ave my pocket money den?'

'You liccle ginall. Der's a pound note in my slacks.'

Royston wasted no time in grabbing the crumpled trousers and rifled through the pockets.

'Wha's de time saying,' asked Biscuit.

197

'Quarter past one.'

Biscuit pulled on a pair of jeans before venturing into the hallway. The scent of generously-seasoned chicken legs wafted throughout the flat. He made for the front room as he picked the sleep out of his eyes.

Hortense, her dome hidden by a black tie-head, was ironing a flower-patterned dress as she hummed a gospel song she favoured. Denise, wearing her favourite seamed jeans and a black polo-neck sweater, was sitting in an armchair, pleasing her eyes on the new garments she had just bought from Petticoat Lane market. On her lap was a new black skirt that was split to just above the knee. Beside her on the floor, inside a brown paper bag, were two pairs of slacks and next to this was a pair of suede, high-heeled shoes in their box.

'You get in so late dese days,' snapped Hortense, collaring Biscuit with her eyes, 'dat you might as well go ah church when you come from party.'

'Sir Lloyd were playing out, innit. Der blues is always ram.' His eyes were attracted by the clothes and shoes surrounding his sister. 'Where d'you get de corn from to buy dem t'ings?' he interrogated.

'Ask no question, me tell you no lie.'

'It's Nunchaks, innit.'

'Who's Nunchaks?' queried Hortense. 'An' wha' kinda foolish name is dat? It sound like ah demon name.'

'You could say dat,' said Biscuit.

'It might be 'im, it might not,' Denise teased her brother, pushing her nose up.

'Don't frig me 'bout, Denise.' He raised his voice, pointing a finger at his sister. 'I told you already not to deal wid 'im. You carry on an' see dat pure tribulation don't lick your behind.'

198

'An' since when you become my daddy?' Denise replied, pushing her head forward and placing her hands on her hips.

'Since you start walk an' talk wid dat terrorist.'

'Stop your noise! De two ah you.' Hortense battled in.

'Well, tell your precious son to stop trying to manners me.'

'Dis ain't 'bout manners, dis is 'bout your foolishness.'

'So wha' is it?' Denise half-grinned. 'Can't tek it dat I don't haffe rely 'pon you for my garments?'

'No!' Biscuit shouted, his face turning very serious. 'De man your dealing wid is dangerous, believe!'

Denise kissed her teeth as Hortense shook her head. 'Why me two elder pickney wan' jus' cuss 'pon each uder? You're coming like Cain an' Abel.'

'Cos he's trying to play daddy. An' as far as I know, Daddy dead.'

'Denise!' Hortense screamed, shocked to hear her daughter speak in this way. 'Hol' your tongue before me cut it off.'

'Yeah, go ahead, blame me,' she taunted her mother.

'Denise!' Hortense slammed the iron into its rack and placed her hands on her hips. 'Don't t'ink you are so big dat me cyan't box you, y'hear me chile?'

Royston appeared in the doorway, matchbox cars in hand, and wondering if the never-ending arguments between his mother and sister would come to a conclusion.

'She's too damn facety,' announced Biscuit, dismissing Denise with a swipe of his hand. 'She don't listen to reason.'

'You jus' don't like me, innit,' Denise said, lowering her voice. Tears began to well in her eyes. 'I can't do nutten to please you.' She glared at her mother. 'Ain't my fault my fader was wort'less, so you keep telling me.' She raised her voice again. 'It's like you don't want me 'ere so! Remind you of 'im, do I?'

Biscuit glanced at his mother, realising the argument was getting out of control. He didn't know what to say.

'Denise, sit down an' calm yourself, girl,' ordered Hortense, ignoring her daughter's crying.

'No! I've 'ad nuff of dese shegarries!' Denise's voice became volcanic and her eyes narrowed to slits of bitterness.

His eyes east-westing rapidly, looking at his mother and sister, Biscuit still didn't know how to calm the situation.

'Denise dis an' Denise dat,' his sister yelled. 'Denise do dis an' Denise don't do dat. You two are fuckeries, man! It's like I ain't related in my own yard. Can't do nutten right! I mus' be de blackest rarse sheep ever! Even so I cook, an mind Royston an' t'ing, but oh no. You always find somet'ing dat I'm doing wrong.' She glared at her mother with such passion that Hortense had to look away. Biscuit raised his palms, thinking for a moment he might have to separate them. Denise continued to print her gaze underneath Hortense's skin. 'Well, I ain't teking dis fuckery any more! I'm shifting.'

Hortense's mouth was primed to say something but her voice was drowned in shock. Denise had never used rude gal language in the presence of her mother before. The intensity of her daughter's argument left one half of her mind in disarray and the other in guilt. At that moment, she would have done anything to get away from her daughter's glare.

'Hol' your backside still!' yelled Biscuit, holding his right palm towards his sister's face.

200

Denise shot out of the chair, brushed past a startled Royston and marched to her bedroom. Hortense said nothing, peering vacantly at the armchair Denise had just left. She then closed her eyes and held her forehead in her palm.

'She ain't going nowhere!' insisted Biscuit, leaving the room. 'Fucking nowhere!' He ran into the hallway and stood outside Denise's bedroom door.

'You ain't going nowhere, y'hear me?'

'You ain't my friggin' paps.'

'Jus' calm yourself an' we can chat.'

'Chat 'bout wha'? Mum wants me out an' you t'ink I'm some kinda leggo beast.'

'No I don't. It's jus' a liccle warning I'm giving you. Nunchaks is ah bad man.'

'Yeah he is. Jus' like you, innit. Maybe I should tell Mummy 'bout your dealings wid 'im. Den she might not t'ink dat de sun rises from your backside.'

'Don't mek me bus' down dis door, y'know.'

'Bus' it down, like I'm scared of you.'

'Lincoln, let her be, man,' Hortense instructed. 'Mek her gwarn an' cool off. She'll soon come back when she realise she der-ya 'pon her own.'

'T'anks for dat, Mum! You get your wish, innit. I'm outta your miserable face. If I go you won't 'ave to t'ink 'bout my daddy's face spoiling your day.'

Biscuit thumped a fist on Denise's bedroom door for a full minute. Then, abruptly, it opened, with Biscuit almost falling against the wardrobe. Denise was wrapped in her beige trench coat. She held on tightly to a bulging holdall. Royston stood still in the hallway, not quite believing his tearful eyes. He clutched his toy cars to him.

For a long second, Biscuit gaped in shock. 'Denise,

man. Jus' cool. You know Mummy loves you an' t'ing, an' me too. You know so Royston will feel it as well. Jus' cool an' we can chat 'bout dis.'

Denise searched her brother's eyes and knew his plea was genuine. But she wanted to cause a little emotional distress for her mother. Mum can't cope without me, she thought. Who's gonna do de cooking four times a week while mum's at work? She held on grimly to her brother's apprehensive gaze. 'You'd better step aside cos der's gonna be one big rarse fight between de two ah we if you don't remove!'

Her tears had reached the corners of her mouth, creeping over her lips. She pushed out her jaw in determination as she fish-eyed her older brother, wondering if she would have to fight to reach the front door. 'Mek her gwarn an' cool off,' a voice maintained from the lounge, and Denise's heart plummeted.

'Don't do dis, Sis,' Biscuit said quietly in a defeated tone. He looked at his sister and for a short moment they acknowledged each other's love. Then Denise looked beyond her brother and saw no sign of her mother. Her bitterness returned.

She palmed Biscuit aside, and three seconds later was walking along the balcony, inhaling deeply on the chilled March air, wondering who would put her up for the night. Somewhere below, a rootsman was playing the Crown Prince's 'Milk And Honey'. She hoped that Frank or Stella would see her and ask what was happening. But all she saw was the white kid three doors away trundling on his scooter.

Back inside the flat, Royston was inconsolable, his eyes clenched tight, not wanting to open them again.

*

'Maybe Pastor Thomas could talk some sense into her,' Jenny suggested.

'No, man. Dat will mek t'ings worse,' Hortense replied. She was sitting in Jenny's front room sipping a cup of nutmeg tea. 'After ah day or two, Denise will come back when she woulda cool off. Her temper too rapid, man, jus' like her wort'less fader. An' she too damn renk. Dis is de first time she swear after me! Me shoulda gi' her two box.' She looked up at the picture of Martin Luther King and wished it was all that simple.

'Dat won't solve anyt'ing, Hortense. Why you nah try an' talk wid her, woman to woman. Get to find out wha' is troubling her, talk wid her like you talk to me.'

Hortense tutted, then sipped her tea, unable to mask her disbelief. She couldn't remember the last time she'd had a conversation with her daughter that didn't end in an argument. 'Royston! 'Ow many times me affe to tell you to stop run up an' down inna Jenny hallway? You carry on an' see I don't cane your foot-bottom wid cheese grater.' She paused, her mind returning to Denise. 'As fe me daughter, 'ow cyan me talk wid her when her mout' so cantankerous?'

'Jus' sit her down an' talk calmly. Hortense, you too much like de old Jamaican women dem who say raise de girls an' love de boys.'

Hortense ignored her sister's remark. 'Royston! Don't mek me come out der.' She wanted to change the subject.

Jenny smiled. 'Let 'im be. It kinda nice to 'ave ah young chile run 'bout de place. I wish mine were at dat age.'

'Royston wan' fe learn some manners,' Hortense riposted.

'So, you t'ink 'bout Royston staying wid me for weekends?'

'Hhhmmm. Wha' you 'ave planned fe 'im? Don't bring 'im ah no blasted church an' mek parson man turn 'im fool. Dem parson or pastor man or whatever you wan' call dem are ginall. Dem always carry on 'bout de poor but dem pocket jingle up wid nuff money. An' I know ah few ah dem 'ave pickney 'ere an' der.'

'You too damn cynical, Hortense!'

'An' you too naïve.'

'So is dat ah yes? Cos me can never be sure wha' you mean. God give you some stubbornness, my Lord.'

'Hhhmmm.'

' 'Member dat time back 'ome when you was staying by Uncle Malcolm? Papa say you needed some work to let go of your talk-back-to-elder-ways.'

'Yes, an' 'im work me like ah mule. Damn slave driver. 'Im use to 'ave me carrying yam heads 'pon me 'ead all over de bush an' planting whole 'eap ah potato slips. Den de slave driver would mek me plant nuff peas an' untold corn. An' backside, 'im never even gi' me ah pair of shoes, cah me affe cover up de corn 'ole wid me bare foot. Den when evening come me would affe cook fe de men dem, sometime all twenty of dem. To backside, me was glad to get 'way from de drop-lip fool.'

Jenny laughed. 'But when you come back, you lef' your talkative ways behind.'

Hortense stirred her tea more than was strictly necessary. The image of her father gate-crashed her mind and recollections of their relationship came thick and fast. She remembered how he used to dote on Jenny, always having her sit in his lap and congratulating her on her school work. Although not quite as good in her classes as her sister, Hortense felt she deserved praise for cooking the family meals and tending to her father's tiny agricultural plot. She could also never understand why her father encouraged her to sing in the church, but banned it in the family home.

She remembered the time she was beaten for losing the family donkey. She had only wanted to impress her father by carrying seeds and agricultural produce to the field where he worked. On the way, she got distracted by other children playing in the bush. When she went to resume her journey, she discovered that the donkey was gone. Her father thrashed her for the loss of the animal in front of all his work mates. Hortense never forgave him, and from that moment tried her best to embarrass him in public. The consequences of this were unfair, Hortense felt. Her father gradually ignored her, and Jenny got even more attention, escorting him on trips to St Anne's Bay and to work in the school holidays. Hortense had to remain home with her mother, a dutiful quiet woman who always left the last word of discipline to her husband.

Still stirring her tea slowly, Hortense set her gaze inside the cup. Jenny looked on with concern. Gradually, realisation dawned on Hortense that her father's sins had passed on to her. Something inside her told her that as a girl she had had the same traits as her daughter. Finally she admitted to herself that Denise's actions were not passed on from her father, but from herself.

'It was only cah me Papa say dat if I ketch ah trouble once more, he woulda sen' me back ah Uncle Malcolm, dat me change me bad mout' ways,' she replied eventually, bringing the cup to her lips.

'Hortense,' Jenny said, using a delicate tone, 'you used to love going ah church back den. I remember how you used to sing out loud inna de choir an' look forward to every Sunday. Sometimes Papa used to cuss cos you used to sing ah night-time when all lights were out. De neighbours did ah love it but it used to drive Papa mad.'

' 'Ow can ah man love 'im daughter to sing out loud inna church but ban it inside our very 'ome?'

'Papa 'as always been ah quiet man who loves de countryside an' t'ing.' Jenny took a generous sip from her tea. 'So we can expect Royston nex' Friday?'

'I s'pose so. But if me 'ear dat 'is backside der-ya inna church, den me an' you will ketch ah cuss-cuss like never before. Y'understand?'

Jenny nodded. 'Sometimes I worry fe you, Hortense. You cyan't keep on vexing God. One day He might tek you in 'and. I will pray fe you an' 'ope dat in time you will see de error of your ways an' come back inna God's 'ouse.'

# 18

# Herb Man Hustling

## 3 March 1981

Soferno Bs record shop blitzed the afternoon with the Crown Prince's 'To The Foundation'. Outside the shop, a woolly-hatted dread wearing a torn anorak bopped his head to the rhythm while peeling an orange with a flick-knife. A white SPG van turned slowly into Railton Road, brimming with eager policemen. To the right of the record shop, inside the market arcade, the scent of recently baked ardough bread wafted through the snapping chill. Three black youths, crowned in different styled berets, ambled towards the unemployment exchange, all clutching their UB40 cards. A teenage black girl wearing a loose-fitting track-suit weaved through the traffic on Coldharbour Lane, constantly looking behind her. Clutched to her chest were five red apples.

Through the entrance of the arcade, about twenty yards from Soferno Bs shack, was another reggae site, the General Record Store, owned by a tall black man with a candyfloss-shaped afro. He was standing in front of a wall that was bedecked in reggae album covers. In the corner of the shop, eating a cocoa bread and meat pattie sandwich and listening to the Crown Prince's 'Sitting And Watching', was Sceptic. Crowned by his tilted white beret, he was dressed in a faded denim jacket and brown corduroys.

He checked his watch. 2.40pm. He watched the entrance and beyond as rootsheads and sound boys raised their hands to the shop assistant to signal a tune they craved. 'Play de new Ranking Joe album,' one demanded, drumming his gold-clad fingers on the counter.

'Nah, boss,' a picky head youth rejected, tapping his right mountain boot to the rhythm. 'Keep on playing de Crown Prince – Dennis Brown *rule*.'

'No, man,' a rootshead disagreed, picking his teeth with a matchstick. 'You cyan't play Dennis Brown all de while. Run some Barrington Levy – 'Robin Hood' is a murderous tune.'

'Ah, true dat,' a bald-headed sound man concurred, fishing for his wallet. 'De Mellow Canary 'as ah voice sweeter dan de sugar inna milo.'

The shop-owner smiled at his audience and proceeded to play Barrington Levy's 'Robin Hood'.

One dub version later, Biscuit appeared, wrapped in his leather bomber jacket and looking very frustrated. He greeted the guys he knew with a respectful nod, then saw Sceptic tongue-polishing his fingers. 'Wha'appen to two o clock?' Sceptic rebuked. 'Been on my jacks since two, man.'

'I was up Myatts Field, checking one of Denise's friends dem, see if she knows where Denise der-ya. Told me she don't sight Denise from time. I feel so she's lying, but bwai, wha' can I do? Can't force her to tell me de trut's an' rights. Where de fuck is she, man? I didn't t'ink she would go missing for dis long.'

'Stop fret,' said Sceptic. 'Denise can look after herself, dread. She mus' be coching wid one of her friends dem, someone you don't know.'

'I 'ope so. Jus' don't want her to tangle up wid Nunchaks . . . By de way, you ain't seen 'im 'bout 'ave you? Don't want 'im to see me, dread.' He dropped his voice to a whisper. 'I'm changing my supplier.'

He had realised that to continue to work for Nunchaks might be dangerous for Denise. Say somet'ing went wrong in his dealings wid de bad man? he asked himself. He didn't want to answer his own question.

'Blowoh. So dat's why you did wan' to check me,' said Sceptic. 'You know so you can't juggle wid any of dem Lineman no more. Not even Herbman Blue will gi' you ah liccle business.'

Biscuit observed the reggae buyers for any suspicious ears. 'Come. Let's step outta 'ere.' He gestured with his head. 'Don't wanna broadcast my business.' He glanced nervously at a black youth in the corner of the shop who was wearing a Slazenger V-neck sweater and a Sherlock Holmes hat.

'Yeah, it's dat,' Sceptic said, looking at the same guy. 'Don't trus' de yout's in dis shop. Informer der 'bout.'

They stepped out of the record shop and turned right, walking deeper into the arcade. They saw middle-aged women inspecting the various fishes on display; black teenage girls gathered around the hair products stall, looking on the multitude of greases and shampoos. At the far end of the arcade, a crowd had assembled around a man who was selling cheap watches.

'I t'ought you could hook me up wid Cutty Narks,' said Biscuit, scanning the shoppers and idlers as he walked.

'Cutty Narks?' Sceptic asked in surprise. Could be dangerous, he thought. 'Blowoh, he's been ratchet sketched nuff times. 'Is face looks like de lace 'pon a rugby ball to rarted.'

Cutty Narks had at one time been the peer of Nunchaks and Herbman Blue, with five dealers working for him. But he had got into an almost fatal fight with a youth who was a member of a dangerous posse.

'Yeah, but he's still juggling innit.' Biscuit said. 'A liccle small-time t'ing.'

'Nutten can stop Cutty Narks from juggling, but he had to remove from 'is spot 'pon de Line,' replied Sceptic, not liking the way the conversation was heading. 'He ketch up inna argument wid de Musketeers posse, innit. T'ree ah dem 'old 'im down an' one ah dem wet up his face like Jimmy Cliff done to dat man in *De Harder Dey Come.*'

'Yeah, me did 'ear 'bout it,' Biscuit said casually. 'Dem man from Stockwell Park sides wid der long piece of knife. But where is he operating from now?'

'Landor Road, dat shubeen where Marxist Hi-Fi used to play. Cutty controls de basement.'

The two friends reached the High Street. They could hear the shouts coming from the bible thumpers at the entrance of the tube station. Cars were stuck in a jam and pedestrians crossed the road, ignoring the green light.

Bus stops were overcrowded as youths peered into the windows of shoe shops.

'You're on your own, dread,' announced Sceptic. 'Cutty don't like man coming wid ah nex' man. He gets all para 'bout it.'

'Some bredren you are.'

'Well, you've got more chance juggling wid 'im if you der-ya 'pon your jacks.'

'I get de drift, man. I'll forward 'pon my own.'

Biscuit had a hunch that Sceptic had got himself into some kind of bother with Cutty Narks. He wondered if Sceptic was one of Cutty's former dealers. But he didn't voice his thoughts; Sceptic always seemed to enmesh himself into tribulation with any juggler he worked for. Mainly because he had a big mouth.

On the other side of the road, Sceptic noticed someone he'd met on the Deptford fire march the day before. 'So why you never come 'pon de march yesterday?' he asked Biscuit accusingly.

'I was looking for my sister. She 'as a sistren called Monica who lives up Kennington sides, near de court-house. Denise went school wid her an' I know so she raves wid her now an' again. She sometimes comes round to my yard looking for Denise. But when I checked her, she told me she don't know shit eider.'

'Wassername? Monica? She fit? She Jamaican? She got man? Do you t'ink you can set me up?'

'Stop sniffing, man. Bwai, you're always t'inking wid your bone.'

Embarrassed, Sceptic returned his thoughts to the march. 'De march was going all right an' t'ing,' he reported. 'Nuff yout' joining 'pon de way, an' everybody was inna vibe. De Deptford fire victims mus' 'ave been

211

well proud. But when we reach up West now some rough-neck bwais start to smash up window an' t'ing. Jus' ah few ah dem spoil de vibe. Untold beastman appeared from nowhere an' start arresting anybody dey could. Nuff yout' get arrested but some beastman get lick up. Blowoh, we 'ad to scatter.'

'So you went wid Floyd?'

'Yeah, lost 'im up West sides. But I'm jus' 'bout to check 'im, see if he's safe an' t'ing.'

'I jus' knew so der would be trouble der.'

'It's dat, but de beast weren't ramping.' Sceptic raised his hand as if he was wielding a truncheon. 'Dey was going on well militant, using truncheon an' t'ing. I sight a bwai get lick up an' he weren't moving, dread. I know so I 'ad to dally.'

Sceptic took his leave opposite the skate-board park, telling his brethren he'd sight him later at Floyd's. Biscuit felt the wad of money in his inside jacket pocket and walked on. Eighty yards later, he turned left into Landor Road. This street was in a worse state than Railton Road, he thought. Most of the terraced housing was falling apart and four skips were on the roadside. He felt confident that he could do business with Cutty because the former Lineman must want to build up trade again, he reasoned. Just need to juggle till summer, he told himself. Then I'll sort out college. Maybe I can take biology again. I'll 'ave to ask Sharon 'bout a grant.

Three hundred yards up Landor Road, he noticed a bruised, blue door – Cutty's place. The windows were boarded up with chipboard and black bags of empty lager cans and bottles rested against the chipped front wall. A voice in his head told him to look Cutty straight in the eye and not be intimidated by the collection of scars. He

212

gathered in a strong breath, then knocked at the letterbox, holding his chin high. The door wailed open to reveal a rather short dread in a black overcoat, chewing on a small stick of sugar-cane.

'Cutty der-ya?' Biscuit asked.

'An' wha' if he is?' snapped the reply.

'Come to chat ah liccle business. I need to control some plants from wholesale.'

The diminutive rasta frisked Biscuit from neck to ankle. Satisfied, he eye-drilled him for ten seconds before leading him into the dimly lit passage. Biscuit's heartbeat accelerated as he was led down a creaking, basement staircase; his steps appeared to be amplified all over the house, and he could feel the ridges of plaster on the walls as he went down into the darkness.

Cutty Narks was parked on a bass-bin speaker box, watching the afternoon's horse racing on a black and white television set balanced precariously on a cardboard record box. The flickering screen was the only light in the room. He was dressed in denim dungarees and crowned by a Panama hat. His locks reached down to the beginning of his throat and his face looked like a road map for the devil. His moustache was the shape of a black horse-shoe, giving him a spaghetti western look. His top lip was about twice the size of his bottom lip, and his cheekbones jutted out of his face like two sticks in a balloon.

A stained brown blanket covered the window, and the smell of lager and rum emitted from the sill. Lengths of sound system wire were piled in a corner, along with tweeter boxes. A naked Action Man, painted in red, gold and green appeared lonesome and discarded in the middle of the dark wooden floor.

'Tek off your clothes to your briefs,' ordered Cutty,

inhaling on a four-incher, imitating the pose of Lee Van Cleef.

Biscuit focused on Cutty. Is de dread serious? he asked himself, his eyes not straying from Cutty's glare. There was a tense stand-off, as Biscuit's brain conjured up visions of being searched in an airport. Nah, he's only doing dis to see if I'm wired to rarted, he thought. Or to see if I'm carrying a blade. He took off his jacket slowly, followed by his burgundy V-necked sweater, revealing a black stringed vest. He felt a print of the short rasta's gaze upon his back as he unhooked the belt holding up his slacks. Seconds later, his trousers plunged in an undignified heap around his ankles. 'I ain't carrying no wire, dread. Brixtonian don't work fe no MI5 or undercover beast.'

Cutty nodded, still maintaining his stern pose, exhaling a rich smoke from his spliff. Biscuit took this as a cue to redress himself; he was sure the dread behind him had had a laugh that he was restraining in his belly.

'Right, my yout',' addressed Cutty. 'You passed de first test, now fe de second. Jus' some liccle question me wan' you fe answer.' He stood up, holding his gaze upon Biscuit, and stepped two paces towards him.

Biscuit raised his head and pushed out his chest, telling himself not to take a backward step. 'Whatever,' he returned, his confidence soaring like smoke from a burning spliff.

'Alright, my yout'. Ah who controls Moa Anbessa sound?'

'Beres.'

'Who's de mic men fe Front Line International?'

'Welton Yout' an' Silver Fox.'

'Who run Small Axe sound?'

214

'Keit'y Dread.'

'Who run t'ings down ah Villa Road?'

'Soferno B.'

'Who operates de sound?'

'Big Yout'. Some man call 'im Chabba.'

'Who's de resident sound inna Cubies?'

'Sir George.'

Cutty smiled as Biscuit kept his pose, daring the dread to question him further. The smaller man appeared in the corner of his eye, and it was only now that Biscuit realised he walked with a slight limp. Cutty switched off the television and set a more friendly gaze upon the wannabe buyer.

'Wha' name dem call you, my yout'?'

'Biscuit. My mudder calls me Lincoln.'

'Irie ites! You name after me bes' singer, Lincoln Sugar Minott. Respect fe dat. So 'ow much collie you want?'

'One ounce, dread.'

The dread tried not to reveal his gratitude, but his raised eyebrows and the whites of his eyes betrayed him. Biscuit tried hard not to grin.

'One t'irty fe dat, my yout'.'

Biscuit couldn't hold back his smile. 'I can 'andle dat, cheaper dan some ah dem Lineman. Some ah charge one sixty.'

Cutty smiled, nodding at the experienced youngster. Dis yout' could mek me some regular corn, he thought. He offered Biscuit a cigarette from the top of the television.

Biscuit accepted and wedged it on top of his left ear. 'I man 'ave de bes' prices in town,' Cutty boasted, gesturing with his hands.

'I don't wanna buy herb dat's already cut up, dread,' asserted Biscuit. 'You never know if it's been sabotaged

215

wid thyme an' t'ing. De brethrens I sell to expect top ranking bush.'

Cutty laughed, exposing his chaotic teeth. 'You know de runnings, my yout'. You know de spud shop inna Stockwell Road?'

'Yeah.'

'Forward der an' ah sistren will soon reach wid your merchandise. Now, show me your corn.'

Biscuit plucked his wad from the inside of his jacket, then carefully counted £130 before handing it over to the flunky.

'Now, 'ear me proper, my yout'. When you mek your nex' order, *don't* forward 'ere so. Jus' call dis number.' Cutty scrawled down a telephone number on a slip of betting paper. 'An' den we can arrange t'ings. Y'understand?'

'I know de score, dread.'

'Irie ites.'

Biscuit presented Cutty with a respectful nod before departing, wondering if he should have negotiated a price of £120.

Ten minutes later, he was inside the shop Cutty had described. A young black woman, pushing a buggy with a gurgling baby inside, entered the shop. She was wearing a light-blue anorak and baggy track-suit bottoms and her hair was in corn-row plaits. She bought a meat pattie for herself and she smiled at the assistant, obviously knowing him. Once the food was served, she turned around and saw Biscuit. 'Lincoln?' she asked.

'Yeah.'

From the baby's buggy she took out a small parcel, crudely covered in birthday wrapping paper. She gave this to Biscuit, and was gone without saying another word.

I s'pose dat meks sense, he told himself. Not even beastman would frisk a baby's buggy.

Walking east on Acre Lane, on his way home from Floyd's place, Biscuit heard the Town Hall clock chime 9.45pm. He was satisfied that the day's trading had gone well. He reached home twenty-five minutes later and his first port of call was Denise's bedroom. She wasn't home. Where she der-ya? he asked himself. Massa God, please don't mek her be wid Nunchaks. He went to the kitchen to fetch himself a glass of water and decided to look in on his mother. She was sleeping, snoring a little with her mouth slightly ajar. He crept over to her and placed two browns underneath her pillow. Then he returned to the kitchen, drank from his glass and gazed helplessly at Denise's bedroom door.

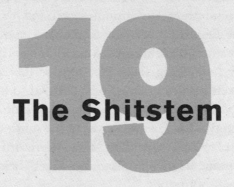

# The Shitstem

**5 March 1981**

Biscuit sniffed the favourable aroma of a burning Thai incense stick. A painting of the Sphinx, hanging over the gas heater, seemed to be watching him. To Biscuit's right stood a teak varnished table, about twice the size of a chess board. Propped on top of this were beautifully carved photo frames, elegantly painted in red, gold and green, housing grainy, creased black and white photographs. In one picture, a woman dressed all in white was standing rigid in front of a hut with a corrugated roof. In another photo, barefoot children posed under a jackfruit tree, dressed in long shorts and T-shirts. The children looked like they had just seen a ghost.

The youth shifted his gaze to Jah Nelson, who was at

218

work, smoothing a chair leg with a wooden block of sandpaper. Nelson studied his work as if he was preparing a gift to his God, Biscuit thought.

He returned his attention to the photos. 'Dey your family?' he asked.

Jah Nelson paused, as if a memory disturbed him. 'Yes. De woman in de white dress an' 'at is me mudder. She was teking de long t'ree mile walk to church dat day. De minister's sister, by some means I don't know, acquired a camera an' tek de pictures dem.'

'Do you keep in touch?'

'Fe ah long time, no. But de last few years me start back writing an' sen' ah liccle money to her.'

'Who are de kids? Your brudders an' sisters?'

'Yeah, man,' Nelson answered proudly. 'T'ree sister an' five brudder me 'ave.' He put down his tool upon the uncovered floor, then set his one good eye upon the teenager, attempting to read the youngster's thoughts. 'Trouble at 'ome?'

'You could say dat. My sister's going on like a rebel. I might bring her come 'ere so to mek you chat to her. See if you can chat sense inna her 'ead.'

'Yes, me coulda do dat. But you affe tell me de root of de fuss.'

Biscuit thought about it, not wanting to disclose family tensions to the sage, even though he thought he could trust him. 'Maybe at a later date,' he answered.

'As you wish. But me ears dem are always trained 'pon de young dem. I affe play my part cos de future will be yours.'

'Some future.'

'You waan fe free yourself from your negativity. Let me tell you dis, if a flat-footed goat find 'imself 'pon ah mountainous land, generations later, de goat offspring will develop a hoof fe 'elp 'im climb de mountain slope. Jah blesses all creatures dat way. An' dat's 'ow you mus' look 'pon it. Mek education your friend, an' like de goat, you will develop ah hoof fe climb your particular mountain slope. Jah know!'

'It's alright fe you to say,' Biscuit argued. 'You've got your trade an' t'ing. Most of us ain't got a friggin chance. Der's nutten der for us, except hustling.'

Nelson collected a wooden chair from the corner of the room and placed it in front of the youth before sitting himself down. Biscuit noticed the thin lines of grey hair that streaked the dread's locks, giving him an almost stately aura. The teenager wondered what he had looked like as a young man.

'Now, listen to me proper, Lincoln. I waan fe tell you 'bout de system. Der is nuff talk of ism, schism an' racism. An' me nah defend 'gainst de charge of racism in dis country. But de main t'ing you affe worry yourself is wid de classism in dis country.'

Biscuit nodded, then delved into his pocket for his rizlas and bag of herb; he had already sold twenty pounds worth to the dread. The rasta stood up and went over to the stereo in the corner of the room. He pressed the play button and returned to his chair. In a low volume, the Congos' 'Children Are Crying' sang out from the set.

'When de children of Africa were dragged to de West,' Nelson continued, 'it was because of money. Cheap labour fe work 'pon de plantations dem. An' it benefited de upper class de most, lining dem pockets. De upper class are doing de same t'ing today, but more subtle.'

220

Biscuit spliced a cancer stick, holding the gaze of his mentor.

'Tek schooling fe example,' Nelson said. 'Inna de inner city you find de most student teacher an' teacher dem who cyan't do dem job too righteous. Seen. Dis is part of ah plan. Cos dis way, wid poor educational 'elp you nah find too many pupils attaining de heights an' forward to university. But dat's de way de system waant it. Y'understand? Consider dis. If every pupil inna de land get top marks, who would waan fe empty dustbin? Who would waan fe sweep road? Who would waan fe mend road? De system relies 'pon someone doing dis work, noble it may be. But de system would collapse if every pupil was qualified to be ah brain surgeon. Y'understand? Dat's why de system will mek sure dat de poor pupil dem inna inner city will nah mek too much progress. Yes, some poor children mek it t'rough. But jus' ah few.'

'Nelson, man. Hol' up, dread. You're going too fast fe me.'

'It's important to tek dis in. An' dat's why me always keep on education. Dat is de key. Don't rely 'pon de wort'less teacher dem who der-ya inna school an' college. Supplement wha' dem teach by teaching yourself. Jah know!'

'Bwai, sometimes you get all heavy 'pon me, dread.'

Nelson laughed as he rose from the chair and went back to his work.

'So dis is wha' you an' dem dread chat 'bout at Twelve Tribes?' enquired Biscuit.

'I used to. But dem kick me out, or me should say me walk out.'

'Why?'

221

'Cos I man cause ah fuss an' ah bangarang when I insisted dat Rastafari start from de civilisation of Egypt, wid Osiris an' de Gods before 'im. I also upset dem cos me question de Bible. Dat cause nuff debate an' argument.'

'Why?'

'Now, how can me put dis? You see de film *King Kong* when it come out ah few years back?'

'Yeah.'

'Well, it is a version of de old *King Kong* film dat come out in de 1930s. An' when you analyse de Bible, you find de same t'ing – ah nex' version.'

'Whadya mean?'

'Tek de story of Noah. Everyone know how Noah buil' 'im ark an' escape de flood waters wid 'im wife, family an' two animals of every kind. Now, listen me proper, Lincoln. All de biblical scholars say dat Moses did write de Genesis part of de Bible, an' dis include de deeds of Noah. But nuh too many people know dat de flood story was written by someone else long before Moses was born. Ah people called Sumerians did ah live near present day Iraq an' Iran, an' it's written an' documented dat dey told de story of dis great flood. De only difference dem 'ave is de names dey used. Ziusudra teks de place of Noah an' so fort'. If you check out de British Museum you can see for yourself, cah dem still 'ave de Sumerian cuneiform writings dat tell de tale. In time I 'ave learned dat der are flood stories, documented an' written from all over de world, saying de same t'ing. It cyan't be all coincidence, so alt'ough me really believe in de flood, I question Moses' version. De important t'ing to realise is dat Moses, if him did write Genesis, was simply copying ah much older script. Jah know!'

222

'So is all de Bible like dat?' Biscuit asked, wondering what his Aunt Jenny would make of it all.

'Could be. Me still finding out. All me know is dat me cyan't tek de Bible word fe word. Yes, me live by it, but nobody cyan be too sure of whoever wrote it an' wha' stories are jus' copies of even older stories. You could say it's been my life's work to solve de mystery.'

'Well, don't go into dat, dread. You mangle up my 'ead wid your stars an' t'ing last time I reach 'ere.'

Nelson laughed again, picking up his smoothing tool and concentrating his eye on the work at hand. Biscuit studied the older man's skilled hands and speculated on whether they had ever caressed a woman. 'You ever been married, Nelson? Or somet'ing like dat? You 'ave any pickney? Joseph Dread who lives in my estate has 'bout twelve wha' he knows 'bout.'

Nelson chuckled. 'Joseph ah fruitful bough! But you find me Achilles heel. Alt'ough me in good company, cah even Solomon, t'ough 'im wise, never know de secret of ah woman. To answer your question, no. Me never tek ah wife an' never even get close. Girlfriends came but quickly gone. Dem could nah tek me ignoring dem when me der-ya inna me book an' meditation. As me reach ah good age, sometime me body 'unger fe ah woman's warmth an' company, y'understand. Me been alone too long in dis life.'

He glanced up to the ceiling, thinking of past memories and his childhood in Jamaica, reminiscing about his teenage sweetheart, the daughter of one of his mother's best friends. They had had to part because her family disapproved of his growing locks. He sighed heavily. I'll 'ave to forward back-a-yard an' visit me mudder, he thought. See her before she passes away to Jah Kingdom.

After all, next year she reaches the glorious age of eighty. I could bless my eyes on the rest of the family, and all the untold nephews and nieces that I haven't seen in the flesh. 'You 'ave ah sweetheart?' he asked Biscuit.

'Sort of. I told you 'bout Carol, innit. She don't like de life I'm leading.'

Nelson noticed how Biscuit's eyes had grown keen. 'It's not fe me to counsel you on womanly t'ings. But if you do develop a relationship wid de girl of your choice, den cherish her an' never let her go. Cah you don't know when Jah will bless you again wid love, y'understand?'

Biscuit nodded. 'Sometimes I think she'd be better off wid someone wid a good job an' t'ing. I can't offer her nutten.' He wrapped his spliff and toked gently, blowing smoke above Nelson's head, giving the rastaman a misshapen halo. 'You're dreaming, dread. Tek a look outside your window an' wha' do you see? Nuff yout' 'bout my age wid nutten to do an' nowhere to go. Ain't nutten in de future for us, except dole office an' inside a beast cell.'

Nelson closed his eyes momentarily in controlled frustration. Then he fingered his matted beard while turning his head to look out the window. He could see seven youths shooting the breeze in the forecourt. 'On your journey, me 'ave planted a sign-post before you, an' you mus' look 'pon de message. Me 'ope is dat you will forward down my route, den uders will follow.'

Biscuit pulled on his spliff once more, exhaling through his nose. He considered on how Denise would respond to a session of reasoning with the dread. Although concurring with Nelson's philosophy, he still harboured itching doubts. 'You say you 'ave sign-posted a route for

224

me. But ain't you giving me corn an' buying my herb? Don't dat mek you a hypocrite?'

Nelson nodded, his mane stirring like a waking lion. 'Good question. But me door is open to you widout de 'erb, y'understand. An' 'erb should be ah free medicine available to all, widout governments meking de people dem criminals if dey use it. It's jus' unfortunate dat you affe do dis hustling t'ing to mek ah liccle money. But I accept your charge. Me ah hypocrite, yes. But my intention towards to you is righteous. Jah know!'

Biscuit offered him his spliff. The dread inhaled deeply and blew his smoke upwards. For a minute they both studied each other silently, with an unspoken respect.

Nelson sensed there was something in the teenager's face that was troubling him. He thought that Biscuit's eyes betrayed a terrible burden and wondered what was at the root of this unease. 'You sure you nah waan talk 'bout dis worry of yours?'

'No, dread. Not ready for dat yet. Maybe nex' time.'

Nelson read his watch; the time was nearing 3.30pm. Biscuit read the time also and rose to his feet. 'Got to go an' pick up my liccle brudder Royston from school. Must dally. Sight you nex' week.'

Nelson watched as Biscuit left the room, not even looking behind. 'Good 'eart 'im 'ave,' he smiled. 'Ah good 'eart.'

Closing Jah Nelson's front door, Biscuit saw a familiar figure stepping stylishly towards him: Yardman Irie, the stepping poet. He was dressed in an army-green camouflage jacket, green corduroys and topped by a black cloth beret with the symbol of the Lion of Judah stitched upon it. '*Me walk 'pon Acre Lane inna de freezing rain, watch out behind you, watch out behind you.*' He pointed dramatically at Biscuit and the teenager's face eased into a wide smile. '*Nuff man inna de bookie shop looking to gain, watch out behind you, watch out behind you, me sight two beastman I swear dem was insane, watch out behind you, watch out behind you* . . . Yo! Me bredren. *Dem tek out der truncheon an' start gi' me pain, watch out behind you. Watch* . . . Wha'appen Biscuit, 'ows runnings?'

'Could be ah liccle better, y'know.'

'Well, life not an easy road.'

'Wha' you doing round dese sides anyway? You 'ave a girl in dis estate?'

'No, dread. Come to check Jah Nelson,' Yardman stated with conviction.

Biscuit's eyebrows soared. 'Jah Nelson?'

'Yes, dread. De teacher.'

Yardman Irie went to Nelson's front door and knocked eagerly as Biscuit looked on. If Yardman Irie reasons wid Nelson, he pondered, the dread must be chatting some sense. 'You seen my sister 'bout?'

'Yeah, I was wondering wha' she was doing wid Nunchaks at a Front Line blues las' Saturday. I was chatting 'pon de mic when I sight her wid Nunchaks an' some uder girl dem. Me nearly choke 'pon me words. Believe . . . She don't know he's ah terrorist?' Yardman looked accusingly at Biscuit.

'Oh, frig my living days,' Biscuit replied, wide-eyed and crestfallen.

Yardman Irie paused and sensed the gravity of the situation. He looked upon his old school-friend with a worried frown before entering Jah Nelson's flat. 'Anyt'ing me can do?' he enquired.

'Yeah, if you sight her again try and chat some sense

226

into her 'ead 'bout de dangers of walking an' talking wid a bad man.'

'Seen. An' if I don't sight her, I'll put de word 'pon de street. Ah serious t'ing dis.'

'Seen.'

Biscuit almost gagged as his heartbeat raced. If only I'd listened to her more, he told himself. I should've sat Denise an' Mummy down an' settled der arguments. Damn! I knew what was going on but I let t'ings drift. If I got dem to chat, Denise would 'ave never lef' de yard. I was too friggin' busy selling herb 'pon street. It's cos of me she's 'pon de street, cos of me, he tormented himself. Wha' am I gonna do? Please, Massa God. He looked up to the heavens and considered going back to Jah Nelson's. He dropped his head to the level of the concrete jungle. 'Oh, fuck. Tribulation gonna mad me,' he muttered.


Coffin Head was clocking the flow of traffic upon Brixton Hill. Parking on a waist-high wall near the junction of New Park Road, he followed the trajectory of a 133 bus, gathering momentum as it sped by the church near Elm Park Road. Thirty yards away to the left, a black man reeled along the pavement, stepping more sideways than forward, like a crab with a toe missing, and topped by a chewed Trilby hat and a sorrowful face. He pined vocally for his lost love, some beautiful woman named Almira. No one took any notice.

To Coffin Head's right sat Sceptic, telescoping the streets for any sign or mark of the Metropolitan Police. 'Don't like coching 'ere so,' he complained. 'Beastman are always up an' down looking black yout' to trouble. Why can't we jus' forward into de pub an' play some pool?'

'Cos I'm checking on somet'ing,' Coffin Head replied. 'I wanna see if de beast 'ave a one- or two-man patrol 'pon dis road.'

'Wha' you chatting 'bout? You talking a trodding beast-man?'

'Frig me! You worked dat one out quick, Scep.'

'Blowoh! You're serious 'bout dis t'ing, innit.'

'D'you t'ink I bought de waster fe puppy show?'

'Dem beastman don't trod up dese sides. Dey trod down de Line now an' again an' in Mayall road, round dem sides.'

'Yeah, but round der is too hot. Char! No chance of blowing away a beastman up der to rarted.' Coffin Head spat the words out, tasting the anger he had inside. 'I wanna see how a beastman's face might look when he's staring down my gun 'ole to rarted. I'm gonna pause jus' for dat, den shoot 'im in his nosebridge. Bloodclaat beastman, dey t'ink dey can get 'way wid anyt'ing.'

Sceptic examined his brethren and saw a pair of eyes with the gaze of the predator. He's really gonna sen' a beastman to de cemetery, he thought. What a blowoh. He'll be one big-time hero, like Yul Brynner in *The Magnificent Seven*. Yardman Irie would mek lyrics 'bout it. But de beast would go fucking cuckoo's nest. Dey would arres' every yout' in Brixton till dey found de murderer, an' in de process nuff yout' would get brutal-ise inna cell. What a blowoh. Beast would patrol de Brixton streets wid M16s in der 'and, firing an' asking questions later. Nuff black yout' would ram up Streat-ham cemetery along wid de dead policeman. They'd be all curfew an' t'ing. No more blues dances an' no more town hall sound clashes.

'Maybe we can size up Tulse Hill, I've always sighted

228

beastman trodding by dem sides,' suggested Sceptic. 'An' der is nuff places to get 'way. Cos, bwai, if you do dis t'ing, de whole of de friggin' police force will tear up de estates looking fe you.'

'Yeah, I know,' replied Coffin Head frostily. 'But we all look de same to dem, innit.'

For the next few minutes the two spars watched the traffic and the passers-by. They recognised one of Carol's friends getting off a bus and Yo'd her. They watched three white men trying unsuccessfully to push-start a car into New Park Road. A green Jaguar, driven by a black man in a green beaver-skin hat, bombed down Brixton Hill. Sceptic followed its direction. 'D'you t'ink Biscuit's sister is wid Nunchaks?' he asked.

'Probably.'

'What a blowoh. I was chatting to Keit'y Dread an' he knows nuff 'bout 'im.'

'Yeah, wha' does he know.'

'Well, dis is 'ow it go. When Nunchaks was a yout' 'im get burn up 'pon his leg. 'Is fader lef' a smoking cancer stick an' der yard ketch ah fire. Nunchaks was sleeping at de time an' dey jus' got 'im out. But his right leg was burn up bad. He grew up 'ating 'is parents cos of it an' fe some reason 'im 'ate woman even more. But it's like fire turn 'im cuckoo. He's obsessed wid it.'

'Don't tell Biscuit dat cos dat will mek 'im stress out even more. Keep your tongue stapled 'bout dat dread. An' don't tell Biscuit 'bout Nunchaks' whorehouse.'

'Im 'ave a whorehouse?'

'Yes, dread. But I dunno where it der. I jus' 'ope dat Denise ain't down der. If she is I'll cry fe her. An' I dunno wha' Biscuit would do if he found out.'

'What a blowoh!'

'Den again,' Coffin Head muttered, watching the road, 'Biscuit would go after Nunchaks. Believe. 'Im don't go cuckoo too much, but if a man fucks wid his family, he would go nuts cadazy.'

# 20

# Brixtonian Females

## 10 March 1981

Janet Kay's 'Don't Feel No Way' mellow-canaried from Carol's hi-fi. Sitting in front of her dressing table mirror, she saw her reflection of rich dark skin and onyx-coloured eyes. I'm getting a friggin' worry line in my forehead, she groaned inwardly.

Dusk was preparing for night and the LED lights that peppered the stereo in the corner of the room, pin-pricked into the dark surroundings. Lovers rock records and cassette tapes were piled on the bed, alongside the latest issue of *Black Echoes* magazine. Looking over the head-rest of the bed was a Teddy Pendergrass poster, and on the opposite wall, above a dirty clothes basket, hung a framed painting of a calypso band. Upon the window-ledge stood a figurine of a black woman, carrying a basket on top of her head. The teak double-wardrobe, standing beside the dressing table, had two suitcases resting on top of it. Propped on the bedside cabinet within a cardboard frame was a Polaroid of Carol's friends, posing in front of the dodgem cars at Clapham Common fair last summer: Biscuit, Sharon, Brenton, Floyd, Carol, Coffin Head and Sceptic all had their arms draped around each other, displaying teenage exuberance and feisty confidence.

Sharon was standing behind Carol, working her hair into braids, talking as she tweezed. 'Bwai, your ends always break off, innit,' she complained. 'Your hair's too fine, man. No wonder your plaits don't stay in. Where d'you get it from? Your mudder?'

'Nah. Got it from my fader. He has ah liccle coolie 'pon his family side.'

'Yeah? He don't look like he has Indian in 'im.'

'Dat's cos he's slowly going a ball 'ead. You wanna see some of his old-time photos dem. His hair straight like anyt'ing. He didn't affe conk it or relax it like most man in his time.'

Sharon finger-scissored a generous helping of hair, admiring its texture and blackness. She combed through it before parting it into three, wishing she also had fine hair. 'Biscuit tell you 'bout Denise?'

'Yeah, I feel for 'im. But wha's Denise up to, man? How can she jus' walk out like dat an' don't come back. Bwai, she 'ave no sense.'

'It can't be as simple as dat,' Sharon argued, resting her fingers for a moment and shaking her head. 'Somet'ing mus' ah gwarn. I 'ear she an' her mudder 'ad some contention going on from time.'

'She still fool-fool though,' Carol insisted, pointing her

232

right index finger to her temple. 'She don't t'ink 'bout how she gonna yam an' keep roof over her head. Biscuit's going cuckoo wid nuff worries.'

'Like I say, somet'ing mus' ah gwarn . . . Biscuit never told you 'bout any cuss-cuss she an' her mudder might of 'ad?'

'Yeah, but it never sounded too serious. It was over a liccle business 'bout Denise getting money from somewhere.'

'Bwai, family business,' Sharon shrugged, shaking her head once more. She went back to work on Carol's hair.

'Oowww. You affe pull so hard?' Carol's face creased up in pain.

'Stop your complaining, sistren,' Sharon answered wearily, her fingers aching from an hour's work. 'You want me to finish dis?'

'Yeah, but don't brutalise my 'ead top, man.'

Sharon kissed her teeth but tried to be more gentle as she continued braiding.

'So,' Carol said mischievously, looking into the mirror and catching her friend's eye, 'you still fighting off Smiley? He seems well interested.'

'De only interest he's gonna get is from my tongue. De man don't understand no. Bwai, me nah know wha' school 'im go to, but his English is seriously basic . . . Can't even understand N.O.'

'Does Floyd know 'bout dis?'

'A liccle. But I won't tell 'im de full score cos der will be almshouse business. You know so how Floyd gets red-eye when ah nex' man tries a t'ing.' She sucked her teeth.

'It's dat. Him mek me laugh de way he gwarn some time.'

'Yeah, mek me laugh too. But at least it shows dat der is

some emotion der . . . Talking of emotion, I can't understand you an' Biscuit.'

'He's deep,' replied Carol, gazing at her faultless complexion again, while Biscuit's image made an appearance in her head. He's so sweet, she thought. And he treats me like there is no other good-looking girl on earth. 'I know he seriously likes me, he's made it clear. I jus' wish he could do somet'ing positive.'

'But do you really like *'im*?' Sharon demanded, gesturing with her hands.

Carol paused, not welcoming Sharon's interrogation. Even though Sharon was her best friend, she felt vulnerable revealing such feelings. Everyone in her posse knew she'd fancied Brenton for a long time, but when Brenton declined the obvious invitation to her heart, she felt humiliated. There was still a flicker of attraction for him, but time had dampened the flames, while her desire for Biscuit was growing like a tree. 'Sort of,' she finally answered, lowering her eyelids.

Sharon sensed her friend's hesitation. 'You know, Floyd tells me Biscuit don't even look 'pon any uder girl. He jus' wants you, sistren. He's got de love t'ing bad.'

'Yeah, I know.'

Sharon glanced at her friend's reflection, thinking she was keeping something from her. 'I'll tell you wha'. If you an' Biscuit ever 'ave somet'ing going, you nah 'affe worry 'bout 'im straying.'

'Yeah, I know.'

'Wid Floyd, all he has to see is a skirt an' ah naked calf an' I start fret. His mudder shoulda call 'im Flirt. Sometimes when we forward to a party or club, I feel like boxing 'im in his head-top. 'Member de last time we went to Nations? I t'ought his eye was gonna drop outta 'im 'ead when he sight dat leggo beast inna de red skimpy frock dat look like some kinda beachwear.'

'Den why d'you put up wid it?' asked Carol, turning to face her pal.

'Good question . . . I dunno. Maybe I t'ink I can control 'im. Like some kinda challenge. De t'ing is, when de posse ain't around 'im, believe me, he can be romantic an' t'ing. Las' Valentine's Day he invite me round his yard an' he 'ad all candles glowing an' t'ing.'

'Floyd lit candles!'

'Yeah. He stuck dem to some saucers. It made his flat look like a friggin' monk-house but de t'ought was der. Him also gi' me ah box of chocolates already opened wid de strawberry ones missing, an' den gi' me some table wine from Tesco's inna coffee mug.'

'Table wine from Tesco's! Nah, I can't believe dat.'

'Ah true, man. De wine tasted like piss-water but again de t'ought was der. Jah bless 'im.' She smiled a glorious smile. 'Him even put in a lovers rock tape an' ask me fe dance.' Janet Kay's 'You Bring The Sun Out' was bringing back sweet memories of their love-making on Valentine's night.

Carol's eyebrows heaved upwards in shock, almost disturbing Sharon's braiding. 'I affe see it to believe it,' she rejected.

Sharon tugged her friend's hair playfully. 'I feel so Biscuit would do dem t'ing fe you if you let 'im.'

'You're probably right. But I 'ate his hustling runnings. Can't go a dance widout Biscuit selling his herb.'

Sharon was about to say something but paused, thinking of her own battle to stop Floyd hustling. She guessed that at least eight out of ten black youths were hustling in some form or other. The other two out of ten were doing jobs they hated. Blinking, she tried to get away from her musings. 'You 'ear 'bout Monica? Her belly get fat.'

'Yeah, who's de baby fader?'

'Dat's de t'ing. She don't know a damn.'

'Wha' a palaver.'

'It could be Ironhead from the Doberman posse, or Elfego Barker, dat cruff who's always following Crucial Rocker sound in his one shirt dat he wears everywhere; Floyd was saying he get wet up de uder day . . . Den again, it could be Joker Smoker who pumped de seed, dat maaga yout' who always gets charge up at Sir Lloyd blues. He looks like an' carries on like Finnley. Bwai, wha' ah tribulation.'

Carol laughed. 'Poor Monica. She can pick her men, innit. Ironhead's a friggin' nutcase, Elfego Barker's always getting inna fight, an' when he ain't fighting he don't know 'bout de invention of deodorant, an' Joker Smoker's a friggin' trodding spliff. Man, wha' ah scandal.'

Sharon laughed out loud and had to place her hands on Carol's back to stop herself falling on to the dressing table. Carol was pushed forward, and almost kissed the hair-grease jar in front of her. 'Get off me you mad woman.'

Sharon stood up and held Carol's head within her palms. 'Look at de mirror,' she laughed. Carol saw two-thirds of her hair in plaits and the other third standing up in apparent shock. 'Who looks like de mad one?' Sharon giggled. 'Mebbe I should leave it like dat.'

'Don't you friggin dare,' Carol raised her voice, play-fully slapping her friend's hand.

Sharon, unable to control her chuckling, pulled up a plait from Carol's hair. 'I wonder if Biscuit's as long as dis?'

236

Trying to restrain herself from laughing, Carol turned around and grabbed hold of Sharon's neck with both hands, pretending to strangle her. Alton Ellis's 'You Make Me Happy' sweet-voiced from the stereo as the two friends fell on the floor in a mock fight, slapping each other on the backside.

A clap of the letterbox disturbed their mirth. Carol, comb in head, stood up and went downstairs, leaving a giggling Sharon in her bedroom. She opened her front door with a fading laugh on her features. A desolate Denise stood before her.

The girl's right cheekbone was swollen and dark, like the colour of a red apple. The right side of her bottom lip was inflated and drooped grotesquely over her chin. Her left eye was bloodshot and half closed. Her hair was dry and lack-lustre. She was wrapped in a dirty green trench coat, buttoned up to her neck. Carol was shocked, and for a minute she found words hard to come by as Denise avoided eye contact.

'I need somet'ing fe my period,' pleaded Denise in a defeated voice.

'Wha's 'appened to you, sistren?' questioned Carol, arms on her hips, scrutinising the wretch before her. 'You know so your brudder 'as been looking for you all over Brixton?'

'Look, me nah 'ave time. Can you gi' me somet'ing fe my period?'

'Come in, Denise, man,' Carol ordered, ushering with her right hand. 'We 'ave to chat 'bout dis.'

Denise peered into the hallway. 'Your people nah der-ya? Lincoln ain't der, is he?'

'No, my parents 'ave gone out, an' no, Biscuit ain't 'ere so. Come *in*.'

Denise followed Carol warily along the hallway and up the stairs. As Sharon saw them troop into the bedroom, she felt a pumping sensation inside her throat. Somehow, she knew that Denise was on the streets and she couldn't quite believe it had happened to someone so close to her. Poor girl, she said to herself.

Denise parked herself on the bed, dropping her gaze to the carpet as her eyes welled up with tears. She sensed the balmy smell of coconut oil and realised she hadn't greased her hair for more than a week. She couldn't remember the last time she had a cooked meal or had a proper night's sleep.

'Wha's 'appened to you?' asked Sharon. 'Who lick you? Why 'aven't you called 'ome yet? Biscuit's going cadazy wid worry 'bout you, y'know. Not to mention your mudder.'

'She don't care a friggin damn!' raged Denise. 'I'm probably up der wid Jesus on who she 'ates de most . . . Are you gonna gi' me a liccle money or wha'? I can't stay long.'

'Why don't I call Biscuit an' he will sort you out,' offered Carol. 'Whatever your story, he'll look after you.'

'No! Do dat an' I'm missing, believe. *Don't* say I was 'ere . . . Promise you won't call 'im.'

Carol looked over at Sharon, silently asking for the next move. Sharon nodded her head and pointed discreetly to the bed. Carol took this as a sign to keep Denise there for as long as possible.

'OK,' said Sharon. 'But can we tek you to de hospital? Get you checked out an' t'ing. Den we can do your hair.'

'No! I 'aven't got de friggin' time! Jus' 'elp me out dis one time an' I'll be back to check you quick time, wid de money back . . . I beg you, please don't tell Lincoln. I will sort myself out.'

238

Carol glanced over at Sharon again, thinking how Biscuit would react on seeing his sister in this state. Oh my God, he's gonna go schizo.

'Denise, man,' Sharon soothed, 'jus' sit down fe ah liccle an' I swear, wha' you tell us we won't repeat to anybody . . . Or you don't need to say anyt'ing, maybe you want a bath?'

'Can't you *'ear*,' Denise yelled, looking at the bedroom door. 'I ain't got de friggin' *time!*' She sounded desperate.

The room was choked by a sudden tension and the dire consequences that it foretold. Denise buried her head into the lapels of her coat as her two friends looked on gravely, both thinking that the sinful hands of Nunchaks had been at work. Sharon moved towards the crying teenager.

'Can't you jus' gi' me de friggin' money!' Denise screamed. 'Jus' gi' me de corn widout de inquest, dats all I'm asking . . . I'll pay you back when I can. An' don't boder judge me cos I know wha' you t'inking.'

Carol went to get her purse which was inside her bedside cabinet. Denise glanced through wet fingers at the photo of the posse, training her eyes upon her beloved brother. Carol plucked out a ten-pound note and handed it to the girl, who took it from her but avoided eye contact.

Once the tenner was banked within her inside coat pocket, Denise got to her feet and rapidly made for the door, escaping down the stairs. 'Please don't tell Biscuit,' she sobbed.

Sharon and Carol heard the front door close and studied each other. 'Frig my teenage days,' Sharon said quietly. 'Biscuit's temper gonna go bionic.'

Carol shook her head in resignation as various nightmare scenarios attacked her brain. 'I'll 'ave to tell 'im. If I don't he'll never forgive me. Besides, she needs 'elp, man. D'you t'ink we should call de police?'

Sharon's eyes responded in the negative. 'If de beast weren't so racist, den yes, we should go to dem. But do you really t'ink dey would do anyt'ing for a black girl who jus' run 'way? An' 'pon de street? Dey would jus' arrest her. Besides, if de police are gonna be called, we should leave it up to Biscuit.'

'Wha' did she mean when she said she's up der 'ated wid Jesus?'

'I ain't got a clue.'

Forgetting that her hair was half-braided, Carol pressed the stop button on the stereo. She caught her friend's gaze and their eyes exchanged fear. 'Y'know, Biscuit never get in too much fight, not like Brenton, but believe, when he gets to 'ear dat a man bus' up his sister, he'll be looking a neck to carve . . . I know 'im.'

# Truths and Rights

**21**

## 28 March 1981

A train rattled over the bridge crossing the High Street and sang violently to a halt at Brixton Station. No one got off. An unleafed newspaper was caught in a tail wind and a few pages ended up embracing the asphalt of the main road, flattened by a bus wheel. A wild-haired black man, who only had one and a half arms, leaned against the railings in front of the tube station, his face a picture of regret. Discovering the lingering scent of spoiled fruit, a limping hound snouted for his supper in the deserted market street.

The Town Hall clock had just chimed 11.15pm. Emerging from the Prince of Wales pub was a cool-stepping Brixtonian. Biscuit had just sold half an ounce

241

of herb to an Indian man he knew. As he walked to the bus stop, he promised himself that he would juggle no more.

Fifteen minutes later, he turned the key in his front door. As had been his habit for the past few weeks, he entered Denise's bedroom, hoping she might be there, playing her favourite lovers rock cassettes while practising her singing. At school, Denise had planned to form her own reggae group, he recalled. Sweet Milo, she had named her singing trio. The dream had come to an abrupt end when Pauline, one of the harmony singers, became pregnant, and the other girl, Panceta, moved to Neasden.

He found his sister's bedroom dark and empty, just like every other night. 'Denise, man,' he whispered, then to himself, 'Wha' de rarse you playing at?'

He moved on into the lounge where he found his mother nestling in the sofa, listening to a debate on the radio. The politicians and crime experts were discussing the Yorkshire Ripper murders and the performance of the police in the investigations. 'Me don't know why me boder cook if you gwarn come 'ome late every blasted night,' Hortense moaned. 'Me jus' see you get up, go out, an' come back when telly sign off.'

He nibbled his bottom lip, thinking his mother should be worrying about something else.

'Royston gone ah Aunt Jenny,' she informed him. 'It seem like 'im t'ink Aunt Jenny 'im mama now. 'Im nuh like stay at 'ome since Denise gone 'bout her business.'

'You should worry yourself 'bout where Denise der-ya.'

'Worry? Me nah kick her out!' Hortense raised her voice, dodging the accusing glare of her son. Her eyes were drawn to the floor, not wanting to reveal any signs of

242

guilt. 'She tek her two foot an' walk out wid vexness. Jus' like her fader she is.'

'Mummy, it's been *weeks*!' Biscuit sensed his mother's remorse and hardened his gaze. 'Don't you wonder where she der?'

'If your sister t'ink she cyan gwarn like big woman an' walk out from her 'ome, den she mus' feel it.' Hortense tried to hide her own fears, but suddenly remembered her father sending her away to her uncle. 'She jus' so impetuous . . . She knows deep down dat me waant her home.'

'*Does* she?' Biscuit walked up close to his mother, scarching her eyes for shame. 'She walked out of dis yard an' you never done nutten!' He felt a punch from his own regrets. 'Say somet'ing 'appened to her? You gonna blame God again an' not yourself?'

'Don't you t'ink I waant her back!' Hortense cried, getting to her feet and squaring up to hcr son. 'You nah see me bawl ah night-time an' LORD GOD! It's *killing* me dat Denise nuh come back 'ome yet. Don't t'ink you is de only one feeling it.'

'While she was 'ere, it never killed you den on 'ow you was treating her. You never bawl over her dcn. Ah puppy tears you ah show me!'

'Lincoln! Mind your tongue! You don't know wha' Denise mean tu me.'

He shook his head in contempt. 'Not much,' he answered coldly, glancing into the hallway as if expecting someone to enter the room. 'Dis is your daughter you're chatting 'bout'!' he hollered again, his frustration simmering and reaching his tongue. 'All over Brixton I've been looking fe her. Checking wid her friends an' people she knows! I was even t'inking 'bout forwarding to de beast. I'm going out of my friggin' 'ead, but all you can worry 'bout is wha' time I reach 'ome an' Royston staying at Aunt Jenny's!'

'Lincoln!' Hortense exclaimed, the shock of her son's raised voice penetrating her senses. 'Wha' do you expect me fe do?'

'TO BE A PROPER MUDDER TO HER! But dat's too late, INNIT.'

'I brought all you t'ree into dis world, an' believe me, it painful. An' me raise you all 'pon me own. Who are you fe tell me to be ah proper mudder! Don't t'ink you grow so big dat me cyan't wash out your mout' wid soap water.'

' 'Ave you ever t'ought why Denise gone? I'll tell you why. Cos she t'ink you 'ate her cos of her daddy. An' sometimes *me* believe it, too!'

'Lincoln! 'Ow cyan you speak such ah t'ing!' Hortense over-exaggerated, knowing her son was right. She dropped her sight to the carpet. 'Me try an' try wid you t'ree. An' it woulda easy if me jus' gi' you up to de social worker dem. But no, me try an' try. Now all you cyan do is run up your mout' 'bout t'ings you nah know. An' Denise decide wid her wisdom to tek her leave. *Dat's* all de t'anks I get . . . Me never did t'ink she would really go an' nuh come back.'

'*Dat's* no excuse. You've never said anyt'ing positive 'bout your one daughter. I 'ope you can live wid your conscience if anyt'ing 'appens to her.'

'So . . .' Hortense paused, realising she would never forgive herself if Denise came to harm. She mentally slammed the door on her guilt again. 'So it's my fault why your daddy dead?' She turned around and raised her arms, as if she was addressing the heavens. 'So it's my fault why Denise run 'way? An' Lord don't fling me down,

244

it probably my fault dat Judas betray de Lord.'

'You got one right,' Biscuit confirmed dryly.

'You t'ink you're so righteous, I don't wan' fe imagine where you get your money from, but you still ah lick me wid morality.'

'But you still tek wha' me gi' you t'ough, innit.'

'Bless me papa. Me nuh gwarn listen to your accusations any more dis-ya night. Me gone to me bed! An' when mornin' come you might show ah liccle respect to de woman who brought you inna dis world.' Hortense swabbed away her tears and steeled herself to look into Biscuit's eyes. She only managed it for three seconds while talking in a whisper. 'I 'ave never claimed dat I am perfect.'

Utterly defeated, she ambled slowly out of the room without looking back. Biscuit heard her bedroom door close gently. He collapsed into an armchair and wept for his family. He thought of Royston growing up with a sister who was a whore, and a brother who was a drug dealer. He despised himself and what he had become. No more! he told himself. From now on he would put his family first. Wha' would his mudder t'ink if she knew dat Denise was a whore? And the link he had with it all? Carol's account of how Denise had looked on that day she suddenly appeared at her home was the worst feeling he'd ever had to confront. I've got to get her back, he vowed to himself.

In the South London night sky, a stubborn thin cloud finally revealed a quarter crescent moon. The trees within Brockwell Park murmured to each other as if they did not want anyone to hear their business. The mild weather for the time of year had enticed the first spring gnats into the air. The irregular swishes of traffic on Tulse Hill didn't quite gel with the hooting of the owls. Two Brixtonians were sitting on a park bench at this hour: 2am.

'Coffin Head, man,' Sceptic addressed his spar. 'I've been jailhouse an' believe, you won't tek to it. Nuff battyman. Leggo dis idea of killing a beastman.'

'Char! It seem like you forget wha' dem did to you an' me. Friggin' pigs dem, all dey do is jus' brutalise us. Why do we affe tek it, man? Der going too far. I wonder 'ow many black yout' dey brutalise. Dey t'ink der so bad wid der government boot an' inna dem uniform. Friggin' uniform won't rarse stop a bullet.'

He delved inside his jacket pocket and his hand emerged with his piece of gun-silver metal. He trained his aim on a nearby tree and imagined it to be a policeman. 'Booyaka!', he cried. 'Fist to fist an' blade to blade days dem done. De *gun* tek over.'

Sceptic looked upon his friend with concern, wondering why Coffin Head couldn't just complain to his brethrens about the police beating he received, rant about it, then accept it as part of life for a black youth living in the inner city. 'Maybe you should forward 'ome fe a while,' he offered. 'Start yam some decent food an' t'ing. You an' Floyd don't cook. You can't t'ink right when you're yamming peanuts for breakfast an' cream cakes fe dinner, dread. An' radication mus' be tired of waiting 'pon your doorstep by now.'

Coffin Head put the gun back in his pocket. 'Went 'ome last night,' he replied. 'Stayed fe an' hour. My mudder wants me to move up Birmingham to rarted, where my uncle lives. Fuck dat shit. Last time my mudder took me der, de black people were seriously backward up der. Dey don't play up to date music, dem dress weird inna dem *Saturday Night Fever* slacks, an' dey can't even chat proper. Can't understand dem a damn. Char! A rarse elocution dem need. Fuck Birmingham, man.'

'It won't affe be fe too long. Jus' till you cool down ah liccle.'

'Cool down which part? I don't wan' fe cool down. Five renkin' beastman boot me up inna cell an' den dey boot me out 'pon street like I'm a rarse football. An' all you say is cool down! Fuck dat, man. Char! Sometimes you don't chat sense.'

'Quaker City comes from Birmingham sides, innit. You could go ah dance an' check dem out.'

'Quaker City? Dey come down to London wid der distorted sound wid der bass sounding like wardrobe dropping down staircase, to rarted. An' der speaker boxes look like de furniture for a shanty town, to rarted. An' dey play tune dat Moa Anbessa were spinning t'ree year ago. Even Slacker Rocker 'ave more style dan dem.'

'Der heavy t'ough.'

'De only t'ing heavy 'bout Quaker City is der trodder boots. Dem sound man look like der 'bout to climb mountain to rarted. An' der locks ain't neat like dem Moa Anbessa man.'

Sceptic accepted defeat on the Birmingham issue. He looked around himself. 'Remember dat day our posse was 'ere, chatting 'bout wha' we wan' fe be when we grow up?'

'Yeah. An' not one of us 'as never even got close. Beastman won't let us do nutten . . . Look at Denise, she was always chatting 'bout being a singer, now she's earning corn fe Nunchaks.'

Sceptic began rolling a spliff, catching a sad, far-off look in his friend's eyes. 'You can tell me man,' he prompted. 'She's always tickled your fancy, innit. Tell me, dread, how long 'ave you been sweet 'pon her?'

Coffin Head peered at the stars as a sudden shyness swept over him. Sceptic could read him well, he thought. He realised he probably exposed his feelings for Denise sometimes. It had hurt him bad when he heard of Denise's plight, and although he would never tell Biscuit, he had always known that Hortense would drive her out of the home. He had witnessed many times the constant arguments in the Huggins household, and this led him to believe that Hortense couldn't give a fuck about her daughter. He knew this helped fuel his wrath towards the police. 'Yeah,' he finally answered. 'I've always kinda liked her. She's got it all, man. Safe. Her facetyness jus' gi's me a . . .' he tailed off, as Denise's current predicament overwhelmed him.

Sceptic dropped his head in sympathy, passing on the burning joint. 'Lick dis. Bought it off Biscuit yesterday. He says he's giving up de juggling.'

'Well' 'im 'ave to. For he knows dat his juggling carries ah portion of de blame for all dese tribulations. An' I'm not innocent eider . . .' Coffin Head felt a guilt within him.

'Blowoh,' Sceptic cried. 'Frig my days, man. Worries never end.'

# Enter the Pimp Don

## 30 March 1981

The smoke of a burning hash and ganga spliff dragon-breathed from a greying glass ashtray, looking for an open window through which to escape. A bare light-bulb illuminated the spider-web-like cracks in the white-washed walls. A crudely built five-foot speaker box lay on its side, a wad of ten-pound notes upon it. Next to the cash were two lighters, both see-through, one tinted black and the other blue. A simple wooden chair, placed in the corner of the room, was draped with a black skirt, burgundy blouse and a woman's underwear. The only other item of furniture in the room was a double bed with an elaborate pink-coloured head-rest. A Chinese-eyed black girl, sporting extensive make-up and burgundy coloured lipstick was naked underneath a flower-patterned quilt. She looked with controlled lust at the tall bare-backed man parked at the end of the bed, studying him as he sucked on his spliff. Just above the waistband of his slacks, the girl noticed the fringes of an ugly scar. I wonder what's below his trousers, she mused.

Nunchaks took a heavy toke of the joint before turning around to face the girl. 'Lie 'pon your belly. Me nah like look 'pon ah girl when I man do my t'ings.'

The girl did as she was ordered. Nunchaks climbed on the bed, declining to take off his trousers. The girl heard him unzip his flies and felt him spreading her legs and roughly palming her backside. 'Can't we play a little . . . Y'know, get me going an' t'ing,' she suggested.

'Shut yer mout', bitch. Ah privilege yer should be feeling.'

Nunchaks pulled the quilt off and threw it to the floor. He then mounted the girl's buttocks, and without warning started ram-rodding away, not listening to his partner's yelps of pain. When he had satisfied himself he zipped up his flies and went to relight his burning cocktail. 'Don't boder mek ah bloodclaat mess 'pon de bed. Customer don't like to spend der corn an' find dutty bed.'

The girl rolled off the bed, keeping her legs tight together, and found a box of tissues resting on the window-sill. She chanced a glance in Nunchaks' direction and observed him playing with the black lighter, flicking it on and off; this habit always disturbed her. 'Do I affe work tonight? I'm really tired, an' I did mek over a hundred last night.'

Nunchaks got to his feet and ambled over to the girl, still clicking his lighter. With his other hand, he raised an index finger and stroked the young woman's face, starting

250

from the right eyebrow to the corner of her mouth. He looked on her with total contempt. The girl's insides quaked, for although she had had sex with Nunchaks many times, this was the most intimate he had ever been with her. She imagined his finger to be a long knife, searching for a suitable place to carve. 'An' you're gwarn to mek ah nex' 'undred tonight,' he whispered. 'De customer dem like you, dat's why me gi' you de privilege.'

He groped under the bed and his right hand emerged with his name-sake weapon. Two lengths of wood, each a foot long, encased inside brutal steel tubes with a five-inch chain linking them. He hung it around his neck and addressed his whore once more. 'You ever see de *Towering Inferno*? Baddest film Steve McQueen ever mek. You remind me of de blonde 'ead bitch who 'ad ah sex session wid ah married man while de building ah burn. Bot' ah dem get burn up wid de girl falling t'rough de window an' drop to her deat' miles 'pon miles below.'

Opening the door, he heard the strains of the Gong's 'Pimpers Paradise' discharging from another bedroom. He strutted along the hallway to a candle-lit living room, wallpapered in an orange and yellow pattern. Upon a tangerine-coloured sofa he saw two of his whores hoover-ing cigarettes while watching as Kojak pondered a crime on the television. Both were dressed in short skirts, white tights and chest-gripping tops, and they acknowledged their boss with plastic smiles. 'You two working 'pon Bedford Hill tonight,' he decreed. 'Don't even bloodclaat t'ink 'bout clocking off till you mek ah 'undred each, y'hear me?'

The girls nodded in unison, getting to their feet while contemplating another night strolling the South London streets. They followed Nunchaks to the front door where the leather-coated Muttley was waiting, pulping his gum with his powerful jaws. Crowned by a black flat-cap, his shoulders seemed too wide to pass through the doorway. The pimp collected his cashmere coat from a peg as he briefed his minder.

'Bedford Hill me gone, me brethren. When Denise come, tell her fe wait fe Ratmout'. She cyan work 'pon de Line tonight, I t'ink she ready now. De white customer dem gonna love her to de bone . . . She young an' fresh an' dats wha' dem like.'

Muttley nodded.

'Ratmout' should soon come. Tell 'im to cut up de herb fine an' weigh it. After dat tell 'im to dry it out ah liccle 'pon de 'eater. Den after dat, he cyan tek Denise down de Line. Tell 'im fe keep ah good clock 'pon her an' be selective 'pon de client dem. Me nuh waan no ragamuffin wid her. Remember, go wid de money an' de money is inna white 'and wearing ah suit.'

'Yes, boss.' Muttley walked into the hallway and disappeared into one of the bedrooms.

Nunchaks departed the flat and peered into the settling night from his fourth floor vantage point. He saw the towering chimneys of Battersea Power Station, and beyond this, bisecting the horizon and blinking red, the Post Office Tower. Within a year, he promised himself, they will fear my name 'pon de uder side of de river. He fondly looked down to his Cortina Mark Two, thought about his future and saw it was prosperous. But the fear of being penniless squatted in a dark corner of his mind. He remembered running away from home when he was only fifteen and living in a squat, full of junkies. The memory of waking up in a Brixton slum, not knowing when he was going to eat, still haunted him to this day. He had learned fast; running small errands for local hood-lums provided money for his supper, and snatching handbags outside Brixton Tube Station clothed him in nice garments.

He recalled the Physical Education lessons he had had at school. The other boys would recoil at the sight of the burn scars on his thighs, and then they would whisper in huddles, glancing at the atrocity. He pleaded with the teacher to allow him to abstain from games, but was told to ignore the jibes and pay them no attention. His mother would say the same.

His life changed when a girl he asked out said no because she didn't want it known that she was going out with the 'burn-up guy', although she said he was alright. That moment had happened fifteen years ago, but Nun-chaks remembered it as if it were just last week. No bloodclaat leggo-beast gonna mek 'im feel dat way again, his emotions insisted.

'Get your backside inna de car,' he commanded. 'An' nah forget to walk wid ah roll. Wine up your hips dem to mek man hungry fe you, y'hear me. An' *smile*. Gi' dem ah smile to mek dem t'ink dey are de best-looking men inna de world. Charge more fe a bareback rider, £5 more. An' don't waste time wid talk. Jus' fock, mek dem shoot dem load an' get 'pon de street again . . . *No* talk. I bought new boxes of tissues today, *use* dem.'

'We know de drill, Nunchaks,' one whore sighed. 'Don't 'ave to keep telling us.'

'Shut your mout', bitch.'

The two prostitutes nodded warily. Muttley reappeared and closed the front door as the two girls made their way along the balcony, whingeing about the cold. Nunchaks placed his weapon inside a custom-built holster within his coat and thought about the money Denise would earn for him. 'She could mek ah 'undred fifty ah night, to rarse claat. Ah ripe cherry dat.'

# The Brixtoniad

## 6pm, 10 April 1981

Rage! screamed a white T-shirt worn by a black youth who had just entered Brixton market. The traders and stallholders were thankful for the sunny weather that blessed the day. A West Indian lady kissed her teeth as the man selling yams and green bananas politely refused any more custom, saying he wanted to go home. Two school-boys playing tag through the market barged into a head-wear stand. Four ladies' hats dropped to the ground. 'You little bastards!' cried a middle-aged white woman, raising her fist. A white teenager clad in a black helmet and knee pads, travelling on a skateboard, skilfully dodged the many empty cartons and boxes on the street. The sound of crashing pots and pans reverberating on the pavement came from beside the Boots store. Next door to the hat stall, a young woman was negotiating the price of a fine, burgundy dress.

'Eight ninety-nine? I'll gi' you seven fifty. It's all I 'ave. Come on, man! I'm 'aving a birt'day party tomorrow.'

'Oh, go on with you then,' the trader yielded. 'As it's your birt'day, give me the seven fifty.'

'T'anks, the lady smiled, passing on the cash. 'You're so sweet.'

The trader adjusted the collar of his shirt and returned the smile, only to see his customer turn around to inspect a selection of hats.

Most of the stallholders had outstripped their usual weekly sales targets, and they were full of hopes and expectations. It was the end of the day, and with contented smiles the marketers were packing up their wares, and even giving away single fruits to passing children. 'So it's the Prince of Wales, is it?' a flat-capped trader shouted to his peers.

'Yeah, 'Arry,' someone answered. 'First round is yours!'

Late afternoon shoppers mingled with returning commuters, offloading from Brixton Tube Station and forming disorganised queues at the bus stops. The rush-hour traffic was stalled by two male drivers who saw each other across the road. Their cars were pointing in different directions, but still they climbed out and began to converse on the central reservation. Other motorists palmed their horns, only to be greeted with Jamaican expletives. The record shops were still open, and local sound men and reggae heads jostled and frenzied for the latest releases, nodding their hatted-heads when a tune they heard licked their pleasure.

The doom-mongers and philosophers, some standing

on discarded fruit boxes, were out in force, competing to gain an audience. Most people ignored them, but a few offered them curious glances that only served to inflame their Armageddon rhetoric. Beggars and finger-flexing, eye-shifting pick-pockets patrolled the steps leading down to Brixton Tube Station, scenting a sympathetic do-gooder or a careless person in a rush. Bad bwai commuters leaped over the ticket barrier with as much concern as they would side-step a banana skin. The aged West Indian ticket collector simply didn't care.

On Atlantic Road, people were entertained by a white bare-backed, dreadlocked man, skanking outside the reggae stall just in front of the entrance to the arcade. His reddened bare feet didn't seem to balk at the heat radiating from the asphalt as he performed some sort of twisty, knee-jerking movement. Sceptic was one of the spectators, bobbing his head to a dub tune while eyeing a passing girl. Other onlookers clapped their hands and laughed with the dancer. Suddenly, the tramp halted his jigging, his attention drawn by something occurring further down the road.

Sceptic followed the white dread's gaze and saw a black youth running down the pavement, passing the Atlantic pub like he was escaping from hell. 'What a blowoh!'

With one hand clutching his breast, the terrified youth looked behind him and panicked when he saw a pursuing constable. Sceptic noticed that the guys he had seen in the record shops were now all around him. 'Wha's 'appening, Scep?' one asked.

'I dunno.' He looked again. 'Blowoh! De bwai's cut.'

Sidewalk trodders stilled their steps; some offered a glance and carried on walking, thinking what's new. 'Go 'way, Babylon,' someone yelled as the policeman caught

257

up with the reeling teenager. The officer immediately realised he had a gravely wounded youngster in his grasp. 'Release 'im!' a teenager shouted behind Sceptic. The officer looked around in alarm, realising what the assembling black youths must be thinking. While holding on to the bleeding youth, he radioed for assistance, wanting to get the victim to a hospital as soon as possible.

The adolescent repelled the officer's touch, thinking he was being arrested. 'Babylon wet de sufferer!' a black man screamed, walking out of the menswear shop with a box of new shoes in his hands.

The injured youth squirmed away from the policeman's clutches and staggered into Coldharbour Lane. Sceptic could hear disapproving protests all around him from a rapidly gathering crowd. He found himself being caught in a mini-stampede up Coldharbour Lane, halting the rush-hour traffic. He heard a car horn as the mob around him wondered where the blooded youth was. 'Where 'im der?'

'Where de beast go?'

'Dey coulda kill de bwai!'

'Bloodclaat beast.'

'Beast haffe dead!'

'Wha' ah gwarn?' asked a beret-topped youth, coming out of the fried chicken takeaway, crocodiling a wing.

'Radication wet up a ghetto yout',' replied Sceptic, trying to look above the heads in front of him. Feeling himself being jostled, he took in the angry faces around him and thought about making a run for it before things got too serious. He saw the DJ, Pancho Dread, his sombrero conspicuous in the crowd, and decided to stay with the flow, not wanting to be called a chicken.

Suddenly he saw a cab bearing the injured youth, who

was flanked by police officers, emerge from Rushcroft Road and head west on Coldharbour Lane. 'Free de yout'!' someone cried. Everyone roared their approval. Within a short second, Sceptic found himself being swept along towards the taxi. Oh my days, he thought. Dis ain't 'appening. He could hear police sirens approaching, and jerking his head to either side, saw ghetto youths picking up bottles, bricks, milk crates and bits of wood. He could hardly see in front of him but reckoned that the cab was surrounded and that the injured youth had been freed from the clutches of the police.

Biscuit, who was in Electric Avenue looking for Denise, heard the commotion. He ran to see what was happening and couldn't believe his eyes as he reached Coldharbour Lane. Youths were hurling missiles at the police vehicles that were rushing to the scene. A car driven by a black man with a youth in the passenger seat, his T-shirt reddened, almost ran Biscuit over. 'Bloodfire!' he gasped. 'Revolution ah start.'

He quickly realised that police reinforcements were coming from the direction of Brixton High Street and north of Atlantic Road, pushing the rioters by the Atlantic pub and up into Railton Road. Thinking he might well be arrested if he stayed where he was, he ran to join the missile-throwing mob, covering his head with his bomber jacket. The sounds of police sirens was almost unbearable as he found himself rubbing shoulders with a now hatless Pancho Dread. 'Wha' ah gwarn?' he asked.

'Babylon cut a yout'.'

They both heard shouting coming from further up Railton Road. Biscuit turned around and saw some people he knew – bad men, Front Line idlers, drama seekers and herb traders, all marching to join the mob. He wondered if Nunchaks was nearby. In the corner of his eye, he saw Sceptic launching a bottle at the now formed police line, twenty yards into Railton Road. He went over to him, pushing his way through the throng. 'Scep!'

'Murder!' Sceptic hollered at the police, caught up in an adrenaline rush. 'Murder!'

'Scep!'

Sceptic looked to his right.

'Come, man,' Biscuit advised. 'Let's go up an' bus' a right into Kellet Road. Dis place is gonna be swarming wid de beast soon. I dunno 'bout you but I don't wanna be inna cell tonight!'

They went over to the pavement, crouching low, wanting to see what was happening ahead. Biscuit decided to stand on a red milk crate. He saw a three-quarter brick obliterate a police van's windscreen and a constable being floored by a Red Stripe bottle. A police panda car was horribly disfigured, all its windows smashed. He glanced to his right and saw a variety of missiles javelined into the air, aimed at the police line. Although he wanted to get away from the scene, it was exhilarating to be a part of this madness. His veins were filling with adrenaline and he joined in a chant. 'BABYLON HAFFE DEAD.'

He saw another police van slowly approach the rioters, as if daring to drive right through them. One protester launched himself on to the bonnet of the van like a body-slamming wrestler. The driver turned sharply and shrugged him off. 'MURDER, MURDER!' Biscuit screamed with the mob. He observed the van assailant tending to his scrapes on the road while being welcomed with glinting handcuffs. In response, Biscuit saw the rabble renew their missile assault with vigour, throwing anything they could lay their hands on. He caught sight of Sceptic tearing down some fencing. Pancho Dread and others were levelling a knee-high brick wall. The policemen could do nothing but raise their forearms in defence. A few of them commandeered dustbin lids to protect themselves. Biscuit heard sirens coming from behind him, and his eyes blinked at flashing blue lights. Frig my living days, he said to himself. I'm removing.

He jumped down from the milk crate and looked for Sceptic, finding him on the other side of the road about to launch a Coke bottle at the swelling police line. 'Come,' he ordered. 'Now!'

They darted into Kellet Road and from there made their way to Floyd's flat. They noticed that the entire area was gridlocked with traffic and police vehicles were racing everywhere. As they walked they could feel the smog of uprising in the air and wondered what would happen now.

Several hours later, Sceptic was eyeing a pot upon a pool table in a pub near Brixton Prison. Middle-aged black and white men sat at the bar talking of the day's riot. Two young women, their faces heavily caked in make-up, sipped on their Pink Lady's, nattering quietly. Three elderly black men, sitting around a table, downing pints of Guinness, pondered on the domino sticks they held in their left hands. A white teenager had just won the jackpot on the one-armed bandit; drinkers looked around on hearing the chink, chink of the coin dispenser. The barman, a twenty-something, long-haired white man, constantly looked out the front window while wiping a pint glass dry. 'They're still going up and down,' he said to those at the bar. 'When we close up I'll think I'll take a cab home. All these bloody police vans about . . .'

'Wha' ah blowoh!' Sceptic exclaimed to his audience, which included Coffin Head and Floyd. 'Man an' man were flinging all kinds of t'ings. Beastman 'ad to tek cover. Blowoh! I couldn't believe wha' me sight today. Beastman inna SPG wagon tried to run over a yout', believe. Nuff yout'man were flinging rockstone an' brick like unruly pickney 'pon coconut shy to rarted.'

'Wha' appened to de yout' who get wet up,' asked Floyd, perched on a bar stool and chalking his cue.

'Word 'pon street says de yout' dead when 'im reach hospital. An' it's Babylon man who gore 'im, y'know.'

'Char! Dey get 'way wid anyt'ing, innit,' Coffin Head scowled, circling around the table to negotiate the shot Sceptic had left him. 'It seem like booting up yout' inna cell ain't nuff fe dem. Now der boring up black yout' 'pon street.' He addressed the cue ball and powered home a long pot. 'We should tek a rarse gored chest fe ah chest. Mek dem t'ink twice 'bout troubling us.'

Sceptic looked upon his pool rival with a deep concern, then glanced over to Floyd who was sipping his lager and sucking a cigarette. Coffin Head parked in his chair, paying no attention to Sceptic's play. He wished he'd been there to take up arms with the other rioters and fling some rockstone and brick in a beastman's direction.

'Coff!' Sceptic clamoured. 'It's still your shot, you jus' sink a ball, innit.'

'Oh yeah. Me forget 'ow *bad* me is at dis game.'

'Wha' 'appened to Biscuit?' Floyd asked. 'Where did he step to? He said earlier he'd meet us in de pub.'

'He might 'ave gone round Carol's, an' he did say he might check out Yardman. See if he knows where Nunchaks brothel der-ya.'

'You know so if he finds out, we'll 'ave to step wid 'im,' stated Coffin Head, poker-faced.

'We'll come to dat when it comes,' answered Floyd, the tension evident in his voice.

Sceptic wanted to change the subject. 'Bwai, wha' ah blowoh. Nuff yout' say der forwarding to Brixton tomorrow an' see wha' ah gwarn. I know so I'm stepping down der from morning. Brixton getting hot to rarted.'

'Der's gonna be nuff beast 'pon street tomorrow,' warned Floyd.

'*Good*,' said Coffin Head, missing his shot but not really giving a damn.

'Bwai, you sound like Mafia man to rarted,' observed Floyd.

Sceptic stared at Coffin Head with scared eyes, waiting for his reply.

'You affe gwarn like Mafia man yes,' Coffin Head said. 'If dey do you somet'ing, den you affe lick dem 'arder dan dey lick you. Renkin' beastman, I 'ope at least one ah dem get a brick inna 'im temple an' ketch coma to rarted.'

'Bwai, Coff, you're getting well militant, innit,' said Floyd, thinking the police beating had fucked his friend up a little.

'You 'ave to, innit,' Coffin Head replied. 'A serious survival dis. Sen' dem to de rarse gravedigger inna box before dey sen' us. Char!'

Floyd munched on his crisps, thinking the beastman boots had inflicted more damage upon his friend than he had first thought. Coffin Head only thought of tomorrow. Yeah, tomorrow I might get my chance, he mused. Yeah, tomorrow's de day.

Next morning, Coffin Head emerged from his sleeping bag at 10am. He pulled on his trousers, slipped on a red

Adidas T-shirt and went to see if Floyd was up. His flatmate's bed was unoccupied and joint butts filled the bedside ashtray. 'Friggin' ginall,' he cursed. 'He 'ad a draw on 'im last night.'

In twenty minutes or so, Coffin Head was ready to seize the day. He stood still, pondering how he was gonna carry his gun. He wanted to place it somewhere secure; it wouldn't look too cool if he was running 'way from de beast an' de gun drop, he thought. He decided to wear his waist-coat bodywarmer. The spacious zip pockets in the lining would be a good place to mask my 45, he reasoned, even though the jacket might prove a little warm in the current climate.

After downing a mug of tea and several Digestive biscuits, he set off towards central Brixton, his gun close to his chest.

The pavements of Brixton were teeming with urban life, and Coffin Head found that every posse had a presence. He also noticed the increased attendance of the police, walking their beats nervously while fish-eyeing the rabble. 'They might as bleedin' well move Scotland Yard to Brixton,' commented a woman who passed him at a road crossing.

Sweat began to ooze from Coffin Head's armpits as the reality of his vengeance mission struck home. If any beastman stops you on sus, den jus' chip, he told himself. As he turned into Coldharbour Lane, the thin sprouts of hair above his top lip became moist. He felt sweat running down his temples and palmed it away. Sensing that eyes were trained on him, he walked swiftly to the Soferno B record shack where he hoped to find one of his own posse. Opposite the record shack, the West Indian barber shop was alive with prediction and bravado. Many black faces looked out of the windows. The usually vocal fruit and veg trader, who was situated under the bridge at the junction of Coldharbour Lane and Atlantic Road, was subdued, his eyes alert.

The sight of Floyd, Brenton and Sceptic standing outside the packed reggae shop made Coffin Head's heart beat easier. 'Wha'appen, Floyd, Brenton, Scep,' he greeted, noticing the many youths idling around, expecting something to happen. 'Wha' ah gwarn?'

'Nutten,' replied Floyd. 'Man an' man are jus' staring out de beast dem when dey pass.'

'The beast would be fool to start anyt'ing today,' said Brenton, nodding his head to Dennis Brown's 'Slave-driver', booming out from the shop. 'Look how many yout's in Brixton today.'

'Yeah, I know,' said Coffin Head, looking east along Coldharbour Lane at the stepping posses coming into central Brixton.

Until the Lambeth Town Hall clock struck one, Brixtonian youths debated on what might happen on this day, and when a pinch of hunger beset them, they satisfied themselves with meat Jamaican patties from more than happy vendors. They washed these down with cans of Special Brew and Tennants.

By 1.30pm, Biscuit had arrived with Sharon and Carol, the two girls filled with curiosity rather than the need for drama. He wondered if he'd see Denise on this day.

The crew greeted and nodded to almost every peer they knew, sometimes seeing someone for the first time since schooldays. Meanwhile, the mist of tension was thickening by the minute. 'I'm gonna check out if de white dread dancer is performing today,' announced Sceptic. 'Coming, Coff?'

'Yeah, might as well,' answered Coffin Head. 'Getting bored jus' standing up 'ere so.'

The two friends made their way to Atlantic Road, where they had to walk near the kerb to avoid the congestion of the pavements. 'Frig my days,' said Sceptic. 'Brixton *ram*.'

At 2pm, they saw two young police officers walking down from Railton Road. Immediately, they drew attention from every youth on the street. The policemen decided to question the black owner of a cab, parked outside the A & M car hire on Atlantic Road.

'What a blowoh,' exclaimed Sceptic. 'Dey 'ave got nuff front!'

'Der friggin' mad,' replied Coffin Head, noticing that youths were spilling out of the market arcade to see what would happen next.

'Go' 'way, Babylon!' cried a heavily bearded dread.

Coffin Head and Sceptic joined a crowd of up to 40 youths who gathered on the pavement outside the A & M car hire. '*Remove, ya!*' a youth wearing a black track-suit top demanded. Next door to the taxi office, the All Star Takeaway emptied as the officers, arrogantly ignoring the assembling hordes, searched the car for drugs or any other incriminating evidence. The cloud of uprising had now become heavy and was about to pour its contents upon the streets.

Cries of objection stung the air, and one black youth stepped into the scene, leant on the allegedly suspect car and stared at the officers with absolute contempt. He pushed up his face, cut his eyes and kissed his teeth. Coffin Head and Sceptic looked on as the crowd wondered how the police would react. The two policemen looked at each other before quickly arresting the youth

266

who mocked their authority. 'Yu racist bloodclaat!' screamed a voice from above. Everyone looked up and saw various youths on the roof of the All Star Takeaway. 'Babylon mus' dead!' the man in the track-suit top shouted.

Coffin Head and Sceptic joined in the protests as they heard the Cool Ruler's 'Mr Cop' playing from an upstairs window. '*Cool down your temper, Mr Cop!*' the mob sang, its members expanding from every walkway and arcade.

The officers hurriedly radioed for assistance. '*Get here now! Right now!*'

Heads fought for space in second-floor windows as the owner of a butcher shop hurriedly slammed his shutters. Coffin Head saw Brenton join the mob, and out of the corner of his eye, he saw Biscuit, Carol and Sharon running with many others towards Railton Road.

A police van, swelling with officers, hot-wheeled into the theatre with the idea of taking the arrested youth away. At once it was surrounded by shouting youths. They rocked the van from side to side, trying to tip it over. The officers inside hastily moved away from the windows. Sirens came from every direction. The crowd surged. Sceptic lost his footing. Coffin Head began to kick the side of the van, and others copied him. Brenton saw a man pick up a half-brick. As Sceptic felt a footprint on his head, he heard a shattering sound. Petrified shouts came from within the van. Another brick landed on the vehicle's bonnet. Coffin Head could see that something had smashed through the window of the vehicle's rear door.

'Babylon haffe dead!'

'Murder!'

'Kill dem, kill dem!'

Somehow, the van managed to escape, screeching away, not caring whether motorists or pedestrians got in the way. The van ran over Floyd's right foot, near to the Atlantic pub, and he fell to the ground. Biscuit had run into Coldharbour Lane, and was standing outside Woolworth's with Carol and Sharon. He scanned the crowd, hoping he might see Denise, but picked out Floyd instead. '*Stay* here,' he ordered. 'I'm gonna see if Floyd's alright.' Going back to the junction of Atlantic Road, he could hear the smashing of shop windows all around him.

On hearing the almost deafening sound of what seemed like a thousand sirens, the main body of rioters had retreated to the junction of Mayall Road and Railton Road. Coffin Head and others ran into an off-licence and helped themselves to bottles of all shapes and sizes. The man behind the counter stood still, utterly dumb-struck. Sceptic was gathering bricks from the crumbling walls of an abandoned terrace. Pancho Dread, his locks free of any hat, was putting stones and small debris into a football sock. Brenton was standing in the middle of the road, looking down Atlantic Road, ignoring the sounds of breaking masonry all around him. Barrabas was standing behind Brenton, testing out his flick-knife. Onlookers peered out of upstairs windows, following the same sight path as Brenton, and a few of them took photos. Shop-owners thought it best to close business early, and in a panic began to board up their shop-fronts in any way possible.

Brenton saw the police reinforcements make their beach-head at the junction of Coldharbour Lane and Atlantic Road. He had never seen so many police vehicles in his life, and judging by the sirens there were more to come. He sensed the unease of the crowd as the police formed themselves into a line and started advancing. 'MURDER!' screamed a youth. A second later, a barrage of missiles darkened the afternoon sun. The sound of bottles smashing on the ground and masonry colliding against vehicles filled the atmosphere. Coffin Head had noticed that Molotov cocktails were being prepared by some residents. Yardman Irie, dressed in green army garb, threw a lump of wood into the police lines. 'ARMA-GEDDON!' he screamed.

The police cowered under the deluge, some officers sustaining wounds to their faces and forearms. They decided to charge the mortar throwers, keeping their heads low. Sceptic was one of the first to turn on his heel and leg it into Kellet Road. Some went with him, throwing missiles at cars while shouting with adrenaline-pumped vigour. Others ran into Saltoun Road, taking out their anger on the vehicles parked there. Coffin Head and Brenton remained where they were. They saw the first Molotov cocktail being launched into the air and smash into the police ranks. As it hit the ground, it ignited and caught alight, causing panic within the police lines. 'JUDGEMENT DAY!' yelled Yardman Irie, grabbing a vessel of promised fire and throwing it. As Coffin Head looked to his right at one of the terraced houses that was supplying this new weapon, he wondered who the fuck was organising it.

Within seconds, he had joined with the Molotov cock-tail throwers, and when he saw that the police were backing up to see to their casualties, his whole body was charged with a weird elation he couldn't describe. He noticed that in their retreat, the police had left behind a van. Smiley, who was dressed in a T-shirt that showed a black fist clutching barbed wire, topped by a black beret, ran to the vehicle with about thirty others. They turned the van on its side with glee, smashing the windows and concaving the bodywork. Coffin Head joined the roar of acclaim when Smiley and his band returned to the main body of rioters.

Brenton, with twenty other malcontents, ran to a small building site that was encircled by corrugated aluminium sheets. He noticed that a few white guys were with him. Together, they tore down the sheets and before them were untold bricks and pieces of wood. While gathering missiles, he sensed a strong burning sensation in the air. He looked down the road and saw the Windsor Castle pub engulfed in flames. He paused and looked on in disbelief. He then became aware of something burning in Kellet Road, but couldn't see what it was. He heard protests from every direction and guessed that there was rioting in all the surrounding streets.

Back at the mob front line, Coffin Head coughed and wiped his streaming eyes. Peering through the smoke, he could see that the cars that lined Railton Road were being drained of their petrol then set alight. He wondered where Sceptic had run to as he heard some residents banging with hammers, boarding up their front windows.

Smiley, who had again encroached on the police lines, saw officers with reddened and bleeding faces. Then he heard sirens of different tones coming from north, south, east and west. Flashing blue lights forced him to blink rapidly. Brenton, gaining a vantage point on a lamp-post, saw that traffic in the area had come to a complete halt, except for emergency vehicles racing to the arena. He lowered his sight and observed a senior ranking police officer trying to quell the anarchy by talking through a loud-speaker. There was a surreal pause as rioters wondered what to make of it.

'*Remove, ya!*' a youth yelled, pointing his finger.

'*Killer beast!*'

'*Murderer!*'

Brenton saw a pair of arms sellotape an image of Che Guevara inside a second-floor window as the missile throwing resumed. As he was about to jump down from the lamp-post, he saw a number 2 bus in the distance, heading for central Brixton. 'Fuck my days!'

Halfway down the road, the driver stopped and stared in complete shock as he realised he was driving into a war zone. For a short moment, he observed the raging battle in acute astonishment, then he gathered his senses, told his passengers that his bus was concluding its journey and suggested to them that they make their own way back to Herne Hill. On seeing the smoke billowing into the horizon, and a crazed rabble flinging all and sundry into the air, the passengers quickly agreed.

Coffin Head saw a member of the Dorset Road posse, Olmek Maya, wearing an Arsenal football shirt, hot-step to the bus with four others. One of them wrenched the keys off the driver, and before Coffin Head wondered what Olmek's crew would do, the big red vehicle was put into gear and charged towards the police line. He bottomed the accelerator and accepted the baying roars of approval by giving a clenched fist salute. 'MURDERRRR!'

A policeman, noticing the approaching red threat, and pissed off with being a target in a mortar shy, picked up a brick and hurled it into the bus's front windscreen. The double-decker swerved, wheel-spun and annihilated someone's front wall. A woman's head popped out of an

271

upstairs window. She stared unblinking at the devastation, then looked up to the heavens, offering a prayer.

By now, insurrection had taken hold of the streets. Fire and ambulance crews were attacked with no apology. Cars everywhere became unwilling beacons as buildings felt the petrol bombs. The heat rose as policemen wiped away rivulets of blood and sweat. Infernos spread to nearby roads as fire vehicles were abandoned and left to the mercy of the mob.

While running down Saltoun Road, Sceptic saw a step-ladder being arsoned as an elderly black man looked out of his blackened bedroom window, clutching a bible in his hands. The streets were carpeted with broken bottles, jagged bricks and masonry as the putrid aroma of expiring vehicles blended with the air.

Biscuit, with Floyd, Sharon and Carol, had helped themselves to new garments from shops in central Brixton. They couldn't believe that the police were offering no resistance. Biscuit glimpsed Herbman Blue boarding up his premises while his crew made their escape up Rushcroft Road.

The windows of every shop that skirted the High Street, Atlantic Road and the adjacent streets, had been smashed to oblivion. A middle-aged white lady ambled up Brixton Hill, holding a baby in her left arm while pushing a pram that held a new television. Sweet-bwais tried on clothes in deserted menswear shops as women fought over gold in a wrecked jeweller's. A suited man sat on a kerb and burst into tears as his shop was emptied of all garments; beside him on the pavement was a new pair of boxer shorts. Ten yards away was a headless tailor's dummy. Woolworth's, situated in the High Street, was not immune to the looters' lust. Food shelves became vacant and tills were pillaged. Stereo systems marched out of the store upon people's shoulders as shop assistants watched in dread. Armfuls of clothes disappeared in all directions as security staff cowered in back rooms. Inside Boots, the pharmacist locked himself into his back room as looters stocked up on cold remedies, face creams, toothpaste, soap and anything else they could lay their hands on.

Marketers hastily boxed up their goods while hungry beggars raided butcher shops and the spicy chicken takeaway. A small boy, separated from his mother, picked up a melted policeman's helmet and tried it on for size. Bible thumpers jumped off their soap boxes and scattered while their cousins, the doom-mongers, stood still in complete awe. Socialist Party activists abandoned their selling of newspapers and joined the looters. Empty shoe-boxes littered the pavement on the High Street as all creeds swapped their footwear for something new. Groups of young men served themselves drinks in the Prince of Wales pub. A little black boy, dressed in a Darth Vader T-shirt, was filling his pockets with chocolate bars. Throwing away his old tatty jacket, a tramp pulled on a new one, tutting at the length of the sleeves. A teenager went by on his new roller-skates. A white guy with three Tesco's shopping baskets ran into a menswear shop. An elderly black gentleman walked casually towards Acre Lane trying on different hats, while packs of youngsters, hearing of the uprising, poured into the district from all avenues.

The encroaching dusk backdropped the numerous fires, especially in the George public house in Effra Parade, the building totally covered in flames that licked the air above the surrounding terraced houses. Passers-by looked up in awe as firemen battled to quell the fire's rage.

The number of fire appliances employed proved woefully inadequate as property owners witnessed their life's work perish in flames. People lay injured in the streets and screams came from every corner; some voices yelled war-cries while others shrieked in pain. Ambulance men didn't know who to treat first, or even if they should dare. Elderly people were reminded of the war as they dispersed as quickly as they could, clutching their belongings to their chests. Residents of every tower block in the area peered over balconies while listening to news reports on radios. The injured of the Metropolitan Police was fast approaching two hundred; no figures were available on the general public.

The Town Hall clock chimed 9.45pm and Coffin Head, realising that the police had finally assumed relative control of the debris-laden streets, hid in the shadow of a burnt-out van in Leeson Road. He had already seen guerrilla-style attacks on police lines in the last hour. His breathing had become almost asthmatic and his face slimed in a blackened sweat. His heartbeat up-tempoed to a ferocious level as he wondered what had become of Sceptic. With a trembling right hand he pulled out his gun, crouched low and waited. He saw the police at the end of the road, sipping hot beverages from polystyrene cups. They were armed with truncheons and holding up their transparent deflector shields. Coffin Head crept forward, sensing the time to seize the moment was upon him.

Twenty yards away, he watched a policeman take a piss against someone's side wall. Coffin Head locked him in his sights, and like a hunting lion advanced stealthily towards his prey. He noticed a bead of sweat drop upon the gun's shaft as he finger-groped for the trigger. He could feel his pulse all over his being, and the perspiration cascading from his eyebrows began to impair his vision.

The policeman zipped up his flies and turned around. He looked up and saw a dark figure in front of him. Open-mouthed and stock still in shock, his eyes widened as he noticed the gun.

Coffin Head trained his aim to the mouth of the constable who was ten yards away. His hand trembled as if there was a wasp in his grasp, forcing the revolver to shake in a drunken circle. The assassin searched the distressed eyes of his prey and felt an awesome power take over him. The power to take a life or grant one. Coffin Head's whole body shook like a pneumatic drill. The wanna-be killer examined the eyes of his enemy once more, but he could not squeeze the trigger. He swivelled around, placed the gun within his jacket and burned his soles to the end of Leeson Road, hot-stepping under the bridge, looking back only when he reached a housing estate by Somerleyton Road. He bounded up three flights of concrete steps before taking time out beside a refuse chute.

Blinking repeatedly to clear the sweat that had marred his sight, he peered over a balcony wall and found that he hadn't been followed. He ran into a crowd of dissidents at the junction of Shakespeare Road and Somerleyton Road, and once he was within the safety of numbers his heart-beat slowed down. He bowed his head, closed his eyes and a rippling shock surged within him. 'Jesus Christ,' he muttered to himself, palming away the sweat on his forehead. He composed himself for two minutes before joining the nearby crowd, wondering if he would ever get another chance.

★

Hortense, who had been listening to the continuous riot reports on LBC radio with increasing alarm, drummed the front door of Frank and Stella's flat. Frank opened the door, wearing nothing but a pair of jeans.

'Frank, Frank. Me worried 'bout Lincoln,' she stressed. 'You 'ear de news? Lord me God, Armageddon ah gwarn in Brixton, an' Lincoln nuh reach 'ome yet. You affe find 'im before somet'ing 'appen. Me dead wid worry.'

'Calm down, Hortense, your son knows how to look after himself. He'll be alright.'

'You nah 'ear de news. De whole ah Brixton is burnt to de very ground. You affe find 'im, Frank.'

'Stella!' Frank called. Stella emerged from the kitchen where she'd just finished the washing up. 'Hortense is worried about Lincoln, I'm gonna take a walk and see if I can find him. But I'm sure he's OK.'

'But will *you* be OK?' Stella asked, offering a displeased glance to Hortense. 'The shit's really hit the fan and we can't afford for you to get arrested, what with you starting that temporary job an' all.'

'I'll be alright, Stell. Can't see the Filth having time to arrest me with all what's going on.'

'T'ank you, Frank,' said Hortense. 'If you sight 'im jus' bring 'im 'ome.'

'As good as done,' Frank replied, pacing towards his bedroom to get fully dressed.

Hortense parked herself on an armchair as Stella returned to the kitchen. 'Do you want a cup of tea, Hor? It will calm you down a bit.'

'Dat would be nice, Stella.'

'Blow me with a fluffy feather,' Stella remarked. 'I'm sure glad I done my shopping dis morning. I was with the kids.'

276

'You're lucky, Stella. Me never seen such ah t'ing in all me days.'

'We saw it on the news. Couldn't bloody believe it. All those bleedin' fires ... It's two sugars you take, innit, Hor?'

'Yes, me love.'

Stella went to make the tea.

The clock at Brixton Town Hall rang in the midnight hour to the accompaniment of a thousand burglar alarms. Off-licences all over the region had been broken into and plundered. Boosted by the luxury of not having to worry about money to buy liquor, spontaneous parties rocked the whole borough, with sound systems offering their services for free. Even the vagrants were well furnished with Hamlet cigars and spirits of their choice. They gathered together in whatever shelter they could find, toasting the shattered windows around them.

In Hayter Road off Brixton Hill, Crucial Rocker sound had set up in a deserted tenement and were swaying the locals. Brenton, Biscuit, Sharon and Carol were all there, along with a drunken Finnley and a cigar-sucking Sceptic. The whole house was jammed full and patrons had brought their own crates of beer and packets upon packets of cigarettes. Even some white neighbours joined in the party, swigging from Thunderbird bottles and downing Skol lager.

Winston, the selector of the sound, spun the Wailers' 'Burnin' An' Lootin' ', whereupon the revellers joined in the chorus: 'Burnin' an' a lootin' tonigh-i-ite.'

Biscuit smiled wryly to himself, remembering that Jah Nelson had given him a different interpretation of the song. The burning and looting meant to rid yourself of negative images in the mind. He noticed a tipsy girl, dressed in a brand-new white trouser suit, singing at the top of her voice. He wondered if Denise was safe.

The crowd roared its acclaim to Yardman Irie who was nearing the control tower, receiving back slaps as he went. Kingsley, the operator of the sound, offered the mic man his half-smoked spliff as Winston played Culture's Rastafari anthem, 'Natty Never Get Weary'. The herds raised their fists in wild salute and hollered their total approval. Winston smiled, glanced at the masses and knew it was time to unleash Yardman Irie on the microphone. The selector opted for Bobby Ellis's instrumental version of the 'Shenk I Shenk' rhythm. Yardman Irie grabbed the mic and addressed the revolutionaries. 'In tune to de great boss sounds of Crucial Rocker. Dis one is special request to all de revolutionary foot soldier, so flash up your lighter if you der-ya inna de uprising. From de murder of Blair Peach in 1979, to de eleventh of April, 1981. An' if you was der-so, bawl FORWARD!'

'FORWARD!' the crowd cried.

'Alright, dis one call de uprising, special request to de man call Grizzly Garnet, Delroy Dyer, an' to de memory of Blair Peach.'

*Uprising dis an uprising, hey!*
*Uprising dis an uprising*
*We're sick an' tired of your ghetto housing*
*An' de friggin sus law an' de police beating*
*Der ain't no work an' we 'ave no shilling*

*We cyan't tek no more of dis suffering*
*So we gwarn riot inna Brixton an' inna Sout'all*
*We gwarn riot inna Parliament an' inna White'all*

278

*You better sen' fe de army an' de 'ome guard*
*Cos we gwarn mash up an' burn down New Scotland*
*Yard*
*So light up your spliff an' inhale de chalice*
*We're gwarn to riot inna friggin' Buckingham Palace*

*In 1979 dey kill de man call Blair Peach*
*It's a guilty verdict de ghetto yout' reach*
*So 'ear wha' Jah Nelson tell me an' preach*
*Babylon affe fall an' dat's wha' I teach.*

*So listen Maggie T'atcher an' William Whitelaw*
*You better do somet'ing fe de needy an' de poor*
*Fe de ghetto sufferer you don't open any door*
*If you carry on dat way den we declare WAR*

*Uprising dis an' uprising, hey!*

Yardman Irie's voice was drowned out by roars of enthusiasm, and youths clicked on their lighters, holding
them up in the air. Car horns outside joined in the praise
as Yardman Irie introduced another ghetto artist.

'Crowd of people I beg you 'ear me. Stepping up to de
microphone is de bad singer wid a voice like mellow canary
call David Miller.' Clenched fists rose as one in recognition
'Winston selector man, play tune mek we bubble.'

The rebel rouser passed on the microphone to the
singer, and without introduction Miller tore into his
Brixtonian anthem.

*Swing an' Dine, dance all the time*
*Swing an' Dine, dance all the time*

*That's how we do it 'pon de Front Line*
*Yes, that's how we do it 'pon de Front Line.*

The crowd needed no encouragement to repeat the chorus, preventing Miller from singing the next verse.

*SWING AN' DINE, DANCE ALL THE TIME*
*SWING AN' DINE, DANCE ALL THE TIME*
*THAT'S HOW WE DO IT 'PON DE FRONT*
*LINE*
*YES, THAT'S HOW WE DO IT 'PON DE*
*FRONT LINE.*

# Confrontation

## 3am, 12 April 1981

Coffin Head walked into what seemed a triumphant celebration. He saw Brixtonian girls swigging from bottles of wine and dressed in brand-new chiffon-type skirts and blouses. He laughed as he looked at guys who yesterday he knew as rough-necks, yet were now wearing reptile skin shoes, waffle trousers and real silk shirts. Dennis Brown's 'Deliverance Will Come' blared from Crucial Rocker's battered speaker boxes, backdropped by the sound of popping champagne corks. A drunken girl kissed Coffin Head on his cheek as he saw his crew beside Crucial Rocker's control tower.

Ten minutes later and suitably refreshed with a couple of free cans of lager, Coffin Head found a willing partner and started to crub the early hours away along to Carol Thompson's 'Mr Cool'. Beside him, bruising the wall, was Sceptic, who had also claimed someone to dance with.

Floyd and Sharon were showing off their new sexy crub as Brenton hoovered a spliff, observing the rejoicing crowd while perched on top of a bass-jolting speaker box. No one told him to get off, fearful of his reputation. Below him, slumped to the ground with his face kissing the mesh that protected the speaker, was an intoxicated but grinning Finnley, who three hours before had contributed a crate of Tennants to the party.

Having said their goodbyes, Biscuit and Carol made their way to the exit, wiping themselves free of sweat. As the still night freshened their faces, they walked arm in arm, happy to be together and sensing their relationship had reached a higher stage.

'Man, what a day,' Carol commented. 'I jus' 'ope my fader don't ask me where I got my new dresses from.'

'My arms are still aching after carrying all dose garments to Floyd's yard,' Biscuit chuckled. 'We affe go der tomorrow an' pick up our stuff.'

'I couldn't believe it when Floyd was in dat shop trying on suit,' laughed Carol. 'An' he got untold pairs of shoes. Most of dem are left foot t'ough.'

'Knowing Floyd, he'll probably go down to de shop Monday morning an' ask to exchange dem . . . If de shop is still standing. I t'ink it was Burton dat was blazing away. It's funny how Floyd recovered from de wheel going over his foot when he sighted de looting.'

'Wha' did Brenton get?' Carol asked.

'A few pairs of trodder boots an' jeans. He 'ad his 'ands 'pon a ghetto-blaster but he gave it 'way to some small yout'. Bwai, Brenton kinda strange sometimes.'

'Sharon got untold rings,' revealed Carol. 'She 'ad to fight off some crusty yout' who tried to drapes her. Sharon kuffed 'im wid a shoe heel for 'im to back off. Man, people were going cadazy for gold.'

'Yeah, I know. Watching dem girl fight made me t'ink of Denise. I 'ope she's safe in all dis. She could be inna cell or anywhere.'

Carol squeezed Biscuit's left hand. 'She'll turn up, man. Believe.'

The couple turned right into Brixton Hill and observed the police ranks in central Brixton going about their business behind roadblocks. Smoke still rose steadily across the horizon and tired firemen tended to burnt-out buildings. Police vans raced here and there, their flashing blue lights illuminating the High Street. TV news crews had set up base near St Matthews church, filming the scene while pricking up their ears, hoping for a new development. Journalists and community leaders stood staring at the destruction by the Town Hall, feeling sorry for the road sweepers who would clock on for work on Monday morning.

'How you gonna get 'ome t'rough dat lot?' Carol asked.

'I dunno. Not sure I want to. Coff was saying dat dey 'ave blocked off de end of Brixton Road by my sides. An' Floyd was saying dat Brixton is blocked off from Streatham Hill sides. A yout' was telling me in de dance dat some Radication squads are patrolling de streets. It's like der's an unofficial curfew going on. Some yout' who was stepping by de George Canning pub get ketch. Dey fling 'im inna van an' he was gone . . . So keep your eyes clocking on de way to your yard. As fe me I'm gonna go back to de dance an' probably coch at Floyd's yard. Or

283

maybe Brenton's . . . Then again, Brenton lives de uder side of Brixton Hill, so he might ketch a problem reaching 'ome.'

'If you want, you could stay by me.'

Biscuit looked upon Carol in shock. 'Stay at your yard? Ain't your parents gonna go cadazy? Your fader will chop off my seedbag.'

Carol chuckled as a shy look spread over her. 'I hope not. I might be needing dat in de future.'

Biscuit's face lit up. 'In de future?' he asked, unable to restrain his grin. 'Like in de nex' hour?'

Carol smiled coyly, offering a sexy glance at the heavens.

Biscuit needed no further invitation and took hold of his girlfriend's arm and upped his walking pace. Ten minutes later, standing outside Carol's front door, he was still concerned about staying intact. 'Is he a light sleeper?' he whispered. 'Wha' time does he get up inna de morning? Do your parents knock 'pon your door when dey enter your bedroom? Don't want your mudder seeing my backside. How far is it down to de ground from your window? Your fader don't keep a bitch piece of gardening tool under his bed does he?'

'Biscuit . . . *Shut up.*'

Carol turned her key inside the mortice lock before inserting her latch key. Biscuit peered through the dark hallway, certain that Carol's father was behind a door. His heart pounded as Carol led him upstairs. When they reached the landing a female voice forced it to vibrate against his chest bone.

'Carol, you alright me dear? Me an' your fader worry 'bout you tonight. But me tell 'im you 'ave sense an' would nah get involve wid all de madness dat ah gwarn inna Brixton. Ah pure newsflash der 'pon TV.'

284

'I was round Sharon's, Mummy.'

'Yes, me t'ought so. She's ah nice girl. We all see de riot 'pon de news an' your fader did ah fret.'

'He should know I 'ave sense.'

'Yes, so me did ah tell 'im. Goodnight me dear.'

'Goodnight, Mummy.'

Biscuit's heartbeat refused to relent until he reached the safety of Carol's bedroom. She turned on a light, which only served to fuel her boyfriend's dread. He sat on the bed and watched, mesmerised, as Carol undressed. Her slight waist led to her deliciously curved backside, and he was transfixed by her toned thighs. The sight of her unbuttoning her pink blouse was too much. He turned his gaze away, conscious of his ecstatic face.

'Sleep in your clothes, do you?' Carol whispered.

'No, er, course not. Jus' chillin' ah liccle. Can you turn off de lights, it's making me nervous.'

Carol switched off the light and dived under the covers, dressed only in her bra and knickers. Biscuit began to pull off his jeans, conscious of any sound he made. Relax, man, he told himself. Don't dive on her like you jus' come from jailhouse. Tek your time an' try to control de rampant t'ing between your legs. Please God, don't mek me shoot before my time. Oh, frig my days, man, I ain't got no dick macs. Oh fuck. I can't believe it.

He climbed into bed, his apology written all over his features. 'Er, Carol . . . I ain't got no caterpillar coats, man.'

She smiled. 'D'you t'ink I'd trust you wid dem t'ing der? Don't worry yourself. I've been on de pill for six weeks.'

'Six weeks? You ginall. Why you never tell me?'

'Cos I wanted it to be a surprise.'

Biscuit held his dream girl in his arms and his mind flashed back to those far off schooldays when he'd tried to gain her attention and walk her home from school. He was jealous whenever another guy chatted to her, and when an opportunity arrived to make small talk with her, he would say something ridiculous.

He kissed her on the mouth, hoping he was doing it right as his hand caressed her back. 'D'you t'ink our pickney will look like you or me?'

'Biscuit.'

'Yeah.'

'Shut up.'

Carol raised herself and unclipped her bra, flinging it down on a bedside chair. Biscuit stroked her breasts with an index finger before wrapping his hands around them, marvelling at their firmness. Carol responded by palming her lover's chest and squeezing his pectorals while kissing his forehead. Biscuit gripped her panties, and in one motion whipped them down to her ankles. Carol kicked them free before brushing his genitals with her right thigh.

Take it easy, Biscuit told himself. Shit! Why did I stay a virgin for so long? No wonder Floyd's always skinning his teet'. I'm coming here every night till I die. Man! Wha' a feeling.

He kicked off the covers so he could truly appreciate the wonder of Carol's body, and he just had to take hold of her buttocks and squeeze them tenderly before excitement got the better of him. Carol didn't seem to mind. Biscuit locked his mouth on her left nipple.

Five minutes later, after they had pawed each other to submission, Biscuit entered her. He could not help but go quicker than he wanted to, and within a minute had climaxed. He palmed away the sweat from Carol's face, rearranged a few of her hair strands and kissed her tenderly on the forehead.

Back at the riot celebration in Hayter Road, a white man entered the terrace and experienced his first Brixton blues. The bass-line of the Crown Prince's 'Here I Come' almost wrecked his unaccustomed ears as a reveller planted a lager can in his grasp. Coffin Head, who was enjoying a flesh-warming crub with a Red Stripe-drinking female, spotted the bewildered crusty frame of Frank, who was comparing the noise to a Who concert he'd once attended.

Coffin Head excused himself from his dance partner and went over to Biscuit's neighbour. 'Frank, man. Wha' are you doing 'ere? Looking a piece of leg-back fe de night? Bwai, if Stella find out you reach 'ere so, she will grate your bone, man.'

'Nah,' Frank objected. 'Come to look for Biscuit. Is he here?'

'No, boss. He walked Carol 'ome 'bout half an hour ago. He ain't reached back yet, so bwai, he might get his t'ings tonight an' break his duck.'

'So he's alright then?'

'Yeah, man. He's more dan alright. Drink up your beer, man, an' find a girl to crub. Ah celebration dis.'

Frank allowed himself a generous swig of the beer. 'It's just that his mother was a bit worried about him. That's all. It kinda gave me the excuse to see what's happening. And fuck me, Brixton's like a fucking war zone.'

'You could say dat.'

'The Filth wouldn't let me through the High Street, so I had to go round the back of Ferndale Road and then on to Acre Lane. There's Filth all over the place, telling people to get off the streets. And fucking journalists all asking questions. I told 'em to fuck off. But some people can't get home. I saw some guys break into an off-licence and take *everything*. I was gonna go up by Floyd's, thinking that you lot were up there, but I saw this little party going on so I thought I'd check it out.'

'I come de same way as you. De beast 'ave blocked up everywhere, even the Camberwell end of Coldharbour Lane. Der is still nuff yout' 'pon street though, 'aving battles wid de beast 'ere an' der. Anyway, we've come to de right place, thank God. Everyone's 'ere.'

Frank looked around him, and after seeing the performance put on by Floyd and Sharon, thought that they might as well go home and shag each other to death. He saw the brooding Brenton, still roosting on his adopted speaker box, draining a Coke can. Frank turned around and spotted Sceptic constructing a seven-paper spliff while ogling the chest of a jigging girl.

Someone else had entered the party and was also looking for Biscuit. Floyd's head sprung into vexed animation as Smiley approached Coffin Head with apparently urgent news. He briefly acknowledged Frank before gaining Coffin Head's attention. 'Where's Biscuit? Me an' 'im affe chat, serious business.'

'He's wid Carol. Why?'

'I know where Denise der-ya.'

'Where?' interrupted Frank.

Smiley glared at the white man. 'Wha's it to you?'

'Char! Cool yourself, Smiley man. He's a brethren of Biscuit . . . Where is she?'

'You didn't get dis from me, y'understand?'

'Smiley, man. Spill de shit or you wan' me fe get Brenton 'pon your case.'

'You know dat tall block of flats by Clapham Road,' Smiley answered hurriedly. 'Near Kennington sides.'

'Yeah,' Coffin Head replied.

'I was driving back from a girl's yard from Oval, an' me sight Nunchaks, Muttley an' Denise getting out from a car. So me park up my car an' see wha' ah gwarn. Me sight dem go to de fourth floor, an' believe, nuff man was around up der, looking over de balcony. It mus' be Nunchaks whorehouse, man.'

Frank's eyebrows pushed up to the middle of his freckled forehead as Coffin Head quickly summoned Sceptic. After a quick briefing they went to inform Floyd, who in turn paced over to Brenton. 'Outside, man. Outside. Can't 'ear a damn you're saying.'

Floyd led the crew into the street, and once they were gathered, addressed them of the situation. 'Someone's gonna 'ave to go up by Carol an' tell Biscuit.'

'I will,' offered Sharon, swabbing her perspiration with a tissue. 'But someone will 'ave to tek me up der. Nuff police der-bout an' der in de mood to jail up anybody tonight.'

'Alright, dat's settled,' decreed Floyd. 'Me an' Sharon get Biscuit, an' de rest of you meet up in my yard, den we'll forward from der.'

'An' do what?' queried Brenton. 'You t'ink we could jus' walk inna de flat an' tek Denise away?'

'It's gonna affe be almshouse business,' remarked Coffin Head.

'Wha' a blowoh,' exclaimed Sceptic. 'Well, I ain't going if Brenton ain't going.'

'Shut de fuck up before I pluck out your tongue,' reprimanded Brenton. 'If anyone don't wanna help, den fuck off an' remove *now*.'

No one moved a limb as Brenton examined all eyes. 'Where's Finnley?' he asked.

'He's charged up,' answered Floyd. 'He ain't gonna be no use to us.'

'Den we'll 'ave to leave 'im,' said Brenton. 'I'm sure Smiley will take 'im 'ome.'

'Nuff bad man work fe Nunchaks, y'know,' informed Sceptic. 'Der is dat mad-up Muttley an' Ratmout' an' some uder crusty youts.'

'Den we'll 'ave to go in tooled,' affirmed Brenton. 'Anybody 'ave a problem wid dat?'

Sharon looked at Floyd, hoping he'd object and come up with a different idea. She glanced over to Coffin Head. What's with him, she wondered. The apprehension was evident in Sceptic's eyes as the enormity of the situation stoked his fear.

'Yeah,' said Frank, nodding his head and feeling the same adrenaline rush he used to get in his boxing days. 'This Nunchaks geezer won't be expecting it.'

'Den dat's settled,' said Brenton. 'Floyd an' Sharon get Biscuit, den go to my yard to meet up wid de rest of us. Der is a few t'ings in my tool bag we could use.'

'Mind how you walk,' advised Floyd as he led the way, Sharon in tow.

Warily, the posse climbed Brixton Hill, then Floyd and Sharon broke off into Elm Park Road. Five minutes later, Carol heard her front door being slapped.

'Who de fuck is dat?' she asked Biscuit, who was laying beneath her.

Before he could reply, Carol had found her dressing gown and was out of the door. On the way down the stairs, she guessed it was Sharon. Maybe the party was raided by the beast, she thought. Perhaps all the crew are in cells, she fretted. Shit! On this night, *anything* could happen.

She opened the door and found Sharon standing before her.

'We know where Denise der-ya,' Sharon revealed, noticing the happy glow on her friend's face.

Floyd took a great interest in Carol's dressing gown. 'Where's Biscuit?'

'Wait in de front room,' Carol said, her expression turning serious. 'We'll soon come.'

Sharon stepped to the lounge, but Floyd took his time, looking up the staircase. I wonder if my man bruk 'im duck, he questioned. Could be, could be. Carol der-ya inna her dressing gown an' no sight of my brethren.

As Carol reached the top of the stairs she heard her mother's voice again. 'Carol, is dat someone fe you?'

'Yes, Mummy. It's a friend of mine who can't get 'ome t'rough Brixton. De police 'ave put up nuff roadblocks. So I'm gonna put her up in my room.'

'Yes, me dear. Dat's ah good idea.'

Two minutes later, Biscuit was treading delicately down the stairs, his face showing a seriousness that his friends had never seen before. Once reaching the lounge, he addressed the two girls. 'Right, you two are staying 'ere. Carol, as soon as Denise is safe, I'll ding you.'

'Use your 'cad,' Sharon advised. 'Don't jus' go in der wid no plan. Tell Brenton to t'ink 'bout it.'

Floyd and Biscuit nodded their heads as they trooped out of the front room and into the hallway, purposefully. Biscuit offered Carol a knowing glance as he headed out into the night. Floyd looked at them both, dying to ask, but the importance of his task over-rode his curiosity.

Biscuit realised that he had arrived at one of the

crossroads that Jah Nelson was always talking about. Sometimes, he recalled, you have to put others before yourself. He was surprised how easily he remembered the dread's words of advice, and he recollected Nelson saying to him that if the root was strong, the tree would bear a rich fruit. Surely the root was his family, he reasoned. So he had to get Denise back and strengthen the root, whatever the cost to himself.

He recognised that he had accomplished nothing in his life. He remembered the first time he went to Nelson's flat and the dread telling him that so many youths didn't know where they came from, so they didn't know where they were going. If I can get Denise back, he thought, at least that will be a start, and I would be heading in the right direction. Even Carol would respect that.

Twenty minutes later, Brenton was handing out lethal weapons from his straining tool bag. Sceptic opted for a claw hammer, Frank chose a mallet, Biscuit decided on a thick screwdriver, while Coffin Head picked out a ball-hammer. Brenton, after pondering about a saw, satisfied himself with a crow bar. Floyd chanced his luck with a sharp chisel.

All tooled up, the crew looked at each other, sensing fear and adrenaline at the same time. 'If we can,' Brenton addressed, 'we'll sneak her out an' we won't 'ave to use dis shit.'

He received nodding agreement, and without further ado they went out into the early dawn where the birds had just started their morning chorus.

Taking a route by Lyham Road, which ran parallel to Brixton Hill, they reached the back of Floyd's block. Coffin Head went to get his car keys from Floyd's flat, and within minutes the posse were cruising around the back streets of Clapham, accompanied by the screams of alarm bells. Coffin Head had to watch the road carefully for lumps of masonry and debris as the crew noticed smoking cars in almost every street. Residents of the various estates looked out from their balconies, drinking beer and sucking cigarettes as if it was the middle of the day.

As the crew entered Stockwell they saw smashed shop windows almost everywhere. Shards of glass covered the pavement and broken bricks lay next to them. The stench of petrol still lingered in the air and they passed small herds of black youths concealing themselves in concrete jungle shadows. Burglar alarms shrilled without answer and isolated shouts came from unseen voices. Spontaneous parties seemed to rock the whole of South London as reggae music rumbled out from every estate.

Coffin Head pulled up thirty yards short of the tower block on Clapham Road. Biscuit climbed out of the car, realising that this block was identical to the place where Nunchaks had threatened him back in January. He was thankful that Nunchaks' brothel wasn't situated on the top floor. Got to get her back, he promised himself. Sceptic, whose entire being was caked in fright, breathed heavily as Brenton led the way. Coffin Head felt the chill of the gun metal against his chest; his back was bathed in sweat. A gathering rhythm played on his ribs as his heartbeat resonated through his neck. He found his mouth drying by the second and the image that formed in his brain was of the cowering policeman backing away from his pointed gun. He prayed inwardly that he wouldn't have to use his revolver.

As they climbed to the first floor, Biscuit thought of his mother and pondered on her reaction on seeing Denise again. A small part of his mind was still inside Carol's bedroom, and reality told him that this could be the best night of his life – or the worst.

Frank thought of Stella and how she was prone to worrying. But I'm doing something worthwhile, he assured himself. For a good friend. Stella would understand.

Brenton had only one thing on his mind: to get the job done, get home and drink a cool beer. In a distant corner of his mind he recalled the savage confrontation he had had with Terry Flynn.

When he reached the fourth-floor balcony, Brenton waved his arm to signal to his brethrens to keep out of sight. He saw Muttley having an animated discussion with someone inside the flat. Not a very good look out, he thought.

He placed his crow bar inside the back of his jeans and covered it with his anorak. Steeling himself, he ambled along the balcony, feeling the crow bar poke into his backside. Muttley saw him. 'Where ya go?' he demanded.

'It's been a bitch of a night, an' I wan' to round it off by boning a fit steak, boss.'

'Who sent you?'

'Me 'ave a white brethren who tell me 'bout dis place. Him tell me 'bout a girl call Denise. Said she well fit an' t'ing. She der-ya?'

Muttley looked on Brenton suspiciously; he didn't reveal that all the girls on Nunchaks' books had changed their names for their life on the streets. Denise's street-name was Cherry Riper; Nunchaks had a thing about fruits. 'We 'ave no Denise 'ere so. G'way yout' an' stop waste me time.'

Brenton noticed Muttley's right hand delve into the breast pocket of his leather jacket. Without hesitation,

294

Brenton pulled out the crow bar, and using a two-handed swing smashed Muttley on his left temple with the forked end of the weapon, sending him witless before he crashed down over the threshold of the abode, spark out.

Biscuit, who had seen Brenton draw first blood, raced to his aid with the rest of the crew in urgent pursuit. Meanwhile, Brenton had stepped into the flat, yelling, 'DENISE, DENISE!' He saw that there were three doors on each side of the passageway and a door right at the end.

Appearing from the first room on Brenton's left were two bare-backed black guys, one of them hastily securing his zip.

All of a sudden, ratchet blades glinted under the red light-bulb as Biscuit, closely followed by Frank, joined Brenton in the hallway. They didn't know which way to go or what to do next. Doors opened, revealing a selection of Nunchaks' crew, and screams began to ricochet off the walls. The smell of cheap perfume wafted in the air as someone bolted from one of the rooms, wielding a long curved blade. Frank suffered a cut on his rib-cage as Brenton tried to count the enemy, holding his ground and swinging his crow bar, daring for any bad bwai to come close.

As Floyd and Coffin Head joined the fray, Floyd was immediately felled by a broom handle across his cheek-bone, stunning him senseless. Coffin Head swung out with his weapon but only ball-hammered the air. From out of nowhere, he felt something blunt crashing against the back of his head, almost felling him into semi-consciousness. Groggily, he turned around and realised some rough-neck had smashed a rum bottle against his skull. He tried to swing his ball-hammer at his assailant, but his strength had left him. Slowly, as shock took a hold, he slumped to the floor beside Floyd.

Biscuit recognised the approaching Ratmout', armed with a baseball bat. He soon realised that his screwdriver was no match for this tool. They met near the front door and Biscuit tried to catch the bat and evade its deadly arc. He was swatted under his armpit and pain rampaged through his torso, but he managed to hold on to the end of the bat while losing his screwdriver. From then on, it was a brutal contest as to who would claim the wooden weapon.

Meanwhile, Brenton jousted with two knifemen as Frank, who by now had lost his mallet, wrestled on the floor with a guy trying to exercise his curved blade. Seizing the hand which held the knife, Frank slammed it into the wall, causing the weapon to drop to the floor. He then went to work with his fists. His unfortunate victim didn't know what he was up against, and in a matter of seconds his face was a bloody mess.

Nunchaks appeared from a bedroom, his skull crackers primed for action. Denise was trying to get out of the room but Nunchaks employed a short swing which connected with her jawbone. She dropped to the floor. Nunchaks raced to the aid of Ratmout', who was still in a struggle with Biscuit. Unaware of Nunchaks' well-practised swing, Biscuit sustained a blow to his forehead. Ratmout' pulled the dazed Biscuit outside as Nunchaks followed.

Frank saw the danger and raced to his neighbour's aid. But it was too late. Biscuit was launched over the wall and dropped 50 feet to the concrete ground below, just missing a parked car. All fear suddenly leaving him, Frank swung a right hook that hit Ratmout's left eye. The sheer force of the impact made Frank stumble back. He tripped over a body near the door.

Coffin Head had come to with the blurred images of the cell beating he'd received. No, not again, he promised himself. Not fucking again. He looked at a dazed Floyd beside him and immediately went for his .45, training his aim on Nunchaks' face as he stood up, strength returning to him by the second. Ratmout' scampered off, trying to stem the blood of his mangled eye socket, leaving his boss to his fate. Shrieks filled the flat. The whores backed away to their rooms of business. Denise was trying to gain her senses by a bedroom door, but the jolting pain from her head stopped her from regaining her feet.

Brenton saw one of his adversaries lose all nerve. He tried to get away but Brenton caught up with him, clobbering the enemy upon his head, neck and back until he was no longer moving.

Nunchaks stood transfixed at the doorway, staring down the gun barrel in disbelief. Coffin Head remained motionless, sweat drenching his face, not realising that blood oozed from the back of his head. Visions of the police beating formed powerfully in his brain. All this is Nunchaks' fault, he felt. This so-called bad guy. Well, he don't look so *bad* now.

Coffin Head's arm began to shake as his heartbeat raced up a gear and quaked his whole body.

'Fire the fucking gun!' yelled Frank.

Brenton turned around and saw the scenario. 'Oh, shit!'

Denise screamed, increasing Coffin Head's tension. His arm started to waver as Nunchaks grew in confidence. He took a cautious step forward while readying his brain killer.

'Fire the fucking gun!' Frank yelled, straining his vocal chords. 'FIRE THE FUCKING GUN!'

Coffin Head fingered the trigger as his eyes became soaked in a downpour of sweat. Nunchaks stopped his advance, thinking he might have been better off running away with Ratmout'. Denise screamed a continuous scream. Coffin Head sensed the odour of blood and deodorant. The trigger of the gun felt extremely cold as he sighted Nunchaks. The man's eyes were stilled with terror. The gun felt heavy, very heavy, as Denise's shrieks penetrated and disturbed his concentration. Nunchaks chanced another step forward.

'FIRE THE FUCKING GUN!'

Nunchaks paced a long stride.

Unable to cope with the tension, Frank scurried to Coffin Head's side, wrestled the gun off him and shot Nunchaks through his left cheek, the bullet forging its way inside his face and coming to a rest near his upper throat. Nunchaks was rendered motionless for a short second, his eyes set deep in total terror. His body fell backwards as blood began to spurt from just below his chin, bloodying his henchman, Muttley, and spotting the door frame.

For a few seconds, a strange lull beset everyone. Denise looked upon Nunchaks' body with her mouth agape, but producing no sound. Coffin Head fell to his knees as shock finally claimed him. Frank, his arm still out-stretched, continued to point the gun at Nunchaks' dead body, afraid he might get up. Then he threw the gun at Coffin Head, offering him a stern glare. 'Know the rules, Coff. If you show a gun then *fucking* use it.'

Brenton clicked into animation and hastened towards Frank. 'BISCUIT!' Frank watched Brenton hurry to the balcony. He then took in a distraught Denise, who was sobbing and groaning. He went to join Brenton on the balcony, and they saw Sceptic tending to a gravely wounded Biscuit on the concrete beside Nunchaks' car. Frank burned along the balcony behind Brenton and bullfrogged down the concrete stairs, thinking Biscuit was dead. When the two of them reached ground level, they found Sceptic kneeling down, crying out loud and holding Biscuit's head. 'Call a fucking ambulance!' Brenton ordered.

Sceptic seemed unable to move. Brenton, suffering acute frustration, punched Sceptic in the face. 'CALL A FUCKING AMBULANCE!'

Biscuit whimpered and Frank was glad to see he was just about alive, but his legs were horribly misshapen.

'No,' Frank said. 'We'll be lucky to get emergency services tonight. We'll have to take him ourselves.'

Brenton nodded, and without further thought, bounded up the stairs of the block once more. He reached the flat, hurdled over wailing bodies, and saw Coffin Head still in the same position as he had left him, his eyes staring at Nunchaks' body. 'Get up,' Brenton demanded. 'You've got to drive, *now*.'

Out of the corner of his eye, he saw Denise crying uncontrollably by a bedroom door, her face swelling by the second.

'Can you walk?' Brenton asked.

'Yeah, I t'ink so.'

'Then come wid me.'

Denise staggered along the hallway and fell into Brenton's arms, her whole body shaking. Brenton realised she was in no condition to walk, so he sat her down and tended to Floyd, shaking his shoulder. Floyd's eyes flicked

299

into life and he slowly gathered his damaged senses. 'We 'ave to go,' Brenton said. 'Biscuit is mash up. See if you can get down the stairs and into the car. I'm carrying Denise down.'

Floyd nodded weakly. Brenton turned around and noticed that Coffin Head had already departed. He picked up Denise fireman-style and made for the exit. By the time he reached ground level, Biscuit was already laid in the back seat of Coffin Head's car, his head resting upon Frank and Sceptic's laps. Brenton placed Denise upon the passenger seat where she heard her brother wailing and groaning in the back. She turned her head and noticed Biscuit's deformed legs. Her breathing cycle halted as she opened her mouth, and without warning her mother's image formed strong in her mind. She could make no sound. A freezing chill of blame and responsibility surged through her as eye-water soaked her face.

Brenton returned to the concrete stairs where he found Floyd reeling, trying to find his feet. He helped his friend to the car, squashed him in beside Denise and told Coffin Head to make speed.

Coffin Head pulled away, pushed into a high gear and disappeared into the gathering dawn, leaving Brenton behind.

Auntie Jenny parked her car outside her home, climbed wearily out, walked around to the passenger side and opened the door. Hortense, who seemed lost in a nightmare, needed every effort to depart her sister's vehicle. Royston was already standing by the front door, staring at the mat with half-closed eyes. Jenny linked arms with her sister and took her inside her home, sitting her down in an armchair. Biscuit had awoken from his long operation the following day and found himself in a rigid neck-brace, his legs covered to just above the knees in plaster cast. As he focused his eyes and sensed the flood of sunlight coming through the window, he felt a strange drowsiness that made him wonder if he was in a dream. He was flat on his back and could only see the high white ceiling. In his condition he couldn't understand why he felt no pain. Then he felt the hand of his mother caress his cheek. She leant over him and looked at him the way only mothers can.

He tried to say something but no words came out as he saw his mother weeping silently. Then Denise, half of her face covered in plaster, came into his vision. Biscuit tried to turn his head but found his neck muscles unresponsive. Denise dropped to her knees and embraced her brother, resting her head against his naked chest. He felt her eyes dampening his pectorals as he tried but failed to touch her head.

Royston climbed on the bed and simply stared at his brother's neck-brace, unable to find words. Hortense pulled her youngest son towards her and hugged him, burying his head into her breasts. Denise closed her eyes and listened to her brother's heartbeat, gradually strengthening her hold upon him.

Biscuit's eyes moistened. It was worth it, he thought, well worth it. The root is now strong.

He heard the door opening and recognised the stride pattern. Standing at the foot of the bed, dressed in a camel coat, her face smudged with tears, was Carol. Hortense went over to her, acknowledged her with her eyes and squeezed her hand.

Indicating to Royston with her head and tapping her daughter on her shoulder, Hortense led them out of the hospital room. Carol stood motionless for a few seconds, looking at Biscuit's legs and neck-brace. He tried to raise a smile, but failed. Carol dropped slowly to her haunches, gripping the metal railings at the end of the bed. Then she dropped her head and wept.

Biscuit cleared his throat, preparing to speak. 'Come 'ere, Carol,' he said in a whisper.

She stood up and walked slowly to his bedside. She knelt down, gently wrapped her arms around his neck and pressed her cheek against his face.

'T'ings gonna be alright, man,' Biscuit said in a weak voice, warming to her touch. 'De worst is over an' I *will* walk again. An' when I get up 'pon my feet, der will be no more juggling an' no more tribulation. I'm gonna forward to college an' t'ing . . . I've loved you since de first day me sight you, an' I wanna marry you badly – if your paps will let me.'

Carol's face broke into a delicious smile but her tears were free-falling. She closed her eyes and placed her left palm upon Biscuit's right cheek. 'D'you t'ink our pickney will look like you or me?'

Biscuit's heart almost sang.

# 25

# The Blessing of Jah Nelson

## 1 June 1981

Jah Nelson was listening to the Gong's 'Redemption Song' when he heard his front door being gently knocked. He got up from his armchair, switched on a light and went to open his entrance. Standing in the warm twilight were Coffin Head and Denise, looking circumspect.

'Come in,' Jah Nelson ushered, extending a friendly arm. 'Lincoln phoned me an' I've been expecting you.'

The pair stepped warily inside, taking in the story of black history that was all around them. Nelson led them to the lounge and cleared some books so that his guests could be seated. Before relaxing into his armchair himself, he lit an incense stick and turned down the music a notch. 'Do you waan ah drink?' he offered.

'No t'anks,' Denise stuttered, not sure of what to expect.

' 'Ave you got any beer?' Coffin Head asked.

Nelson smiled and indicated no with his eyes. 'I'ave some juices if you prefer – apple or orange?'

'Nah,' Coffin Head declined. 'Too sweet.'

Nelson sensed his visitors' unease, so he displayed his palms while keeping up his friendly gaze. 'So you is Denise, an' your brudder sen' you to me. How's he keeping?'

'He seems to 'ave adjusted to his situation better dan any of us,' she answered. 'Especially my mum – she's completely devastated. But de doctors say he will walk again an' he'll 'ave to go t'rough one of dose rehab programs when dey tek off de plaster. He seems 'appy enough t'ough, chatting 'bout forwarding to college when he gets better.'

'Dat is good to 'ear. 'Alf de battle is de determination fe walk again . . . He asked me to 'ave ah talk wid you,' explained Nelson.

'Yes,' Denise answered hesitantly. 'Biscuit feels so you can do some good.'

'It's not me dat cyan do some good. Dat is up to you.'

'Wha' you mean?'

'Well, your brudder 'as told me de full story, an' it seem dat you need ah boost. Need to feel better widin yourself.'

'An' you're gonna give it,' interrupted a sceptical Coffin Head.

'I 'ope so . . . You see, in life everyone needs to know dat sometimes we tek de wrong options in life, mek bad choices. An' I'm not an exception to dat rule. Not ah single man or ah woman 'as learnt anyt'ing widout meking mistakes. Y'understand? An' everyone 'as de resources to rise up from any tribulation.'

304

Denise found herself nodding her head. Nelson continued, satisfied he had at least one attentive listener. 'So, me say to you, sistren, dat you might feel bad an' blame yourself for recent t'ings. But let me tell you dis. You are ah strong African woman, first an' foremost, let no one tek dat 'way from you.'

Denise managed a half smile. Jah Nelson resumed. 'An' when you realise dat, you will rise from your pit of low esteem.' The dread's features changed from a smile to the countenance of a historian. 'Fe dat reason alone you should walk proud. Great men an' women 'ave come fort' from your loins an' history is blessed wid dem. De great Isis herself was born in Africa. Shaka Zulu was once a babe who suckled from his African mudder's breast. Toussaint L'Ouverture, de great slave leader, could nuh 'ave lived if it wasn't fe 'im African mudder an' de mudders before her. Yaa Asante of Ghana, de woman who led de fight 'gainst de British, was proud of her African heritage. Nanny, national hero of Jamaica, 'ad African blood flowing t'rough her veins. Frederick Douglas, once a slave but became part of de implement dat wiped out slavery from America, recognised his African roots. Marcus Garvey was suckled in de rural parish of St Anne's, Jamaica, by an African mudder. Nina Simone, Maya Angelou, Angela Davis, Martin Luther King, Malcolm X, Richard Wright, Nelson Mandela, Muhammad Ali . . . I could go on an' on.' He never let on that he had been rehearsing this speech for the last few days. 'An' even de Tuff Gong 'imself, may Jah bless 'is soul, all came from de same source, from African seed.'

Coffin Head acknowledged Nelson's citing of the Gong.

Bob Marley had passed away on the eleventh of May,

and although the concrete jungle dwellers declined to talk about the loss of their spiritual leader, there was a disheartened acknowledgement in everybody's eyes that was all too clear. Pirate radio stations were still playing the Gong's music 24 hours a day. Devout rastas wept openly in the streets, and recent sound system sessions had a mournful vibe.

Nelson paused as the Gong's 'Time Will Tell' played from his stereo, and even his face yielded to a grievous bane. He went on, 'An' you Denise, come from de same source, an' de same blood courses t'rough your veins. You should walk tall wid de knowledge of de Nubian heritage you ah carry. Jah know . . . You can achieve anyt'ing an' rise over any stumbling block.'

Denise looked upon the dread with fascination and then offered a stunned glance to Coffin Head. Nobody had ever called her a great African woman before, and she found it hard to avoid Nelson's determined gaze.

'You're young an' in need to know of de resolve inside you,' he continued. 'Education will bring dat out, an' also de knowledge of your great history. Don't blame yourself fe nutten, cah sometimes de most High mek Him plans fe us. An' Babylon put 'pon de pressure so much dat sometimes we lose ourselves. But believe me, sistren, de seed dat runneth t'rough you has given you great capabilities. All you affe do is recognise it an' use it wisely. Education is de key.'

'Dat's all an' good, Nelson, but I still feel responsible, an' my brudder might not walk again. I know de doctors are saying different but I dunno wha' I would do if de worse comes to de worse.'

'Wid time, dat burden will pass . . . Ah builder began to buil' his 'ome wid nuff stone all around 'im. He decided

306

to reject a particular stone dat was rough an' looked like it wouldn't quite fit. But, later, de 'ouse came crumbling down. So de builder start again, dis time using de stone 'im reject. Before 'im set de stone he once rejected in place, 'im polish an' shape de stone so it could be good. An' de 'ouse was strong an' sturdy wid de rejected stone being used as de cornerstone. Jah know!'

Denise, fully understanding the parable, smiled and nodded.

# Acknowledgements

I would like to thank the Hon. Lord Scarman, who conducted and published an honest and creditable inquiry into the 1981 Brixton riots that proved to be a valuable source for this work. Thanks to all my friends of that era who swapped memories with me of the uprising.

A big thank you to my childhood brethren, David Miller, for allowing me to use the lyrics of his Brixtonian anthem *Swing and Dine*. (Yardman Irie, Pancho Dread and Prester John lyrics by Alex Wheatle.)

Sincere gratitude to Mrs Carmen Tipling, my PR in Jamaica, Franklyn McKnight of Radio Jamaica and Ian Boyle of Television Jamaica.

Shouts out to Mikey Hibbert of Pure Jam, Jackie and Debbie Timol, Sharon Wheatle, Mrs Lilleth Clarke, Mrs Hermine Timol, Mr Alfred Wheatle.

Respect to my 'producer', Leo Hollis, my agent Laura Susijn, Steven Thompson, Courttia Newland, Vanessa Walters, Linton Kwesi Johnson, Gaverne Bennett, Raymond Stevenson, Jerry Cole, Shane Donnely, Clyde Minott, Mikey Maha, Marby Brah, Clive Banton, Floyd Windett, Errol Findlay and the Tupper King sound system crew.

**A revolution will find a solution.**

**Bob Marley**

**P.S.**

Ideas,
interviews
& features ...

# Unfinished Stories

*Joanne Finney talks to Alex Wheatle*

**How did you start writing?**
I never thought about being a writer when I
was growing up. In my misspent youth I was
a DJ, a member of a sound system called
Crucial Rocker. Somehow I became the one
who wrote jingles and rhymes to chant over
the music. That's when I first started
thinking about words. I ended up with
notebooks stuffed full of lyrics. When
performance poetry exploded in Brixton in
the early nineties, I got into that. There was a
venue on Acre Lane called the Brixton
Brasserie (now the Z Bar) and on one Friday
every month, they'd have a Poetry Jam.
They'd have established poets, and then a
free hour for anyone to get up and do their
stuff. First I just watched and then, after a
while, I made that step and got up and read
my stuff. That's how I learnt my craft. It was
a bit of a culture shock to perform to people
who were there to listen to me rather than
the music, but I loved it. When that time in
my life was over, I still had the desire to put
what I was thinking and feeling down on
paper.

**Why did you write your first novel *Brixton
Rock*?**
I was inspired by the experiences I'd been
through as a child and a teenager, growing
up in children's homes, and by what was
happening in my life and my friends' lives.
These were stories that were worth telling
and I had to get my story out. I didn't feel
there were many books out there which

spoke to me or of my experiences. At the time I was reading a lot of Harlem Renaissance writers, like James Weldon Johnson, because I couldn't find any modern British writers I could relate to and that seemed wrong. When I first started writing I didn't really have publication in mind. It was only when friends said I was on to something that I even considered it.

**Several of the characters in your previous novels reappear in *East of Acre Lane*. Is the book meant as a continuation?**
It's not, but I felt I had unfinished business with several of them. In the earlier novels, you might only see one aspect of a character or they might only play a minor role so I wanted to develop them further. The book is part of a trilogy, though. My latest book, *Island Songs*, is actually a prequel to *East of Acre Lane* – it's Hortense and Jenny's turn to tell their stories. The trilogy isn't in a chronological order but I don't think I was mature enough to write *Island Songs* when I first started writing. I think readers like to find out what happens to characters.

**Your work comes across as working-class writing, rather than 'black urban' writing – would you agree?**
Definitely. I write from the point of view of the average person on the street. In the book, Jah Nelson says that 'classism and elitism in this country are much more dangerous than racism'. That's definitely something I ▶

6 Music was everywhere – on the streets, coming from people's houses – music is what made Brixton so vibrant 9

Alex Wheatle was born in London to Jamaican parents on 3 January 1963. He lives in South London, near to where he grew up, with his wife Beverley and three children. He won the London Arts Board's New Writers Award for *East of Acre Lane*.

## Unfinished Stories *(continued)*

◄ believe; Jah Nelson's voice is mine. I still think there's a big divide in the UK between those who have and those who have not.

**Jah Nelson acts as a mentor to Biscuit. Who influenced you as a teenager?**
I spent a lot of time with rastas when I was at an impressionable age. They gave me good advice about how life works and a real pride in my background.

**Brixton in the early eighties is very much brought alive in your novel. How did you carry out research for the book?**
I didn't actually do that much research, I just drew on my own life. A lot of people I knew were selling drugs to make ends meet like Biscuit and his mates and were involved in the riots. A lot of it was still vivid in my memory. Spending time with other people who were there also helped. I had some friends from that time round one evening and I taped us all reminiscing about being teenagers in Brixton.

**Like the clubs where Biscuit and his crew hang out, *East of Acre Lane* is heaving with music. Could you imagine writing the book without referencing songs and lyrics?**
The soundtrack came to me almost as soon as I started writing the book. Not only because I love music but because music was central to my experiences in early eighties Brixton. It was everywhere – on the streets, coming from people's houses – music is what made Brixton so vibrant. I also think certain music works as a fast connection to a

4

period of time, and plays on people's memories and nostalgia.

**April 2006 is the 25-year anniversary of the Brixton riots – how do you think the situation has changed for Brixtonians and the area?**
The area's changed a lot. It's much more multi-cultural than it was in the eighties and a lot of it's been done up. Railton Road, where the riots and a large part of the book take place and which used to be really run down, is now full of wine bars! Obviously, there are still people living without much and problems like drugs and violence but that's pretty much true anywhere. I don't think Brixton is the 'trouble spot' it used to be. They're all over London, the whole country even, now. I can't see a repeat of the riots in Brixton but I can see parallels between what is happening now in the UK to the Asian community and how my friends and I felt we were treated at the time. We felt we weren't being heard and it got to the point where we had to do something about it.

**What advice would you give to anyone who wants to follow in your footsteps?**
To keep at it. I still think it's hard for young male black writers to get published. Especially those who are writing about the working class and life on the streets, as I do. But I still think you should write about what you know and what you believe in. Hopefully the successes in the last few years of black women writers like Andrea Levy ▶

## TOP TEN BOOKS

*The Black Jacobins*
C.L.R. James

*Pimp*
Iceberg Slim

*East of Eden*
John Steinbeck

*Soul on Ice*
Eldridge Cleaver

*The Autobiography of Malcolm X*
Alex Haley

*Catch a Fire: The Life of Bob Marley*
Timothy White

*The Grapes of Wrath*
John Steinbeck

*The Color Purple*
Alice Walker

*Brighton Rock*
Graham Greene

*The Souls of Black Folk*
W.E.B. DuBois

## Unfinished Stories *(continued)*

◀ will open up the way for the boys!

**Some of the scenes in the book, particularly those that take place during the riots, read as accurate documents of history. Would you ever think of writing non-fiction?**
I have considered it. I read a lot of non-fiction myself and always have. To be honest, my ideal non-fiction book would be a sports book, especially cricket. I'd love to follow a tour and write about the characters as well as the game.

**What's your next project?**
I'm working on the last book of the trilogy that started with *East of Acre Lane* and *Island Songs*. It's Biscuit's son's story this time … It's still early days though. I've also contributed to a documentary made by Blast Films for BBC2 which is going to be broadcast in April 2006 for the anniversary of the Brixton riots. ■

# A Writing Life

**When do you write?**
Always mornings. I start the day with a quick
cup of coffee and a fag while I read the
papers but I like to get going as soon as
possible.

**Where do you write?**
I've got a desk in my bedroom which is set
up for writing.

**Pen or computer?**
I jot down a basic plot and a few character
sketches on paper but I always write on the
computer.

**Silence or music?**
I have to listen to music – it can be anything
from old standard R 'n' B to reggae. I find it
difficult to write in silence. I think that goes
back to my DJ days.

**How do you start a book?**
The characters always come first. Then I plan
a basic plot, and have a vague ending in
mind before I start to flesh it out.

**And finish?**
With relief.

**Which writers do you most admire?**
John Steinbeck, C.L.R. James, Chester
Himes, Alice Walker, Toni Morrison, Maya
Angelou, Paddy Clarke.

**What or who inspires you?**
The people I've come across in my life, the ▶

## A Writing Life *(continued)*

◄ struggles they've faced and how they've survived. I'm also a great people-watcher.

**If you weren't a writer what would you do?**
I'd like to teach creative writing. I've tutored a few Arvon courses and been on a few school visits to talk about creative writing but I'd like to do more.

**What's your guilty reading pleasure or favourite trashy read?**
*The Thorn Birds* by Colleen McCullough and anything on the ancient civilisations.

**Which book do you wish you'd written?**
*Absolute Beginners* by Colin MacInnes. It perfectly captures the London of the streets, something that I try to do in my writing as well. It was the book that showed me that you have to write about what you know and see, rather than trying to write in someone else's voice or trying to fit into a specific genre. ■

# Brixton Hot!

*by Alex Wheatle*

*10 April 1981*

THE SUN HAD set over a balmy evening and the battle for Railton Road was raging. About fifty yards down the road, scores of police were employing dustbin lids as makeshift shields to protect them from missiles that rained towards them. They were trying to advance in an ordered line. As we hacked down low brick walls that fronted terraced housing for more ammunition, we heard the screams, yells and curses, backdropped by sirens, coming from every direction. We noticed some rioters preparing Molotov cocktails ready to launch into the massed police ranks. As I peered upward, everything seemed to be orange. The street was a carpet of broken glass, petrol, burning cars and fractured bricks and as I looked around, the determination to 'hold' this slice of Brixton was evident on the sweat-encased faces of the people around me.

From constant throwing, my arms were almost spent but someone told me that the police were attempting to catch us by surprise from behind. They were moving down the Herne Hill end of Mayall Road, a route that ran parallel to Railton Road. About sixty of us, armed with all the bricks and missiles we could carry, ran to meet them. We turned left into Shakespeare Road and we quickly decided to employ a tactic that had proved successful for us earlier in the day: fifty or so would remain hidden in back gardens or 'friendly' houses and about a dozen of us would engage the police, ▶

### Brixton Hot! *(continued)*

◄ throwing our missiles into their positions and then luring them into an ambush. I was one of those that formed part of the 'carrot' for I was a swift runner.

Thirteen of us marched up Mayall Road, knowing that the rest of our group were lying low in two terraced houses. All lights were switched off. We saw the police about a hundred yards away and all that lay between us was a number of busted, smoking cars. As soon as they were in range we hurled all and sundry into the air. They immediately charged at us. Feeling great fear and excitement, we turned on our heels and ran for our lives. We were only too aware of what might lie in wait in a police cell.

As we sprinted by the junction of Chaucer Road and Mayall Road, the police were caught in our trap. Some rioters had even climbed on top of the community centre to better launch their missiles. But a few of the police carried on chasing. With panic coursing through my veins, I ran left into Chaucer Road while the rest of my guerrilla group hurtled down Mayall Road. To my alarm, five policemen were still in pursuit. As I approached the perimeter fence of Brockwell Park, I considered trying to clamber over the fence and into the darkness of the park. But my arms were too tired. I had to rely on my speed of foot. I carried on running into Brixton Water Lane, almost tripping over myself. They were still hunting me.

Turning left into Tulse Hill, I made for the nearest council estate I could find. My heart was racing ferociously and as I glanced behind, the police had yet to turn the corner from Brixton Water Lane. Upon entering the estate, without thought or hesitation, I leaped into one of those grey metal council rubbish bins. I was exhausted and just had to rest so the stench emitting from the black garbage bags meant little to me. There I remained for half an hour, not daring to peep over the bin wall. Perspiration was dripping down my face.

Fearful of police snatch squads driving up and down Tulse Hill and Brixton Hill, I made my way to my hostel off Brixton Hill via the back streets. Once inside I drank greedily from the cold tap in the kitchen. Then I took a quick cold bath. Getting dressed, I noticed that my hostel mates had been busy looting. New clothes were everywhere, alongside boxes of cigarettes and untold bottles and cans of liquor. Downing a Special Brew, I tried on a new pair of Farah trousers. They fitted perfectly.

Being a sound-system DJ, known by the moniker of Yardman Irie, I wanted to write a new lyric. My small notepad was full so, on the back of a Dennis Brown 12-inch record sleeve, I wrote the lyrics for 'Uprising'. Little did I know that 20 years later the same lyrics would appear in my novel, *East of Acre Lane*.

Wanting to recapture that adrenaline rush, I made my way to central Brixton again, via the back streets. I noticed that in the council estates, people were peering over balconies. Militant reggae music was booming out of every street and, despite the police cordoning off Brixton from Streatham Hill and Kennington, packs of youngsters ▶

6 The street was a carpet of broken glass, petrol, burning cars and fractured bricks 9

### Brixton Hot! *(continued)*

◀ were pouring in from all avenues, all wanting to be involved in the uprising. There seemed to be a thousand alarms ringing out in the night. I smiled as I realised that the looters were now targeting the off-licences, preparing for the parties.

Returning to Railton Road via Brockwell Park, I noticed that the police had gained relative control of the front line. They were housed in numerous green coaches, sipping hot drinks from polystyrene cups. Fear was written over their faces. It was an empowering sight to behold. Sudden movements of police on the ground informed me that rioters were still throwing their missiles at the fringes of the police presence.

Tumper, the proprietor of a 24-hour West Indian food store on Railton Road (his premises were untouched by rioters), was gaining a roaring trade selling fried dumplings, cheese and bun sandwiches, carrot cake and fish fritters. Queuing up to buy a snack, I bumped into a friend of mine. 'Dey took a raas beating, innit,' he said.

'Yeah,' I agreed. 'They did.' ■

# Have You Read?

*Other titles by Alex Wheatle*

*Brixton Rock*
Alex Wheatle's first novel is the story of
16-year-old Brenton Brown who's spent
most of his childhood in children's homes.
Being reunited with his mother brings the
promise of a better future, but the discovery
of a half-sister he never knew he had
threatens to change that.

.................................................

*The Seven Sisters*
Brought together by a tough childhood in
children's homes, Glenroy, Bullett, Curvis
and Carlton have a plan of escape – they'll
run away together and finally be able to feel
'normal' – but their freedom comes at a
price.

.................................................

*Island Songs*
The prequel to *East of Acre Lane* tells the
story of sisters, Jenny and Hortense, from
their childhood in Jamaica to their twilight
years.

# If You Loved This,
## You Might Like ...

### Small Island
Andrea Levy
*Small Island* is the story of the first wave of Jamaican immigrants who arrived in Britain after the Second World War.

### A Lazy Eye
Donna Daley-Clarke
Geoffhurst's life is going well until he is forced to relive what happened eight years earlier in the long, hot summer of 1976. Everything was OK – his dad was one of the first black footballers to be signed, his mum was the most glamorous woman in the neighbourhood and Geoffhurst felt invincible – but all good things must come to an end.

### Saturday Night and Sunday Morning
Alan Sillitoe
A lathe worker by day, a womaniser by night, Arthur Seaton is a young rebel without a cause. An insightful look at working-class life in 1950s Britain.

### Down and Out in Paris and London
George Orwell
In this, his first book and the one which found him fame as a writer, Orwell documents his life on the breadline.

***Nickel and Dimed: Undercover in Low-wage
America***
Barbara Ehrenreich
Journalist Barbara Ehrenreich spent six
months seeing if it was possible to survive
on the minimum wage. Her humorous,
politicised findings make interesting reading.

# Find Out More

READ ...

*Scarman and After: Essays Reflecting on Lord Scarman's Report, the Riots and Their Aftermath*
John Benyon

*The Scarman Report: The Brixton Disorders, 10–12 April, 1981*
George Scarman

*Harlem Stomp!: A Cultural History of the Harlem Renaissance*
Laban Carrick Hill

SURF ...

www.arvonfoundation.org
The Arvon foundation for writing offers courses for songwriters, poets, novelists, script- and screenwriters, playwrights and journalists. They also do work in schools and youth groups, encouraging young people to think creatively.